MW01134665

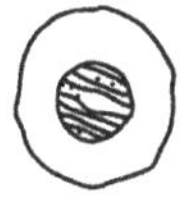

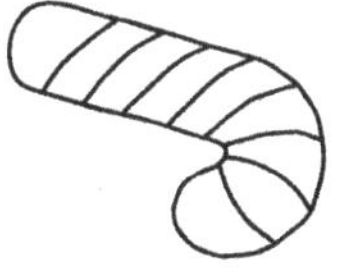

Books by Alina

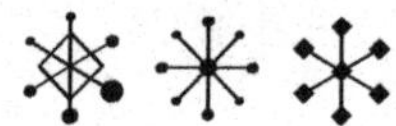

The Holbrook Cousins
- The Successor
- The Screw-up
- The Scion

The Frost Brothers
- Eating Her Christmas Cookies
- Tasting Her Christmas Cookies

The Svensson Brothers
- After His Peonies
- In Her Candy Jar
- On His Paintbrush
- In Her Pumpkin Patch
- Between Her Biscuits

Check my website for the latest news:

http://alinajacobs.com/books.html

EATING HER
Christmas Cookies

A HOLIDAY ROMANTIC COMEDY

EATING HER

ALINA JACOBS

Summary: Broke and alone for the holidays, I need to win The Great Christmas Bake-off. Though I am faced with a stalker mall Santa, a bake-off saboteur, and a crabby, sexy billionaire who hates Christmas, my holiday cheer will not be snuffed!

This book is a work of fiction. Names, characters, places, and incidents either are products of the author's imagination or are used fictitiously. Any resemblance to actual events or locales or persons, living or dead, is entirely coincidental.

To my grandmother, whose cookie recipe inspired this story.

On the first day of Christmas,
my true love gave to me...

CHAPTER 1

Chloe

I could tell New York City was preparing for Christmas as I rode in the Uber on the way to Frost Tower. Even though Thanksgiving had only been yesterday, workers were hanging garlands on buildings and wreaths with big red bows on lamp posts. The advertisements on the sides of the various kiosks screamed reminders about holiday shopping, and there were light snow flurries in the air.

"It's so magical," I sighed, gazing out of the window. I'd always wanted to live in New York City, ever since I'd come for a middle school trip. Now I was back—broke, desperate for money, but back.

"You're going to be singing a different Christmas carol after you've lived in this city a few months," the driver said. "Or maybe not if this is where you're living."

"Is this Frost Tower?" I asked him. We had stopped in front of an all-glass tower that reached up to the cloudy sky. It was beautiful, like an ice sculpture, but it did not inspire warmth or Christmas cheer. In fact, unlike the other buildings we had passed in which Christmas trees and other holiday decorations were visible in the lobby, Frost Tower was barren.

"Don't forget to give a five-star rating," my driver said and winked as I stepped out of the car.

"Spare some change?"

I turned to see a tipsy-looking Santa Claus waving a coffee cup in my face.

"Get outta here!" the driver yelled at him as the homeless man staggered off. "You'd think a fancy building like this would have better security." The driver carried my suitcase and my crate of high-end cookware to the door, waved, and then returned to his car.

I entered and looked around. The lobby was completely empty. There were no people, no artwork, and no Christmas decorations. It was all glass and polished concrete with clean white walls. On the wall near the elevator lobby was a handwritten sign that said ROMANCE CREATIVE PRODUCTIONS 37th FLOOR.

I stepped in the sleek elevator feeling slightly apprehensive. What if they didn't want me to be in the show anymore? I couldn't go back to the Midwest. There wasn't anything for me there, and besides, my credit cards were almost maxed out.

"I guess I found all the people," I said to myself when I stepped off the elevator. The large elevator lobby was packed with people pushing carts, carrying cables, and toting heavy lighting.

"Are you Chloe Barnard?" asked a tall, elegant woman with long, dark hair. I nodded and held out my hand.

"Hi, I'm Dana Holbrook. I'm one of the producers. We talked over email. That's my co-producer, Gunnar Svensson." Dana gestured to a tall blond man talking intently on the phone. "We're very excited to have you. Let me show you to your room." She tapped the elevator button, and we rode up another twenty floors.

"Your Instagram is very impressive," Dana said as we walked down the hall of one of the upper residential floors. "You have hundreds of thousands of followers, and they all seem quite active. *The Great Christmas Bake-Off* isn't airing on network or cable TV, it's only on the web, so we'll need you to leverage your social network to make this show a success. Make sure you send out lots of photos of the contest!"

"That's what I'm planning on," I told her. "I want to use *The Great Christmas Bake-Off* as a platform to hopefully star t my own café or at least be offered a cool job."

"We anticipate this show will be very popular," Dana said as she punched a number. I tried to memorize it but failed.

"I emailed you the code," she said and opened the door. The apartment was beautiful, with big windows, a large kitchen, and a view over a nearby park.

"Believe it or not," Dana said, "this is considered a big apartment for New York City."

"It's perfect," I told her, setting my bag down.

"Pick a room. You're the first contestant to arrive. You'll have to share, unfortunately, but it's only a five-week contest. We'll be done filming by Christmas."

By the time I had unpacked my things, no one had arrived yet. I sat on the small bed in the room I had chosen and checked my email. There was a message from Dana with a scant amount of information, just a tentative shooting schedule and the key code.

When I had auditioned for this contest, the paperwork had said there would be a cash prize of $20,000 for the winner. It wasn't enough to open my own restaurant, but it would at least let me pay off my credit card debt. My druggie cousin had stolen my money, and against my oma's protests, I had filed a police report. That had been the only way the bank would refund my money. Though it returned a few thousand of what I had lost, it still hadn't refunded the full amount, and almost a year had passed since the incident. After my oma had passed away, I hadn't had the energy to fight with the bank. Now I was slowly trying to build a life without her.

I was starting to feel morose, so I snapped a selfie in front of the window and edited it, then posted it to Instagram. I was immediately rewarded with dozens of likes.

"That's all you needed, a nice ego boost," I told myself as I headed downstairs. Maybe I could make friends with someone who could help me win or at least navigate the contest.

"What am I supposed to do with all of this garland?" someone was yelling as I stepped off the elevator.

"Just hang it up, Zane!" I heard Dana shout.

"I am not an interior designer!" the man yelled back. He had on a headset that held back his long hair.

"I guess this isn't a polished production," I joked, walking over to him.

"What gave it away?" he said, shaking his head. "The decorator quit—was offered a better job. So now I have all of these Christmas decorations. I'm supposed to put everything up in the soundstage, and I don't know what to do." He made a disgusted noise. "We're starting filming tomorrow morning. They better pay is all I have to say."

"Yeah," I agreed, "I need the prize money." I started pawing through the boxes.

"There's nice stuff in here," I told him and started pushing the loaded cart toward the double doors. "Come on, I'll help you deck the halls."

The camera guy followed me gratefully. "You're a lifesaver. You're Chloe, right? I've seen your Instagram—it's super cool. I'm glad you're helping. I can make a camera shot look good, but I just don't have the decorator's touch."

We spent the next several hours putting up decorations, and when we were done, the studio set looked like Christmas. Zane looked around in awe.

"You really did an amazing job," he said. I had arranged bunches of pinecones and ribbons, hung big fat strands of garlands, sprinkled fake snow, tucked little ornaments here and there, and put up lights to make the place sparkle.

"Are the fairy lights going to mess up the cameras?" I asked in concern.

"Nah," he said. "I have them plugged into the lighting board, so the lighting guy can adjust as needed."

I took out my phone to take a picture for my Instagram account. Dana said we should be promoting, so I hoped it was okay. It was the only thing going right in my life right now, especially since this contest was clearly not a Food Network–level production.

There were some decorations left over, so I hung them up out in the lobby to make it feel more festive. As I was returning from stacking the boxes in a storage room, I heard more yelling.

"It stinks!" a deep voice said. "My whole tower smells disgusting."

"It smells like Christmas," I heard Gunnar reply.

In the lobby off of the soundstage was a gorgeous man. He was tall and broad shouldered with silver-white hair and icy blue eyes. Framed against the Christmas decorations, he made a perfect picture.

I snapped his photo. I knew who he was. Jack Frost—the billionaire owner of Platinum Provisions. I thought his company made some type of very expensive, highly specialized surgical equipment along with drill bits for mining and other applications, but I only knew them for their line of cooking tools and molecular gastronomy equipment. It was high precision and expensive.

I had my own special collection of thousands of dollars' worth of Platinum Provisions cooking and baking tools, and they were among my most prized possessions. My collection contained tiny knives that rarely needed sharpening, distillery equipment to extract the flavor from various ingredients, and high-precision frosting guns and icing pipers to make intricate decorations. Some of my most-liked Instagram posts were of the perfect miniature cakes I had made with these Platinum Provisions baking tools.

Speaking of Instagram—I snapped Jack Frost's picture again. He was too perfect.

"Don't take my picture!" he said, his attention snapping to me.

"Holy smokes, Jack, calm down!" Gunnar said.

"I can't believe I let you rope me into judging this competition. You know I hate Christmas," Jack said.

"You don't like Christmas?" I blurted.

"*I hate Christmas*," he snarled, "I hate the scented candles and the decorations and the holiday baked goods."

"Not even Christmas cookies?" I asked, flabbergasted. Who didn't like Christmas cookies?

He walked up to me, closing the distance between us and invading my personal space. I was sure my eyes were wide in my head. I was wearing boots, but he was still tall enough to loom over me, his icy blue eyes boring into me.

Wouldn't it be great if he was boring something else into you?

I told the naughty elf living in my subconscious to shut up.

"I don't like cookies," Jack said, "and I don't like little girls who believe in the magic of Christmas."

"You'll like my cookies," I told him, not sure where that surge of courage had come from.

"Don't bet on it," he replied and turned on his heel, followed by Gunnar.

A bake-off judge who hated sweets. Awesome.

CHAPTER 2

Jack

The day had not gotten off to an auspicious start. My younger brothers, Matt and Oliver, had left that morning, and I already missed them. I was never able to spend that much time with them now that they were away at college, and they didn't even want to stay all of Thanksgiving weekend to see me. Instead, they wanted to return to Harvard early and play video games with their friends.

Now I had to contend with this bake-off that was going to start filming tomorrow. I already regretted agreeing to allow Gunnar and Dana to film in my tower. The whole place reeked of sugar, butter, marzipan, and spices. And Gunnar didn't have enough money to pay a third judge, so I had been enlisted as a judge–not that I was qualified.

To make matters worse, now the short little blonde was taking my picture. *I better not see it plastered all over the internet,* I thought.

As I loomed over her, I could smell the sugar wafting off her, mingled with the scent of fresh pine boughs. She smelled like Christmas, and when I said I hated cookies, she gaped at me, eyes wide with shock, as if I was the Grinch personified.

"I cannot wait for Christmas to be over," I muttered to myself as Gunnar ran after me and grabbed my upper arm.

"You need to remember why it is that we're filming here at all," he hissed. "You can't find tenants for this tower, and no tenants equals no rent money. Romance Creative is a paying tenant—"

"You haven't paid me a cent yet," I said to him.

"But we will, as long as this show is popular. You want the rent money? We can't have any more problems. The decorator quit, I barely have enough money to make payroll, and now you're threatening Chloe, who is the contestant with the most popular Instagram account by a wide margin."

So Chloe was her name. Not that I cared, of course.

"It's *The Great Christmas Bake-Off*, Charlie Brown," he said, patting me on the shoulder, "and you need an attitude adjustment and a heaping tablespoon of Christmas cheer. This is going to be good publicity for both of us. We'll have fancy establishing shots of the tower and B-roll of the contestants in that beautiful lobby. Speaking of which, we need more decorations outside and in the lobby to make it seem festive."

Though this was far from the ideal situation, I knew Gunnar was right. This bake-off was my last shot at drumming up paying tenants for Frost Tower.

I walked with Gunnar down to the lobby to try and find someone who could procure and install Christmas decorations inside and out. I needed the tower to look impressive. I glanced over at the empty retail space off of the lobby. It was an expansive two-story space. I had envisioned it as an upscale restaurant, but now it sat empty.

The security guard was nowhere to be found.

"I can't believe I pay that useless man," I said irritated.

And to pour a tanker's worth of gasoline on this dumpster fire, along came the person I despised most in the world aside from my parents: Hartleigh, the girl who had been obsessed with me and had stalked me since I was a young teenager.

She saw me, shrieked, and made a beeline in my direction.

"What is she doing here?" I yelled.

"Seriously, Jack, you need to stop accosting contestants," Gunnar said.

"Hartleigh cannot be a contestant, she's my stalker!" I protested.

Hartleigh looked at me as if I was a piece of meat and she was a hyena.

"Jack," she purred, sidling up to me and wrapping her arms around me. She was wearing some sort of vintage fur stole, and it made me sneeze.

"As soon as I heard this show was filming in your tower, I had to be a participant." She grabbed the lapels of my suit and pulled me in, rubbing our noses together. I pushed her away.

"We're meant to be together, Jack," Hartleigh said, making a kissy face at me.

"If you'll just check in upstairs," Gunnar said, and Hartleigh sashayed away. Not that she did it convincingly. She was thin, bordering on scrawny.

"She'll make for great TV," Gunnar told me while I brushed little pieces of fur off of my suit. "Is she really the girl who's been stalking you?"

I nodded, and Gunnar looked thoughtful.

"I guess she does look kind of unhinged," he said. "Still, if she tries to murder you, wouldn't that put the show on everybody's radar! Romance Creative needs all the publicity we can get."

I glowered.

"Kidding, Jack," Gunnar said.

The elevator dinged, and a familiar blonde walked out—Chloe. Her eyes narrowed at Hartleigh as my childhood stalker blew me another kiss.

"Dana said you needed more decoration down here," Chloe said, looking around at the space. "But I don't think we have enough."

"We should buy more," Gunnar said. I looked at Gunnar. He looked at me. I frowned then sighed and handed Chloe a credit card.

"Oooh!" she said, taking it in her hand. "It's heavy."

I looked at her, and she blushed. "I mean it's a very thick credit card."

"It's American Express Black," I said. "They make them special."

"Will it even fit?"

Gunnar was silently laughing.

"I mean in the card reader," she clarified, her face almost as red as her holiday sweater.

"Go shopping!" Gunnar said, spreading his arms. "We need to fill this place with Christmas cheer."

"I'll make it look like a winter wonderland," she said, smiling up at me.

CHAPTER 3

Chloe

I hadn't had time to shop the day before, but Zane had said they weren't releasing the first episode for about another week, so there was still time to decorate the lobby and produce the establishing shots.

We had had orientation the previous day, which went late and barely left any time to learn more about the other contestants.

Now it was early the next morning, too early, and I was on set for the first day of the bake-off filming.

As I took my place at my station, Nina, another contestant and my roommate, said, "I'm so nervous."

"Me too," I told her, inspecting the long worktable that would be my kitchen home for the next five weeks.

"I'm not," Hartleigh announced. She was at the workstation on my other side. "Jack and I go way back, and I know he's going to give me the best score." She tossed her hair, or she tried to at least. Hartleigh had straw-like hair that looked like it had been blow-dried, colored, and straightened within an inch of its life. I itched to give her a honey leave-in conditioner treatment.

I also wanted to redo her makeup. It looked caked on and gave her skin a chalky texture. The production didn't have the budget for makeup artists, so we contestants were on our own. I checked my makeup in the compact mirror I had put in my apron. I looked okay, if a little tired.

A pretty, willowy young woman practically waltzed over to me. Her makeup and hair were stunning.

"You're Anastasia from the blog Whimsical Dining!" Nina exclaimed. Anastasia air kissed us.

"I love you!" I gushed. "I wish I could travel all over and eat at Michelin-star restaurants. Your blog is amazing!"

Anastasia did a proper hair toss, her chestnut locks cascading down her back. My curls and I had come to an uneasy truce, but they would never look like Anastasia's hair.

"You're so sweet," she said. "And I just adore you! I love your Instagram feed—you're so cute!"

"Are you judging the bake-off?" Nina asked.

"I'm hosting," Anastasia replied.

Before we could ask Anastasia any more questions, Dana walked into the room, followed by the three judges. She motioned to Anastasia, and the camera crews moved into position.

As Dana, Anastasia, and the judges talked in low whispers, I studied the judges. More importantly, I studied Jack. He looked amazing in a deep navy-blue suit with a very subtle pattern. The billionaire seemed irritated that he had to be here. His mouth was a cold line, and a frown interrupted his smooth features.

"Don't even think about it," Hartleigh hissed at me. "He's mine. We have a history."

"Yes, I heard you the first time," I told her.

Dana left the studio, and Anastasia turned to the contestants as the judges took their seats on stools at a long butcher-block table.

"Welcome to the first episode of *The Great Christmas Bake-off*, sponsored by Trader Mike's," she said. "This show is about watching expert bakers create beautiful holiday-inspired desserts. We don't do gimmicks, weird contests, sabotaging, or timed rounds. We give our contestants the space and time they need to create the most beautiful and tasty Christmas desserts possible. This is a five-week contest, with two episodes a week."

She turned to the judges, the cameras following her movements.

"For our judges, we have Anu Pillai, a chocolatier and baker from Lil' Masa bakery in NoLiTa. Then we have Nick Mazur, a pastry chef and restaurant owner with businesses all over the New York area. Finally, we have Jack Frost, founder and CEO of Platinum Provisions, a global company that designs and produces, among other things, a line of specialty items for cooking and baking."

I felt charged and anxious while Anastasia talked. I knew about the two chefs who were judging. They were critically acclaimed and made award-winning desserts. They would be tough.

"For this first challenge," Anastasia continued, "we'll ease everyone into the holidays with the Santa's Christmas Cookie challenge. Everyone has the experience of selecting the perfect plate of cookies to leave out for Santa Claus. Now we want you all to create the perfect plate of cookies for the judges. Do the judges have any advice before the contestants start?"

"What I look for in a cookie is that it needs to be soft but have some yield," Nick Mazur said. "I don't want to just taste sugar. It needs to have a complexity of flavors."

"I concur," said Anu. "Cookies are quite deceptive. They are finicky, and to make the perfect cookie, all steps in the process need to be completed perfectly. Since this is Christmas, we will also be looking for cookies that evoke the memories of childhood and holidays spent with family. Food has a power in that it can be transportive and take you back to places, memories, and people you thought were long gone."

Anastasia nodded then said, "Jack, do you have anything to add?"

Jack looked even more annoyed, which I didn't think was possible.

"*Jack*," Anastasia repeated.

He looked right at the camera and said, "You have ample time to make beautiful creations. This evening, when the round is over, don't show up with something that looks homemade. My company has products that can help you create high-precision decorations with icing and other edible fluid ingredients. There is a range of equipment at each of your stations. I suggest you make use of it."

"Don't forget," Dana said as she walked around us as we were gathering ingredients, "the aim here is viral videos and beautiful pictures for Instagram. This show won't sell well with advertisers if you all just hack some horrible cookie together. We want beautiful desserts. You have all morning and most of the afternoon. Keep in mind we may ask you to redo something so we can get a better shot. This is supposed to be more like the Buzzfeed food shows you see on YouTube, not a scripted Food Network production. Do good work. There's a fan favorite prize as well, so make sure you are promoting the show on social media."

I gathered the flour, butter, sugar, eggs, and almond extract I would need for my cookies. I had a perfect recipe for a sugar cookie—it had some bite, but it was fluffy, and the almond made it taste a little nutty. I mixed the dough, put it in the fridge, and contemplated the best way to make a winning plate of cookies.

Baking the same types of cookies wouldn't be enough to win, but I didn't want to go wild and make a thousand different types. That wouldn't photograph well, and I always liked to keep the photograph in mind—my Instagram fans wanted to see gorgeous photographs. I decided to use the same dough but make different shapes and sizes and decorate them differently.

"Do you mind talking a little about what you're planning?" Anastasia asked, coming over to my workstation trailed by two cameramen.

"I'm making an assortment of sugar cookies," I told her as I rolled out my dough. "I don't want to overdo it, I just want a tasty, pretty cookie, but I also don't want it to be too precious. I'm using the cookie cutters to make some, and others I'm freehanding. I want big cookies and small ones to compose a balanced plate."

I didn't mind talking to Anastasia. We had most of the day to work, and soon the thoughts of Jack and Hartleigh and the contest faded away, and it was just me and my baking. The cookies came out of the oven perfectly. The snowflakes I had hand-cut held their shape, thankfully. You could never tell with an unknown oven. I let them sit on the baking sheets to bake the rest of the way with the residual heat. Then I prepped the icing. I was debating between a stiff buttercream and a royal icing. The royal icing would let me draw more intricate patterns by hand compared to buttercream, but I personally liked the taste of buttercream better.

Fortunately, I had the Platinum Provisions icing piper.

The tips were very tiny and made the most intricate patterns. The icing piper was easier to use than the bags because it was run by forced air. I plugged it in and did a few tests, making sure the consistency of the frosting was right.

It wasn't magic, though, and it still took me longer than I had hoped to decorate the hundred or so cookies we had to make. Each judge needed to have a plate, and we had to make additional plates for the camera teams to film and photograph.

I arranged each plate of cookies and taste-tested one. It was perfect. It had some bite, and while I could taste the almond, it wasn't overwhelming. The buttercream was a light layer, but it made intricate patterns on the snowflakes, reindeer, bells, and other shapes I had chosen for my cookies. I snapped a few of my own pictures while Anastasia checked that everyone was finished.

I looked over at Nina and Hartleigh's workstations. Their plates of cookies looked well made too. This was going to be a stiff competition.

"You can all go to the waiting area," Anastasia told us, "except for Chloe. You're first up."

I took a deep breath and picked up my plates of cookies. Jack, the ice prince, was perched on a stool, watching me as I walked up with my plates of cookies and presented them to the judges.

CHAPTER 4

Jack

When Anastasia said that the contestants had all day to bake, I half considered grabbing one of the candy canes that decorated the studio and stabbing myself in the eye with it. Thankfully, we were allowed to leave after the cameras took the shots they needed of the judges reacting to the start of the bake-off. Anu and Nick actually stayed to give more narration and talk to the contestants. I could tell they were really into this baking stuff.

I was not into baking, and I fled to my penthouse. My husky needed to be walked, plus I had work to do.

"I cannot believe I'm wasting my time on this," I complained to Milo, my dog. He was excited to go out, and I knew it was better for him that I was stuck at the tower a few days a week. He would see more of me that way. The husky strained at the leash as we walked out the door. He sniffed at a homeless Santa slumped outside, and I yanked the dog away. I really needed better security for Frost Tower.

The day passed too quickly, and soon I had to report for bake-off judging duty in the studio. As I took a cursory glance at the finished products, I was begrudgingly impressed. I saw intricate frosting work, impressive variety, and generally very professional-looking cookies. One girl had even made 3D cookies, which even I could see would photograph nicely.

I looked at Chloe. She was intently taking pictures of her cookies. From far away, they didn't look as impressive as the others. I hoped she knew what she was doing. She couldn't be sent home already—I still needed her to decorate my lobby.

After the rest of the contestants filed out of the studio, Chloe approached the judges' table. She was covered in frosting; it speckled her Christmas apron and her hair. There were streaks of it on her face, and I wanted to reach out and lick a little green dollop off of her nose.

I crushed that thought. Since when did I want to lick icing off of anyone?

The other two judges smiled at her. I did not. I didn't want to spend the rest of my already wretched day stuck in this studio eating cookies.

"Can you tell us a bit about yourself?" Anu asked as Chloe put the plate of cookies in front of us.

"I'm from the Midwest," Chloe said. "I learned to cook from my *oma*. She loved Christmas! She loved the decorating, the large gatherings, and cooking. But she really loved baking. She passed away a few months ago." She wiped away a tear.

Here we go, I thought, *the desperate ploy for sympathy.*

I ignored her sob story and inspected the cookies. Though I had originally thought they were plain, on closer inspection, I saw that they were intricately decorated. I studied the frosting work on the cookies. Chloe had some sort of lace design that looked like patterns of frost on a window. It was a subtle nod to the holiday season and very clever.

"I'm using this contest as a platform to show the breadth of the types of desserts I can bake," she told the judges. "I would like to one day open my own line of cafés like Christina Tosi and Milk Bar Bakery."

Nick smiled at her, and he and Anu each chose a cookie. I picked out the smallest one I could. It was a tiny, perfect snowflake.

"I hand-cut that," Chloe told me.

"It's very nice," I said begrudgingly. They were really pretty.

"Cheers," Nick said, and he and Anu tapped their cookies against mine, raining crumbs and sugar all over my expensive designer suit.

I scowled.

"Don't make that face, or it's going to freeze like that," Chloe said.

"Is that so," I said.

Anu took a bite of the cookie. "This is a perfect cookie!"

Nick broke off a piece and put it in his mouth, chewing slowly. "I love how there's some give and how I have a complexity of flavors. I mean, my mom didn't make cookies that tasted like this, but it still feels like coming home."

I didn't want a transformative experience. After Nick's reaction, I was worried the cookie was going to cause me to do something rash.

"Don't you want to taste my cookie?" Chloe asked me, her eyes wide and innocent. The apron clung to her body, emphasizing her curves. I wanted a taste of something of hers but not the cookie.

Don't sleep with a contestant, I chastised myself. *That sounds like a sexual harassment suit waiting to happen.*

I looked at Chloe's cookie. It looked like it was sweet and sugary. I took a bite. It wasn't bad. It *was* sweet, but I could also taste a hint of almond. Chloe's snowflake had a deeper flavor than store-bought cookies. Thankfully, I didn't feel the need to break down in tears and rehash my less-than-ideal childhood. I scraped my teeth with my tongue. I could feel them start to rot from the sugar.

"You know sweets are bad for you, right?" I said to Chloe.

Chloe looked upset, but she calmed her features and replied, "You just need a little milk with it."

Was she flirting with me? I couldn't tell. Hartleigh had ruined that for me. I couldn't trust any woman.

"I don't like sweets," I said, wiping my mouth, "but your decoration is perfect, and Anu and Nick seem to think your baking is superb. So..." I swallowed, trying to get the taste of the frosting out of my throat. "Good job."

Each of the other nine contestants came up and explained their cookies. They seemed expertly baked to my untrained eye, though Chloe's decorating was still the best, I thought.

We had to take a bite out of each cookie, and by the time we were down to the last two contestants, I had a headache and was probably prediabetic.

Contrary to Chloe's cookies, the rest were very sweet—cloyingly so. They had some flavor, but mainly I tasted sugar of varying consistencies.

The girl whose workstation was next to Chloe's, Nina, was the second-to-last contestant. She had made the 3D cookies that were a sleigh and reindeer. She had fresh berries and whipped cream piled in the sleigh. I was glad to have the fruit if only to cut the sweetness of the cookies.

Finally, Hartleigh, the last contestant, stepped up. Her boobs were pushed up ridiculously high, and I was afraid they might pop out of her apron. Speaking of nightmare material, Hartleigh was the reason I didn't date. We had grown up next door to each other, and she had stalked me in earnest since high school, when I would find her in my room rifling through my things. She even showed up at Harvard periodically while I was a student there. And here she was again.

Dana and Gunnar clearly were running some sort of substandard operation if they couldn't even complete a simple background check.

I wished Belle was here. I wished for the thousandth time that my sister hadn't cut off contact with us. If she were still in the area, Hartleigh wouldn't come near me. My sister was the only person Hartleigh was afraid of.

I took a bite of her cookie.

"Not as great as Chloe's," I said. "Also, while I see you used my company's icing piper, Chloe had a better mastery of the tool. Her cookies look like art, and yours don't. You and Chloe did basically the same cookie, but hers were better. "

I could tell she was furious.

"I have to agree with Jack," Anu said. "You need to step it up if you want to win."

After Hartleigh stomped off, Anastasia said, "Now that you've reviewed every contestant's cookie, could the judges please discuss the best and worst."

"I actually really love this 3D cookie idea," Nate said. "It should be cheesy, but it's executed so well. I could serve this at my restaurant. "

"It's not a plate of cookies," I countered. "Anastasia said a plate of cookies like you would leave out for Santa." I was so annoyed at this whole bake-off. These people didn't even follow their own rules!

"Chloe's decorations were technically very perfect," Anu said.

"Yes, but she used the machine," Nick added.

"What's wrong with using a machine?" I countered. "You didn't have the contestants start their own fire. It's not as if my company's product is a magic wand. For example, Hartleigh clearly didn't do as great a job as Chloe."

"Chloe definitely has a mastery of the tools," Anu said.

"I do agree with Jack, however, that the 3D sleigh isn't really a cookie. It is inching more into a general dessert for me," said Nick.

After we had reached a verdict, the contestants all filed back into the studio. The middle-of-the-pack people were told they were safe. We sent the contestant who had made a stack of lackluster chocolate cookies home, then it was time to announce the winner.

Nina and Chloe stood together, holding hands.

"And the winner is..."

CHAPTER 5

Chloe

"I won the round! I can't believe it!" I exclaimed. After the camera crew took all of the shots they needed, Nina and I went back to our stations to clean up.

"And you're runner-up," I said to Nina. She looked pleased. I was glad she wasn't mad that she hadn't won the round.

As I cleaned my equipment, I watched Jack talk to Anastasia.

"It's too bad Jack didn't have a transformative experience," I said to Nina.

"Just be glad you won," she said, "and that we weren't sent home."

"Maybe I just have to find his favorite cookie. Do you think he would like gingerbread? Or a linzer cookie? Maybe more of a shortbread?" I mused.

Jack looked in our direction and scowled.

"What's his deal?" I whispered to Nina.

"I don't think he's scowling at us," she replied and looked pointedly at Hartleigh.

"What's up with you and Jack?" Nina asked Hartleigh.

"We have a bond, a connection," Hartleigh said imperiously.

That made me annoyed. I shook off the feeling. I wasn't jealous, was I? I didn't even like Jack; he was a meanie who hated Christmas.

"Now that we're in the same tower, I bet we rekindle our romance. I didn't win this round because Jack doesn't want to play favorites," Hartleigh told me as we dumped the bowls and spoons in a large bin to be washed by some unknown staff person.

"Could you all come shoot interviews?" Dana called, waving us over. "We don't need much since Anastasia talked with you guys during the round."

"I need a shower," I complained.

"You're fine," she said.

"I'm covered in frosting."

"This is supposed to feel looser and more authentic than those highly scripted reality TV shows," Dana said. "It's a positive that you look like you just spent all day baking."

While we waited, I made a silly face and took a selfie and posted it.

I immediately received comments. One said,

You still look beautiful even covered in frosting

I replied,

Thanks!

The person wrote back,

Can I send you fan mail?

That made me excited. I loved receiving mail!

Sure! Send it to Frost Tower. That's where we're shooting.

I received a smiley face wearing a Santa hat in return.

"Someone's sending me fan mail!" I squealed to Nina.

"Be careful," she warned. "There are a lot of nutcases in the world."

"It's fine," I said, waving her concerns away. "I have a baking Instagram. How crazy can baking fans be?"

When it was my turn to sit in front of a decorated Christmas tree and be interviewed, I talked about the decisions I had made, what I hoped to do next, and how I felt about the judges' comments.

By the time we were done, the whole day had passed, and I hadn't even eaten a real meal.

"There are no places to eat around here, unfortunately," Anastasia said when she heard Nina and me complaining about our hunger. "We're between subway lines in this weird sort of Bermuda Triangle."

"Leave it to Jack Frost to find the only place in New York City that's not booming," I said as Anastasia waved and stepped onto the elevator.

After we showered and changed, Nina and I cooked a simple dinner of broiled fish and charred Brussel sprouts in the shared kitchen. Then we both posted pictures and interacted with our followers on social media. My fans were clamoring for the first episode. I didn't know when it would be online, but I promised them it would be out soon. Jack's photo came up as I scrolled through my phone to find more bake-off pictures to post. He looked elegant and delicious, like a perfectly artistic cookie, glazed in frosting.

"He's really handsome," Nina said, looking over my shoulder.

“Don’t even think about it,” Hartleigh snipped, coming into the room.

“Look here, you crazy b—”

“Let’s go out,” I said, standing up and grabbing onto Nina. “I need to buy Christmas decorations.” I still had Jack’s credit card, and I was itching to spend money.

“You have his credit card!” Nina said when I showed her in the elevator.

“It’s the closest I’ll ever be to a billionaire’s kept girlfriend!” I said with a giggle.

The mall was crowded. It was nothing like the dead malls filled with discount stores in my hometown. This was a high-end mall catering to customers with no-limit credit cards and expensive tastes.

Jazz renditions of Christmas carols played over the sound system, and the expansive atrium in the center of the mall was filled with holiday décor. In the middle of the large space stood a giant Christmas tree decorated with oversized glass ornaments and big wrapped boxes underneath. As we walked along toward the cluster of home furnishing and decorating stores, Nina pointed.

“It’s Santa and the elves!”

We stopped to watch the kids be placed on Santa’s lap. He seemed jolly and happy to be interacting with the children. Nina and I cooed at the kids. Some of them seemed excited to be meeting Santa, and some of them were completely freaked out.

Santa saw us looking and waved. We waved back then headed on our way.

The first store we stopped at had a huge amount of décor to choose from.

"Did Jack give you a budget?" Nina asked as we walked to the display of Christmas decorations that took up most of the back half of the store.

"Nope," I replied, fingering a wreath festooned in gold ribbon. "We shouldn't go crazy, but we do need to buy enough so that the lobby looks decorated." I pulled up a picture of the space on my phone and started choosing items.

"I like these white-painted abstract Christmas trees, but I think we will need a few more in different sizes," I said to Nina as I snapped pictures. I thought I saw her nod out of the corner of my eye.

"Maybe we can ask a sales associate if they have any more," I said as I turned around to look at Nina. Then I screamed.

"Santa!" I said with a nervous laugh. The red-suited man gave a fake chuckle.

"Shopping for Christmas decorations, I see," he said.

"Something like that..." I replied. Had he followed me here? Where was Nina?

"Are you on break?" I asked him. Wasn't he supposed to be doing pictures?

"Come have a drink with me," he said.

"Uh, I'm busy. I have to decorate for Christmas. You know how it is," I said, starting to back away. Santa reached out and grabbed for me, pulling my hair out of its loose bun. At that moment, Nina came running over with a sales associate, and Santa hurried away.

"Are you okay?" the salesperson asked.

"Sure," I said, patting my hair back into some semblance of order. "I think he's just filled with a bit too much Christmas cheer."

We finished our shopping. Nina and I found several large wreaths, garlands of different styles, and sets of candles.

"I think we should buy three Christmas trees," I said. "The lobby is such a large space. We can intersperse it with these abstracted Christmas trees in white and metal." They were pretty, they had little lights on them, and I was envisioning creating a sort of forest in Frost Tower. The lobby was a somewhat cold space with polished concrete and glass, and I wanted to keep the same restrained, almost industrial nature and complement it instead of trying to hide it.

"You should add some of these," the salesperson said, pointing to large metal letters etched in tiny lights. They spelled out words like JOY and HOPE.

"Perfect," I said.

The sales associated helped us carry our purchases to the garage. I had to call three large SUVs to hold everything.

"Do you think this is too much?" Nina asked.

"I'm thinking this might not be enough," I said as we loaded in the last of the boxes.

Our next stop was a Christmas tree lot. I picked three of the largest, fullest blue spruces I could find.

"Do you have garland as well?" I asked the seller.

"Yes, miss," he said, loading up several bags' worth. "Have in-laws to impress?"

"Ha!" I laughed. "I'm just decorating for a TV show."

He strapped the trees onto the cars, and we loaded up the boxes of garland. I was turning Frost Tower into a winter wonderland, and Jack the Grinch could suck on a candy cane.

CHAPTER 6

Jack

I pulled one of the prepared meals out of my fridge. I had a personal chef make them, but it wasn't as if he had them waiting for me whenever I wanted. He made them every few days, packaged them, and had them delivered to my penthouse. It was convenient and probably better than takeout every night. I dumped one of the containers on a plate and heated it up. Milo whined for food as I ate standing up at the kitchen counter. It wasn't that enjoyable, but it was energy.

Speaking of energy, Milo looked like he needed another walk. Huskies had an insane amount of energy. They probably shouldn't be kept in cities, but Belle had given him to me a few Christmases before she left, and there was no way I was letting the dog out of my sight, let alone sending him off to the suburbs.

Milo was happy to run around in the park, and he was tired but content on the walk back to Frost Tower. As we approached the lobby, I saw a caravan of cars pull up.

"What on earth?" I muttered.

As I approached the entrance, I saw Chloe and Nina chatting to the drivers. They were unloading bags and boxes and carrying them inside.

"What is all this?" I demanded, hurrying into the lobby.

"Christmas decorations," Chloe said. Her cheeks were rosy, and she was wearing a red coat with a fur hood. She looked cuddly, and I just wanted to scoop her up and snuggle her. I shook my head. Clearly the stress of the financial situation of my tower was affecting me.

Milo head-butted Chloe, wagging his tail and acting like she was his long lost-friend.

"You're the worst guard dog," I told him as Chloe and Nina petted and cooed over my husky. I watched helplessly as the drivers finished unloading the cars and propped the Christmas trees up in the lobby.

Yes, trees. Plural.

"Who needs three Christmas trees?" I said in disbelief.

"This space does," Chloe said, giving Milo one last pat.

"Those need to go in water," one of the men helping to move the boxes inside told us, pointing to the trees.

"Right."

Chloe looked at me.

"What?"

"Aren't you going to tip them?" she asked.

I slipped the men a few twenty-dollar bills while Chloe and Nina started rummaging through their purchases.

"I hope this didn't cost an arm and a leg," I said.

Chloe handed me the credit card and a wad of receipts then gave me a slightly guilty smile.

"It's for a good cause," she said.

"Is it?"

"Now you'll have a lobby full of holiday cheer!"

As I watched Chloe and Nina ooh and ahh over their purchases while I waited for the elevator, I felt a small smile creep onto my face. I immediately stamped it down. This sight should not inspire cheer, Christmas or otherwise. Chloe had spent what looked like thousands of dollars on decorations. That was money I shouldn't be throwing at Frost Tower.

I knew that financially the best decision was to cut my losses and find a buyer for the tower. Though it was illogical, I didn't want to give up, and a part of me hoped Chloe's Christmas magic worked. I hated losing, and signing away the tower felt like admitting defeat.

When I returned to the penthouse, I forced myself to prep for the morning meeting with Svensson Investment. They were partial owners in Frost Tower, and they were not pleased with the performance of their investment.

The next morning, I took the subway to the Svensson Investment tower. I knew this was not going to be a pleasant meeting.

"There's our Christmas-baking-loving judge!" Liam Svensson, my Platinum Provisions cofounder, said when I walked into the lobby of the Svensson Investment tower. He threw an arm around my shoulders.

"You really are grasping at candy canes," he said jovially, "if you're judging a baking competition to try and convince my brothers not to force you to sell that tower."

"I just need a few more months," I told him. "I don't want to lose. I don't want that black mark on my resume."

"Who cares if Frost Tower goes under?" Liam said. "It's the real estate business. These things happen."

"It's my first real estate venture," I told him. "I can't fail on my first try."

"Everyone fails their first real estate venture," he said as the elevator door opened. "When I was eighteen, I bought this car wash, and it hemorrhaged money. I finally burned it down. It was a complete disaster. "

"Yes, but this is a skyscraper that cost hundreds of millions of dollars to build. There is already an uncomfortably long section on my Wikipedia page about what a failure it is," I told him.

The elevator for the top floor pinged. I tried to steel myself.

"You should move to Frost Tower," I told Liam.

"I'm living rent free in one of my brother's condo towers," he said. "And the rest of my brothers are there. Besides, Frost Tower doesn't even have a restaurant. What would I eat? I would starve."

He must have seen the dejection I was trying to hide.

"I'll see if we can't convince them to keep your tower on life support for another quarter," Liam said, clapping me on the shoulder. "But my brothers are going to want results soon."

"I know," I said. "I should have stuck to the industry I excel at—making products people can buy and use. Real estate is nothing but dark magic."

Walking into the large boardroom at Svenssons felt like going to a funeral. There were two broad-shouldered blond men, spitting images of Liam, seated at the table, and they did not look happy.

Greg Svensson stood from his place at the head of the table and came over to me to shake my hand.

"You smell like frosting," he remarked.

"It's *The Great Christmas Bake-Off*," I explained. "It permeates the air."

"I don't care about the bake-off," Greg said, sitting back down. Carl, Greg and Liam's other brother, tapped at his tablet. A screen descended from the ceiling, and the lights dimmed.

"As you know," Carl began, "I handle a large portion of Svensson Investment's real estate portfolio."

A graph popped up on the screen.

"Your tower is our worst-performing asset," he said. "By quite a large margin."

"I know," I said through gritted teeth. It was like a punch in the gut to see such low numbers on the screen.

"There is an eighty-seven percent vacancy," Carl said. "The tenants you promised to deliver never materialized—"

"The financial technology firm that was going to lease several floors the building is having difficulties right now," I said, cutting him off. "The Securities and Exchange Commission has them under investigation, and the senior leadership is probably all going to prison. Our other big tenant declared bankruptcy because they were defrauding their investors. That's hardly my fault. It's just one of those things. I promise I'll find more tenants, better tenants."

Greg looked at me steely-eyed.

"Furthermore," Carl continued, "only two of the luxury condos were sold, one to yourself and one to a young woman named Anastasia."

"I had foreign buyers lined up, but they were from Russia, China, and Brazil, and with the sanctions against those countries, the deals fell through. Some of the condos the feds are still sitting on because they froze the transactions. It's just bad luck," I said, "but this is New York City; we'll find buyers eventually."

"We don't have until the end of time," Greg said. "In real estate, you live or die by your pro forma. You are wasting too much time and energy on this tower, Jack," Greg said. "You're neglecting your real company, Platinum Provisions."

"I'm not neglecting it," I countered. "We are bringing in more revenue than ever."

"Be that as it may," Carl said, "the tax bill on Frost Tower is going to be due soon. And Svensson needs a return on our investment. I have a Canadian buyer who is interested in the tower as well as a Qatari buyer."

I looked to Liam.

"Just give him one more quarter," Liam said. "It's Christmas, and it's not like much is going to happen this month that would be ready to go in the first quarter."

"I just don't see how you can turn it around," Greg said, shaking his head.

"Look," I told them, launching into my spiel. "Frost Tower was well designed, though currently it comes off as a bit bland. It lacks character and a sense of place, but I think if I could find the perfect ground-floor tenant, like, say, a popular restaurant, it would attract the type of creative companies and pique the interest of residential buyers looking for new property next year. Gunnar's Romance

Creative holiday production should help put Frost Tower on everyone's radar."

Greg rolled his eyes, and Carl smirked.

"Our half-brother is half crazy. I can't believe he and that Holbrook are filming a web show in your tower," Greg said.

"They're paying tenants," I countered.

"Are they?" Greg said, his mouth quirking slightly in disbelief.

"They will be," Liam assured him. "Jack's having the tower decorated for Christmas, and there will be nice establishing shots. The contestants were picked because they have huge Instagram and social media followings. This one girl, Chloe, has hundreds of thousands of very active followers. I had one of our marketing analysts take a look at her profiles."

Greg looked at Carl, who shrugged. "Okay, fine, you have another quarter," Greg said.

I walked out of the meeting feeling lighter than I had in weeks.

"Thanks, man," I told Liam.

"We'll figure something out," he said. "Maybe you can convince Starbucks to come into that vacant retail space you have."

"I just need a Christmas miracle," I said.

"Or you need a Christmas lay," my friend replied with a wink. "That girl, Chloe, is cute. You could dress her up in a sexy Mrs. Claus outfit."

That was a tantalizing thought. I could feel the heat rush straight to my groin.

"Or there's always Hartleigh," Liam said impishly.

I grimaced. At least my boner was gone.

I had hoped to avoid Hartleigh for the duration of the contest, but luck was not on my side. She was down in the lobby with Chloe and Nina. The space looked... well, it looked magical. I could appreciate how the décor might make this space more desirable. Chloe was snapping pictures, for her Instagram I presumed.

She jerked up when Hartleigh saw me and shrieked, "Jack!"

I ignored her and asked Chloe, "Are you quite finished spending my money?"

Chloe glared at Hartleigh, then she turned to me. She had bits of tinsel and pine needles in her hair and on her sweater.

"We're only partially finished, but I think it's coming along nicely. Aren't you feeling the Christmas spirit?" she asked, running her hand under her ample chest. Her tits strained against the sweater. Liam's words banged like a bell choir in my head. *Christmas lay... Chloe in a sexy Mrs. Claus outfit.*

It took me a second to register that she was not in fact implying that her tits were there for my Christmas cheer. Instead, she was referring to the blinking reindeer on her sweater.

"You know I hate Christmas," I told her. "Also, you have garbage in your hair."

She patted her head, fluffing the glittery pieces of ribbon clippings and tinsel out of her frizzy blonde hair.

I swept around her, catching a whiff of pine and sugar.

Concentrate on saving the tower, I told myself. *Chloe will only be a distraction.*

But I bet she would be a tasty one.

CHAPTER 7

Chloe

The next day was another early morning. I stifled a yawn as I listened to Anastasia tell us about the day's challenge.

"This is the Home for Christmas Signature Challenge," she said. "Everyone has a Christmas dessert that is steeped in family tradition and that people associate with you. This is an opportunity to let your personality and family holiday traditions shine."

I knew exactly what I was going to make—an Austrian wedding cookie my oma made at Christmas. I went into the studio pantry and gathered pecans, French imported sea salt, and some of the best butter I had ever seen. At least Dana and Gunnar weren't skimping on ingredients.

"This challenge is again sponsored by Trader Mike's," Anastasia concluded. "Make fabulous desserts at home."

I wondered how they had convinced the chain to sponsor an unknown web series. Then I remembered Dana was from the billionaire Holbrook family, and she probably had all sorts of connections.

As I arranged the pecans on the roasting pan, I thought about what I would do if I won the contest. I knew my cousin would come begging for money. I also knew I would probably give him some, even though I knew he would spend it on drugs. I was turning into an enabler like my oma. But that was a dark thought, and I was here to bake tasty Christmas desserts.

I toasted the pecans to bring out their nutty flavor, salting them slightly before putting them into the hot convection oven. I wanted to win, yes, but more so, I wanted to impress Jack. I had selected this cookie recipe because it wasn't super sweet. This dessert would be just the thing to break through Jack's icy exterior and stoke the flame of holiday cheer.

You want to stoke something else too, the naughty little elf in my subconscious said. *Maybe lust? Sexual desire?*

No, I told it, *I only want to see his eyes roll back in his head when he bites into one of my cookies.*

You want his eyes to roll back when he pushes inside of you with that thick, hard—

"Rolling pin," I said out loud. Nina looked over at me, and I blushed.

"Do you need a rolling pin?" she asked me, holding out one from her station.

"Uh no ..."

Yes...a big, thick—

Shut up, naughty elf.

"These cookies don't need a rolling pin," I muttered to myself.

Nina walked over and felt my forehead.

"I hope you aren't turning crazy like Hartleigh," she said with a grin.

I swatted her hand away and busied myself chopping nuts, mixing the loose, crumbly dough, and pressing the cookies together. The trick was to not pack the mixture too tightly. The cookie needed little air pockets for one to fully taste all the flavors.

While these cookies were somewhat time intensive to assemble properly, they weren't actually all that difficult. I didn't have to decorate them, only roll them in confectioners' sugar.

While the cookies baked, I looked around. Anastasia was chatting with the other contestants. Normally I felt bad for chefs in cooking shows when the host would take up three of the twenty minutes contestants were allotted to make a complex dish, but the Romance Creative producers gave us enough time that I didn't mind chatting with Anastasia about my cookies and listening to other people talk about their signature desserts.

"I think Jack will love these," Hartleigh said as she talked about her pomegranate scones.

Even though I despised Hartleigh and how she acted around Jack, her scones did sound amazing.

Ethan, another contestant, was making a cranberry-pear pie. He seemed a little frazzled as he tried to cut an intricate pattern out of the pie crust and make sure his filling was cooking correctly.

"You want some help?" I asked him, going over to his table.

"I swear I'm usually better than this," he said, his face flushed.

"You need cold hands to make pie crust," I told Ethan as I dumped the runny dough in the trash and cleared off his space to start a new dough.

As the dough chilled, I took my cookies out of the oven. They smelled amazing—nutty and savory with a hint of sweetness. Jack was going to love them.

I let them cool and went back to Ethan's workstation. The pie dough was chilled, and I rolled it out and braided a Christmas wreath pattern around the pie. I also cut out little sprigs of mistletoe and holly. Finally I cut out a winter Christmas scene with a tree and several animals and placed them over the pie filling.

"Wow!" Ethan said. "You're really good at this. Thanks!"

I was proud of the pie crust. After taking a few pictures, I rolled my Austrian wedding cookies in confectioners' sugar, giving them a layer of white powdery sweetness to contrast with the savoriness of the nuts and butter.

As I arranged them on a platter, I watched Jack walk in. Hartleigh made a kissy face at him, and he looked annoyed. I was starting to feel weirdly protective of Jack Frost. He clearly didn't like it when Hartleigh made advances towards him.

I knew he would like these cookies, though. With the last ones, he had complained about sweetness. Though the wedding cookies were covered in sugar, it was just a coating before the blast of the more savory, almost umami taste of the nutty cookie.

I was one of the last contestants to present my dessert, and I waited nervously in the back room for my turn.

After her presentation to the judges, Nina came in beaming.

"They loved my dish," she said. "I'm so relieved!"

Then it was my turn. I approached the butcher-block table as the judges each took a cookie. But my eyes were only on Jack. I wanted him to fall to his knees after tasting my Christmas cookies.

He took a bite of the dessert. I saw a smile break through the ice.

CHAPTER 8

Jack

The Austrian wedding cookie was the most amazing thing I'd ever tasted. It was like love and family and Christmas. It wasn't too sweet, even though it was covered in sugar. Instead, the cookie was nutty and rich. I swallowed. I thought I had powdered sugar on my suit.

Chloe wore a triumphant smile, like she had planned this whole thing and was waiting for me to cry or fall to my knees and worship her baked goods. The sick, mean, Grinch part of me didn't want to admit that I loved the cookie.

"It tastes like garbage," I said. Her face fell. "Also, didn't you make cookies last week?"

Might as well go for broke, Jack, I thought.

"Come to think of it," I said coldly, "Maybe you should lay off the cookies." I let my eyes roam her body. She didn't need to lay off anything—she had a cute, sexy figure. She was curvy and had a pretty face, which was just what I liked.

Chloe looked upset. Anastasia seemed pissed, and the camera guy made a shocked noise. Anu, to her credit, kept her face perfectly neutral as she took a bite of the cookie.

"This is a very nice cookie, but everyone else made something a bit more impressive," she said. "This was the signature challenge. While these taste amazing, they don't look that pretty."

"They seem very homemade," Nick added. "They are called wedding cookies because it's something simple for relatives to make for a younger relative's wedding. This isn't a pastry chef–quality production."

"Maybe you should have spent more time on your dessert instead of helping other people. Ethan said you made his pie crust," Anu told Chloe. "That was something worthy of a chef. Your pie crust was amazing. It was flakey and buttery, and the decorations you put on it were just beautiful."

"I agree. You spent more time on Ethan's dessert than your own," Nick said.

Chloe looked upset, but she didn't say anything else.

All I could think of was scoring more of those cookies. She had made extras, right? I could just sneak some more off of one of the plates. Even so, then they would be all gone. I needed a long-term cookie plan.

Anu and Nick declared Nina and her stollen *crème brûlée* the winner. Chloe made it to the next round, but she was in the bottom two. Ethan was kicked out since the part of his dessert the judges liked best, the crust, Chloe had made.

When I walked out of the studio to do postproduction commentary, Gunnar and Dana were waiting for me.

"You are not allowed to be rude and misogynistic," Dana snapped.

"I'm sorry," I said. "I'm under a lot of stress." I saw one of the production assistants walk by with the extra desserts the contestants had made. Chloe's cookies passed not even two feet away from me.

"Are you even paying attention?" Dana hissed.

No. No, I wasn't.

"Sure, yeah, I'll be better next time," I told her and walked off to follow the cookies. There were some left out for photographing. I swiped two while the camera guys weren't looking.

In the elevator, I took out one of the cookies hidden in my suit pocket and ate it. Heaven. It was amazing. The cookie wasn't too sweet, and I could taste the individual ingredients. The nuts made the cookie savory and slightly salty, which balanced out the sugar. It was addicting. I needed another one.

I walked into my apartment chewing the last of the swiped cookies. I looked down; my suit was covered in powdered sugar and little crumbs. Milo jumped off of the sofa and padded over to me, licking the sugar off of my suit as I brushed off the crumbs.

"I need more of those cookies," I said to the dog. They seemed to be a fairly standard cookie according to Nick and Anu. It shouldn't be hard to find a cookie like the one Chloe had made, especially in New York City. I checked online. Several bakeries had similar wedding cookies. After making sure my suit was powdered sugar-free, I put on a light overcoat and went out.

This should have been a job for an assistant, but my assistant was gone—she had gone to California with her new husband, and between my company and the disaster of Frost Tower, I hadn't had time to find a new one.

Under the pretense of finding a tenant for my tower, I visited bakery after bakery.

Each bakery had wedding cookies that looked similar, but none of them tasted like Chloe's. They were poor imitations. Was it really that impossible to find a decent cookie in New York City?

While waiting for my car to swing around the block, I searched for a recipe online. The cookie used only four main ingredients. It couldn't be that difficult to make. I went to a store and picked up what I needed.

I'm a billionaire, I went to Harvard, and I run a global company. I can make cookies, I thought.

CHAPTER 9

Chloe

I couldn't believe I was in the bottom two.

"Your cookies were fine," Nina assured me. "Jack was just a douche."

I was lying on my bed in our shared room, feeling depressed.

"Jack said I didn't need any more cookies," I whined. "And the judges were mean to me."

"Jack Frost is a horrible person," Nina said, patting me on the head. "He's basically a monster. I mean, he doesn't like Christmas and he doesn't like desserts. Who does that?"

"I made those especially for him! Why didn't he like them?" I wailed. "I was sure he would like those cookies!"

"Some people can't be saved," Nina said. "That's what all those billionaires are like. Did you know that something like twenty-one percent of all CEOs are sociopaths? He's a fundamentally awful person."

"Don't talk about my future husband like that!" I heard Hartleigh yell from the common area.

"I am not staying in the apartment with her," I said to Nina, standing up and putting my shoes on.

"Let's go finish decorating the lobby," she suggested. "Gunnar told me that he needs to take the shots of the space tomorrow morning."

I collected my decorating supplies while I stewed about Hartleigh and Jack and the unfairness of it all.

"Jack and Hartleigh deserve each other," Nina said as we rode the elevator to the lobby. "They can make freakishly tall, freakishly scrawny babies."

"You're just saying that to make me feel better," I said.

"I speak the truth! Her skin is sallow, and her chest is a bit flat. You'd think Jack would want actual boobs on an actual woman."

"At least Hartleigh seems to fit into New York City, though," I said as we walked off the elevator into the partially decorated lobby.

"That's probably why her hair looks so bad, all the binging and purging and cosmos for dinner. She can't even cook."

"That's good, because Jack doesn't even appreciate good cooking," I said, ripping open a box of lights. "My oma said not to trust a skinny cook, and I certainly don't trust Hartleigh."

Nina and I tacked up the rest of the garland, decorated the trees, and strung up lights.

"It's beautiful," Nina said.

It did look nice. All the decorating had cheered me up a little bit. I snapped more photos and posted them. The comments came immediately. There were lots of Christmas emojis as well as phrases like "Beautiful" and "Christmas magic."

"Did some weirdo write, 'You'll make a great wife'?" Nina asked.

"It comes with the territory, unfortunately." I sighed, putting away my phone.

People were stopping outside to look at the decorations and snap selfies in front of the window.

"We certainly made this a popular space," I said as I rearranged the chairs that I'd bought around the lobby space. The space was cozy but elegant. It also didn't feel so sterile.

The glass walls that had previously made the lobby feel like a goldfish bowl now made the decorated space feel as if it was a magical portal to another world where it was always Christmas.

"The trees definitely help to scale down the space," Nina remarked as we picked up the remaining packaging.

"Perfect!" Gunnar told us as he paused to take a few pictures on his way out of the lobby. "Go team!"

"And of course they aren't paying us for helping," I muttered.

"Yes," Nina said, "but we had an awesome time shopping, and it was all on Jack's dime."

"I hope he has a heart attack when he sees the credit card bill," I told her.

"You're still crabby," my new friend said, putting her arm around me. "Come, I'll make us something good to eat."

"Sit," she ordered when we returned to the shared apartment. She started making a creamy pasta carbonara dish.

"You shouldn't eat that. It's bad for you," Hartleigh said from her spot on the living room couch. "I'm eating salad."

"You're eating lettuce leaves," Nina said. "Salad has dressing and cheese and artichokes."

Hartleigh picked up her bowl and went to her room in a huff.

"Maybe I *should* eat a salad," I said, resting my head in my hands.

"I'll make you a nice creamy Caesar salad with croutons and fresh grated parmesan cheese tomorrow," Nina said. "But right now, you need carbs. You've had a rough day."

"I mean, I really shouldn't. I—" She stuffed a generous forkful of pasta into my mouth.

"That's really good," I said around the mouthful of pasta. The little bits of pancetta were crispy and fatty, the sauce was rich, and the pasta was salty and flavorful. I grabbed the whole bowl.

"Hey, we have to share!" Nina exclaimed, gesturing with her fork.

We both ate out of the bowl then curled up on the couch while Nina searched for a movie to watch.

My Fitbit beeped, reminding me that I had had no exercise that day. I dragged myself upright, drunk on pasta.

"I'm going to take a walk," I said, standing up.

"It's dark out," Nina protested. "And cold, and we were going to watch a movie."

It did look cold outside, but Jack's words had cut more than I wanted to admit.

"I'll be fine. It's New York City. There are still people out on the streets at night," I said.

I checked my Fitbit. I hadn't gotten in that many steps today. Determined to do some walking, I put on my coat and wrapped my scarf around my neck. I told myself I wasn't exercising because Jack made a mean comment about my weight, I was doing it for my own health.

The women in my family tended to hold onto the pounds, except for my mother, who had been an opioid addict. In her final days, she had been as thin as a rail. My grandmother had raised me, and when she found out my older cousin, who she had raised and who was like a brother to me, was also an addict, it broke her heart. He proceeded to steal from both of us, and when I reported it to the police against my oma's protest, I think the grief killed her, though it could have been all the baked goods.

That thought spurred me to up my pace in the chilly night air.

CHAPTER 10

Jack

After shopping for ingredients, I received a call from Liam.

"Where are you? Gunnar said filming was done for the day."

I looked at the bags of ingredients beside me in the car.

"I was caught up looking for restaurant tenants," I lied.

"Did you forget about the meeting?" Liam asked.

Shoot. I had forgotten that the marketing director and his team wanted to meet with Liam and me. I had the car turn to head towards the Platinum Provisions tower.

Unlike Frost Tower, this one was in a great location and had a well-reviewed Japanese restaurant, a café, and a high-end retail store at street level. It was also completely occupied. Of course, my company was the one and only office tenant, but still, Platinum Provisions tower was a success.

I walked in, glad that the ingredients were in a nondescript brown bag without logos. Liam was waiting for me in my large office.

"I know this meeting is a bit late in the day," he said, "but with your filming schedule…"

"It's fine," I told him.

"What's that?" he asked, pointing at the bag.

"Just samples from potential tenants," I lied.

"Look at you, selling your retail space like a boss," he said as he reached for the bag, "Anything good?"

"No," I said, snatching the bag away.

"Okay." My friend and business partner gave me a weird look. "I heard about your outburst during filming, I guess you're going to be a weirdo today. Whatever. As long as your craziness makes us money."

"I'm not crazy," I said as I followed him to the elevator.

"Sure," he drawled as the elevator dinged. I wondered if I should refrigerate the butter, but maybe it would be fine. The meeting wasn't going to be that long, was it?

When I walked into the board room, the marketing team looked as if they were settling in for the long haul. We spent the next few hours going over the projections and ideas. I was more of the product and operations guy, whereas Liam had more of the creative interpersonal flair. We made a good team and had built a successful company.

The first part of the meeting was fairly straightforward. The sales of our medical equipment were growing, and I told the marketing team about some of the new types of surgical equipment we were working on patenting, and they took notes on the benefits. We also discussed the company's push into taking a greater share of the specialized drill bit market.

"Now on to something more fun," the director said. "Christmas baking."

Liam chuckled at my expression.

"The sales of our baking equipment have been growing steadily, as everyone is aware, but after Thanksgiving we saw a spike in sales. Sometimes these spikes happen, but this one seems to have legs. We haven't been doing any big marketing campaigns. At first, I thought maybe our competition was buying our product for some reason, but then we traced it all back to this girl."

He pulled up Chloe's Instagram feed. There were pictures of her smiling broadly, wearing cute clothes, or displaying elegant baked goods.

"Every third picture practically is her either with our Platinum Provisions cooking product line or her showing off something she made using our products. We're not paying her anything, yet she's driving a lot of traffic to us," the marketing director said.

"She has some of the best social media engagement I've ever seen," said another young woman on the marketing team.

Liam was smirking. I could tell he was struggling to hold back a comment.

"Just say it, Liam," I growled. "You know you want to."

"Jack is judging a bake-off competition, and Chloe is a contestant. Also, he insulted her so don't count on any more sales," he said in one long run-on sentence.

The marketing director's eyes bugged out. "You insulted her?"

"It was an accident," I said.

"You can't do that!" he protested. "Look at her followers. She adds hundreds of new fans a day. *Oprah* retweeted her.

One negative comment from her could set off a chain reaction of nuclear proportions!"

"I'm going to fix it," I said, trying to keep the annoyance off my face.

"What is this competition, by the way?" another senior marketer asked.

"My half-brother and one of the Holbrooks are doing this reality web TV series," Liam said.

"We should sponsor a few episodes," the director said.

"It was supposed to be more about promoting Frost Tower," I said. "I didn't want to involve Platinum Provisions because it seems sketchy."

"There's nothing sketchy about Chloe," the marketing director said. "She's like a pure fluffy cinnamon roll."

"I'll give you Gunnar's contact," Liam said. "I think it's a great idea. Jack's already a judge, so it makes perfect sense for us to be a sponsor."

After another hour of talking about marketing, I was finally able to escape. The food in the brown sack felt a little warm, but I stuck the butter in the fridge when I returned home. Then I set to work toasting nuts, measuring ingredients, and baking.

After several frustrating hours, I realized I could not, in fact, make the cookies. Oh, I was able to follow the recipe and make something vaguely cookie-like, but it didn't match the contradictorily perfect cookie that Chloe had made that was both fluffy and dense, sweet and savory.

The whole place smelled like sugar and charred nuts. I opened the French doors that led out to the large balcony to air out the penthouse.

It was freezing cold outside as I looked out over the city from the balcony. I was in a T-shirt. The cold numbed my skin, just the way I liked it. My husky liked it too. I looked down and saw a figure in a red coat walk out of the building. It couldn't be.

I ran and grabbed the antique telescope my sister had given me for my birthday a few years ago, one of the last times I had seen her, and focused it on the figure. Yep, it was Chloe. What was she doing alone at—I checked my watch—11 p.m.? She could be hurt.

Not my problem.

I stood on the balcony and watched her disappear down the street.

What if she was killed?

No more cookies.

I pulled on my boots and a light jacket—it was rarely too cold for me—snapped the husky into his harness, and set off. I made a few wrong turns, but I eventually found her. The red coat she wore made Chloe easy to spot.

I followed her from a distance. I didn't want to spook her, just make sure she was okay.

CHAPTER 11

Chloe

New York City at night was magical. The snow fell softly, providing an attractive backdrop for the well-dressed people walking down the street.

When I'd come to New York City the last time, I had been a young girl, but I'd fallen in love with the glamor and the sights. I promised myself I would move here permanently, and here I was. I had also thought I would have money, a swanky apartment, and a handsome, wonderful boyfriend, but that was clearly unrealistic. At least I was here in the city though.

For how long, I wasn't sure. If I didn't win the competition or if I was kicked out too early, then I wouldn't have enough time to build my platform. If no one wanted to hire me as a pastry chef, I couldn't stay. My vision, of course, was my own bakery franchise, but that was looking more and more like an unrealistic pipe dream. I would settle for a job making cookies for hotel guests if that was what would help me stay in New York City.

I stopped in front of a Kate Spade window display. I loved Christmas window displays. No one did them anymore in my dinky little Midwestern town, but here in New York, they were drool worthy. Kate Spade had purses shaped like Christmas ornaments hanging from the ceiling just inside the window. White and silver scarves of wool, fur, and gauzy silk were draped on the floor like snow. It was simple yet elegant.

I strolled down the street, going from window to window. My selfies looked awesome. I wasn't the only person out—there were tons of people out on the street, even though it was late. I was posting my latest selfie when I saw red out of the corner of my eye. There was a man dressed as Santa. He waved, and I waved back.

"Don't give crazy people the time of day," said a woman hurrying past me. "You won't last long in this city with that attitude."

Her comment shook me out of my Christmas haze. What was I thinking waving at that Santa? What if he was the same one who had followed me at the mall?

I hurried back in the direction of Frost Tower, the wind tugging at my hair. I heard footsteps behind me. Was the Santa was following me?

I turned a corner to take more of a diagonal route back to the tower. The street was quiet. Some people had lights on their balconies, but I could feel I was alone. Picking up the pace, I checked the map on my phone. I was still quite a ways away from the tower; I had walked farther than I meant to. My Fitbit beeped, and I shrieked, clutching my chest, as I realized it was just telling me that I had met my goal.

Go me.

The footsteps behind me sounded louder, as if a man was running towards me. I started jogging, cursing all the cookies and pasta I had eaten that day. In front of me, I saw a figure jump out of an alley. It was a Santa.

I screamed, and a dog barked as someone grabbed me, pulling me back against a muscular chest. I froze for a second then attacked the man holding me.

"Ow! Don't fight me! I'm trying to save you!"

I clobbered him with my bag.

"Spare some change?" the Santa slurred.

"Leave or I'm calling the police," said the man.

I realized that the deep voice was familiar. It was Jack. I stopped struggling.

The Santa took a swig of his drink then staggered off. The growling husky started to go after him.

"Heel, Milo," Jack commanded. The dog circled back to his master's side.

"Are you following me?" I yelled as Jack released me. My heart was pounding, and I tried to calm down.

"I'm trying to protect you," he said, visibly annoyed.

"From *Santa Claus*?" I huffed. Now that I wasn't alone, I was feeling more confident.

"I don't need your help, especially after you insulted me and almost had me eliminated from the competition," I said, hands on my hips.

Jack stared down at me. He looked like the prince of winter, the wind blowing his silver-white hair, his eyes narrowed, his nose imperious. The beautiful husky stood next to him, snapping at snowflakes.

"You have no idea what you're doing," Jack growled. "You're wandering around on side streets in a foreign city."

"It's a grid," I scoffed. "You can't lose your way."

"But you could be hurt," he said.

I could see the outlines of his abs and pecs through his thin T-shirt. His light jacket was unzipped, though it was freezing cold. His breath clouded around his mouth, which I wanted to kiss.

He stepped closer to me. He was so tall! He leaned down slightly. Was he going to kiss me? His mouth was a thin, cold line, and instead of kissing me, he grabbed me by the arm and started guiding me down the street.

"You need to go back to the tower."

"I can walk just fine, thank you," I said, tugging away. He pulled me back towards him. I decided to just let him have his way this once. It had absolutely nothing to do with the fact that his arms were strong and the feel of his hand on me sent sparks through my body.

"Where is your coat?" I asked him.

"I don't mind the cold," he said. "It's good for your circulation."

We walked in silence for a few blocks. I had to walk quickly to keep up with his long strides.

"In the future," he said, breaking the silence, "don't leave without an escort. New York has changed, but Frost Tower is not in the most desirable of locations."

"Then why did you put it there?" I protested as I followed him.

"It was cheaper."

"Probably for a reason. A lot of people use fake vanilla because it's cheaper, and it also has a cloying aftertaste. It's better to just pay for the real thing. Otherwise you'll be paying more because you have to dump your whole batch of cookies."

"Did I get the right vanilla?" I heard him mumble.

"What?"

"Nothing." We walked a few more blocks in silence, then he said, "You remind me of my mom. She's a scientist and has weird facts that she blurts out as non sequiturs."

"You have parents?" I said in mock surprise. "You didn't just pop out of a snowdrift and into my life as an aggravating villain?"

"I'm not a villain," he said.

"You weren't very nice," I told him. "Didn't your mother teach you any manners?"

His face went dark. "I don't want to talk about my parents."

"Fine," I said. "Let's talk about the fact that you said my cookies were garbage and that I'm dumpy and ugly."

"You aren't ugly," he said. He stopped and turned to look at me. His eyes flicked from my nose to my mouth down to my chest and back up. "You're cute," he said, taking my hands. "And I'm sorry."

"Well," I said. He did make a pretty picture. "I forgive you. But you have to let me find a cookie or a dessert you like. We're humans. We are evolutionarily primed to like sweet, salty, fatty foods. I was sure you would think the wedding cookies were yummy."

He released my hands and turned away from me.

"I told you I don't like sweets," he said.

"Yes, but they weren't that sweet. That was the point," I said. I scurried after him and his dog Milo, who was trotting along.

When we reached the tower, Jack escorted me inside. The security guard was snoring at the desk. Jack shook his head.

The lobby looked even better at night. The Christmas trees and the lights made it look like a fairy kingdom and Jack its prince. He turned to me and took me by the shoulders.

"Don't go walking around in the dark," he said. "Promise me. You could be hurt, and then who's going to bake those cookies?" His eye seemed to sparkle slightly in the light when he mentioned cookies.

I smirked at him for a moment, then I crowed, "I knew it! I knew you liked my cookies!"

CHAPTER 12

Jack

"I knew it!"

"No, you don't," I protested.

The security guard woke up with a snort. "Mr. Frost," he said. "Package for you, Ms. Chloe." Then he went right back to sleep.

"You liked my cookies," Chloe said, poking me in the chest. The lights in the lobby glittered off of the melted snowflakes in her honey-blond hair. I had this sudden desire to kiss her, but I fought it back.

She danced around the Christmas decorations with glee.

"You loved the cookies, you loved them!" she whooped, then she ran over and hugged me. It was startling, and she released me as soon as the warmth and softness of her registered.

Then she skipped to the elevators, singing a little made-up song about how Jack Frost liked her cookies.

Watching her so ecstatic that someone liked something she had made stirred something in me. Was my icy heart starting to melt? I couldn't let that happen.

Though the lobby looked warm and inviting, the retail space mocked me with its cold emptiness. I needed to focus. I only had until the next quarter to show Svensson Investment that Frost Tower was a viable business proposition and shouldn't be sold off to the highest bidder.

I picked up Chloe's package and followed her to the elevator. She did this little wiggle when she saw me, and I took the liberty of resting a hand on her lower back to guide her into the elevator. I didn't have to, and I shouldn't have, but I needed to feel that connection again.

Chloe leaned back against the wall and grinned up at me as we rode up. The elevator dinged for her floor, and I handed her the package as she stepped into the hallway.

"You should follow me on Instagram," she said, blowing me a kiss. "Cookie lover."

Chloe was right, I did like her cookies. As I scrolled through her Instagram, I could see why she had hundreds of thousands of followers. There was something about her; it was as if she reached through the page to give the viewer a hug. I wanted her to reach somewhere else... That was a dangerous, distracting, and tantalizing line of thought.

A notification popped up that she had posted a new shot.

Just got this awesome gift from a fan! the caption read.

There she was in a low-cut top that said KISS THE BAKER. It hugged her curves and showed off a slight peek of midriff. Her friend must have snapped the photo, because she was on her bed raised up on her knees. In addition to the skimpy shirt, she was wearing these ridiculous reindeer antlers and black yoga pants. Her mouth was smiling and slightly open. I hastily closed the app. I wanted more than Chloe's cookies.

"I can't believe she's posting that on the internet for everyone to see," I muttered. I wanted to walk right down there and rip it off of her. No, not like that, just because it was a very revealing shirt. Not because...

I threw the doors open and let the winter inside.

The cold air focused me. The comment to Chloe about my mother made me think of my family, which made me think of Belle.

For a brief moment, I considered writing to Belle, but the final email she had sent before she disappeared had made it seem as if she didn't want anything to do with us at all. I certainly hadn't been a great brother. I sighed, letting the cold air sear my lungs.

Belle would have liked Chloe, since they both loved Christmas. But maybe Belle had just been pretending. Maybe the whole thing had been a lie.

I turned back to my sad attempt at baking. The cookie monstrosities I had made were mocking me from my kitchen counter. I swept them into a Tupperware container and thought about how I could convince Chloe to come bake more for me.

Thankfully we weren't filming the next day, or at least I wasn't. I was sure Dana had something planned for the contestants, since they were all gathered in the lobby when I left the next morning.

I saw Chloe and immediately imagined her in the tight little T-shirt. She smiled at me, but I didn't trust myself to smile back.

"Good morning, Jack," Hartleigh cooed. Chloe's eyes narrowed from across the room.

"I have to go to a meeting," I told her, pushing past her. She latched onto the arm of my suit jacket.

"You work too hard. You should let me come visit you. I could help you…" She let her hand drift down the front of my suit. "Relax."

"No, thank you," I said through gritted teeth and pushed her away.

"I love a forceful man," she said, letting out a half moan.

"Why is my life so crazy?" I muttered as I hurried to the waiting car.

I tried to clear my mind as I walked into the Platinum Provisions corporate office. Here at least I was in control and things were going well. After the marketing meeting yesterday, I had scheduled a meeting with the cooking equipment design team.

"The marketing team wants more of a Christmas push," I told them. I could see annoyance on people's faces. I knew they didn't like surprises.

"The marketing department wants a special cooking product we can market as a limited-edition Christmas item."

"It will take a while to develop that," said one of the engineers.

"Let me clarify," I told him. "We already have the products manufactured, we're simply providing a little extra bonus item along with them. That small item is the only thing we need to develop."

"Are you going to help?" the engineer demanded.

"Do not speak to me like that," I growled. "I understand that it's a lot to ask."

The engineer looked angry.

"But of course I will help develop a product," I continued. "We all work here, and we all have to pitch in."

"We can't design and test a whole new product and manufacture it in time for Christmas," another engineer complained.

Honestly, dealing with engineers was like herding cats. I resisted the urge to massage my temples.

"I'm not talking about a new product," I said. "Just maybe an add-on for an existing one, like the sprinkle maker or the icing piper. The marketing team is thinking we can produce a limited-edition Christmas set with our normal product plus a few of these little add-ons, mark the price up, you know the drill."

"I was working on some add-ons for the sprinkle maker," one man said sheepishly. "I've designed an attachment to create little multicolored snowmen and reindeer." He showed me photos of the samples on his phone.

"These look ready to go!" I said, smiling at him.

"Yeah, I guess they are. I made them for my daughters. They've been using them a lot recently, so I know the design works."

Of course he had done that for his daughters, because he was a good father, unlike my own.

"Perfect," I said, trying to shake off any feelings of resentment. I was a grown man and a billionaire. I shouldn't still have issues with my father.

"Anything else?"

Another woman piped up, "I have a few frosting nozzles. I wanted them to make more natural plant-like decorations.

My partner uses them for her wedding cake–decorating business." She showed me pictures.

"Looks like Christmas garland," I said, studying the picture of the elaborate cake.

"Yes, I was thinking that's what we could market the attachments as."

"How did you make these?" I asked her.

"I 3D printed the prototypes then machined the final."

"We'll work with these and start talking with the machine shops," the chief engineer said. "The factories are more than willing to work with us, since they know we keep the lights on. Plus it's Christmas, and everyone needs extra money. I'll talk to operations, but I believe there are at least two factories that should have capacity."

"I'll come up with a couple more ideas," I said, "and run them by you all. The marketing department wanted to have at least three different sets they could advertise."

When Platinum Provisions had first introduced the cooking equipment line, I hadn't been all that interested in it. I cared more about the lifesaving surgical equipment and expanding our drilling products. But people seemed to respond well to the chef products, and if the marketing department thought it was a good idea to pay Romance Creative to market these products and it helped me keep control of my tower, then I was all for it.

In the car on the way home, I sketched out ideas for new cooking tools. Chloe used these in her baking, so maybe she had some ideas for a special Christmas product. I smiled thinking about having her alone.

Just for business, of course.

CHAPTER 13

Chloe

We had a slight break between shooting the challenges. Most of the film team was finalizing edits and show structure for the web premiere. Romance Creative did assign Zane and another camera guy to follow us around and film us while we shopped for the next contest.

"Tomorrow's challenge is about Victorian desserts, so keep that in mind when you grocery shop," Anastasia said to us when we were all assembled in the lobby. "We thought you might have some interesting ingredients to use that we didn't think about. Plus Trader Mike's wants some footage of its stores in the show."

"I thought we have to figure it out on the fly?" I asked.

Anastasia laughed. "No, but we have to make it seem that way. We'll have shots of you leaving and coming back into the studio with your purchases. Also, Dana said to tell you all that the trailers for the show were released already and to please share them with your followers."

While Anastasia answered questions, I tweeted the preview clips of *The Great Christmas Bake-Off* out to my followers. Not even ten minutes later, my phone was blowing up with messages about how great my desserts looked and how delicious Jack looked. Speaking of everyone's favorite billionaire bake-off judge, when he walked through the lobby, Jack didn't seem all that pleased to see me even though I smiled at him.

Whatever. I knew his secret. He wanted my cookies, and he wanted them bad. Too bad Hartleigh was determined to ruin his morning.

"What is your problem?" I asked her after Jack disentangled himself from her. "He clearly doesn't like you."

"Yes he does! We are *in love*," she said.

"She's nuts," Nina said.

"Speaking of nuts," I said and showed her a picture someone had sent me early in the morning. "Check out this crazy picture." It was of Santa wearing only his hat, a fake beard, and sunglasses.

"Goodness gracious!" Nina said and crossed herself.

I sent out another message to let my fans know that the first episode of *The Great Christmas Bake-Off* was going to be uploaded that evening, and then it was time for shopping.

"Too bad we don't have Jack's big, thick credit card," Nina said, giggling.

"He gave you his credit card?" Hartleigh screeched.

"Just to buy decorations," I said. "Calm down."

That woman irritated me. I couldn't believe she and Jack had a history. If she was his type, then I didn't want anything to do with him. I shook my head. As if that was even a possibility. He wouldn't even admit he liked my cookies, though he didn't deny it.

The grocery store was a few subway stops away. When we walked in, I felt immediately relaxed. This was my happy place. I smelled the different fruits, inspected ingredients, and tasted the spices.

As I browsed through the shelves, I thought about what I would make. Victorian desserts tended to be a little more basic. You didn't want to overly excite people—they might get *ideas*. The Victorians were fond of trifles and puddings, which weren't that impressive. I wondered if the Victorians were trying to distinguish themselves from the sinful excess of the Renaissance period with their marzipan animals and molded ice creams and such. Still, Victorian desserts were sugar intensive, and I knew Jack wouldn't like that.

I was leaning towards a twist on a Victorian pudding, which could be sweet or savory. However, I was a bit wary because I didn't want to be yelled at again for doing something too simple and basic.

As I gathered my ingredients, the hair on the back of my neck stood up. It felt like I was being watched. I whirled around, and sure enough, there was a man in a Santa Claus suit staring at me from the other end of the aisle. I gasped and dropped my basket in shock as he advanced towards me.

"What is your problem?" I yelled.

One of the cameramen came into my aisle, and the Santa ran out of the store when he saw him.

"Do you know that Santa?" Zane asked in concern.

"No, I don't know him!" I snapped, picking up the ingredients that had rolled out of my basket when I dropped it.

"You should have a security detail," Zane said.

"I don't need a security detail. I'm not that high maintenance. He was probably just a homeless dude," I said.

But what if he was the same Santa from the mall? No, it couldn't be. It was probably just my imagination. Even if it was the same Santa, it wasn't as if the show had any money to deal with him.

My shopping high was ruined. One of the production assistants swiped a credit card, then we took our purchases back to the tower. I was still slightly rattled as we stored our ingredients. Part of me wished Jack had been there. I hadn't felt unsafe at all with him the night before.

"You guys done?" I asked Dana when we left the storage area. She and Gunnar were stretched out on a couch in the studio lobby.

She flashed a thumbs up. "Done! It's so good. Don't forget, tonight we upload the first episode!"

"I already told my followers," I told her.

"Oh, before I forget, another box came for you. The security guard was wandering around looking for you. I think he put the package in your apartment."

"A present!" I said.

The box was waiting for me when Nina and I walked into the apartment. I opened it up. It was another cute outfit.

"It's a gingerbread girl costume," I said, putting it on. "It's a little snug."

"Are you sure you want to put that on Instagram?" Nina asked.

"Someone went to the trouble to send me a gift," I said. "It's not food or anything, so what's the harm? Plus I look hot in this outfit. Come help me take pictures! I want to do it in the studio with all the Christmas decorations."

Nina followed me down to the kitchens.

"Are you sure we're supposed to be down here?" she whispered.

I shrugged. "We're not going to cook anything and mess up the space. I just want to set up a nice photo. Besides, it's good publicity for the bake-off."

I posed with the giant stuffed gingerbread man that came in the box. I had done my makeup to look like Christine Baranski in *The Grinch*, and I struck campy poses.

"These are cute pictures," Nina said. "I'm jealous of how many followers you have."

I didn't answer because I was doing an over-the-top suggestive photo, sticking my butt out and caressing my boobs, which practically heaved out of the too-tight outfit.

"I hope you aren't putting that online," she said with a laugh. "It's a bit much. Your cup of peppermint mocha runneth over."

I adjusted my boobs as someone coughed.

"Jack," I said, my hand half stuck down the front of my dress.

"I don't think you're supposed to be in here," he said.

"I'm just, you know, Instagramming for the debut episode tonight," I said, hastily smoothing down the dress. "We want everyone excited."

"I'm sure they will be," he said, blatantly staring at me.

I adjusted my top again. He made me frazzled. The dress was too tight, and I could see my chest heaving with every breath. Jack's eyes flicked down to my chest then immediately back up to my face.

"Can I help you?" I asked.

"I'm trying to come up with an idea for an attachment for one of the Platinum Provisions cooking tools."

"More sprinkle shapes!" Nina said. "And more icing tips."

"We have a few of those already in the works," Jack said. "We were looking for one more that could be a Christmas-themed attachment on another device. We're trying to market them for the holidays."

I thought for a moment then said, "I know exactly what I want!"

I dragged him upstairs to my room.

"Let me just find my equipment; I have it under my bed," I said, crouching down on all fours to fish out the box. "Sorry, it's stuck. Hold on."

"I'll wait outside for you," Jack said. His voice sounded ragged.

"I hope you're not sick," I said, my voice sounding slightly muffled. "All that time out in the cold without a coat isn't good for you."

Nina collapsed in laughter as soon as Jack left the room.

"What?" I said, blowing a lock of hair out of my eyes.

"You are such a tease!"

I gave her a confused look.

"Bending over on all fours wearing that," she cackled. "You should have seen his face! If I hadn't been here, I think you two would have been making fondant."

"Oh," I said. I looked down. "Oh! Good gracious, that's not…I didn't mean to flirt with him!"

"It wasn't even flirting," Nina said. "It was more like foreplay."

I groaned. "I swear that is *not* what I meant to do."

"We'll give him a minute to get that raging boner under control."

"He wasn't…"

Nina laughed. "Not that I saw, but his suit jacket probably hid some of it."

I changed into something less suggestive then walked out with the box.

"So what I need," I said, "is a fluffer."

Nina stifled a giggle.

Jack cocked his head. "Come again?"

"I want to make whipped sugar."

"Like cotton candy?" he asked.

"No, like whipped, fluffy icing, like snow. For a gingerbread house, people dump powdered sugar all over the plate, but I want fluffy whipped icing."

Jack looked thoughtful for a moment then nodded. "I'll see what I can do."

CHAPTER 14

Jack

Watching her bend down, her ass wiggling in that ridiculously sexy costume, was almost too much.

I am in control, I chanted to myself. *I am a block of ice, cold and unfeeling.* But Chloe threatened to melt right through me and ignite my inhibitions.

She had given me a good idea at least for an attachment on the air injector pump. Chefs used the device in molecular gastronomy to infuse scented smoke into candy balloons or delicate dumplings. They also used an attachment to whip liquids or create foams. Chloe's request for fluffy frosting snow wasn't out of the realm of possibility.

I had a work room in my penthouse where I kept my tools and such. I changed out of my suit, put on my goggles, and set to work. Milo snoozed at my feet. I hadn't been doing as much tinkering lately. My days seemed to be taken up with meetings and the minutiae of corporate life. It was nice to actually create something, and I was soon in a flow state.

I carved the nozzle out of wood first to see if the shape worked. Once I had molded it to my liking, I would scan it into my computer to have a 3D model, and then I would hand it all over to the engineers.

I looked over the air injector pump. It only needed a few modifications to fluff the frosting. I spent the rest of the afternoon alternating between conference calls and working on the add-on for the air injector pump.

To test the nozzles I was making, however, I would need to make frosting. I found a recipe online and set to mixing. It wasn't as hard as I thought it would be. It didn't look like professional frosting, but it would suffice to test the nozzle. I spooned the frosting into the chambers and switched on the machine. The air pump purred, and the foamy icing came out of the nozzle like a cloud. I tasted it, and it was like pure sugar. I spit it out, unhappy with the sugary taste, but the texture seemed to be what Chloe had asked for.

My whole condo reeked of sugar, and I opened the French doors out to the balcony to air out the penthouse while I scanned the nozzle then set the 3D printer to make a metal version of the latest iteration. I wanted Chloe to test it before I sent it to the engineers.

Milo barked as someone knocked on the door.

"That better not be Hartleigh," I muttered, checking the camera. Gunnar and Dana were waving at me.

"Happy premiere night!" Dana said as she and Gunnar walked into my living room. "I thought we would all watch together. You need some socialization."

"You seem calm," I told her.

Milo barked again, and Liam barged in.

"I never should have given you the code," I told him as he roughhoused with Milo.

"Someone has to have access," he said. "What if you freeze to death from leaving all the windows open?"

"Milo doesn't like the heat," I retorted.

Dana rubbed her arms. "I should have brought a hat and a coat."

"Are you baking?" Liam asked, laughing as he surveyed my kitchen.

Right, the frosting.

"No," I said hastily, sweeping everything into the trash. "I'm testing a new add-on for the air injector pump for the Christmas baking tools packages."

Liam looked over my work.

"This is pretty cool," he said. "Does it work?"

"Yes, but I need to borrow one of Dana's bakers to see if it's up to a professional's expectations."

"I should have brought one of them up here to cook," Gunnar said. "You have no food in your house. Just these sad little meals."

"They aren't that bad," I said. "Food is for fuel."

"You live such a gloomy existence," Gunnar told me in pity.

Dana tapped on her phone. "I've ordered for us."

"Sounds like a viewing party!" Gunnar said.

"How many viewers are you expecting?" I asked them.

"Honestly, I'll be happy with eight hundred thousand tonight. I think between the contestants' social media followings and the advertisements we've run, we should hit that number tonight. If we can make it to two million within a few days, then that should be enough to convince other advertisers to come on board."

"Did you already tell him about Platinum Provisions?" I asked Liam.

"Yes, the marketing team's already in talks with us," Gunnar said. He was setting the TV to the webpage and had a viewer counter up on his laptop.

"Is there a countdown until it's live or anything?" I asked as the security guard knocked on the door with our food delivery.

"No. It's the internet, so we just wait for it to be uploaded."

Gunnar was pacing around my apartment while Liam and Dana sat on the couch eating. I was nervous too. I was delaying Romance Creative's rent on the promise that they would pay me once the advertising checks came in. If this web series was a hit, then they would be able to pay. If not, Svensson Investment was going to be very angry.

"It looks like it's live!" Gunnar said, refreshing the page and hitting the play button.

We watched the show. The episode was about thirty minutes long. It was beautifully shot and well-paced. It also made me look like a dick.

"I think it was decent," Liam said.

"We need it to be viral," Dana replied.

Gunnar pulled the counter up on the large screen, and we watched it. The numbers on the viewership counter were already at two hundred thousand.

"That's not bad," Liam said.

"We need more traction," Gunnar said, resuming his pacing around the living room.

I was also watching Chloe's social media feed. She had been tweeting and Instagramming about the bake-off premiere all day. I saw that Chloe had tweeted to her followers that the show was live and they needed to watch immediately.

The counter refreshed, and the viewer numbers jumped up about the same number as Chloe's followers.

"Yeah, we need her to make it to the finals," Dana said. She was monitoring all the other contestants' social media as well. The video page refreshed again; the comments were coming in fast and furious.

"They all loved Chloe," Liam said then chuckled. "Her fans hate Jack for being mean to her."

Dana wagged her finger at me. "You need to play nice."

"I have been."

"Some of these comments are harsh," Liam said, "and really sexually suggestive." He was scrolling through the thousands of comments. Chloe's followers seemed to have jump-started engagement on the video.

"They're posting it on Reddit," I said. "It's on the front page."

The viewer numbers were closing in on five million when I shut down the TV.

"I have several emails from advertisers," Dana said, grinning. "We're going to be busy tomorrow."

My penthouse was quiet after they left. I went outside to stand on the balcony again.

"You're waiting for her," I admonished myself. I checked my phone. Chloe still seemed active on Instagram and Twitter. She was replying to people and posting more pictures, and it was unlikely she would leave the tower tonight.

I went back to tinkering with the pieces for the frosting fluffer. It needed a better name, something less suggestive.

The 3D printer was done with its work, and I polished the pieces and made sure they fit on the device. Now I just needed to find Chloe to test it.

CHAPTER 15

Chloe

Everyone was excited about how successful the pilot episode had been. We had had a little viewing party in the apartment, and now all the contestants were glued to their phones and tablets.

"Thanks for the shout out," Maria, another contestant who was talented but down to earth, told me. "I just netted twenty thousand new followers thanks to the picture of us you sent out!"

"Chloe's Miss Popular," Nina said as she read through the comments.

I snorted. "Too bad I don't have any brand deals."

"You should be happy," she said.

I felt myself tear up. "I just wish my oma was alive to see this. She would have been ecstatic. She loved baking shows, and this is my first Christmas without her."

Maria came over and hugged me. "She's here in spirit."

I stayed up late interacting with fans. I only managed to sleep a few hours before it was time to film the next episode of *The Great Christmas Bake-Off*.

As I was groggily dressing and fixing my hair, my phone rang.

"Jack wants to see you," Dana said. "It's about a new product."

When I walked into the studio, Jack was sitting at the judges' table, looking amazing in a charcoal pinstripe suit. He stood up and buttoned his jacket when he saw me.

"I think I have your icing fluffer working," he said, setting a box on the table. "I want you to test it out before I hand it over to the engineers."

"You want me to come up to your apartment and fluff your icing?" I said and winked. I could see him try not to smile.

"I brought it with me," he said. He was close. Dangerously close.

I tried to ignore him by tying on an apron and making icing at my workstation. I spooned some into the chamber of the air injector pump and squeezed the trigger. It worked perfectly.

"This is amazing!" I said, scooping up some of the light, fluffy icing with a finger.

"Want to try?" I teased Jack, holding the finger out to him.

He took my hand and licked the frosting off my finger, not breaking eye contact with me. The sensation went straight down to my toes. I was practically salivating as he released my hand. The naughty elf in my subconscious was shrieking.

"Okay, well, I'm just going to clean this up for filming," I said, my voice sounding unnaturally high. "I'm sure you're busy with phone calls and meetings. Being a billionaire must be exhausting."

The rest of the contestants were starting to arrive, and Jack walked over to the judges' table.

My gaze kept flicking between him, my workstation, and Anastasia. Every time I looked at him, he was watching me. I tried not to think about his tongue and lips and teeth on my skin and instead tried to focus on what Anastasia was saying about the next challenge.

Maybe I was tired or wrung out from the emotion of last night, but my mind insisted on imagining all the naughty things Jack could do to me. Was he flirting, or was it just about the frosting?

I couldn't deny the fact that licking frosting off someone's finger was more than just business. There hadn't been anything modest or prudish about his behavior. The Victorians definitely wouldn't have approved. Which was fitting, since today's challenge was Victorian Christmas.

I gathered my ingredients and tried to focus on my dish.

"Can you tell us about your dessert?" Anastasia asked as the camera crew panned over my station.

"Puddings are classical British Victorian dishes," I told them. "The Victorians had a sweet tooth, but there was still a sense that restraint and modesty should be strived for. Unlike, say, a lot of French desserts, puddings are quite humble. They are versatile, and anyone can make one—you don't need years of culinary training."

"And how are you going to turn a stodgy pudding into a winning dessert?" Anastasia asked.

"The Christmas pudding is what we in America traditionally think of when we talk about puddings," I replied. "A Victorian Christmas pudding is made with dried fruit, eggs, and suet, which is an animal byproduct. Once the dough is made, it is wrapped in linen cloth and boiled for hours. It's quite heavy and is sort of the precursor to the American fruitcake."

"So for your dessert, you're going to be doing a twist on a Victorian pudding," Anastasia said.

"Exactly. I want it to be light and flavorful. I don't have the time to let it cook for an entire day. Plus, we want beautiful desserts, and even if you put the pudding in a mold, it never looks that hot."

After Anastasia left, I opened the box holding the icing fluffer. The ideas were bouncing around in my head. I knew I needed something light, and the fluffer would create the perfect texture. I wasn't sure what to use for the liquid. I needed something that I could fluff, so it needed to be about the consistency of frosting. Maybe I could make a custard base? I wished I had tested this dish before attempting it live. Oh, well. I would either win or be eliminated.

The traditional pudding used eggs, nuts, dried fruit, spices, and brandy. I decided to make five different puddings that reflected these main ingredients. I gathered pistachios, figs and oranges, a variety of spices that felt like Christmas, and an expensive Italian liquor. The whipped puddings needed to be less sweet so that the sugar didn't overwhelm the taste of the other ingredients.

I chopped fruits and nuts, separated eggs, and measured spices. Finally I was ready to make the custards. I ran each of the five custard mixes through one of the small blenders Jack's company had supplied. Their blenders gave me a smooth consistency without becoming so hot that they cooked the mixture. Zane, camera on his shoulder, made me move around and repeat the mixing so he could have a good shot of the logo from several angles.

"Can I use one of your burners?" I asked Nina.

"Sure." She looked back at me as I placed my pots and turned up the burners.

"You're making a lot!"

"Five different kinds of puddings," I said. "Hope this works!"

"Fingers crossed."

I had all the pans sitting in double boilers, and I stirred them two at a time, alternating among them.

"Wow, look at your acrobatics!" Anastasia said.

"This challenge is on the shorter side, so I have to work quickly," I explained, my face red from the exertion. I couldn't afford for my custards to burn. Finally the consistency was thick but smooth, and my whisk faced a bit of resistance. I set the custards to cool.

For the final touch, I made a sprig of holly out of a type of fruit leather. Another Platinum Provisions tool allowed me to infuse the fruit leather with the scent and taste of holly. The cameras focused in on me while I worked.

"I hope Jack Frost is paying you to showcase his products," Nina called to me.

"I'm sure it's part of the show budget," I said. "I doubt I'll see any of that money."

I tried to stay focused on the desserts and not become depressed about my abysmal financial situation. The bank still hadn't refunded me the money my cousin had stolen. At least the show was providing food and a place to stay, since my credit cards were mostly maxed out.

"Focus," I told myself. I needed to win. The prize money would help me pay off my debts, and maybe one of the judges would be impressed enough to help me find a job somewhere.

Using a thermometer, I checked the custards to see if they were cool enough to fluff.

"This thing better work," I said, spooning some of the pistachio custard into the air injector pump.

"Please work," I said and pressed on the nozzle. Out came beautiful, fluffy custard.

"It's like fairy moss!" Nina said, watching over my shoulder. Zane shooed her away so he could film me filling little shallow square bowls with the colorful fluffy custard. I placed a sprig of edible holly on the corner of each little bowl then arranged them on long rectangular wooden trays.

"Don't drop those," I warned the production assistant.

She smiled and gave me a thumbs up. "They look amazing!" she said.

"I hope the judges like it."

CHAPTER 16

Jack

I was trying to be a nicer judge. The pilot episode hadn't shown me in a sympathetic light, and people hadn't even seen the latest episode, in which I told Chloe her cookie tasted like garbage and implied she needed to lose weight. No wonder she had looked like a scared little rabbit this morning. Or maybe that had something to do with my licking the frosting off her finger. It had been an impulsive decision, but it was an experience I wanted to repeat. Minus the frosting, of course.

"The desserts in this round are so imaginative," Anu said. "I can tell everyone is stepping up their game."

The production assistants placed trays of beautiful colorful little custards on individual spoons in front of us as Chloe stood on her mark in front of the table.

Nick took a bite of the green custard while I tried the pink one. It was an explosion of flavor.

"The texture on this is so intriguing. It's not foam, and it doesn't taste whipped. It's like a cloud, it's like eating a cloud," Nick said.

"I used the Platinum Provisions air injector pump with the—"

Please don't call it a fluffer, I thought.

"With the snow-maker." That was a good name for it.

"It's very clever," Nick said. "It almost reminded me of the texture of Japanese shaved ice except this was room temperature. I wish the viewers could try this. We talk a lot about taste and smell, but texture is usually relegated to crunch. This is something new and different."

"Also," Anu said, "the flavor. It's almost a cliché at this point to talk about hating Christmas fruitcake that's been sitting around for months, but with this dessert, I can taste the fruit and the nuttiness."

I took a bite of the green custard. It was pistachio, but it wasn't too sweet. It was more nutty and salty.

"It's interesting how you deconstructed the dish, but it's still a pudding," I said.

Nick and Anu nodded appreciatively at my comment.

It didn't take us long to figure out the winner and loser.

"Chloe's dish was amazing," Nick said. "She's the clear winner."

"You made the snow-maker?" Anu asked me.

"Yes," I said.

"Where can I buy, like, ten of them for my restaurant?" Nick asked.

"They're in production now," I told him, feeling pleased that my invention had worked so well.

"I'm serious. You have to make sure to deliver several of them to me."

"Of course," I told him.

"Also, can we make requests of Platinum Provisions?" Anu asked.

"I don't see why not," I said. "Let's set up a meeting. We're always looking to innovate."

I wished Hartleigh was being sent home, but the two pastry chef judges had thought her tiny tarts in chocolate, lemon, and almond were well executed.

A girl who had made a rice pudding was sent home. She cried when Anastasia told her to say goodbye.

"It was really terrible," Anu remarked after we did the interviews in the late afternoon.

"The texture was really unsettling, wasn't it," Nick said, handing in his microphone.

After the filming ended, I waited around for a few minutes, hoping to talk to Chloe. I knew the contestants had a grueling schedule. Chloe was probably too busy doing post–bake-off interviews.

Gunnar saw me standing there.

"I just need to talk to Chloe about the new equipment," I said.

He gave me a look. "They aren't going to be out for a little bit. Maybe you can schedule a meeting with her tomorrow."

"Of course," I said, trying to ignore the part of me that did not want to talk to Chloe about business and instead wanted to do more than lick frosting off of her fingers.

The filming had ended early that day, so I was able to have another meeting with the Platinum Provisions marketing team.

"These are impressive," I said as they showed me the ads and packaging they had created for the Christmas baking sets.

One of the operations managers was in the meeting, and he said, "The factory thinks they are going to have the first shipment ready by next week if we send them the 3D model by tomorrow. We already have preorders on this stuff."

"Your girl, Chloe, has been Instagramming it," Liam added. "People are clamoring for these products. Platinum Provisions' cooking line is going to be a hot Christmas item."

"The show just filmed a whole episode centering on our snow-maker attachment," I informed the team.

"At least that's a better name than fluffer," Liam said with a snicker. "It sounds like the holidays."

"We're prepping a handout for proper terminology for our products," the marketing director said. "We need the contestants on *The Great Christmas Bake-Off* to use the proper language when referring to our products."

"I'll make sure Dana and Gunnar are aware," I promised.

It was dark when I returned to Frost Tower. Hartleigh was waiting for me. I wouldn't have put it past her to have been waiting in the lobby all day for me to return. Frost Tower didn't have money in the budget to hire a full-time security guard or even a doorman. Of course people weren't renting space here—this tower was a complete disaster.

"I'm busy," I said, brushing past her. She tried to follow me into the elevator.

"Jack, please talk to me!" she said. "Your parents want us to be together."

The elevator doors closed on her. Hartleigh and my parents conspiring against me—that was a chilling thought.

My mind circled back to Chloe. When I was alone in my penthouse, I pulled up her Instagram. Yes, I was now following her on Instagram. I was stalking her like Hartleigh was stalking me.

Chloe was wearing some Christmas pajamas her fans had sent her. She posted a picture of herself wearing them on Instagram. She was in bed with a large mug of hot cocoa with marshmallows cut in the shape of snowflakes. I scrolled through the app back to the pictures of her in the tiny T-shirt and the sexy gingerbread girl costume. I felt my pants grow tight.

"Don't go down that road," I told myself. "She's a contestant." I whistled for Milo and went out for a run to let the cold give me clarity.

CHAPTER 17

Chloe

I could still feel Jack's lips on my skin, the way he licked my finger.

"If that's enough to send you into a tailspin," Nina said after I gave her the play-by-play, "then you really need to get laid."

"Yes, by Jack." I clapped a hand over my mouth.

"Hartleigh is going to have a real problem with that," Nina said with a snicker.

"Yeah, and they have some sort of previous relationship." I sagged. "I need to concentrate. I can't afford to be chasing after unattainable men. I need to fix my life; it's in shambles."

"You won the last challenge," she said.

"I wish they had sent Hartleigh home."

"Pray for a Christmas miracle," Nina said as she turned on *White Christmas*, one of my favorite movies.

❄✳❄

The next day was shopping again. I was tired and grouchy. Jack had haunted my sleep. Even though his last name was Frost, he left me hot and bothered.

Anastasia was waiting for us in the lobby.

"The next challenge is Medieval Christmas," she said. "But when we film in the studio tomorrow, remember to pretend like it's a surprise."

Shopping was fun. Zane cracked jokes with me and Nina in between filming us selecting fruits and imported chocolate. The creepy Santa didn't show up, though I half expected to see him there.

"This is going to be a tough challenge," Nina remarked. "The medieval period was a lot of smoked meat, plum pudding, and mincemeat pie."

"They did have things like pepper, ginger, cloves, and saffron," I said. "They also had spiced wine and sugar creations in weird, random shapes."

"No chocolate though." Nina sighed.

"At least they had sugar," I told her.

I decided I was going to go very avant-garde with my dessert, and I filled my basket with honeycomb, pears, and some pungent cheeses. While I took pictures for Instagram, the hair on the back of my neck stood up. I felt as if someone was watching me, but when I whirled around, no one was there.

"I'm seeing things," I muttered and took my basket up to the front to check out. Through the window, I could see a Santa Claus ringing a bell.

"He's not the stalker, he's just a Salvation Army volunteer," I said to myself. "No need to be spooked."

When we left, I put a few quarters in his pot just to prove to myself I wasn't afraid of Santa Claus.

"Ho, ho, ho! Merry Christmas!" he said.

After I had stored my purchases from the shopping trip, Anastasia cornered me.

"Your social media game is on point," she said. "Come have drinks with me. We should talk. I want to hear about your plans for the future."

"I'd love to," I replied.

"Meet me downstairs in two hours," she told me.

"There isn't much around the tower," Anastasia said as we sat in the car on the way to a restaurant she had recommended. "Jack keeps asking me if I know people who could open a restaurant in that retail space." Anastasia made a slight face. "All these billionaires think that just because they made their money in one area, suddenly they're going to be great at everything. Real estate especially is a huge gamble. I can't believe that Svensson Investment went in with him on a skyscraper. And in this location!"

The drive to the restaurant had been long, and I was starving when we were finally seated. The servers looked a little shocked to see Anastasia. She glanced over the menu, her lips pursed.

"It's my treat," she said and turned to the waiter. "We'll have the honey pear cocktail, the scallops, the bone marrow, and the pasta."

My stomach growled.

"This place is owned by Nick Mazur," she said, "one of the judges."

"Is he here?"

"No. He owns about thirty restaurants in the city."

"Wow. How does he manage that?"

"He delegates," Anastasia said.

"How come he's judging?"

"He and Dana are friends. Dana can convince anyone to do anything. She's very persuasive. All those Holbrooks are quite charismatic."

"So that's why Jack is judging," I remarked.

The food arrived, and it smelled divine. I picked up my fork.

"Wait!" Anastasia said. She took out her camera and proceeded to carefully photograph each dish.

"Are you—"

"Shh."

"Are you going to review them?" I asked when she was done photographing.

"Just a quick one," she said. "Not in depth. I need more content for my blog."

The scallops were buttery, and the bone marrow was meaty and creamy. I spread it on the little bits of crusty bread.

After I swallowed a mouthful of pasta, I said, "Can I pick your brain about the restaurant business? My dream is to be a pastry chef or open a chain of little bakeries."

Anastasia took a sip of wine. "It's cutthroat. You'll need backers. Honestly, this whole business is pretty misogynistic. The banks and the big restaurateurs don't like to give women financing, though they'll make donations to sketchy nonprofits to make themselves look better."

"Oh," I said, feeling dejected. Maybe my dream was just that—a dream that would never be a reality.

"Don't let it bring you down," Anastasia said. "There *are* women who run successful restaurants. There's not a big dessert movement in New York right now, however. No one wants to spend money paying a pastry chef to create desserts unless they are aiming for another Michelin star. Instead they head down to Trader Mike's and buy tubs of ice cream and serve that."

"That's sad," I said, slowly running my finger through the condensation on the wine glass.

"I know you want to be the next Christina Tosi with her Milk Bar franchise," Anastasia said, "but remember that she had a major restaurateur as a backer, and she worked almost a decade in fine dining to pay her dues before she started her bakery."

"I know," I said.

"It's difficult, but not impossible," Anastasia said. "I don't want to discourage you. Sometimes all you need is a lucky break. People won't believe in you until you've proven yourself. Then they'll all act like they were your biggest fans the whole time."

I was slightly tipsy when I returned to the apartment. Hartleigh was in the living room taking selfies. She had on a skimpy outfit and a Santa hat.

"It's for Jack," she said in response to my disgusted look. "He won't be able to resist."

Nina was talking to her family in our bedroom, and I didn't want to sit in the living room with Hartleigh. I needed to think about my future. It was seeming less and less likely that I could make my dreams come true.

Only you can change your life. No one can do it for you.

That was what my oma would always tell me. She had made me believe that hard work and dreams would take me far. Anastasia had put a damper on those beliefs. But I had to try.

I checked my Instagram; I had gained more followers thanks to the bake-off show. At least that was something I could leverage. I looked out the window. It was snowing lightly outside, which would be perfect for more photos.

People were still out on the streets even though it was late. I took a few selfies in front of the building, but I already had several shots like that. I decided to go to the nearby park. It was too bad I didn't have another person to take the full-body shots I wanted of me wearing my red coat against the snow falling on the landscape.

"Don't you know it's late?" a man said. "Also, you need an escort."

"We have to stop meeting like this," I said, recognizing Jack's voice.

He smiled at me.

"Out in the snow without a coat on, I see," I said, poking his chest, trying to ignore the fact that it was a very well-muscled chest.

"Milo doesn't have a coat," he said, smiling at me as if he knew exactly what I thought of him and his barely clad body. The husky did look happy to be out in the cold, though.

"More Instagram photos?" he asked, gesturing to my phone.

"You know it! Since you're here, we can go to the park."

"It's closed at night," he replied.

"It closes at one a.m. I can use the internet too, you know," I told him.

He sighed, and Milo pulled against his leash in the direction of the park.

"I'm surprised to see you out here," I said as we walked the few blocks to the park. "Hartleigh's all alone, and she's dressed up in something skimpy for you."

Jack made a sour face. "There is nothing going on between us."

"I thought you two had a history," I said. My tone was teasing, but I really did want to know what the deal was between the two of them.

Jack seemed pensive for a moment, then he said, "Her family is friends with my parents. Hartleigh is...she's overbearing, I guess you might say. She was always a terrible fixture in my childhood. My parents forced me and my siblings to be friends with her. It was just one of many self-serving decisions on their part."

"Good to know she's not your type," I said, feeling oddly giddy that Hartleigh was in no way in competition for Jack. I mentally hit myself. There was no way Jack wanted anything to do with me.

But he licked frosting off your finger, the naughty elf reminded me.

"Of course she's not my type. She should be locked up. You haven't even seen her at her worst. She's clearly trying to be on her best behavior for the bake-off," Jack said.

"I can't believe your parents just forced you to be friends with her," I remarked. "Didn't they care about your feelings?"

He scoffed. "As if. They don't care about me. My parents wanted a big family for no other reason than to say they had one. They had no intention of taking care of us. My sister..." His mouth snapped shut. "Never mind."

"I know something about shitty parents," I said, trying to put Jack at ease. "My dad and mom were both major druggies. They were probably some of the first casualties of the opioid epidemic." I didn't know why I was telling him this. He had opened up to me, but his rich-kid problems probably paled in comparison to my life. But I couldn't cut myself off. It felt natural to talk to him as we walked through the park.

"Practically my whole family are addicts. My aunt and two uncles died from overdosing. Even my cousin and his druggie friend stole my identity and wiped out my savings. I reported him—I had to because that was the only way for the bank to give me my money back. I did it even though my oma begged me not to. The police showed up and arrested my cousin. My oma was so upset she died a few weeks later from the shock." The grief and the horror and the betrayal felt as if they had happened only yesterday.

"I'm sorry," Jack said as he unclipped Milo's leash. "Sometimes you have to make difficult choices."

"I think I made the wrong choice, though," I told him. "I shouldn't have reported my cousin. My oma would still be alive. The bank didn't even return my money. They were supposed to refund it all, but it has been months, and still they've only returned twenty percent."

"Your grandmother was an enabler," Jack said, stopping to look at me. He placed his hands on my shoulders, turning me to face him. "She enabled your cousin, and she wanted you to enable his addiction too."

I looked down at the snow and scuffed it with my boot. "I think she probably enabled me too," I said softly.

"What do you mean?" he asked.

"I should have done a degree in, oh, accounting or something stable. Instead I went to a culinary institute for an associate's degree, which I didn't even finish, and now I'm trying to be a baker." I shrugged unhappily.

"You're a good dessert chef," Jack said. "You are the only person in the world who makes desserts I want to eat. You made those amazing cookies."

"You really liked the Austrian wedding cookies?" I asked softly, looking up at him.

"I loved them," he told me with a small smile.

I sniffed. I needed to stop feeling sorry for myself and start taking cool photos. Instagram followers were fickle. I had to keep them supplied with new content if I wanted them to stick around.

I dabbed at my face. "I'm splotchy," I said. "I can't take photos like this; I'm a mess."

"I think I know something that would help you," Jack said.

"What?"

Jack wrapped me in his arms, and I shrieked as he whirled me around and around in the falling snow.

"I'll drop you in this snowdrift," he growled playfully.

"No!" I yelped, which caused Milo to run over to us, barking.

Jack set me down. "Now you're happy and you can take photos."

I was pressed close against his chest. There were snowflakes on his eyelashes. We were so close I could count them.

"I should get those pictures," I murmured. He released me, his hands lingering on my back. I handed him my phone.

"Make me look like a star!" I said.

He snapped photo after photo as I spun around, threw snow up into the air, and played with the husky.

"Classic Instagram poses," I said as I flipped through the pictures. "These are great! When you're tired of being a billionaire, you can be a photographer."

He smiled, and it seemed a little bit dangerous.

"Okay, I helped you," he said. "Now, what do I get in return?"

"What do you want?" I asked him, my heart yammering.

"Cookies."

CHAPTER 18

Jack

When we stepped out of the elevator on the top floor, I grabbed her by the hand and led her to my front door. Her hands were warm, and she didn't pull away when I laced our fingers together.

"You have a keypad too," she said.

"Every condo in the building does," I explained. "It was supposed to be state of the art. This tower was such a mistake."

"It's nice. It just needs some playfulness and people," she said, stepping into my penthouse.

"I'm working on it," I told her. I didn't want to go into the details of my hubris. The tower, like my parents, was going to be a sore point the rest of my life.

"Let's talk about happier things, like cookies," I said to her.

"I'm shocked that you are so enamored of them," said Chloe, her face lighting up in a smile. Her whole presence warmed my apartment, chasing away the chill of self-doubt and past hurts.

"I tried to find these cookies at other bakeries," I said as I helped her out of her coat, "but they don't have your magic touch."

"Your touch is pretty magical," she said under her breath.

"What was that?" I asked, grinning at her.

"Nothing." She headed toward my open kitchen.

"The Austrian wedding cookies don't take long to make," she told me as she tied her hair back, "but I need the ingredients."

"I already have them."

"You do?"

"I tried to make them myself, but…" I sheepishly pulled out the box of disasters.

"Oh my," she said. Chloe picked up one of the sad little cookies and broke it. She sniffed it then tasted it. She made a face and threw away the whole box.

"Wow, that bad, huh?" I said.

"Yes, that bad," Chloe told me. She pawed through my cupboards and started taking out ingredients.

"You don't have the right nuts," she said finally.

"My nuts are great." She blushed, and I smirked.

"I need pecans, not almonds," she told me. "I bet you just pulled this recipe off of some random junk SEO blog, didn't you?"

"It was the first thing on Google," I admitted.

She wrote out a list for me. "I need these ingredients. Pecans, good pecans from Georgia. Unsalted. They are in season right now. And I need French sea salt from *Guérande*—not table salt. At least you didn't buy self-rising flour," she said, shaking her head.

"I didn't realize it was so complicated," I said.

"Baking is science," she explained. "It's not like regular cooking. The ingredients have to be measured precisely and be of a high quality. There is no margin for error."

"So no cookies." I sighed. I didn't need the sugar, but they were mainly nuts and butter, and that was practically keto, wasn't it?

"Not these cookies," Chloe replied. She poked around in my cabinets. All of my meager spice collection was placed on the counter so that she could smell each one. Then Chloe pulled out the bags of sugar I had bought to test the frosting for the snow-maker attachment.

"I can make gingerbread cookies," she offered.

I wrinkled my nose then forced my expression to smooth down. "I don't like gingerbread," I said. "We had to eat it in school. It's gross. It has a weird aftertaste."

Chloe laughed. "I bet the cookies came out of a can and used fake vanilla and a spice liquid blend. You'll like my cookies," she said with a wink. "I promise."

She set everything out and started to bake.

I held as still as I could while I watched her. She was completely focused on the task at hand. What was interesting was how much she tested and tasted as she baked. She reminded me of the way I worked when I was designing a new product. I could see why she had such an enthusiastic fan club.

As the gingerbread dough came together, my apartment smelled like a Turkish bazaar. Milo sneezed while Chloe rolled out the caramel-colored gingerbread dough.

"You don't have the right pans either," she said as she checked the thickness of the dough. "Where's that list? Write this down—I need an insulated cookie sheet. You only have plain ones."

"These cookie sheets were expensive!" I protested.

She sniffed. "Expensive doesn't mean it's any good. Hopefully these cookies don't burn. At least you have a convection oven and not just a microwave."

"I'm an adult; I have a kitchen," I said.

"Do you even cook?" she asked skeptically. I glanced over at the window then back at her. She raised an eyebrow.

"I bet the most cooking you've done is when you were butchering those cookies."

"I have a chef who makes food," I told her.

"Was that what was in those sad little containers? I should come back here and make you a nice home-cooked meal. You're making me feel sorry for you," she said, wagging her finger at me.

"What can I say? I'm a busy man. I don't have time to cook. Food is fuel."

"Food is home and family and tradition," she retorted.

"I don't want a lot of emotion wrapped up in my food," I countered. "I can't afford to have an existential crisis every time I eat a hamburger."

"You need to have a nice meal with people you care about," she said. "It will reset your internal food counter. Human beings are programed to gather and share around a meal." She waved me over to stand close to her. "You didn't have a cookie cutter, so I hand-cut them," she said, showing me the cookies. They were works of art.

"See, there's Milo, and there's you before you ate a cookie." She pointed to a grouchy-looking gingerbread man.

The figures weren't the rounded gingerbread people I was used to. They were more lifelike. Her creations looked like a graphic design project.

"And there's you after you ate my cookies," she said, pointing to another character that seemed looser and more relaxed.

I was so close to her. The smell of spices mingled with the slight honey scent from her hair.

"This is me." She pointed to another cookie shaped like a girl wearing a dress and holding a tray.

"They're beautiful," I murmured in her ear.

She hurried to put the gingerbread figures in the oven. She had to brush past me, and it wasn't my imagination when I felt her shiver as her body pressed against mine for the barest moment.

"Scoot," she said as she closed the oven door. "I need to make icing."

I watched her mix the frosting. She did it deftly, measuring the correct proportions of sugar, meringue powder, and water, then whisked it by hand until it was foamy.

"Come put in the icing sugar," she said, looking at me. She continued to whisk as I carefully spooned in the heaps of icing sugar.

I was behind and slightly to the side of her, and her hip pressed into my groin. I could feel myself growing hard, so I stepped back.

"That's enough!" she squeaked.

The timer dinged. The gingerbread people were done. She moved them onto a cooling rack.

"Where's your icing snow-maker?"

I handed her the tool. She placed some of the icing she had made into it, then squeezed the whipped icing all over a plate.

"It's just like snow," she said. "This is amazing."

She had little bits of icing on her cheek. I watched her as she placed a few of the gingerbread people in the icing.

"It's like they're playing in the snow. This is really cool." She scooped up some of the frosting with a gingerbread girl and held it out to me. I took it from her and bit into it.

"Again, the spices you had weren't a hundred percent up to my standards, but see how you like it."

"This is amazing," I said. The gingerbread wasn't cloyingly sweet, and I could taste the spices. The cookie had a zing that tickled my nose.

"I thought you were going to eat it out of my hand again," she joked.

I scooped up a dollop of frosting and held it out to her. Her tongue darted out, and she licked it off my fingers.

"I make really good frosting," she said.

"You do."

She laughed nervously. "It's really warm in here, isn't it?"

"You have frosting on your cheek," I said and kissed it, licking it off. "And your neck," I said, nuzzling her. I could feel her pulse racing. Chloe was soft, like a pillow stuffed with marshmallows. "And it's on your mouth," I said, kissing the corner of her lips. She was spicy like the gingerbread.

I pressed her against the wall, letting my hands caress her as I kissed her. The smell of the spices and sugar was making me a bit dizzy. Chloe moaned when my hands slid down her back and lower. She immediately pushed me off.

I think I drooled a little watching her adjust her skirt.

She swallowed. "I, um, I have to go because we have this contest, you see, and I should, um, you're the judge. Okay, bye!"

She ran out of the apartment, leaving me alone with a mountain of frosting and some of the best cookies I had ever eaten.

CHAPTER 19

Chloe

Once again, Jack Frost had brought me to a boiling point.

"You're back late," Nina said when I quietly came into our shared room. "The competition is tomorrow."

"I know." I lay down on my bed and closed my eyes. It wasn't my imagination. Jack Frost wanted me. It was very obvious. I opened my eyes. Nina was looming over me.

"You have to tell me everything," she said, her eyes wide in the darkness.

She gasped when I told her how he had grabbed me.

"Hartleigh is going to flip her lid," she said. "Oooh, this is too good!"

"She can't know about me and Jack! What if she tries to, I don't know, have me kicked out of the competition?" I said, panicking.

"You can't keep this a secret!"

"I could lose my one shot at being a famous baker!" I protested.

"You want him, though," Nina said. "Jack's a billionaire; he could solve all your problems." She looked thoughtful for a moment. "I guess your cookies really are magical."

"I don't know," I said with a frown. "Maybe he's just bored."

"Or frustrated. Or high on sugar," Nina said.

"I can't deal with this right now," I said, lying back down and pulling a pillow over my head. A part of me wished I had stayed, while the other part was glad I'd left.

I felt as if I was charged with electricity as I prepped my station the next morning. Anastasia walked in, looking perfect as usual, with Jack trailing behind her. Both of them were elegant New York City money types.

I looked down at my apron. It was streaked with sugar from two days ago because I hadn't had the energy to wash it, and my hair was a rat's nest. What did Jack really see in me? Maybe he was just teasing me or playing a game. Sleep with the baker, another candy cane in the billionaire's collection.

Zane came over to film reaction shots.

"I can't today," I complained, hiding my face. "I'm a mess."

He smiled. "You look great!"

"For today's contest," Anastasia said, "we're making a dessert for the ages. The Middle Ages, that is."

Then we had to pretend to go shopping and come back with the bags of food we had bought yesterday.

While I unpacked my ingredients, I started to envision the dessert in my head. I also thought about how I could make it so that Jack would love it.

The dessert I was planning was supposed to make each person feel as if they were having Christmas in medieval times. Skewers of cheese and fruit were a common Christmas dessert during that time period. I was going to make something similar but pump up the volume. To really evoke the feel of the period, each plate would have a spire made of colored melted sugar like stained glass, and the plan was to pump smoke under each one.

The timing on this dish was everything. I needed to make sure all my ingredients were prepped. I would have to fry the bits of fruit and cheese then quickly place them under the spires and pump in the smoke. They would need to go to the judges immediately.

I laid out little molds using square dowels, melted the sugar, colored it then poured it. While the pieces cooled, I made a spiced wine reduction to drizzle over the skewers and carefully cubed my cheese, apples, and pears.

"What's all that bacon for?" Nina asked, looking over from candying rose petals and various fruits.

"The smoke," I said. "The Middle Ages were all about fire. They didn't have ovens or gas or even chimneys in their houses, just big open fires. Smoke was everywhere, and I want my dessert to capture that."

"Do you need my smoking gun?" she offered.

"No, I want real smoke. Those little smoking guns make cool smoke, which is fine, I guess, but I want to burn wood and char meat."

I pulled out another piece of equipment from Platinum Provisions. Unlike the little smoking gun, this one was much larger and looked similar to what one would use to smoke a beehive.

Zane and another camera guy were buzzing around me, watching me as I snipped off the plastic tie holding a small cord of cherry wood together and selected a piece.

"Whoa, whoa! You can't burn that in here!" Gunnar exclaimed, running over.

"I need it for my dish," I told him. "You want a viral dessert, don't you?"

"You're going to burn the tower down!"

"No I won't," I scoffed.

He glared at me then said, "Let me talk to Jack."

I was antsy waiting for Jack. Everything needed to be timed perfectly. I needed that man to hurry up!

When Jack finally sauntered over to my workstation, he smirked when he saw my fire setup.

"So tell me, Mr. Big Shot Tower owner, is it going to set off the alarms if I make smoke in here?"

"Are you actually making your own fire?" he asked, a smile playing around his mouth.

"She can't burn that in here," Gunnar said.

Jack looked up at the massive ducts on the ceiling.

"We have a robust air-handling system," he said. "It should be fine."

Gunnar shook his head. "The last thing we need is for the sprinklers to go off. I cannot afford any setbacks."

"I need the smoke," I told them. I was not compromising on my dessert.

"Why don't you use the cool smoke gun?" Gunnar asked.

"I need the richness of the charred wood and bacon. It's like the difference between barbeque from a smoker and barbeque chicken made from a sauce packet and a crock pot."

"Maybe she can light it outside and bring the embers inside in the bowl of the smoker," Jack suggested.

I scowled. "I guess I'll have to."

"Come on. I'll help you," Jack said.

"I'm blaming you if my dessert fails," I said.

Jack smiled and picked up my wood, bacon, and equipment.

"I look crazy!" I complained as I stood outside in front of the tower. The drunk Santa was slumped against the wall, and he waved at me. At least it wasn't the same creepy Santa from the mall.

"Trust me, this is one of the least strange things happening in New York City right now," Jack said. "Do you need help?" He gestured to the pan that I was going to use to keep the wood from burning the sidewalk.

"I can light a fire," I snapped.

"You're feisty when you're angry."

The wood had started to burn. I laid the pieces of bacon on a metal grill over it. The cameramen panned around the fire while Jack and I watched.

The bacon had started to cook. I put the charred pieces in the smoker then hacked off some embers into the tempered glass flask that attached to the smoke gun.

I left Jack to put out the fire and raced back upstairs to finish my dessert.

Nina, bless her, babysat my embers while I assembled my skewers. I flash fried the perfectly ripened pears and the breaded cinnamon- and nutmeg-infused apples. Then I skewered the fruit, the various cheeses, and gooey pieces of honeycomb. Finally, I drizzled the spiced wine reduction on the skewers and topped each plate with a delicate sugar spire and used the smoking gun to pump bacon and wood smoke under each one.

Nick spontaneously applauded when I had finished.

"I think we'll let Chloe go first since her dish seems to have a short shelf life," Anastasia said.

"Wow!" Nick gushed as he broke the little stained-glass candy spire and the smoke poured out. I was giddy as I watched them eat.

"You know," I said, "in the Middle Ages, people were actually pretty loose compared to the Victorians. There was a lot of sleeping around and general debauchery. The desserts, limited as they were by the available ingredients at the time, were also pretty wild."

I could feel Jack's gaze on me. He ate a piece of the honey-covered cheese with a snap of white teeth.

"Debaucherous," he said.

I half wondered what would have happened if I hadn't left his apartment last night.

"This is amazing," Nick repeated. "I'm speechless."

"This is the type of dessert you would expect at a Michelin-star restaurant," Anu said. "There's so much to unpack—the layers of smoke, the way each piece on the skewer is thought out and prepared. The timing of this dish was perfect, and the stained-glass spire evokes the medieval tradition of soltetie. This is exactly what you want when the challenge is medieval dessert."

CHAPTER 20

Jack

Chloe's dish was blowing up Instagram. She had pictures of herself posing with the smoking gun, and everyone wanted to know what it was.

One of the Platinum Provisions social media people was on Chloe's Instagram answering questions about our products. Buzzfeed picked it up, and several stores upped their orders of our products.

"Are we ready to launch?" Liam asked at the marketing meeting the next day.

"The engineers didn't have changes on my design for the snow-maker attachment," I said. "It's been sent off to a factory in the Midwest. We should have the product in stores within the next couple of weeks."

"Are you going to be able to make the deadlines?" Liam asked. "It seems like a short timeline. Also, is it enough time to even market the limited-edition Christmas products?"

"We already have a ground game in place," the marketing director said. "And we're featuring the devices on the show."

"There were millions of viewers," I told them.

The marketing director laughed. "You haven't seen the latest numbers. The show has gone viral. Ellen DeGeneres talked about it; the Kardashians put it all over their Instagram. The first episode has 200 million views."

I whistled. "That's impressive."

"It's an advertising gold mine. Your brother is a genius," the director said to Liam.

"Hopefully Gunnar's genius turns into a check for rent," I said to Liam after the meeting.

"Have you had more interest in the tower?" he asked.

"I'm afraid that because we're in that dead period between Thanksgiving and Christmas, I won't have much interest. I still don't have a restaurant lined up."

"Your lobby looks nice. It's very festive," Liam said, throwing an arm around my shoulders. "Has your heart grown three times its size? Are you going to be the Christmas cheermeister?"

I shrugged off Liam's arm. "I don't do Christmas."

"But do you do Christmas bakers?" Liam asked.

I stopped in my tracks. "What are you talking about?"

Liam wagged his finger in my face. "Midnight photography sessions. I saw the photos on Instagram. I know what your dog, Milo, looks like. No billionaire in the world does a late-night photo session in a park in the dead of winter unless they really like someone."

"It's just business," I told him. "She's selling our products."

"Uh huh."

As my car drove me back from the office, I passed by a familiar blonde in a red coat. I told the driver to stop and let me out.

"I'll walk the rest of the way," I told him.

Chloe was so engrossed in taking pictures that she didn't notice me come up behind her. I couldn't resist kissing her neck just behind her ear. She had her hair up in a bun, and her neck was smooth when I pressed my lips to her skin.

She screamed and whirled around.

An older woman passing by looked at us in bemusement.

"You know," she said to Chloe, "a homeless man kissed me like that this morning. Count your blessings it's someone who looks like him." She gestured to me.

"Sure, yep," Chloe said. Her cheeks were rosy from the cold. I couldn't tell if she was irritated with me or not.

"You're wearing a coat," she said.

"Just an overcoat."

She reached out and ran her fingers down the front of the coat. "Nice," she said.

I wished she would run her hand down something else.

She bounced up and down on the balls of her feet.

"Come back to the tower with me," I told her.

"No."

"No?"

"I have to make more pictures," she said. "I have to feed the Instagram beast. I don't suppose you know of any places filled with Christmas cheer? In fact, I probably shouldn't hang around you if I want nice Christmas pictures. You're like a black hole of anti-Christmas. What's that Christmas monster? The Krampus? That's you."

"Really," I said, as she turned to leave. In two strides, I was next to her, and I matched my pace to hers, which earned us dirty looks. True New Yorkers did not walk right next to each other because it blocked sidewalk traffic. But I had to be next to her.

After the third dirty look, I wrapped an arm around her, pulling her close to my body. She made a little squeaking noise and started to pull away.

"Someone's going to stab us," I told her, pulling her back against me. "We take up too much room on the sidewalk."

"It's because your shoulders are really wide," she replied. She was tucked neatly under my arm. "It's weird being this close to you."

"Chloe," I said in mock admonishment. "This is a public place. Get your mind out of the gutter. Besides, we fit perfectly together."

She rolled her eyes. "Where are we going?"

"I was following you," I told her.

"I need pictures," she whined.

"So demanding."

"My followers are all I have," she muttered.

"What do you mean?"

"Never mind." She seemed grumpy.

I hesitated for a moment then said, "I know of this place. No one else will have pictures like this. It's a bit of a subway ride, though."

"Where are we going?"

"It's a surprise, Chloe."

I pulled her down the stairs of a nearby subway stop, and we took the train to Hell's Kitchen. When we resurfaced, I led her through several alleyways.

"I feel like I'm following the big bad wolf or something," she said, sounding slightly nervous.

"You are wearing red," I said with a slight smirk. "But honestly, this area has been cleaned up. Lots of rich people live here."

I hoped the secret place was still there, though. Otherwise I would have to think of something else to impress Chloe.

We ducked through a brick archway and down another alley then through another doorway, and the view opened up.

"Wow!" Chloe said.

"This was my sister Belle's favorite spot," I said, looking around. The tiny garden was exactly as I remembered it.

"Who did all this?" she asked me. I shrugged.

"I don't know. But it's always well maintained."

A little miniature horse trotted out to greet us, the bells on his harness ringing.

"This is too pure," she said and took a cookie out of a bag in her purse.

"Of course you have cookies," I remarked, watching as the horse gratefully took a cookie out of her hand then followed us as we walked through the garden.

"It's like a fairytale!"

The owner or caretaker had decorated for Christmas. There were miniature trees with tiny ornaments, little glass snow globes floated in the ponds, and pots of poinsettias were tucked here and there around the garden. Hidden lights gave the place a magical glow.

"This is why I love New York!" she exclaimed. "Little hidden moments like this." She looked a little tearful. "It's so beautiful."

"Aren't you going to take a picture?"

"No," she said, shaking her head. "This is just for us." She reached out and took my hand. We sat on a bench and petted the pony while he begged for more treats.

"Where is Belle now?" Chloe asked.

"Gone," I said simply.

"She didn't...pass away, did she?" Chloe asked carefully. "Sorry. I don't mean to pry."

"It's fine," I said. "She's fine, she's just gone. She...my parents... It's hard to explain. I don't want to ruin this place."

"I understand," she said, resting her head against my arm.

CHAPTER 21

Chloe

The outing with Jack left me feeling rejuvenated. I loved New York City, and I had to stay here by any means necessary. I hadn't taken any pictures of the little garden. I didn't think I could properly capture it without the right lens. Besides, it felt wrong, like if I tried to photograph the garden, it would disappear.

I also didn't know exactly what was going on with Jack. It sounded as if his family was horrible. I didn't know what his parents had done to run off their daughter, but I could sympathize. My relationship with my own parents was terrible—I hadn't even gone to my own father's funeral.

"What's for dinner?" Maria asked me.

We were in the kitchen of our apartment, preparing a shared dinner. The contestants liked to swap off cooking duties. Only Hartleigh didn't participate. She ate weird stuff like yogurt with bee pollen and shaved zucchini that looked like noodles. Give me real pasta any day of the week.

"Handmade sausage with garlic, cheesy fennel mashed potatoes, sauerkraut, Caesar salad, and chocolate raspberry lava cake for dessert."

"Yum!"

"How was your date?" Nina asked as she grated parmesan cheese for me.

"I know I should be concentrating on the bake-off, but I can't stop thinking about Jack." I looked around in a slight panic. "Hartleigh isn't here, is she?"

"She's out," Maria said. "So you were telling us about your perfect man?"

"I don't know about perfect," I said. "He doesn't like Christmas—in fact, I think he hates it. He needs some cheering up."

"I suppose you could always give him a blow job," Nina said.

I choked on the piece of lettuce I was eating to taste the Caesar dressing. Slapping me on the back, Nina handed me a glass of water.

"Geeze, I was thinking I would make him dinner."

"He's a billionaire. I'm sure he has people to do that sort of thing," Nina said.

"Maybe. He doesn't seem all that excited about food. He probably drinks that Soylent stuff, you know, you mix up wheat protein, oil, and vitamins or something, and it replaces meals."

"That sounds disgusting," Maria said as she stirred the potatoes.

Nina took a bite of the mashed potatoes. "Perfect."

After dinner, I went for a walk. Even though I had been out with Jack, I was still shy of my step goal.

It was freezing, and there weren't any Santas out. I stayed close to Frost Tower, walking briskly down the blocks surrounding the building.

"I thought I told you not to be out here at night by yourself," said a man's gruff voice.

I yelped. A husky barked.

My hand clasped to my chest, I laughed. "Jack! You can't keep scaring me!"

He was grinning down at me, his silver-white hair reflecting the lamplight.

"Are you stalking me?" I demanded.

"No, of course not," he said.

"Then how did you know I would be out here?"

"I didn't," he protested. "Milo wanted to go on a walk."

"The next time I'm in your penthouse, I'm going to check out your view. I bet you can see everything from up there."

"The next time," he said, a crooked grin on his face. "So I didn't scare you." He reached out, pulling me closer to him. "You want to come back up and finish what I started?"

The palms of my hands were pressed against his chest. He smelled clean, like melted snow and basil. He looked down at me, his eyes daring me to tilt my head up and close the distance between us.

"I was just going to cook you a nice meal," I said.

"Cook me food?" His expression changed from hot desire to curiosity.

"You seem like you need it," I told him. "Lonely bachelor with only his billions and his dog to keep him company."

He tucked me under his arm again and escorted me back to the tower.

"I have"—I checked my Fitbit—"like a thousand more steps to go. I thought you were walking your dog anyway?"

"Fine," he said and turned us around in the opposite direction. "So tell me what you're going to make."

"It's a surprise," I said, "but I'll make your special cookies."

"You want to make special cookies with me?" he asked, nuzzling my neck.

"It sounds so dirty when you say it like that!"

"Yes," he said with a grin.

"Do you and your neighbors have get-togethers? Maybe you could take them some cookies."

"One, no one touches your special cookies except me. And two, I don't have neighbors, with the exception of Anastasia."

"No neighbors? But it's such a nice tower!"

"Yeah, well, between half of the buyers being thrown in jail by their foreign governments and the other half being affected by various Western governments freezing all their money, there's not a lot of buyers for top-of-the-market, high-end luxury condos."

"But this is New York City!" I couldn't fathom why people weren't lining up to buy.

"There's a hot new tower opening in New York practically every quarter, it seems, and this is not the greatest location." Jack ran a hand through his hair. It was snowing again, and the motion sent glittering sprinkles into the air. "The feds are really screwing me over. A few people bought places, but the feds took control, so I couldn't sell those even if I wanted to. The condos are in a weird limbo, and no one wants to lock their money into a tower with such a black reputation."

"You'll find buyers eventually," I assured him. Though what did I know? I couldn't even manage my own measly bank account.

Jack shook his head. "There's office space in the tower, and unfortunately, people normally want all residential or office plus hotel, which I didn't do. I never should have jumped into real estate. It has been a huge, expensive, frustrating mistake."

"Sorry to hear it."

"Gunnar claims this show will help the tower," Jack said.

"It's sure helping Platinum Provisions," I told him, rubbing a hand over his back. "Everyone on my Instagram wants the product."

"Yes, Platinum Provisions always does well. I should have stuck with what I knew."

"I'll post some more shots of the lobby and the outside of Frost Tower," I promised him. "You'll figure something out. You just need better branding."

I took a few shots of the tower and the lobby from the street when we returned. The homeless Santa was slumped on a bench opposite the tower. The security guard was nowhere to be seen.

"Yet another thing wrong with this place," Jack said in disgust.

"Christmas Chloe!" the Santa said, waking up with a snort. "Spare some change?"

I gave him a few nickels. "Sorry. That's all I have."

"You shouldn't give them money," Jack said to me when we were in the warmth of the lobby.

"It's only a few cents," I told him, my voice tight.

"He's an addict, and you're enabling him," Jack said flatly.

"I know he's an addict," I snapped back. "Trust me, I know about addicts. My father and my mother and my cousin are all drug addicts, or were in my parents' case. They died of their addiction. So yes, I'm well aware of addiction. But I don't let the bad things in my past affect the rest of my life and color my perception of people and make me cold and aloof and emotionless."

Jack looked stunned. I shook my head. I couldn't believe I had just gone off on a tirade. Jack was a billionaire—he didn't care about my petty problems.

I walked away before he could say anything.

CHAPTER 22

Jack

I was obsessing about Chloe. Was she really that attached to the homeless Santa? Wasn't he the one who had screamed at her in the alleyway? Maybe she felt guilty over her parents. I knew how that was—I was still wracked with guilt about Belle.

I needed to stop thinking about Chloe and start obsessing about finding tenants. Ever since Chloe and her Christmas baking had come into my life, she was proving to be a major distraction. She was drawing my attention away from both saving my tower and making sure my actual company remained successful.

"Earth to Jack!"

I shook myself. I was standing outside of the Platinum Provisions tower.

"Is Chloe some sort of magical Christmas elf who put a spell on you?" Liam joked.

“How did you know I was with her last night?” I practically yelled at my friend.

“I didn’t,” Liam said, looking slightly miffed. “But now that you mention it, I would say sexual frustration and a lack of Christmas cheer are making for one crabby billionaire.”

“I’m not crabby,” I muttered. “I’m just thinking about how this tower is so much better than Frost Tower.”

“You mean besides the fact that it’s all one tenant and we have a boutique hotel and the best Japanese restaurant on the East Coast and a public parking garage which, I don’t know if you’ve seen the numbers on it lately, but that thing brings in mad cash. I guess it’s true what they say—sex sells, but nothing sells like a parking space in New York City.”

“Are you ready for the board meeting?” I asked Liam.

“Of course!” he exclaimed. “I love how they all just fawn over us.”

“All of the board members are your brothers,” I retorted as the elevator stopped on one of the upper floors that held the main conference room. Someone had decorated for Christmas since the last time I’d been there. The diffused winter light shone in through the floor-to-ceiling windows, making the fake snow on the garlands glitter.

“*I’m dreaming of a—*” Liam started to sing.

I socked him in the stomach.

“Ooof,” he gasped. “You’re lucky I work out and have the most amazing abs, or you could have done some serious damage.”

“I didn’t hit you that hard,” I retorted.

Greg Svensson and his half-brother Hunter Svensson were waiting inside the conference room. They both had the same dirty-blond hair and tall, broad build. They looked as if they were descended from Vikings except that now they were corporate mercenaries.

"I was told there would be snacks," Liam said by way of greeting. I shook hands with Hunter while Greg snapped at his younger brother.

"There will be lunch, but only after you two give your reports."

Liam fiddled with the presentation equipment. A Christmas carol blared over the sound system, and I winced.

"Greg is a Christmas Grinch too," Liam said over the din.

"Turn it off!" Greg yelled.

"Both of you need some Christmas in your life," Liam said as little naked Santas danced across the screen. Liam flipped to the next slide, and the music shut off.

"Honestly, Liam," Greg said.

"Is this what you all are up to in Manhattan?" Hunter said quietly. "Why am I not surprised?"

"I don't need your judgment," Greg snapped at his half-brother.

"Can we please move this along?" I said. Chloe was supposed to make me dinner tonight.

"He has a hot date," Liam said.

"I don't!"

"*Children*," Hunter said in a low voice.

"So basically our report is that Platinum Provisions is rolling in money," Liam said, "and we're giving out hefty Christmas bonuses." The screen flipped to a slide of Chloe in that revealing gingerbread-girl costume blowing a kiss at the camera and icing a cookie with one of the Platinum Provisions tools. I grabbed on to the arm of the chair.

"That is inappropriate," Greg said.

"This is what sells," Liam retorted. "We are making so much money, all thanks to this girl and Gunnar's web show."

"We will basically sell as many of these as we can produce," I interjected. "We will beat our projections from last quarter by twenty percent thanks to the limited-edition Christmas baking product line. With *The Great Christmas Bake-Off*, people are taking a renewed interest in high-end kitchen products."

"We'll need a way to keep interest up past the Christmas season," Hunter said.

"We make medical equipment and drills." I told them. "The baking stuff is a side venture. It shouldn't overwhelm our main focus."

"Yes, but if there's money, you all need to go after it," Greg added.

"Let's move on and discuss your progress on the pharmaceutical production tools," Hunter said, flipping to a new page in his notebook. "There's a need in Svensson PharmaTech for products that Platinum Provisions could design and produce."

The rest of the board meeting went on longer than I thought it would. Hunter and Greg insisted on reviewing the production schedule for the Christmas baking items.

"What absolutely cannot happen," Hunter said, "is that your company fails to meet these promises you've made to consumers. There's marketing everywhere. Everyone who wants a cooking device needs to be able to buy one. Failure is not an option."

"We'll make it happen," I promised.

"Will you?" Hunter said. "You're so distracted by the tower, and Liam mentioned a girl—"

"I am not distracted."

"Good," Hunter said. "Platinum Provisions is your first priority, not my brother's stupid reality show, not your tower, and certainly not that baker. Understand?"

"Of course," I said firmly. But Chloe was taking over my life and my headspace.

"Where are you off to?" Liam asked after the board meeting. "Come eat with us so I'm not alone with my brothers."

"Chloe was supposed to make me dinner," I told Liam. "But she's mad at me. So maybe it won't happen."

"So you can come for a drink."

"I don't know. I have filming and my dog."

"When are you going to hire another assistant?" Liam asked.

"Someday. I have a lot on my plate."

I took the subway back to the tower. There was a major accident, and traffic was worse than usual. Homeless Santa was outside the lobby entrance. He gave me a half salute, and against my better judgement, I put a donation in his cup.

"Much obliged, sir," he said in thanks.

Maybe it would bring me good luck.

Chloe was walking out of the tower when I arrived; she almost ran right into my arms. I wanted to kiss her, but I didn't know where we stood.

"Off to take more pictures?" I asked, trying to scrub clean the image of her in that costume from my brain.

"I'm going shopping for your dinner," she said.

I wondered if she saw the lust in my eyes. "I was afraid it might be canceled," I said.

"No." She looked down at her shoes then down the street. "I'm sorry I yelled at you."

"It's my fault," I said in a rush. "I'm trying to be less mean spirited. I gave Homeless Santa ten dollars just now."

"That was a bit much," she said with a frown then checked her watch. "I need to shop or it's going to be too late to cook for you."

"I'll come with you," I said. I didn't want her to pay for ingredients.

"The grocery store where we shop for the show isn't far," she said as we wove through the rush-hour crowds. There was a Santa outside ringing a bell collecting for the Salvation Army.

"Ho ho ho! Merry Christmas!" he said.

I expected to be in and out of the store quickly, but Chloe had to stop and inspect every single item. She looked over every turnip, examined every potato, and spent an insufferable amount of time arguing with the butcher. I wandered around in the area, bored. There was a Santa looking at the pasta. Christmas just couldn't leave me alone.

When the butcher handed her the meat wrapped in wax paper, I thought we were finally finished. But no, Chloe wanted to go back to the fruit and vegetable aisle.

"Are you buying eggplant?"

"I might," she said, putting the eggplant back and picking up an identical one and placing it in one of the baskets she had me carrying. She smiled at me. "I like having a handsome man following me around and carrying my stuff."

"Speaking of following," I said. "I don't want to alarm you, but I think that Santa is watching us."

"Of course he is," she said, turning to glare at the Santa. He noticed us staring and hurried towards the exit.

"Do you think it's Homeless Santa?" I asked.

"Who knows," she said.

"You just attract the crazies, don't you," I joked.

"Yeah," she said. She didn't seem her usual bubbly self. Instead she seemed lost in thought as I paid for all the food.

She was silent on the walk back to the tower.

"I want to cover you in frosting and lick it off every inch of you," I said, trying to rouse her.

"That's nice," she said.

"What's wrong?"

"Nothing." We walked the rest of the way in silence.

"Speaking of crazies," Chloe said when we returned to the tower. Hartleigh was waiting in the lobby.

"I knew I saw you two leave," she said.

"I hope she won't make things too difficult for you," I murmured to Chloe.

"I'm used to crazy people," she said, her mouth a flat line.

CHAPTER 23
Chloe

I really couldn't catch a break. I knew exactly who that Santa Claus in the grocery store had been: my cousin Cody. I thought he was supposed to be in jail. I itched to look him up online. Maybe they had released him early.

I steamed as I prepped dinner.

Jack was sitting on one of the barstools near the counter watching me work. His suit jacket was off, and his sleeves were rolled up. I wanted to trace my fingers along the veins of his forearms.

He seemed concerned. I didn't want him to think I was mad at him. I just wished real life wasn't intruding on my Christmas fantasy. Oh well, there was nothing I could do about Cody's sudden appearance right now. I was safe in Jack's penthouse making a nice meal for a wealthy, handsome man who might hopefully, maybe, like me.

"Did you say you were going to cover me in frosting and lick it off?" I asked him.

He smirked. "Every inch."

"I thought you didn't like frosting," I said coyly.

"I like it on you."

I couldn't believe I was blatantly flirting with this guy. In all my severe lapses in judgment, this had to be the worst.

"What are you making?" he asked me.

"Some real food," I said, concentrating on slicing vegetables for the ratatouille. "Tonight you will be eating steak, truffle mac and cheese, veggies, and a nice salad."

"Sounds rustic," he said.

"My oma used to say, 'Chloe, do you know what a man wants?'" I said, gesturing with my knife the way she always would. "'He wants you to fuck him, not fuck with his food.'"

Jack laughed at my impression of my oma. "She had a bit of a potty mouth," I said sheepishly. "She said she was old and a grandmother and had therefore earned the privilege."

"I think I would have liked her," Jack said, still chuckling.

"Yeah. I think she would have liked you too."

He looked at me in concern.

"Sorry," I said. My eyes were tearing up, and I wiped my hands off to blow my nose. "This was supposed to be, if not a romantic evening, at least a fun one for you. You work too hard."

Jack came around the large kitchen island and wrapped me in his strong arms. They really were ridiculously buffed.

"I'm sure she would be proud of you," he said, kissing me on the cheek.

I leaned against him for a moment until I felt more in control.

"Let me finish cooking," I said after he released me. While the ratatouille and the macaroni and cheese bubbled happily in the oven, I prepped the steaks.

"This is another reason I never want to leave New York," I said. "The cuts of beef are amazing." I stuck a piece of the raw meat in Jack's face. "See this marbling?"

"It's really impressive," he said.

I inhaled. "Dry aged, just some salt and pepper and a dab of butter." The oven beeped, and I pulled out the pasta and veggies to settle. Then I put the nuts for the cookies in the oven and cooked the beef in a piping-hot cast iron skillet, which I was shocked to see that Jack owned.

"I can practically see you salivating," I said as I set the steak on his plate and dished up the sides for him.

"It looks amazing," he said. "It's better than any restaurant."

"Oh, look, you set the table!" I exclaimed. There were candles and linen napkins and a bottle of wine out. "This is too perfect!"

He waited impatiently while I snapped a few pictures.

"I think I need you to move in," Jack told me after inhaling his plate of food and going for seconds. "After living off of takeout and reheated prepared meals, it's the ultimate luxury to have you here serving me home-cooked food."

I was pretty pleased. "The best compliment is someone taking a second helping or a fourth cookie," I said, trying not to sound giddy that he liked my cooking.

"Speaking of which, you did promise me your special cookies," Jack said, grinning impishly.

"I thought you wanted me covered in frosting for dessert," I said, innocently sipping my wine. Then I jumped up before he could take me up on the offer. The grin on his face was practically hazardous.

He followed me and watched from the other side of the island as I busied myself chopping nuts and measuring flour.

"I should have gotten you an apron," he said as a wayward pecan escaped my knife.

"One of my fans will probably send me another one I can keep here," I told him. There was that dangerous grin again.

"You want to stay here," he said slowly.

"You have a very, very nice kitchen," I told him. "And you don't even cook! It's the height of unfairness."

He walked around the counter and there he was, back in my personal space.

"I don't know why your name is Jack Frost," I said, "because you're smoking hot."

His hands rested on my hips as he said, "I want to kiss you."

"I thought you wanted Christmas cookies."

"I do, but there's something else I want more," he said. "I want the Christmas cookie baker."

He had me pressed up against the length of his body. I could feel the bulge in his pants. We were so close that I could feel his breath cool against my lips. *This is a bad idea*, I thought, but the naughty elf was sitting on my shoulder, cheering me on.

I let my hands roam up his dress shirt and grabbed him by the nape of his neck and pulled him down. Our lips met in a kiss. It was long and slow, his hands caressing my back, sliding down, down to my hips and slipping under my skirt. I was wearing stockings, and they were preventing me from having what I needed, which was his hand there, stroking the hot flesh between my legs. I moaned, bucking lightly against him, pushing against the hand that pushed at my tights.

"I want to lick you like I licked the frosting off of your finger when I saw you in that outfit," he said, kissing my neck. "I need you to be wearing that the next time we fuck. But right now, I want to fuck you bent over the counter."

Well, that had escalated quickly. I pushed him off. The elf was not happy.

"Your special Christmas cookies!" I gasped. "I have to make your cookies." I was grasping at candy canes, trying to get my bearings. Jack stepped back, looking at me with one eyebrow raised.

"I can't tell whether I should be insulted or flattered," he said as I furiously finished chopping the nuts, little pieces flying everywhere like something on *The Muppet Show*.

"I'm just going to finish your cookies," I repeated.

"You seem flustered," he said. "I can't imagine why."

The only guys I had been with were the future meth heads in my oma's small Midwestern town. They had always liked to think they were hot stuff with their trucks and their taxidermied deer heads, but they were nothing compared to Jack.

"You kiss like you mean business," I told him.

"Am I scaring you?"

"No."

"You're lying."

He was gazing at me from across the kitchen, his arms crossed as he leaned back against the counter.

"You're awfully smug," I told him.

He pushed off to stand close to me again, his hands sliding down my backside.

“You know,” he said thoughtfully, “I think it’s better this way. I think the first time I fuck you, I do want you to be in one of those sexy Christmas outfits.”

“I thought you hated Christmas,” I said, feeling frazzled.

He let me go, and I turned back to the cookies. I was afraid my skin was going to be too hot to make them.

CHAPTER 24

Jack

The cookies were as transformative as usual. I ate three. Okay, five.

Chloe smiled as she watched me eat.

"Don't look at me," I said, covering my face. I was rewarded with peals of laughter.

"You're covered in powdered sugar," she said, giggling. She leaned over and kissed me, then playfully licked my mouth.

"Yum," she said. "Sugar. You taste like Christmas."

I pulled her close to me and kissed her not so playfully. She practically melted against me. I wrapped her legs around me.

"I need to take off your tights," I said.

"I thought," she said, her voice breathless, "I thought you wanted to fuck me in my sexy costume."

I kissed her, pressing her against me, and she ground her hips against my crotch.

"I don't think I can wait," I told her.

Her phone rang.

"Ignore it," I said, continuing to kiss her. The phone stopped ringing, then it beeped.

"Someone is trying to reach me. It could be about the bake-off." She pushed away from me somewhat reluctantly then went to grab the phone.

"It's Nina," she said. "Dana wants to talk about the marketing plan and product placement."

"Seems late."

"This whole Reality Romance production is a mess," she said, grabbing her bag and her coat.

Before I let her leave, I pressed her against the door, kissing her one last time. I didn't want to let her go, but she slipped out of my grasp.

"Come back anytime," I told her, watching her skip down the hall to the elevator.

The room was warm from the oven. Milo was eyeing the leftovers from dinner with alarming intensity.

"No," I told him. I was way too hot, so I threw open the doors to the balcony and let the snow come in. Then I plotted how I was going to get Chloe into my bed. Chloe was like her cookies: once I'd had a taste, I wanted the whole box.

Deciding I might as well do something productive, I took Milo for a walk and took a call with our Australia office. I saw a familiar red coat waiting in the lobby when I returned. Chloe? The woman turned. No, it was Hartleigh.

"You need to leave me alone," I told her.

She sniffed me, and Milo growled.

"You smell like baking," Hartleigh said. "I bet I know who it was." Her voice had taken on a high-pitched, lilting quality. She sounded really unhinged, and she wasn't blinking, just staring at me.

"It was Chloe, wasn't it?" She started to cry.

"It's not any of your business," I told her.

"You and I," she said, gesturing wildly, "Jack, we have something special. We always did."

"No, we don't. There is nothing between us. Go back to your apartment," I told her. I wished I had my sister Belle's authority. She could look at you, and you jumped to do her bidding.

"I'll tell Belle what you're up to," I threatened.

She flinched then smiled. "Belle isn't here, Jack, she's gone. But she'll come back for our wedding!" Hartleigh said with a laugh.

"We will never marry," I told her. "You're insane."

"I don't know why you treat me like this, Jack. I am the only person who loves you," Hartleigh said, wrapping her arms around my neck.

"No, you don't," I said, unwrapping her limbs. Where was the security guard?

Someone banged on the glass. It was the drunk Santa.

"I have to deal with this," I told Hartleigh.

She latched onto me, physically trying to drag me back. I couldn't hurt her; that wouldn't look good. Then I really could kiss my tower goodbye. Milo snapped at her, and she let me go.

As I opened the door, I had a deviously clever idea.

"Are you looking for Hartleigh?" I asked the homeless Santa, turning my head meaningfully and looking back at my stalker.

The Santa gave me an exaggerated wink.

"Sure," he slurred.

"Great. Hartleigh, your friend is here to see you!" I called out, pushing him in her direction.

She shrieked as the drunk stumbled over to her. "Jack!" she yelled, trying to get around him. I smirked as she cursed when he patted her shoulder.

"We're meant to be together," Hartleigh said. "I talked to your parents. They want me to be the mother of your children."

"My parents are crazy. And honestly, I'm crazy for even interacting with you."

"You're mine, Jack Frost," she said with unnerving intensity right before she swept away into an elevator.

"Thanks, man," I told the Santa and handed him twenty dollars. "You can sleep in here if you want. Just don't mess with the decorations."

"I wouldn't," he said. "That girl, Chloe, did them. I like her."

I smiled at him. "I like her too."

"I thought that pretty baker was your girlfriend," Santa said. "What're you doing with that witch?"

I looked in the direction of the elevators and replied, "Just a ghost of Christmas past."

CHAPTER 25

Chloe

Jack had left me frazzled. Even though I took a shower when I returned to the shared apartment after the meeting Dana had called, I still felt off kilter.

"What is he playing at?" I asked Nina.

"I don't think he's playing at anything. He's a billionaire. He knows what he wants, and he's going after her."

I groaned and flopped down on my bed. I sort of wished I had given in and slept with Jack. However, I had lied when I said he didn't scare me. Being the center of attention on social media was one thing. The screen was a buffer between me and my followers. But Jack was right there in the same room. He saw *me*. What if he didn't like the real Chloe?

The next morning, after very little sleep, we assembled in the studio for the next challenge.

"Welcome back for another episode of *The Great Christmas Bake-Off*," Anastasia said to the cameras.

"Alcohol in various forms has been served during Christmas. Be it eggnog with rum, spiced wine, or the special family Christmas punch, alcohol plays a part in making the holiday season bright. If you have trouble with your family, then alcohol makes the holidays bearable."

"Amen!" Nick said. I chuckled along with the other contestants then made the mistake of sneaking a look to Jack. He wasn't laughing. Instead, he was staring intently at me. I felt flushed again.

"Bakers, grab your ingredients. We look forward to seeing what you create."

I grabbed bottles of rum, whiskey, and bourbon. As soon as I returned to my station, I poured myself a sip of each.

"It's nine in the morning," Nina teased.

"I have to taste the ingredients to have a sense of the flavor profile," I told her.

"Uh-huh," she said as I poured myself another sip of bourbon. "That looks like more than a taste."

Jack was still sitting at the judges' table. I watched him over the rim of the glass. Why was he still here? Normally he left to go do whatever billionaire things he had to do. Was he honestly going to sit here the entire day and watch me? He looked at me and smiled in a self-satisfied way.

"Do you even know what you're making?" Nina asked.

"No, but the alcohol is starting to infuse itself in my brain, and I feel an epiphany coming on."

"Drunk epiphanies can lead to really terrible results," Nina warned. Jack was still watching me.

"I need a dessert, a boozy Christmas dessert," I chanted to myself as I racked my brain.

Eggnog. I had to have eggnog. But what to eat with it?

Jack, the naughty elf chanted. *You should eat Jack! He tastes like pure snow and pine and sex.*

I finished off the rest of the whisky in the glass. Jack stood up from the table and walked over to me. One of the cameramen hurried over to film our interaction.

"And what are you making?" Jack asked, a smile playing around his mouth. "Your last dessert was very impressive. Hopefully you can top it."

Top it... top Jack...Jack on top of...

"Can you tell us what you're making, Chloe?" Zane repeated. "I need footage."

"Sorry," I told him, blinking. That whiskey sure was strong.

"I'm making eggnog."

"With lots of alcohol," Jack said, his smile widening. He stepped closer to me.

"Yes."

"Anything to eat?" Zane prodded.

I looked around and sighed. "Bacon."

"Bacon," Jack repeated, one eyebrow raised slightly. "Sounds interesting."

He was too close to me. Suddenly I needed air. I stepped away from him.

"This isn't working for me right now. I need to concentrate."

"Did you even eat breakfast?" he asked as Zane walked over to film Nina.

"Jack!" Hartleigh called. She made a pouty fish face and stuck out her chest. "Jack! Come look at what I'm making."

Jack grimaced. "I'll see you later," he said to me, lightly touching my hip and letting his hand slide down. He hurried away as Hartleigh stomped over to my work table.

"I know you're after Jack! I know you're trying to steal him from me."

Maybe it was the alcohol on an empty stomach, but Hartleigh looked unhinged. It seemed as if her eyes were twitchy and not really focused on me.

I poured myself another sip. "Jack is a grown man," I said. "He can make his own decisions."

"I am supposed to marry him. His parents said I could."

"This isn't the Middle Ages. People's parents can't dictate who they marry."

"You want to marry him?" Hartleigh screeched.

One of the production assistants hurried over. "Stop talking so loudly," she said. "You're messing up the sound quality."

"Sorry," I mumbled and gave Hartleigh a dirty look.

Dessert. Right. I knew I was making eggnog. It needed to sit and let the flavors blend, so I decided to make it first. I stirred together egg yolks, sugar, nutmeg, vanilla, and cloves in a saucepan on low heat. Once I started moving and taste-testing the creamy custardy mixture I'd made for the eggnog, I felt a little more clear-headed. The eggnog thickened to a creamy consistency. I wanted the flavor of the rum but not the bitterness of the alcohol, so I flambéed it in another saucepan. Once a sufficient amount of the alcohol was cooked off, I stirred it into the eggnog as well.

Using a spoon, I took a taste.

"Delicious," I declared. The eggnog was still slightly boozy but not overpowering. I set it aside to cool.

What to cook? Remembering that I had promised Jack bacon, I cooked some and ate a piece. Then I needed some more whisky to wash it down.

"Are you eating or cooking?" Nina asked.

"Cooking!" I said. "Watch me go!" I was just freestyling it at this point. What went well with eggnog and bacon? Booze, obviously. I took another sip of bourbon. Then I made a sponge cake.

Satisfied that it was delicate and light, I set it aside to cool. Then I made a cranberry gelatin. Straining it, I let it set in small, circular molds. Then I made a thick citrusy custard and let it set as well. While the pieces of the trifle I had decided to make set, I candied some whole cranberries. They sparkled with granulated sugar, and I set them aside to harden.

Pleased with how my dessert was progressing, I took another sip of bourbon. I was really on fire now. I carefully cut circles out of the sponge cake and soaked them in a sugary alcohol mixture, then used a torch to caramelize each one.

To bring in the bacon, I made donut balls fried in bacon grease and glazed each with a salted bourbon caramel and sprinkled bacon pieces on top. While I assembled my trifles, I noticed Jack had returned. He was sitting at the long butcher-block judges' table. His eyes followed my every move. I had another swig of the whisky. It was smooth going down my throat.

Don't think about smooth things, or smooth man chests, I told myself. I needed to win this next round, and I couldn't afford any distractions. But Jack was a distraction I desperately wanted.

Once the trifles were assembled, alternating with the sponge cake, the custard, and the cranberry gelatin, I garnished each with a toothpick holding one of the donut holes and two of the candied cranberries.

As we waited in the holding room, I shared the last of the bourbon with Nina.

"Happy boozy Christmas," Nina said, clinking our glasses together.

CHAPTER 26

Jack

As soon as Chloe stepped up to present her dessert, I knew she had been sneaking sips from the container. She was definitely buzzed.

"I made for you," she said a little too loudly, "dessert. You have eggnog, a cranberry sponge cake parfait, and a bacon caramel donut."

The donut was superb. The rest of the dish seemed a little scattered.

"This is like a two a.m. snack after you've been drinking all night," Nick said.

"I agree," Anu replied. "It's a little all over the place. Each piece by itself is superb, but there's a lot going on with this plate."

The contestants had gone all out on the boozy desserts, and Anu and Nick had a difficult time deciding on a winner.

"Chloe's dish was interesting," Anu said, "but Nina made that cranberry cobbler with eggnog ice cream that was divine."

"It also felt more thought out," Nick said. "Nina's flavors were a little more cohesive. I think she is our winner."

"That was a good donut, though," I added, though they really weren't supposed to take my comments into consideration, since I had no experience cooking, let alone baking.

"Why didn't you make them pick me?" Chloe said when she saw me outside of the studio.

"I can't just tell them who to pick," I whispered to her. She was close to me, her hands fiddling with the buttons on my suit coat. I could smell the bourbon on her as her fingers laced into my tie. I let her pull me down until our faces were inches apart, then she stood up on her tiptoes and kissed me on the mouth. People might see us, but I didn't care. I pulled her close and let her melt into me. One of the production assistants giggled, and I drew back. I might not care if people saw us, but Chloe might. At least she might when she was sober.

"Everyone's going to see," I told her as she reached up to kiss me again.

"I'm sloshed," she said as she leaned into my chest.

"I can tell. Maybe you should go sleep it off."

"I had to taste the eggnog," she said, "and the brandy sauce. It was very alcoholic."

"I see that. Maybe you should eat something," I told her.

"I'm drunk!" she said again, giggling. I wondered if that was the only reason she was kissing me in public. Maybe she would think I was taking advantage of her.

One of the production assistants came over and led her away for post-challenge interviews.

Filming had ended a bit late that day. Instead of going into the office, I went to my penthouse and answered emails then looked in my fridge. Chloe's leftovers were still there. I smiled to myself when I thought about how tipsy she was.

There was a knock on the door. Milo barked.

"That better not be Hartleigh," I said as I checked the security camera.

Liam waved.

"How's my favorite Christmas Scrooge?" Liam said, slapping me on the back when I opened the door. "Missed you at the office today."

"Were you even there?" I countered, following Liam into my kitchen.

"Of course," he said. "Someone has to make sure Santa has enough Platinum Provisions baking equipment to put under every Christmas tree. Not that I'm not happy to see you in the Christmas spirit."

He rummaged around my kitchen and found Chloe's leftovers.

"Who made you this?" he demanded. He grabbed a fork and speared a piece of the leftover macaroni and cheese. "This is so good."

"That's mine!" I said.

"Sharing is caring!" Liam said, blocking me from taking back the container. I wanted to fight him for the food, but I didn't want it to end up on the floor. "Did that crappy chef delivery service make this?"

"No," I said, taking the container away from him and cradling it. It seemed wrong to beg Chloe to cook for me, but that was what I wanted: her here every night making dinner, wearing one of those ridiculous outfits, and drinking an eggnog martini.

Liam made a face at me. "So…"

"So what?"

"Who made it? You're acting like that's the last meal you're ever going to eat."

"Chloe made it," I told him, "and it might be the last meal she makes me."

"Why?"

"Just…" I didn't want to explain, so I changed the subject. "Why are you here?"

"So this Christmas stuff had me thinking," Liam said. "We rely too much on factories that we don't control to manufacture our product."

"We outsource it because it's cheaper," I said.

"Is it, though? My half-brothers have all that land out in the western part of the state. They have the hydropower infrastructure in place, and there's an active freight rail that goes there. What if we built a factory out there and started in-house production?"

"I don't know," I said. "That seems risky."

"You're just being overly cautious because you're being burned on this real estate deal." Liam motioned around the tower. "We should be in control of some baseline of our production."

"I'm not moving out to the country," I said flatly.

"Harrogate is only two hours outside of New York City," he countered.

"I don't care," I said. "I'm not moving out there. Are *you* volunteering to move?"

"I can travel back and forth," Liam said.

"What does Greg say?" I asked.

"We have to present a united front. You know he and Hunter don't get along all that well. I don't want Greg to perceive it as some sort of weird power play. You know how paranoid he can be."

"I don't know if I can survive Christmas and deal with a temper tantrum from Greg. I'm already on thin ice with him over this real estate deal," I told Liam.

Liam looked a little disappointed, but I said, "Why don't we hash out some more details, then we can really pitch it and sell him on it."

"Yes! This is going to be great!" Liam said as he grinned and pumped his fist.

"I bet you start singing a different tune once you're stuck out there with all your younger brothers. How many half-brothers do you have out there anyway?"

"I think it's like close to fifty," Liam said. "The older ones go off to college, but my father keeps shipping the younger male children across the country."

"There's nothing anyone can do about your father?" I asked. As bad as my parents were, they paled in comparison to the Svenssons' father. The man should have been locked up.

"Hunter has been trying. He and Greg report my father to the authorities every other month, it seems. The state, of course, says my father can raise his kids however he wants. They have running water and beds, so the state doesn't care beyond that." Liam looked frustrated. I knew his family was a sore subject for him.

"Change of topic?"

"Yes, please," Liam said then waggled his eyebrows. "Let's talk about Chloe. How are you going to have her wrapped and waiting under your tree? Have you even tried to make yourself enticing? It's such a tragedy that you have absolutely no game."

"I don't want to drive her away," I admitted.

"You really like her," Liam said.

"She made me special cookies."

"Chloe made you special cookies? What does that mean?"

I showed him the box.

"You're eating cookies?" Liam waved a hand in front of my face. "Where is Jack Frost, and what have you done with him?"

"You don't understand," I said. "These cookies are amazing! They're salty and melt in your mouth."

Liam took a cookie. I resisted the urge to snatch it out of his hand. He ate the cookie, and his eyes closed. "This is amazing."

"Right?" He reached for another. "Okay, that's enough," I said, taking the box from him.

"Now I see why you like her," Liam told me, dusting the powdered sugar off his hands. "As much as I want to stay here and eat Chloe's food, I have to go."

"Have a hot date?" I asked him.

Liam barked out a laugh. "Hardly. I'm too busy. No, unfortunately, I have to meet Greg. Not here," he said in response to my concerned face. I couldn't face Greg Svensson today. "It's something about some Holbrook drama he's caught up with."

"That man has his fingers in every pie in this city."

After Liam left, I wandered around the penthouse. I felt restless. All the talk of Chloe had sent my thoughts barreling back to last night when she was here in my kitchen, cooking, baking, and making insane noises while she melted like butter in my arms.

There was a knock on the door. "Did you forget something, Liam?"

But it wasn't Liam—it was Chloe.

The door swung open, and she walked in on impossibly high platform stiletto boots. She posed in front of me, and my eyes wandered up, up the thigh-high boots, up to the very short skirt and low-cut top of the sexiest Santa outfit I'd ever seen.

"Cute," I replied, my cock throbbing.

"One of my fans sent it to me," she said. The little pompom on the Santa hat she wore bounced as she talked.

"Do you like it?" she purred, striking a little pose.

"You're drunk."

"I am," Chloe said, walking over to me and resting her hands against my chest.

"I don't want to take advantage of you," I said.

"You're such a gentleman. The prince of winter. It's freezing in here; I should warm you up." She pressed up against me. I was very close to losing all sense of control.

"You're too drunk for this," I told her.

"Correction. You're not drunk enough," she said, leading me to the kitchen.

"You know what this outfit didn't come with?" she said, walking over to the counter. Her ass was tantalizingly perky with the heels.

I swallowed. "What didn't it come with?" I asked her.

"Matching lingerie."

CHAPTER 27

Chloe

I bent over the counter slowly. The skirt, though short, was full from the starched layers of lace underneath. *Everything* was exposed when I bent over, and I felt the chill of the air on my thighs and the glistening darker pink flesh. I looked at Jack over my shoulder as I bent over.

"I can't believe you came here without any underwear," he said. His voice sounded ragged.

"It's constraining," I said in my best sultry voice. "I'm also not wearing a bra."

"How did you get your tits to look so good in that outfit?" His voice was an octave lower, and it purred through me.

"Are you hard?" I asked as I watched him unzip his pants.

"What do you think?"

He walked over to me and let his hand travel down my back, let his fingers slide up my warm inner thigh. His hands were a counterpoint to the blazing heat that went through me.

"I know you want to taste my Christmas cookies," I told him, the alcohol giving me the courage I hadn't had the last time I had been in his apartment. He leaned over to kiss my neck. I felt his cock, hard through the silken boxer briefs, press against my bare thigh.

His hand circled around my chest, working one of my breasts out of the low-cut top. He rubbed it, pinching and teasing the nipple. I wanted his mouth on my nipple; I wanted his mouth everywhere. All the tension of the past few days had reached a boiling point, and I needed relief.

Jack let a hand sink into my hair then tugged me lightly upright. I turned around, and he kissed me deeply, promising pleasure. His mouth moved down, kissing my neck, my collarbone, and the breasts that now spilled out of the too-tight top. I gasped, my chest heaving.

"This costume is too much," Jack said with a huff of laughter.

"It's a little too small," I said, pulling his head back down to my breasts, letting him kiss and lick them.

His fingers found the silky wetness between my legs. I moaned, spreading my legs, inviting him to fuck me with more than his hands.

"I thought you wanted to fuck me bent over the counter," I told him.

He straightened, his fingers still working on my clit. I moaned and bucked against his hand.

I gasped, "Don't you want to fuck me? I want you to fuck me."

"Yes, I want to fuck you," he said. "I want to fuck you just like this." His hand was still making that steady, infuriatingly slow motion that was slowly pushing me to the edge. "But you have to be methodical about these things." His hand moved up to my jaw, tilting my head up to kiss me. My back was arched, and my hips made little circles against his hand. "I need to watch you come undone first."

"Please, I need—"

"Oh, I know what you need," he said. "Turn around. Put your hands on the counter."

"Are you going to fuck me?"

"Better," he said.

Drunk on boozy eggnog and Jack Frost, I leaned over the counter, the flesh between my legs pulsing from his touch. My heart was racing, and I felt hot and charged.

I felt Jack moving behind me. He grasped my hips, hauling me upwards and forwards so I was splayed with my knees spread on the counter.

"I think I found my favorite cookie," Jack said as he pressed his mouth between my legs. His tongue traced every fold, and he kissed and sucked my clit. I hung onto the counter, pressing back against him.

"Faster," I whimpered. He obliged, his tongue and mouth bringing me to the edge of pleasure then throwing me off the cliff.

I cried out as I came.

"That was amazing," I slurred as he pulled me off the counter and wrapped me in his arms. "I came so hard I was singing Christmas carols."

I reached for the bulge in his pants, fully intending to repay the favor, but between the lack of sleep and the alcohol and the post-orgasm haze, I was feeling a little loopy.

Jack picked me up easily and took me into his bedroom.

"You didn't..."

"Next time," he said, kissing me softly as I settled back against the pillows and drifted off to sleep.

I woke up with a start.

"That was an insane dream," I said out loud. The sun streamed through floor-to-ceiling glass. My bedroom sure had a lot of windows all of a sudden, and I didn't remember it being this big.

"Wait a minute," I whispered. I was not in my apartment. Where was Nina? More importantly, where were my clothes?

Drunk Chloe and the naughty elf had conspired against me. I slowly inched over to the edge of the bed. On a far closet doorknob, I saw my sexy Santa costume hanging up. Had I really shown up wearing that? No wonder I ended up naked in a strange bed. I eased out from under the sheets, tiptoed over, and ripped the little costume of the hanger.

"Where is my underwear?" I muttered.

"You weren't wearing any," Jack said from the doorway.

I turned and stared at him, clutching my costume towards me. It did not cover much.

Jack looked me up and down, grinned, and sipped the mug of coffee.

"What happened?" I asked cautiously.

He looked at me, a little surprised. I hoped I hadn't insulted him.

"I just didn't remember..." I said, blushing. "I don't want to be the type of girl who sleeps with a guy and doesn't even remember."

"We didn't sleep together," he said, coming over to me and setting the mug on the nightstand. He pulled the dress out of my hand and threw it on the floor, pulling my naked body against him. "You were a little drunk to fuck."

"We did something," I said. "I remember you going down the chimney, so to speak. Eating my cookies." I was hungover and couldn't think of any other terrible innuendos, and his hands were doing distracting things to my body.

He smirked.

"It was a very nice cookie."

He leaned down and kissed me; it was deep, his tongue tracing inside my mouth. His hand moved between my legs.

"I had my dessert, and now I want the full meal," he whispered to me.

My body remembered what had happened last night even if my mind was a little fuzzy on the specifics. All my body knew was that it had been good, and it wanted to go again.

"You know," he said, kissing down my neck to my nipples, "I think you're sober enough for a fuck this morning."

Yes, I thought, but better judgment prevailed.

"I um…" I pulled away from him and grabbed the coffee and took a sip, hoping to calm down.

"Blech," I said when I tasted it. "What is that? It's bitter and cold."

"It's iced green tea," he said. "It's good for you. It's much healthier than coffee and milk."

The booze was long gone, and I wasn't feeling as adventurous as I had been last night. The desire in his eyes scared me.

"I'm going to, uh, shower, and then I'll make you some breakfast, pile of French toast, butter-pecan maple syrup."

I slipped into what I hoped was the bathroom and closed the door. My last sight of Jack was of a slightly stunned-looking billionaire.

"What the hell?" I heard him say. To avoid thinking about him and his frankly lustful proposition, I started the shower. There was scratching at the door, and I let the husky inside with me.

"He's allowed to watch you?" Jack called out.

"He likes baked goods," I called back.

"I like baked goods!" Jack protested.

So did I, I thought, *Jack's baked goods, that is*. Why was I being so cautious?

"It's a lot to take in," I told Milo. But I still felt slightly guilty.

"I'll make him something nice," I told the dog. "Maybe not French toast." I stepped into the shower. "I'll make him something savory, nice winter baked goods. He likes bacon, so maybe soup and bread? Soup and muffins? Soup baking? Soup muffins!" I said. "Bacon and cheese and potatoey muffins. I bet Jack would like that."

I felt more clearheaded after the shower. I wrapped the biggest towel I had ever seen around myself then peeked around the door. The bedroom door was closed. There was a robe on the bed. It was enormous, and it draped off of me while I pawed through his drawers looking for something else to wear. His boxers were a little snug on my hips, but they would do.

"I can't believe I showed up here without a bra," I muttered to myself. My boobs were not small and perky. They were voluptuous, to put it nicely, and needed a bra to contain them. I settled on an undershirt and a T-shirt.

"It's not like he hasn't seen it before," I told myself, running my fingers through my hair while Milo licked the lingering droplets of water off my feet.

"Feeling better?" Jack asked. He was frowning.

I walked over to him and kissed him lightly, and he held me close.

"Sorry," he said. "You were drunk. I should have—"

"I'm an adult. I can make my own choices," I told him seriously. "It's not like you hit me over the head and dragged me back to your cave. Here, I'll make you something to eat."

The pickings were slim. He didn't have a lot of food in his fridge. There were some eggs left, and I cut up the rest of the steak and added some leftover veggies and the rest of the cheese.

"I have a surprise idea for something nice to cook for you," I told him as I made his breakfast. "But of course you don't have the right ingredients." I scraped the omelet onto his plate.

Jack grinned at me. "Guess you'll have to come back here another night."

CHAPTER 28

Jack

After my latest encounter with Chloe, she was all I could think about. Even just seeing her walk around my apartment in my T-shirt and barefooted like she belonged there, I just wanted to wrap her up in blankets and make her stay with me always.

She had returned to her apartment, but she left the costume in my bedroom. It smelled like her and sex. My cock was hard in my pants.

"You didn't even fuck her yet," I told myself.

She was supposed to get a taste of me and become smitten, but instead, I had only succeeded in whipping myself into a frenzy. I couldn't stop thinking about her. Unfortunately, I needed to, because I had to give Greg and Carl Svensson an update on my progress with Frost Tower.

When I walked into the conference room later than morning, Chloe was still permeating my brain.

Focus, I told myself. I had to spin my lack of progress somehow.

"So, *The Great Christmas Bake-Off* is proving to be a lucrative marketing avenue," I began. "Platinum Provisions projections are up, and—"

"This is not a meeting about Platinum Provisions," Greg interrupted. "What is going on with the tower? Gunnar told me you've been distracted with one of the contestants. I don't see sleeping with the only person making that show profitable anywhere in your business plan."

"I haven't slept with her," I told Greg, which was true. Sort of.

"I don't want a play-by-play of your bedroom activities," Greg said, scowling. "You need to make progress with this tower."

"You said I had until the end of the next quarter," I countered.

"Yes," Greg said, "*until the end of*, meaning you can't show up here at the end of March with a handful of potential leads. I need to see condos sold and tenants booked by the end of the quarter. I will know as early as the end of January whether you will hit that target or whether I have to do all the work. From the looks of things, it seems I *will* have to do all the work."

I glowered at him. Greg was unfazed.

"Get out of my office and go find tenants. Trust me when I say I will sell your tower if you don't deliver."

I stepped out of the Svensson Investment tower into the hazy winter light. It was still early afternoon, but it already felt as if it was starting to grow dark.

Greg was right, though. Chloe was a distraction. I couldn't stop thinking about her, especially in that outfit. I wondered if she had any more.

She hadn't been wearing any underwear.

On a whim, I stopped at a boutique lingerie shop I passed whenever I came to the Svensson Investment tower. Previously, I had never had a reason to buy any woman anything of the sort. It felt weird to buy something so intimate for someone I had only met a few weeks ago. But I felt as if I had to see Chloe in one of the sexy scraps of fabric in the window. I craved it.

"We have a special Christmas sale," the associate said when I entered the store. "What size is your special lady?"

"I'm not sure," I admitted. That earned a patronizing look from the sales associate.

"Don't worry, you're not the only man who comes in here and doesn't know his girlfriend's size. Is she bigger or smaller than me?" she asked, motioning to her body.

"I'm not stupid enough to answer that question," I told her.

"Maybe a picture, then?" the sales clerk said with a small smile.

I pulled up Chloe's Instagram on my phone. She had a picture of herself in the sexy Santa outfit. I was suddenly furious that she had shared the picture with the world.

"Ah, I have just the thing for curvy girls." The associate winked at me.

She pulled out several options for lingerie that she said would work on Chloe. I picked one that was made from a soft velvet and had a furry white trim.

"She'll love it!" the clerk said and wrapped it up for me.

I hoped so. I was starting to second-guess the purchase. Maybe I should have bought her some baking tools. But then maybe that would imply that I just wanted her to cook for me, and while that was true, that wasn't all I wanted her for.

The subway was down, again, and traffic was backed up. I could walk faster than the cars were moving. People were hurrying against the cold, but it made me feel energetic. It was cleansing, purifying.

"Buying that for a special lady?" someone asked. "Do I see grandchildren in my future?"

My heart sank. I spun around, and another walker cursed at me for stopping in the middle of the sidewalk.

"Get lost!" I yelled at him and faced the woman I despised perhaps more than Hartleigh—my mother, Diane.

"What do you want?" I asked cautiously.

"I want to see my son!" she said. "You never call, you never write."

I could feel my blood pressure spike. "After everything you did to us," I hissed, "how dare you try and talk to me?"

"Mrs. Henderson's daughter-in-law just had a baby," my mother said, oblivious as usual to my anger. She was a scientist who liked facts and figures and seemed not to have any real emotion. Oh, she tried; she could play the part well enough to fool colleagues and the neighbors, but I had lived with her and my father for years, and there was nothing behind that façade.

"Did you know that there are approximately 2.7 million grandparents acting as the main caregivers for the grandchildren? Isn't that wild? I can't wait for you to give me grandchildren." She patted the box. "I'm glad to see you're working on it. We should have Christmas dinner like the old days. You can invite my future daughter-in-law."

"We will never have Christmas together," I said flatly. "Especially not after what you did to Belle. You basically stole her life because you were too selfish to be a real mother."

"Quality time with grandkids while they're children improves mental health of grandparents, according to one study," my mother chattered. "That's how I want my old age to be—surrounded by a big, happy family."

"Then you should have been a better mother," I growled. It was as if she didn't even hear me!

"That's why your father and I had six of you, so we could have a big family!" she continued as if I'd never said a word.

"You never raised us!" I said loudly.

"We did a wonderful job with you!" she said, finally seeming to listen.

"No," I said. "No, you didn't."

"You're a billionaire, all of you went to Harvard. Except Belle, of course, which is a shame." She shook her head.

I was seething. "You can't claim that! You never spent a cent on our education! Belle was the one—" I was yelling now. People were staring, and in New York City, you knew you were acting crazy if people were bothering to stop and turn their attention to you.

I forced myself to relax. *I am cold. I am ice, I am unfeeling. This interaction means nothing to me.*

"I have to go, Mom," I said and turned to walk quickly away from her.

Hartleigh was waiting for me in the lobby.

"Oooh! Did you buy a present?"

I ignored her.

"Maybe we can do something special tonight?" she asked, batting her eyelashes.

"I'm busy. I have a meeting."

The drunk Santa knocked on the window, and I let him inside. Once she realized what I was doing, Hartleigh scowled and went back upstairs. The drunk Santa didn't seem quite so out of it today. It was still early, though.

"Hey," I said to him, "do you want a job?"

He shrugged then said, "Sure."

"Fifty bucks a day to sit here, and if you see that woman"—I gestured in the direction Hartleigh had gone—"shoo her away whenever I have to walk past her, okay?"

"Sure thing, boss," he said and saluted. The motion sent the smell of garbage, sweat, and stale beer over to me. I tried not to gag. If that was what would keep Hartleigh from ambushing me, then so be it.

CHAPTER 29

Chloe

As soon as she walked into the apartment, Hartleigh demanded to know what I was doing with Jack.

"Are you in love with him?" she cried.

"Go away," Maria told her. "You're being obnoxious."

"He's the judge. You can't be friends with him," Hartleigh said, ignoring Maria.

"That's rich coming from you. What do you have going on with him?" I demanded. "You were all talk about how you were going to rekindle a romance with longtime beau Jack Frost."

I knew I shouldn't engage with her, but I was sick of her creepy possessiveness of Jack, especially now that I knew he disliked her.

"I know better than to sleep with a judge and compromise the integrity of *The Great Christmas Bake-Off*," Hartleigh huffed at me.

"Yes, because this is some sort of PhD defense and not a half-rate reality show that's not even broadcast on TV. It's really not a life-or-death situation," I told her. "The show is a platform to sell people on your brand."

"Except there's only one person you're trying to recruit as your fan. You're trying to steal Jack from me," she replied.

"Whatever," I said, standing up and putting on my coat. "I need to go take some pictures."

I did wonder if Hartleigh was going to make a stink. I couldn't afford to be booted off the show so soon. The bake-off was finally starting to gain some traction; I had tens of thousands more Instagram followers. I just needed to win, then I had the feeling my dreams would start coming true.

The drunk Santa was sitting in the lobby when I walked out of the elevator.

"The boss said I could sit in here," he said in response to my questioning look. "Gave me a job."

"Jack gave you a job?"

"Yes, ma'am."

"Congratulations," I told him, "Mr… I'm sure your last name isn't Claus."

"You can call me Eddie, ma'am," he said.

"Don't call me ma'am, call me Chloe," I told him. "Does the security guard know you're here? I don't want him to shoot you or something."

Eddie, the Santa, grinned. "He was arrested two nights ago. The police just sped by and snatched him up."

"Well," I said, "that's not very charitable."

Eddie shrugged.

"Do you need anything? Food? A shower, perhaps," I asked.

"Boss wants me just like this." He pulled out a flask and took a sip.

"I must be off," I told him, trying not to gag on the smell. Jack really didn't want the man to shower?

It was bitterly cold outside. Not as cold as the Midwest but still chilly.

As I walked around taking pictures, a man wearing red grabbed me and I shrieked. Was it the mall Santa? The Santa pulled down his beard.

"Chloe, it's me, Cody."

"I know who you are," I snapped. "I saw you following me in the grocery store." I had hoped if I just pretended I didn't see my cousin, the problem would solve itself. That clearly hadn't happened.

"You have some nerve to come and find me, especially after you stole my money," I told him.

"I'm sorry, Chloe," my cousin said. "It was an emergency. They let me out of prison early."

"But they let you out on parole, right? Which means that you were supposed to stay in state."

His eyes shifted. "I know," Cody whined. "Look, I didn't come here for you to give me a hard time, I just need you to lend me some money."

"You already took all my money!" I screeched at him.

Another Santa walked up to us.

"Cousin Chloe," he said.

"Who are you?" I said. I liked Christmas, but this Santa business was starting to be a bit much.

"This is my new friend, Kevin," Cody said by way of introduction. Kevin looked like a drug addict. He was the scrawniest Santa I had ever seen.

"I can't help you," I told them. "Please leave."

"Oma said family is important," Cody wheedled. "Do you hate your family? I'm all you have left! Is this what Oma would have wanted, for you to let me go hungry and cold on the streets of a strange city?"

"You're just going to spend it on drugs," I said.

"You do have money," Cody insisted.

"I don't have a lot," I said, mad at myself for still continuing the conversation instead of walking away.

"Please, Chloe!" Cody begged.

His tone reminded me of when we were kids and he would beg me to do something for him. I would always give in. I sighed and pulled out my wallet. Even though he had stolen from me, I supposed I could give him five dollars to buy a cheeseburger.

"Just buy food, please," I said, handing him the cash.

"Thanks, Chloe," he said, grabbing the cash greedily and hurrying off with Kevin.

Angry at myself for giving in, I started walking. How could I be so stupid? Then I started second-guessing my actions with Jack. What I had done, going up to his penthouse in that outfit, was dumb. Maybe Hartleigh was right and this thing with Jack was going to blow up and ruin my chances in the bake-off. I bet he wasn't even that serious about me. Wasn't that what billionaires were like—playboys who seduced unsuspecting women so they could brag to their friends about it?

Looking up, I found myself in front of the grocery store. I did want to make soup muffins, and Jack did have a nice kitchen.

There was a Santa out in front ringing the bell.

"Sorry, I don't have any money," I said.

Because I gave it all to my junkie cousin and his friend. The soup muffins wouldn't be expensive, at least.

I shopped quickly. Grocery shopping had formerly been my safe space, but now I couldn't help but look over my shoulder for a Santa Claus. I grabbed cheese, potatoes, and chives. Jack really needed to stock up his kitchen. Did he have a muffin tin? I needed one and didn't want to take the chance that he wouldn't have one. I scurried to grab a muffin tin, and there he was—the Santa Claus. I was sure he was the one from the mall. The large, red-clad man made an exaggerated bow. I grabbed the muffin tin and practically ran to the cashier.

"Oof," I said. I tried not to look at the total on the screen as she rang me up.

"Credit or debit?" the lady asked when I presented my card.

"Credit." I was so far in debt, what did a little extra matter, right?

As I walked back to Frost Tower, I could swear the Santa was following me. But when I turned around, there was no one there.

"I'm seeing things," I muttered to myself as Eddie opened the door to the lobby for me.

"Thanks." He saluted me.

"Have you..." I licked my lips. I didn't want to sound crazy. But then I remembered who I was talking to. "Have you seen any other Santas around here?"

Eddie looked at me oddly, or maybe he was drunk. He reeked of booze.

"No, Chloe," he replied.

"Keep an eye out, okay?"

"Sure," he said, nodding slowly.

I went up to Jack's penthouse, determined to put all thoughts of Santas and my junkie cousin out of my mind and instead focus on whatever this thing was between me and Jack.

"I hope he likes muffins," I said and knocked on his door.

CHAPTER 30

Jack

I left the present for Chloe in my penthouse on the kitchen counter and told the dog not to chew it, then I went to the Chamber of Commerce holiday party. Greg was there, and his mood didn't seem to have improved any.

"I hate Christmas parties," Greg said, glowering.

"I'm only staying for a little bit," I told him. "Just seeing if anyone is expanding."

There was little interest until Mark Holbrook walked in. I hurried over to him, elbowing aside other real estate company representatives looking to land his company as a tenant.

"I heard your new company is looking for some space," I said after introducing myself. "I have some unique space that was designed for creative firms like—"

"Look," Mark interrupted. "My company is still in the startup phase, so there's a lot of experimentation we're doing. My engineers and I do serious research and development for robotics, and we have specific requirements for our work area."

"And I have the perfect space for it," I said smoothly.

"*If* I were to put my company in New York City, I could just put the company in my uncle's tower," Mark retorted.

"You could," I said, "but Frost Tower has FM 200 fire-suppressant systems. It's specially configured for technology manufacturing and design companies. Each floor is high bay space, perfect for engineering and testing new products. You wouldn't have to spend money reconfiguring the space to meet fire and other safety requirements."

Mark seemed intrigued, but then he said, "You're in that weird dead space though, right? There's no restaurants or anything over there."

"I'm working on bringing in more amenities to the area," I told him. "Frost Tower is brand new, it's near a park, and there's good natural light. I could give you a great leasing deal."

He looked at me.

"You don't have to give an answer right now," I said, "but think about it."

There were several other developers waiting to talk to Mark when I headed back to Greg.

"They'll probably offer him a better lease than you will," Greg said and downed the rest of his drink. "I talked to a shared workspace company, and the representative said she would come see the space in Frost Tower. They would lease at most two floors, which means you have another forty to fill."

"Mark's company could occupy a significant chunk, especially with the amount of money the Defense Department is throwing at robotics," I told him.

When I returned to Frost Tower, I was feeling more optimistic. I looked up at my building, hoping it would still be Frost Tower in four months.

Once at the door to my penthouse, I punched in the key code and took off my suit coat, letting the door slam behind me.

"Milo!" I called as I unbuttoned my dress shirt and took off my tie. I heard the dog bark. What was he up to? Normally he ran to greet me when I returned home. For a brief moment, I thought Chloe might have let herself in to surprise me.

Unfortunately, I was having no such luck. There was Hartleigh in my living room, wearing the skimpy lingerie I'd bought for Chloe. She didn't fill it out as well as I knew Chloe would have.

"You need to leave," I told her, furious. "I don't know how you even snuck in here!"

"The security guard gave me the code. I was *very* persuasive," she said.

"I guess some people have low standards," I said coldly.

"You're so bad to me, Jack," she said, trying to walk seductively towards me. "And all I want is to make a baby with you. We could make a Christmas baby. Your parents would be happy."

"You are the last person in the world I would have a baby with," I snapped at her.

"I saw your parents," she told me, her eyes wide. They didn't seem like they were even that focused on me. "Your parents want grandkids. We could do that for them."

"There is no us!" I roared. "You can't keep stalking me!"

She took off the lingerie and stood there stark naked. I didn't feel a thing. Instead, I picked up her coat from the couch and threw it at her.

"Out," I ordered.

She blew me a kiss, put on the coat, and left.

Angrily I walked through my space, furious that she had been there touching my things. I looked at the expensive present I had bought for Chloe. It was lying on the floor. There was no way I could give it to her. I picked it up and threw the lingerie in the trash.

As I tried to force myself to calm down, there was another knock on the door.

"I swear, if that's Hartleigh..."

I wrenched open the door to find Chloe standing there, a big bag in her hand, looking up at me. She seemed a little scared, and I tried to tamp down my anger.

"What do you want?" I asked more harshly than I intended. "I mean…" I blew out a breath. "Sorry. I've had a difficult evening."

"Sounds like it," she said and smiled at me. "Can I come in, or is this a bad time?"

"No, of course." I stepped aside.

"There's a recipe that's been bouncing around my head that I wanted to make for you," she said, walking towards the kitchen.

I took a few cleansing breaths. Chloe was here, but of course I had done something to screw it up. So much for my merry Christmas.

As I joined her in the kitchen, I heard Chloe say angrily, "What's this?"

Oh no.

CHAPTER 31

Chloe

When I walked into Jack's kitchen, I emptied out the bag and started laying out the ingredients to chop. I didn't see a muffin tin in my cursory glance through his cupboards, so I ripped the paper off the one I had bought. As I opened the trashcan to dispose of the wrapping, I saw it.

Lingerie.

There was lingerie in the trashcan—a very expensive, very sexy-looking set of lingerie. It was red with white furry edging.

"*What is this?*" I yelled. Was this why Jack was acting so strangely, why he looked disheveled and half dressed?

Jack ran into the room, and I picked up the knife.

"Explain," I said to Jack. His eyes were wide as he gaped at me.

"Hartleigh—"

"Hartleigh was up here?" I screeched. I sounded crazy and irrational, but I'd had a hard day. And if Jack was banging Hartleigh…

"That harlot!" I yelled.

"It's not what it looks like," Jack pleaded.

"Really? Because it looks like I interrupted something between the two of you. I don't need you to waste my time."

"That's not…" He blew out a breath and sat down on one of the stools at the counter. "She's… she finagled the key code from the security guard and snuck in here. She's been stalking me. I guess it's escalated."

"Stalking you?" I said, shocked. I remembered him saying he didn't like her, something to do with being an annoying family friend, but stalking was a whole other situation. "If she's stalking you, how is she working here? Don't you have a restraining order?"

Jack barked out a laugh. "Look around. Romance Creative is some half-baked production company. I mean, they had you helping set up decorations. It's not like this is some streamlined enterprise."

"But they have tens of millions of views!" I protested. "They could have at least done some due diligence, for goodness sake."

Jack looked upset, and I felt bad for yelling at him. I set down the knife and went around the island to him. I hugged him to my chest.

"The lingerie was supposed to be a gift for you," he mumbled. "But she broke in and took it."

I petted his hair.

"It's been like this for decades," Jack said. "I can't escape her. If only Belle were here…"

"That's your sister?"

Jack nodded. "Hartleigh was afraid of her. Belle must have threatened her or something."

I wanted to commiserate, tell him about my crazy cousin, but then I wondered if that might scare him off. Drug addict with a criminal record was different from an upper-middle-class family friend turned stalker. Cody and his junkie friend might be a little too real for Jack. I didn't want him to think I was a trashy drama llama.

I stroked his hair until he seemed to calm down. He wrapped his arms around me then pulled me down to kiss him.

"What are you making?" he asked, standing up to look over my purchases. "You didn't have to buy all this, Chloe."

"It's not a problem," I said.

"I thought you were broke," he said.

"I said it's not a problem!" I huffed. "I'm cooking for you. Just sit tight. I'm going to make you something delicious. It's a new creation. I'm calling them soup muffins. You'll like them; I thought them up just for you."

I draped the bacon over the back side of the muffin tin and set it in the oven. It would make little cups of bacon that I would use instead of muffin liners. Then I chopped onions, cubed potatoes, and shredded cheese.

"I hope this works," I told him as I mixed up my batter.

I wanted the muffins to be crispy on the outside and gooey and savory on the inside. After spooning the mixture into my bacon baking tins, I wacked the pan a bit to release any lingering air pockets.

As they baked, I watched the oven nervously.

"You're like a little cat or something with those muffins," Jack said.

"Don't call me anything inane like kitten or goose or mouse or something. People who call their significant others animal names weird me out."

He laughed. "You would hate my parents, then. My father calls my mother bunny duck."

"Wow, okay, well. Are they still together?" I asked, then I mentally kicked myself. "Sorry, I know you don't want to talk about them. I was just curious," I told him.

He sighed. "I ran into my mother today. She was the same as always, but yes, to answer your question, they are still together, very much in love, and completely absorbed with each other." Jack said the last part through his teeth. I wanted to ask him what he meant, but I could smell cheddar-and-potato soup.

I opened the oven and jiggled the muffins. "I'll let them cook a little longer in the residual heat," I told him as I set them on the cooling rack on the counter. "That's the secret to baking things like muffins or chocolate chip cookies. Undercook them then leave them on the pan to cook the rest of the way."

"How long?" he asked.

"Maybe ten minutes," I said.

Coming around the counter, he wrapped himself around me and brought his head down to kiss me. "It's a shame about the lingerie," he said. We kissed again, our hands running up and down each other's bodies, until the timer went off.

Jack released me, and I grasped at him blindly.

"I want a muffin," he said with a grin.

And I wanted him to continue doing delicious things to me. Instead, I pried a soup muffin out of the pan and watched him nervously as he broke it open, steam rising from the baked good and swirling around his face. Jack blew on it then popped a piece in his mouth.

I clapped my hands when the expression of pure bliss bloomed on his face.

"This is amazing!" Jack said, smiling broadly. "I feel like we need to drag one of the camera guys up here just so I can show everyone in the world this muffin."

Shoving half of the muffin into my face, he said, "So you see that? Look at that! It's gooey and cheesy in the center and covered in bacon."

I took it from him and bit off a piece. "That is really good," I said around the piping-hot food. "It's like eating soup. But it's a muffin."

"You should open a bakery," Jack told me.

I laughed. "I would like to, but I can't think about any of that until after this show is over."

After taking the rest of the muffins out of the pan so they didn't become soggy, Jack and I snuggled on the couch.

"I feel like I should have made you something more substantial than muffins," I said to Jack as I looked around for a remote.

"I use streaming," he said and pulled out a box of remotes, rummaging through it. He handed me a tablet; I stared at it and poked it.

"This seems unnecessarily complicated."

Jack pressed a few buttons on the giant tablet, and a menu came up on the TV.

"Just pick whatever you want." He brought the entire plate of muffins to the coffee table, along with the rest of the cookies I had made, while I picked a movie.

"*Elf*?" he said in disbelief as the movie started playing.

"You'll like it," I told him. "The main character is crabby like you."

"I'm not crabby," he said, pulling me against him as Will Farrell bounced around the screen.

Jack actually laughed at a few parts of the movie.

"Look who's embracing the Christmas spirit!" I told him. "We should have a Christmas movie marathon."

"I don't know if we want to do all that," he said.

The muffins and the movie were making me sleepy. Jack had a blanket wrapped around us, and Milo was half sprawled over our laps. I felt cozy and safe.

"I love Christmas," I told him with a yawn as the movie ended. "I love the smells and the food and the warmth inside while it's cold and snowy outside. My oma and I would cook for days before Christmas, then she would have all her friends and neighbors over—you know, the ones who were lone wolves or recluses or who didn't have family nearby. They would all come to her house."

"It sounds great," he said.

I turned my head to kiss him. "I think I should throw a Christmas party for you."

CHAPTER 32

Jack

"I don't need a Christmas party," I told her. "My mother would always throw them."

"Was that part of your holiday traditions?" she asked me.

"Yes, my mother liked Christmas. She liked to have a big holiday party. She said you had to have a big party at Christmas, and she always took pride in the fact that her parties were fancy affairs. Of course, she was always too busy with work to actually plan and execute the party herself, so she would make my sister Belle decorate and cook. When we were younger, Belle would enlist me and my brothers to help. We would decorate the whole house, indoors and out. Belle was good at decorating—she had these special cookie cutters and boxes of antique glass ornaments." I shook my head at the memory.

“My mother would make us wear matching outfits when we were little. She liked to show us all off to her friends and make everyone see what a perfect mother she was.” Chloe murmured sleepily. I didn’t know if she was really listening, but it felt good to say everything out loud.

“My mother liked to pretend she was perfect, even though Belle did all the work. My parents liked the idea of a big family but not the reality. Belle would always seem excited at Christmas, and I thought she loved the holiday, but then two years ago, she just left right after Thanksgiving was over.”

I heard a slight snore from Chloe. It was probably for the best; I was becoming morose.

“I guess that means no steamy evening,” I said. After dealing with Hartleigh and my mother today, though, I wasn’t really feeling it. I picked up Chloe then carried her to my bed, stripped to my boxers, and crawled in bed beside her. It felt right to sleep next to her. Milo curled up on my other side. All the good things in my life came together in one moment.

I wished I could love Christmas. I used to like it before I realized the whole thing had been a lie. Belle had been practically kept prisoner by my parents due to their own selfishness and Belle’s selflessness. Christmas was just one giant money grab, made for narcissists to preen for an audience and massive corporations to sell products. My corporation included.

Still, if it made Chloe happy, maybe I could let her throw a party. As I pulled her close to me, I could feel the ice on my heart melting.

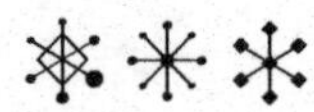

Chloe was still in my arms the next morning. I had never had time to date, and between my apprehensions with running into someone like Hartleigh, I actively avoided forming relationships with women. I looked at Chloe. We should have been too different to be compatible, but here we were.

I let my fingers run through the tangle of honey curls. Chloe murmured sleepily then stretched like a cat and flipped over to face me.

"Good morning," she said.

I kissed her, letting my mouth linger on her bottom lip.

"You're not wearing any pajamas."

"This building is too warm, and it makes me too hot to sleep in a lot of clothes," I whispered, taking her hand and trailing it down my bare chest. She cupped the bulge in my boxer briefs. I wondered if she had done this before, but it seemed rude to ask. I straddled her, pressing down against her. Her arms wrapped around my neck, and her fingers tangled in my hair.

"I want to fuck you, Chloe," I breathed. She made a little whining noise that made me harder than I already was. I ground my hips against hers and let my mouth drift down to nuzzle her breasts. I wanted to rip off the fabric that kept them from me.

Her phone rang.

"Don't answer it," I growled.

"It might be the contest," she protested.

I kept kissing her but allowed her to push me off so she could run into the living room. I heard the sound of a bag being dumped out.

"Hello? Yeah, okay, I'm coming."

I rubbed the bridge of my nose and tried to come to grips with the fact that Chloe and I would not have hot morning sex.

"We're filming early today," she said. I saw her look longingly at me.

"Sorry," she said.

"No need to apologize. I don't want to rush this. I want to take my time with you." Her eyes went wide again, and I smirked as I watched her gaze drift downward.

"I need to win this contest." It sounded as if she said it more to herself than me. She licked her lips. I closed the distance between us, crushing her against me. She moaned.

"A taste of what's going to happen," I told her after releasing her. Milo was whining; I knew he wanted to go out.

Chloe left in a daze. I knew she wanted me, and that was enough for now. I could wait.

I still wished I had seen her in that lingerie. Her Pinterest was public, and I scrolled through the images while Milo ran around in the park, making note of the items I thought she might like.

CHAPTER 33

Chloe

"You need to stay away from Jack," Hartleigh said to me when I walked into the apartment.

"I'm in a rush," I told her, "and I can't deal with your hysterics right now."

She grabbed my upper arm, her nails digging into my skin. "I know you were up there with him. I waited up to see if you would come back to the apartment, and you didn't. Admit where you were! You're trying to steal him from me."

I yanked my arm away from her. "Jack said you have been stalking him and that he doesn't even like you. In fact, he despises you."

"That isn't true. *We are soulmates*. We're meant to be together, and he would see the truth if you weren't trying to steal him from me," Hartleigh said, her face screwed up in fury.

"I'm late for the contest," I told her. "I need to change."

I quickly showered but didn't have a chance to dry my hair properly. I wound it into a bun and ran downstairs. I slid behind my workstation and put on my apron just in time. Dana gave me a look.

"Sorry," I mouthed.

I wasn't the last person to enter the room, though. Jack sauntered in, cup of cold green tea in his hand. Despite our steamy session this morning, he looked cool as ice.

"We all want Christmas dinner to be perfect," Anastasia began. "And what more to demonstrate what a perfect host or hostess you are than to create a perfectly executed dessert? That's why this next task is the technically perfect holiday challenge. As you can see, we're starting very early today. You have until this evening to bake. We want to see your most impressive desserts."

As Anastasia went around to start talking to the remaining contestants, Hartleigh came over to my workstation, her face screwed up in anger and jealousy.

"Jack is just using you because you're an easy lay," she sniped at me as I gathered my ingredients. "He is my future husband. Our parents want us to be together."

"Go back to your own station," Nina yelled at her.

I had to put Hartleigh out of my head. To me, the technically perfect holiday challenge meant French pastries, and nothing was more difficult than macarons.

I was making holiday-inspired macarons. To make the dessert impressive enough to win the competition, I would need to make an array of flavors, which meant I needed to have separate batters and fillings for each flavor. It was good we had the majority of the day, because executing each step perfectly was going to take a while.

For the flavors, I decided on several different fruity macarons, including cranberry, spiced orange, and apple cider. In addition, I would make chocolate macarons, peppermint bark, vanilla bean, eggnog, ginger, and salted caramel. I made a mental note of everything I needed and grabbed ingredients. I couldn't rush macarons; everything had to be exact.

As I worked, Zane came over to take close-ups. Because I had so many different-colored shells, I had to make separate batter for each macaron shell. After sifting the almond flour and the powdered sugar to make sure there weren't any coarse bits, I weighed each dry ingredient carefully. If the weight was off by even a fraction of a gram, it could undermine the integrity of the macaron.

Before I started the wet ingredients, I made sure my parchment paper was perfectly flat and laid out. I didn't need a template. I could make perfect circles with my eyes closed.

The next step had to be executed flawlessly. The day before I had left my egg whites in the fridge to age, since Anastasia had let us know what the challenge was ahead of time.

I started to beat the egg whites. They were frothy, but to my eye they looked a little odd. I started to add the sugar, hoping they would form the glossy, stiff peaks I needed. I beat and beat. The egg whites would not stiffen. Nina looked over.

"What's wrong with them?" I asked in a panic. "I can make meringue, but this stuff in my bowl is the consistency of cheap marshmallow fluff."

Nina came over to inspect the bowl. "These are definitely not the dramatic glossy peaks of good meringue," she said.

"What's wrong with them?" I wailed, looking at the clock. Today, time seemed to be flying by.

"Did you use aged egg whites?"

"They are. I let them set overnight."

Nina looked over to Hartleigh, who was smirking.

"You!" I screeched. "You messed with my ingredients!"

"I did no such thing," Hartleigh said haughtily.

"Yes, you did! You put water or oil or something in the bowl." I picked up my spoon to throw it at her, but Nina grabbed my arm.

"Just start over," she said. "Everything has to be perfect, or it won't work. You don't have any other choice but to keep going."

I took a deep breath and tried to relax. Macarons seemed to know when you were unsure or nervous.

Fuming that Hartleigh would just escape any blame for sabotaging me, I went to grab more eggs. It took me time to carefully separate all the egg whites. I also had to use a completely different bowl, because there was no telling what Hartleigh had done to the original one. If it had oil in it, that would just ruin the new batch of egg whites.

This time when I made the meringue, it held its peaks.

"I hope this works." The camera guys were hovering over me, trying to get close-up shots of my folding the mixture together, the food coloring turning the mixture a deep red.

"If you so much as breathe on these cookies, I'm going to stuff you in the oven," I warned Zane as I carefully piped the mixture onto the parchment paper. I didn't like big macarons. They should be one bite or two small bites. I made mine about the size of a dollar coin. They were perfect little dabs of color on the parchment paper.

Hartleigh had me paranoid. I checked and double-checked my ingredients while I made the next batch, carefully mixing in the food gel coloring.

After the first set had sat for half an hour, I checked it, making sure a skin had formed over the top. The oven claimed it was the proper temperature, and the thermometer made by Platinum Provisions confirmed it.

"If these are ruined, I'm blaming Jack Frost," I half joked to the camera.

Zane and I camped in front of the oven, watching the macarons slowly rise.

"Hey, these look perfect!" Zane exclaimed, camera glued to the oven door window.

"Shh!" I hissed at him. "No loud noises." They were forming perfect little feet. When the timer dinged, I took the macaron shells out of the oven and set them to cool.

I eased one off the parchment paper and ate it.

"Perfection," I said. "Now I have to do this a dozen more times."

Over the next few hours, I made the rest of the macaron shells and slowly rotated them into and out of the oven.

"I think I was too ambitious," I told Anastasia when she came over to ask me what I was making. I had all the macaron shells made. Now I had to make the filling.

"Are you making your own fillings?" Anastasia asked.

"Of course!" I said, offended that she thought I would do something crass like spread jelly inside.

She looked at the clock. "You better hurry!"

The fillings were supposed to be light but still flavorful. I cut up all the fruit and ingredients then set the multitude of double boilers going on the stove. For the fruit fillings, I made a series of almost translucent gelatins. I also made a glossy chocolate ganache and a tangy orange custard.

I let the pots simmer low and slow, stirring constantly, both hands alternating between the saucepans. Every so often, I glanced at the clock. Time was not on my side.

"Are you going to make it?" Anastasia said, coming over to my station.

"I will if you stop distracting me," I snapped.

"Okay, let's leave her to it," she said, smiling at one of the cameras.

My hair and face were sweaty from the exertion and the hot stove. Finally, things were the consistency I wanted. I strained the fruit fillings and made sure the orange custard was the right uniformity and color. The colors had to match. That was important.

After setting up an assembly line of macarons, I carefully piped a very thin layer of the fillings on their respective macaron shells. I hated a big pile of filling in a macaron; the filling should be unobtrusive, just a thin glossy line between the two shells.

The cameras were back in my face.

"*This is a delicate operation!*" I screeched. "Sorry, please don't put that in the show!"

Zane laughed. "Too late! You're hilarious when you're harried."

"It's just these macarons. They make me crazy," I said as I carefully assembled the tops, my tongue between my teeth. The shells had to match exactly. They couldn't be even slightly askew. Everything had to be impeccable.

Originally, I had wanted to hand-paint some, but looking at the clock, I saw that I just didn't have the time.

I arranged the macarons carefully in a line down the center of a long rectangular plate. I wasn't going to add any garnish. Each judge would receive a simple, perfect presentation.

The judges applauded when Anastasia called time. Nina rubbed my shoulders as we walked into the holding room. I looked at other people's dishes—they had beautiful, more avant-garde–type desserts. Mine was the most basic.

I chewed on my lip. I hoped the macarons were good enough. I also hoped Jack liked them.

CHAPTER 34

Jack

"These are perfect," Anu said as she ate one of Chloe's macarons. "They are quite simply technically perfect."

"Also, can I just say I'm glad you didn't make cute little animals or something," Nick said to Chloe. "These are just perfectly round little bites of flavor. The texture, the variety, the consistency, everything is flawless."

I looked at the macarons. The only thing my mother ever baked were macarons. The rest of the cooking Belle had always done. My mother liked to make macarons because she liked to show off what a great chef she was. I knew what a technically perfect macaron was, because my mother was of course able to produce them. Chloe's macarons were perfect. However—and maybe it was my history—they felt soulless.

"Jack," Nick said. "Comments?"

"I see the Platinum Provisions equipment didn't let you down," I teased.

Chloe blushed. "You heard that?"

"Cut her some slack," Anu said. "Macarons will drive you mad. But you did well, Chloe."

"I need a drink!" she said with a laugh.

"After all that, I would say you deserved it," Nick said.

The rest of the contestants had made amazing dishes. One girl, Chloe's friend Nina, had made a twist on a croquembouche. She had little towers of tiny puff pastries filled with orange cream. The tower was layers of the little tiny puff pastries and little wafers studded with candied cranberries and orange peel then draped with spun caramel. It looked like a tree.

"That dessert was clever," Nate said. "But the macarons were technically perfect."

"That's the name of the challenge," Anu agreed. "And she made technically perfect macarons, and in a variety of flavors that still had the sense of Christmas."

The two judges seemed to like Chloe's macarons the best, so I went along with it. I knew she wanted to win. A guy who had made panaforte was sent home.

It was late, and the contestants still had to sit for post-challenge interviews. I wasn't sure if I would be able to spend time with Chloe that night. Then I saw her coming down the hall towards me.

"Did you like the macarons?" Chloe asked me, her face rosy.

"Uh..." I was such a terrible liar.

Her face fell.

"You know I don't like sweets," I said hastily. "They were great, just, macarons aren't my favorite."

"I worked really hard on them," she said.

"I know you did, and it shows." I felt bad for not being more enthusiastic. There were a ton of people around, so I didn't want to get into the long, drawn-out, painful explanation.

"But you know something else I like to eat," I whispered in her ear. Her face went beet-red, and I grinned.

"Tonight?" she asked, her voice cracking a little.

"Rain check, unfortunately. I have a meeting tonight. It's a family thing."

Speaking of painful family memories. I had a dinner scheduled with my older brother.

Owen was waiting at the bar when I arrived later on that evening.

"Are we drinking our dinner tonight?" I asked him as I sat down. He raised his glass in greeting.

"How are the Svenssons treating you?" I asked him. His firm and Svensson Investment were collaborating on some projects.

"Can't complain," he said.

"Of course you can't, Mr. Bitcoin billionaire extraordinaire," I said.

Owen looked angrily at his drink. "Belle is the one who made it happen," he said. "I hate Christmas."

"Tell me about it," I said as I signaled to the bartender to bring me whatever my brother was drinking.

"Have you talked to her?" I asked him.

"Nope. I think she hates us."

"Can you blame her?"

We were silent. Belle had left right after Thanksgiving two years ago. My brothers and I kept thinking she would come back, but she never did. Then she sent out that email saying she didn't want anything to do with us, that she was tired of enabling Mom and Dad to have the perfect family, and that she was done with us forever.

"Have you written her?" Owen asked me.

I shook my head. "I figure she didn't want to hear from me after that email she sent. Belle will come find us if she wants to talk."

"*If*," Owen emphasized. "She talks to the youngest two."

"Not often, though, it sounds like," I said. We were silent for a moment.

"Friend of yours?" Own said, jerking his head towards the large window at the front of the bar. A Santa stood on the sidewalk, watching us.

"Maybe," I grimaced. "I've been paying a homeless Santa to be my security guard. It's just because—"

Owen held up a hand to cut me off. "I don't even want to know. So why did you want to meet?" he asked. "Wait, let me guess: it's that tower."

"I'm not asking for money, I just need the Svenssons to give me more time," I pleaded. "Or maybe you can at least help me find tenants."

"You know, Jack, sometimes you have to let things go. You're always so emotional."

"I'm not emotional," I argued.

"Yes, you are. You have an emotional connection to that tower."

"I spent a lot of time on it—"

"And it didn't pay out," he said, "so you need to walk away. That's what Belle did."

"Please, I just... Maybe you could buy a condo there?"

Owen barked out a laugh. "As if. I'm not enabling your bad decisions. That's what we did for years with Mom and Dad."

The bartender brought him another drink, and he drained half of it then said, "Do you know when you were a baby, they never once came to comfort you when you cried? Belle was the one who did it. Or I did since I had to share a room with you. Mom and Dad were oblivious, of course, or they just didn't care. Mom's friends would always remark on how well rested and fresh faced she looked, all while her elementary-aged kids were picking up her slack."

"I'm not asking you to pick up slack," I said.

"Yes, you are," Owen said. "You need to man up."

I glowered at my drink then downed it and signaled for another one. It was turning out to be yet another terrible Christmas.

"Did I tell you I saw Mom?" I asked him, hoping to break some of the tension between us.

"Really?"

"She just randomly saw me in the street," I said.

"Let me guess, she wants grandchildren," Owen said.

I looked at my older brother in surprise.

"She told me all about it when I saw her and Dad," he explained.

"Why would you see them?" I asked.

"It was against my better judgment," Owen said sourly. "They said they wanted to make amends. I think Mom is baby crazy. She had the blueprint for the perfect life, and now her oldest kids are at the age when her spreadsheet is telling her it's time for grandchildren, so grandchildren there must be."

I scowled, and Owen looked at me seriously. "Mom said you were buying lingerie for Hartleigh. Are you seriously together with her?"

"Never!" I said. "I'm shocked you would even think that!"

"That's a relief," Owen said. "Dad went on and on about how Hartleigh and you were going to be a perfect couple and their friends' daughter and their son were going to have babies. Somewhere in the word vomit, I heard Mom say you were going to move back home with Hartleigh."

"Absolutely not!" I couldn't believe my mother. No wonder Hartleigh was after me—my mother was stirring up the pot of crazy in her head.

"Then who were you buying the lingerie for?"

"I..." I snapped my mouth shut. Owen smirked at me.

"Jack," he said, "you deserve to be happy, but do me a favor and make sure this girl isn't anything like Mom."

CHAPTER 35

Chloe

I was so hot after all the baking and from Jack's comment about eating something other than my cookies that I needed some air. Eddie wasn't in the lobby; he had probably gone to buy alcohol. I hoped he wasn't in a ditch somewhere. I looked around cautiously but didn't see any Santas waiting outside.

A few blocks away, there was a pop-up Christmas market, and I wanted to take some photos. The booths had cute decorations, and several sellers displayed gorgeous Christmas ornaments.

"I really don't have the money for this," I muttered as I looked longingly at the ornaments.

"It's buy one get one," the woman at the stall said. "These will add Christmas cheer to your home!"

"I don't really have a home," I said, feeling slightly embarrassed. "I was thinking of buying one for a male friend."

The seller winked at me. "Maybe these will bring you a Christmas engagement ring."

I laughed but handed over my credit card anyway. It was a good deal, and they would add some much-needed Christmas cheer to Jack's penthouse. I had just given Cody five dollars; surely I could buy something for Jack.

As I meandered through the market, trying not to feel guilty for spending money I didn't have, a Santa approached me. I thought it was Eddie for a second. But as the Santa came closer, I saw that he was much too tall to be Eddie or my cousin Cody. The Santa stopped right in front of me. I didn't even think it was the stalker Santa from the mall. Why was I attracting so many men dressed up as Santa Claus?

"It's you," the Santa said.

"Excuse me?"

I could see him smile through the fake beard. "I'm here to watch over you. You're being stalked. I'm here to protect you and the Christmas bun in the oven."

I peered at him. Something about him seemed familiar, something in his voice and his eyes. Was he someone I knew? I wracked my brain. The Santa smiled enigmatically.

"Don't fear, little one."

"Okay, thanks," I said, starting to feel apprehensive.

"You! Leave her alone!" someone shouted from a nearby stall. The Santa turned away, his long stride carrying him off into the crowds.

"You're new to the city, aren't you?" a stall owner said. "You can't give these nutcases the time of day. You need to be forceful."

"I will, thank you," I told the woman. I had been raised in the Midwest, and we were not at all confrontational there.

If being followed by crazy Santas was my new normal, I would need to grow a backbone.

Eddie was back in the lobby when I returned. He had a little bottle of vodka he was sipping from while contemplating the Christmas trees.

"Package for you," he told me. It was another large box, probably from a fan.

"You have nice fans," he said.

"I was worried about you," I said seriously. "It's crazy out there."

"I just slipped out," he said, grinning at me. "Got back right before the boss."

"Jack is back?"

"Yes ma'am."

When I returned to the apartment, I opened the box. Inside was an even racier outfit than the last one. This one was a sexy candy cane outfit with thigh-high striped stockings, a red-and-white corset, and a little lacy fluffy skirt. It also came with a striped hat. I posed in the outfit, cropping the picture strategically so it wasn't too revealing.

I was immediately rewarded with a comment.

Thirst pic!

Dozens more poured in, along with tons of likes. I didn't stay online to interact with my fans because there was one very important like I wanted first.

The desire and anticipation made me slightly nervous when I went upstairs to Jack's penthouse. I wished I had taken a swig of brandy to calm my nerves.

Milo barked as soon as I knocked on the door. Jack opened it. He was shirtless and looked a little drunk as his eyes roamed over me.

"I was about to apologize and say I needed to put on a shirt," he drawled, "but clearly that's what you're here for."

"Are you going to invite me in?" I asked, arching my back as much as I could in the corset to make myself seem as enticing as possible.

His smile was possessive. "Did you dress up on my account?" His voice was deep, and I could tell he was aroused.

"A fan gave me this outfit," I said as I waltzed into his living room as if I owned the place. "I thought you might like it." His hand rested on the curve of my waist, and I felt it slide down and gather up the short skirt.

"No matching lingerie?"

"I didn't think it was necessary," I said. He laughed, his voice husky in my ears.

"Your pulse is racing," Jack said. "Are you nervous?"

"No," I lied.

"I think you're a little scared," he whispered in my ear, "but then why did you come up here if you didn't want my big thick cock?"

His hand pressed lightly between my legs.

"Too bad you don't like Christmas," I told him, "because I could give you one hell of a present."

"I could give you one any day of the week."

"I want to see your cock," I said.

"And I want to see your tits." He pulled me around to face him and kissed me deeply and powerfully. I knew what his mouth could do. I felt as if maybe I should have worn panties, he was making me so wet.

I unbuttoned his pants and pushed them down as he kissed me. Greedily, I let my hand run over his bare chest then down and around his silky boxer briefs.

"You're amazing," I said to him.

"You haven't seen anything yet." Then Jack picked me up and took me into his bedroom. I was sprawled on the bed, and he was half over me.

He took the corset in both hands then ripped it, exposing my breasts.

"Your tits," he said, kissing and licking the nipples, "are amazing."

He ripped the flimsy skirt off of me, then his tongue was back. He kissed my torso, his hand working between my legs. He kept kissing down, down, and I laced my fingers in his hair, coaxing him. Jack was slow and deliberate as he dragged his tongue in the hot pink flesh between my legs, going daringly close to my clit but not quite there. I was panting.

"Faster," I told him, rotating my hips in little circles, trying to make him go where I needed him to go. Jack laughed then flicked his tongue, eliciting a moan from me. He inserted two fingers in me then kissed and sucked my clit until I was a sweaty, moaning mess.

I came too soon.

"You didn't." I ran a hand down the length of his cock.

"You want my cock?" he asked, pressing it to the hot wetness between my legs.

"Yes, you promised." He put on a condom, looking at me while he rolled it onto his cock. Then he flipped me over, pulling my hips up. I was still relaxed and wet from his hands and tongue, and he was able to slip inside me in one motion. He pushed in and out, finding a rhythm, as his fingers worked furiously on my clit while he fucked me.

"You're so tight," he said, talking dirty in my ear. "Your pussy is so hot and tight."

I couldn't say anything intelligible back. My hips didn't know whether they wanted to push against his hand or back against his cock. My breath came out in mewling gasps as he fucked me methodically.

I knew he was close when he started jackhammering. The bedframe creaked against the wall as his balls slapped me with every thrust. I came in a jumble of ohmygods and curse words, and he fucked me a little longer, drawing out the aftershocks of the orgasm, then he came too.

Sweaty, he held me against him, kissing my neck.

As I came down off the endorphin high, I realized that I had slept with a competition judge, for real this time. If anyone found out, I could lose my spot in the bake-off and my chance at the prize money.

Jack nuzzled my neck. "This was perfect," he said.

No, it wasn't! I thought in a panic. *It was a disaster!*

CHAPTER 36
Jack

Waking up next to Chloe, I felt more relaxed and at peace than I ever had. I kissed her, reveling in the fact that I could, that she was finally mine.

She blinked at me and kissed along my jaw to my ear. "I'm going to make you something good for breakfast."

"I already know what I want," I said, pushing her back down against the pillows.

She was just as hot and tight as she had been last night. Her moans as I thrust into her were intoxicating.

"I think I could fuck you all day," I told her as she panted and whimpered against my mouth. She let out a cry when she came, and I drew out her pleasure, loving that I was the one who made her come undone. She was soft and loose in my arms, and I trailed kisses over her face and chest.

"I still want to cook something for you," she said, wrinkling her nose as I kissed it softly. "I have nightmares about those cookie abominations you made."

"Let's take Milo on a walk," I said after we showered, "and we can order something when we come back. I can tell he's anxious." Milo was doing his little wiggle.

"I guess I need to go grab something to wear from downstairs," she said then covered a yawn with her hand.

"Wait, I have the perfect thing," I said, going to the closet and pulling out the boxes that had been delivered yesterday.

"Oooh!" Chloe exclaimed. "You shouldn't have bought this for me, it's too much."

"They were on your Pinterest," I explained as she opened the boxes. I had bought her a long-sleeved sweater dress and very nice lingerie that, while it wasn't the velvet Christmas-themed stuff, was lacy and white and very sexy.

"I know, and they're so expensive." Chloe seemed almost reverent as she put on the lingerie. "It's so soft; it's like a kitten. Feel it," she ordered, and I reached out and caressed the breast encased in the lacy bra. It was soft.

"And it's exactly my size." I could see the light pink of her nipple against the white fabric. I just wanted to rip it off of her. "Don't even think about it," she warned, wagging a finger. "This is the nicest underwear I have ever owned." Then she corrected herself, "Worn."

"It's yours. I bought it for you," I said.

"I don't like handouts." She made a face. "I work hard."

"I know you do," I said, "but really, if you think about it, I bought the lingerie more for me than for you."

She pursed her lips.

"I'm not patronizing you," I said. "I wanted to do something nice for you. Christmas spirit and all that."

"I suppose I'll accept your gifts," she said dramatically and put on the sweater dress. It hugged her curves, and the deep V showed off a slight amount of cleavage. I gave her the next box.

"More?" she said. She opened it and yelled, "Boots!"

After tugging the knee-high dark-brown leather riding boots on, Chloe posed.

"You'll have to take my picture," she said then fussed with her hair in the mirror. "I should have brought some makeup."

"You look great," I told her, snapping a few pictures.

"You're just saying that," she said, sticking her tongue out at me. But she really did look good. The eyeliner from last night was a little smudged, and she looked radiant.

"You look very New York City," I told her as she inspected the photos.

"Let me borrow a coat," she said. "It looks like it's snowing."

She started rummaging through my closet.

"I have something better," I told her and pulled out the last parcel. It was a huge white box, and I whipped off the lid and held up a voluminous fur coat.

"Ta da!" I said.

Chloe screamed and sank to the floor. Milo ran up to sniff the coat.

"It's so beautiful!" Chloe said, wiping away a tear. "I can't accept that."

I wrapped the coat around her shoulders.

"No, take it back, it's too expensive," she told me.

"I already took the tags off, and if you don't take it, Milo will use it as a bed."

She pressed the silver-grey coat to her cheek.

"So soft," she purred. "This was too much money."

I was starting to wonder if I hadn't gone a little overboard. The coat had been front and center on her Pinterest page, however, and she even wrote a comment under the image that she would literally sell a kidney for this coat. Maybe she hadn't meant it. Why pin the coat on her Pinterest if she didn't even want it?

Chloe stood up. "I can't wear this outside. It should be in a museum."

"You have to take it for a spin at least, take a few pictures," I told her.

"Do I look okay?" she asked me after I helped her slip her arms into the coat sleeves.

"You look—" She looked mysterious and sexy and almost erotic in the coat. It gave me a huge rush of pleasure to see her in items I had bought for her.

"Nice coat!" Eddie said, flashing her a thumbs-up as we walked out of the lobby.

Icy, snowy flakes were falling when we walked outside. I saw our reflection in the window of the Frost Tower lobby.

"We look like a pair of celebrities." Chloe laughed.

"You look like a celebrity," I corrected. "I look a bit slovenly." I wasn't wearing a suit, having opted instead for boots, thick canvas pants, and a long-sleeved T-shirt.

"Nonsense," she said, taking my arm. "You would look great in anything, though in this weather you look like an alien. I can't believe you're not cold."

Milo tugged towards the park. No one was out when we arrived, so I let him off his leash.

Chloe modelled while I took pictures of her in the falling snow. I took a great shot of her and Milo. She wasn't posing, just playing with the husky, pure joy on her face. I couldn't help but smile as I watched her.

The coat was huge on her. I loved how she looked like a puffy sticky bun or something. Tucking the phone into my pocket, I jogged over to her and swept her up. I ran my hand over the coat, feeling the curves of her body underneath.

"I want to take you home and rip those clothes off of you," I said, kissing her.

She looked up at me balefully. "You can carefully, gently take these lovely clothes off of me, and then you can have your way with me, Mr. Frost."

"I suppose we'll have to compromise," I murmured against her mouth. I pressed the fluffy Chloe ball against me and spun her around.

"It's like a Christmas movie," she said. She pulled me down for another kiss then snapped our picture.

"Hartleigh can suck on this," she muttered.

"Trouble in bake-off paradise?"

"It's nothing; it's petty. It doesn't matter. I won last round."

I saw a flash of red in the trees. Milo looked in the direction and sniffed.

"Let's go," I said, my voice tense.

"Oh, wait, you don't have any food," Chloe said as we left the park.

"I told you I would order in something."

"No takeout for you while I'm around," she said emphatically. "I'm cooking."

We walked to the store, and I braced myself for a long food shopping session. We left Milo tied up outside, and Chloe handed me a basket.

"I'll be quick," Chloe promised.

She wasn't.

I threw worried glances to the window and sighed as she picked out potatoes, argued with the man at the fish counter about the state of the salmon, and picked over the cheese selection. I paid for the groceries, and she went to untie Milo. When I walked out, there was a skinny Santa talking to her. Chloe looked angry.

"Leave her alone," I snarled at him.

"Sorry, man," he said, holding up his hand.

"Do you know that Santa?" I demanded.

"Why does everyone assume I know them?" she yelled. She seemed frazzled, and I didn't want to ruin the day by pressing the matter.

"It's just that you're the self-proclaimed queen of Christmas," I joked.

She smiled slightly. "I guess I am."

When we arrived back at my penthouse, Chloe went to my bedroom and slowly took off the coat, the boots, and the sweater dress.

"I thought you were making eggs," I said, watching her, "but I'll take you for breakfast."

"I don't want food to get on my clothes."

"So you're going to cook in these?" I asked, unhooking her bra. Her tits spilled out, and I bent down, taking one in my mouth, rolling the nipple with my tongue.

She moaned and said, "I was going to put on one of your shirts."

"Yeah, I think I could get behind you walking around my house in a T-shirt, no bra, and the barest panties," I said.

"I'm supposed to be cooking," she said, the words coming out a little breathless.

"But it will be so much more satisfying after this," I told her.

I hooked a finger in the panties.

"Don't rip it!" she gasped. I slowly pulled them down, past her thighs, then let gravity carry them to the floor. By that time, I had my fingers between her legs, one thigh hooked up around me.

"Not fair! You still have all your clothes on," she protested.

I ripped the T-shirt off then kicked off my boots and pants and took her back into my arms.

"You weren't wearing underwear," she said, stroking me.

"I had high hopes for this morning," I said and rolled on a condom then rubbed my cock between her legs, coating it with the slickness. Then I hoisted her up onto the dresser in the bedroom and encased myself in her.

"You're so tight," I whispered to her.

Her legs were wrapped around me, coaxing me deeper. I pressed my face to her tits, sucking and nuzzling them. The little whimpering and moaning noises she was making were driving me to the brink of my self-control. I angled her forward so that my cock would rub her clit every time I thrust. I could feel her nails in my scalp. She was so close.

"You're mine," I told her as we came. "I don't care if you're stalked by Santas, you're all mine."

CHAPTER 37

Chloe

"You really can bring the heat," I told Jack. Our lovemaking had been quick, and I was feeling a little lightheaded.

He caressed my thighs, letting his hand come up to rest on my hips.

"You smell like sex," he said.

"I guess I better shower then," I replied, leaning into his touch.

"Don't. It smells good," he said, kissing my neck.

His touch was addictive, but I wasn't quite sure if I could go again.

"I'm showering," I told him, "then I'm cooking."

He followed me into the shower. The water was cool, but Jack felt warm. I guessed that was how he could run around without any underwear. I closed my eyes and let the water wash over me. Jack's hands and mouth were counterpoints to the flow of the water, and under his ministrations, I was aroused.

I opened my eyes, and it hit me suddenly that this was real—Jack was real, and right in front of me. I reached out and ran my hands down his chest to grab his cock.

"Put it in me," I told him.

He turned me around and gripped my hips. Between the shower and my own desire for him, he slipped in easily. It felt wanton to have sex in the shower. Jack's fingers were on my clit, and I bucked back against him. I reveled in the feel of his breath on my neck, the slight half moans he made, letting me know he took pleasure in my body and that I, Chloe, was making this man—this billionaire with an ice-cold demeanor—come completely undone.

"Add showers to the list of things that are a thousand times better with you," Jack said as I put on a pair of his boxers and one of his T-shirts. He watched me for a moment then said, "I thought you were wearing your new panties?"

"No."

"Why? I thought you liked them." He looked a little hurt.

I kissed him to make him feel better. "I do love them. That's why I'm saving them."

"For what?"

"I don't know, a special occasion," I replied.

"I can buy you more underwear," he said after a moment.

I stuck my tongue out at him. "I'm cooking your breakfast," I said and slapped him on a bare, very perfect and very firm, buttock. "After all that, you deserve something good."

I was chopping vegetables when Jack walked into the kitchen. He was only wearing boxers, and he threw the doors to the balcony open. Milo ran outside into the cold.

"It's hot in here, isn't it," I heard him say to the dog.

I sighed. We were going to have to come to a compromise about the window opening. I started the stove. Maybe I would warm up.

Speaking of big warm things, I was sure seeing a fair amount of activity in the man department lately.

"Everything all right?" Jack asked, coming around and wrapping his arms around me. I didn't think I would ever grow tired of it. But he might become tired of me if he ever figured out how trashy my family really was. Jack had his own family drama and didn't need Cody and his druggie friends screwing everything up.

At least Cody hadn't asked Jack for money. He had seen the fur coat Jack had bought me, and he knew it was expensive. I knew, now that Cody thought he could scam money through Jack, he would be back. I cursed my lack of a normal family as I chopped vegetables.

"I'm great," I told him. "Hungry."

"Can I help?"

"Sure." I handed him an onion to chop and winced while I watched him butcher it.

"Stop!" I yelled as he was about to chop off a finger. "Curl your fingers like this over the onion then slice horizontal to the counter then perpendicular." I demonstrated, and perfectly chopped pieces of onion cascaded off my knife.

"Wow, Chloe has skills," he said. "You're more than just a baker."

"I'll have you know that desserts are the hardest foods to make," I told him, launching into my lecture. "They are about precision and technique. You have to know exact measurements and how humidity and air pressure will affect your creations. If you're any good as a pastry chef, then you aren't just a baker. Making desserts is very technical; it's not something drunk sorority girls do for fun."

"Sorry," he said after a moment. "I didn't mean it like that."

"Go sit down," I said, more harshly than I intended. I felt bad as I watched Jack slink away to the couch in the living room. Across the open floor plan, I watched him fiddle with the remote-control tablet thing.

The TV turned on, and *Rudolph the Red-Nosed Reindeer* blared from the speakers.

"You're voluntarily watching Christmas shows?" I asked with a laugh.

He turned to grin at me. "I have to keep the chef happy."

The frittatas didn't take long to cook, and I arranged a piece of the egg dish on plates with sausage, potatoes, and fruit. Jack wolfed down the food as Milo looked on longingly.

"Can he have some salmon?"

Milo whined as Jack pretended to glare at him.

"I guess so."

Milo snapped up the fish from my fingers.

"You didn't even chew it," I admonished the dog.

"This is so much better than the chef-prepared meals," Jack said with a sigh. He leaned back against me. On TV, Rudolf was prancing around in the snow, singing a song with Frosty the Snowman.

"I love these old Christmas shows," I said. Jack Frost appeared on the screen in puppet form. I laughed, clapping my hands. "That's you!" Jack made a face, and I kissed him. "You need some Christmas cheer in your life."

"I have you," he replied, his hand moving up under the T-shirt.

"We just need to decorate your penthouse," I said. "You need a tree and garlands. Oh, that reminds me, I forgot your present."

"You're supposed to wait for Christmas to give presents," Jack said, smiling up at me. "Besides, I already have my present from you."

He pulled me to straddle him on the couch. I took off my shirt, exposing my bare breasts. He combed his hands through my hair then let his hands drift to my hips to pull my shorts down.

"I guess it's good you're already shirtless," I gasped and arched over him, running my hands down his muscular chest and his arms.

"I want you," he murmured.

Rudolph was still chirping away in the background. I tried to ignore it and concentrate on Jack. His fingers eased between my legs, stroking me.

"I want to feel you," I told him. I wanted to reach for his cock, but it was all I could do not to tumble down on top of him. The sensations from his mouth and his hands were disrupting any chance my brain had of forming a coherent thought.

Jack eased down his boxer briefs, and I felt his cock hard and warm against my thigh. I ground against him. I heard him fumble a condom on, then he eased me up, then pushed inside of me. I rode him, his cock running against my clit every time he thrust into me. I spread my legs, wanting to take all of him.

The pleasure was so much. Jack was basically holding me up now, his large hands pressed into my hips, his fingers digging into my ass. He was controlling the rhythm, and I was along for the ride.

My back was arched, and my head tipped back to expel moans and cries whenever he thrust into me. He was keeping me right on the edge.

"Faster," I said, my voice low and throaty. "I need to feel you."

His movements became more erratic, and he was practically jackhammering into me. My teeth were vibrating. My whole body clenched, then there was release.

"Fuck, Chloe," Jack said as he came.

I lay sprawled on top of him, panting.

"*Merry Christmas*!" Rudolph shrieked on the TV.

CHAPTER 38

Jack

"Sex with you is amazing. I think I could fuck you all day," I said, kissing her sloppily on her neck then sucking on her bottom lip.

"I hope Milo wasn't scared," she said.

"He can handle it." The dog wasn't even in the room. I heard him whining, then I heard knocking at the door.

"Mr. Frost!" I heard a man call through the door. "I hear you in there. Would you please answer the door?"

"Is that Eddie?" I asked incredulously.

Chloe giggled. "That's what you get for hiring a drunk Santa as your security guard."

I slipped on my boxers. How dare he interrupt me? Who was paying his—well, not his salary, but I did give him cash. I threw the door open.

"Eddie, what the hell—"

"Mr. Frost," said Mark Holbrook.

Shit.

"I trust you're enjoying your Saturday," he said.

"How can I help you?" I cursed myself for not at least putting on pants.

"I was in the area and decided to take you up on your offer to look at the space you have for rent," Mark said smoothly.

Right. Of course he did.

"Okay, uh," I scrambled for a way to salvage the situation.

"Hey, Eddie," Chloe said, "do you need something to drink? Oh..."

She had at least put on a bra. She was still wearing a T-shirt and my boxers though.

"I see I've come at a bad time," Mark said. He was in a suit and looked polished. I knew he came from old money, and he was too well bred to make any sort of off-color comment. Instead he introduced himself to Chloe. She shook his hand.

"Would you like to come in?" she offered. "Jack can go put some clothes on."

I hurried back to the bedroom, muttering swear words under my breath. Why had Mark Holbrook chosen *now* to come by?

I heard Chloe talking to Mark. He was eating the last soup muffin as I walked out. Milo was sitting at Mark's feet, whining. Eddie was standing at the bar cart in the living room, drinking some of my expensive scotch.

"Eddie," I growled. "You are supposed to be in the lobby."

"Sure thing, boss," he said shambling to the door.

There was no way Mark was going to rent space in my tower. He clearly saw what kind of poor-quality operation I was running here at Frost Tower.

"This is an amazing muffin," Mark said when he saw me. "Have you had one of these, soup muffins, I think she calls them? It's amazing."

"They're a little bit better fresh out of the oven," Chloe said. "Sorry, it's all I had on hand. Jack doesn't keep food in his condo, so it's a constant struggle to make sure he's not eating takeout or sad little precooked meals."

Mark smiled. "Sounds like every billionaire bachelor I know. He's lucky to have you. Thanks for the muffin," he said, standing up and following me to the elevators.

"You have quite the eclectic bunch here," Mark said as we rode down to the creative office space.

"Yes, it's a work in progress. The tower is still somewhat new."

"I'm assuming Eddie is temporary," Mark said.

"Yes, my other security guard was arrested." I mentally hit myself. That didn't sound good.

"Arrested." Mark sounded mildly shocked.

"Not for anything terrible," I said. Actually, I didn't know exactly why he had been arrested, but Mark didn't need to know that.

"If I move my operations here," Mark said as the elevator stopped on the empty floor where I had the high-bay creative space, "we need an actual security team."

"Not a problem," I told him. "Frost Tower can provide whatever security accommodations you and your company need."

Mark looked around appreciatively at the space. I was proud of it. Normally in a tower, the developer would have the architect design the ceilings as low as possible to cram in as many tenants as they could. Instead, I had had the ceilings built as high as possible while still minimizing the number of columns.

"You could have a crane in here if you wanted," I boasted.

"We don't need a crane," Mark said, walking through the space. Even though it was cloudy outside, the two-story windows let in an astonishing amount of natural light.

"I imagine it's hot in the summer," he said.

"We've already mitigated any summer heat gain issues," I said and pulled out my tablet to click a button. Shades rolled down, diffusing the light but still allowing us to faintly make out the New York City skyline through them.

"These creative work floors have a double skin," I told Mark, clicking another button. The shades went up, and in between the exterior and interior panes of glass, another set of large stiff blinds came down. "If you don't want the shade, you can have blinds to totally block the light."

"Very nice," Mark said.

"It's also part of the ventilation system to keep the dust down," I explained.

"I do like the fact that you have some condos in the building as well. We would probably need to purchase a few of them. I'll have to talk this over with my board. I'm also looking at some other properties both in the New York City area and in Connecticut, so I can't make any promises," he warned.

"I understand," I told Mark and walked him to the lobby.

"My mother really likes your Christmas decorations," he said with a slight smile. "She insisted I come and at least look at the space."

When I returned to the apartment, Chloe was baking furiously.

"Did you make the deal?" she asked. "Sorry, I hope I didn't ruin it by giving him a muffin."

I danced her around the penthouse.

"He loved your muffin, and the only reason he came by at all was because his mother liked the decorations in the lobby."

"Well, that's promising," she said.

"Promising! It's the best lead I've had all year! If I can convince Mark Holbrook to take space in Frost Tower, tons of other tech companies will follow suit." I kissed her. "Maybe this will be a merry Christmas after all!"

She giggled. "You should send him some of these soup muffins. Actually, wait, I know! I'll make an assortment, and you can send them a whole box. I'll decorate it and brand it and everything."

"You're a genius!" I told her. She smiled, and I kissed her under her jaw.

"I want to fuck you right now," I said, pushing my hands under the shirt to cup her breasts.

She rapped me on the head. "Not now. I have to bake."

CHAPTER 39

Chloe

It was magical staying in Jack's penthouse. I made another version of soup muffins—French onion with a bubbly layer of *Gruyère* cheese on top. I had extra pecans, so I also made Jack more of the wedding cookies.

"I think my work here is done," I said, proudly surveying all the baked goods arranged on the counter.

Jack grabbed a muffin and a cookie and ate them while I sketched out ideas for presenting the muffins and cookies to Mark Holbrook.

"I'm thinking two separate boxes," I said. "The muffins will be nestled in nice tissue paper, and the box should be blue. We'll write Frost Tower on it. Do you have any ribbon? What am I saying, of course you don't! I have some calligraphy pens already, though, so I'll think of something. The cookies I think I'll arrange nicely in a smaller box. Then it's like a little present in addition to the muffins."

Now that I had a way, no matter how small, that I could help Jack land a major business deal, I was dedicated to proving that I wasn't some freeloading thief like my cousin.

"You're the expert," Jack said. "I defer to you." He handed me his credit card. "Buy whatever you need for the muffins."

The next morning, I was back to the grind of the bake-off.

"Tomorrow is the Meet the In-Laws challenge," Anastasia told us as we assembled in the lobby to go shopping. "So, if you need anything special, now's the time to buy it."

Dana Holbrook walked into the lobby, her high-heeled shoes clicking on the polished floor. I wondered if she knew her cousin Mark had been here that weekend. I hadn't ever heard her talk about him, but then it wasn't as if she and I were besties.

"We're going to a different grocery store today," she said. "We have a deal with a high-end specialty food store. I'll be there to make sure we fulfill the terms of the marketing contract. There are also a few food brands that we need to showcase the labels on as well. I have outlined statements on these products, so if we ask one of you all to showcase a brand, act natural. We will redo shots until they look good."

"I've already met my in-laws," Hartleigh whispered to me. "Jack and I grew up together. I'm the girl next door."

"You're the insane person next door," Nina said.

I wasn't sure what I was going to make for the Meet the In-Laws challenge. It implied something remarkable but still conservative so as not to scare the parents you were trying to impress during the first meeting.

As we rode in a large SUV to the specialty grocery store, I wondered about Jack's parents. He didn't seem to like them. It was something to do with his sister. As I perused the store, pulling stuff not just for the contest but also for soup muffins, I wondered about Jack's family. I wanted Jack to have a happy Christmas. I vaguely remembered his talking about his childhood Christmases with fondness, and I wanted to put his family back together. I couldn't do that with my own family, but maybe I could do it with Jack's—bring them all together and show them the true spirit of Christmas.

The specialty grocery store was much nicer than the one the bake-off show usually took us to. And an added bonus was that there wouldn't be any Santas here to follow me around.

As I perused the high-end foods, I wondered, if I were meeting Jack's parents for the first time and had to bring a dessert, what would I make? Something with chocolate ganache, perhaps? Maybe with some sort of tart fruit? I was thinking little pieces of candied pears. I did like flourless chocolate cakes, but were they Christmassy enough? Maybe I could make a crepe cake. People liked those, and they did look impressive, but they weren't off-the-wall crazy. I couldn't use whipped cream, though. That was too pedestrian.

"Are you making a potato dessert?" Nina asked me, looking into my basket.

"Just working on a side project," I told her softly.

"For Jack?" she asked me.

"Yes, so shhh."

Hartleigh was watching us, clearly suspicious. I pulled Nina away to another aisle.

"I'm making him muffins," I told her. "I mean, most are for him to give as gifts."

"You're like a corporate wife without the ring," she said.

I rolled my eyes. "I'm just helping him out as a friend."

"I know you slept with him. You're basically his girlfriend!"

"He doesn't even know me." I snorted. "You might consider us friends with very generous benefits."

Nina snickered. "You don't need to win the bake-off if you win Jack."

"I don't think I'm going to win him," I said. "I think he's a little gun-shy with serious relationships thanks to everyone's favorite crazy stalker. I'm pretty sure the only reason he keeps me around is for my cooking and baking."

"I'm sure those ridiculously sexy outfits you post on Instagram also have a lot to do with it," she told me with a wink.

"I guess."

"I bet he's sending them to you himself," Nina said as we perused the cheeses. "Side note: You need to make a grilled cheese–and–tomato soup muffin." She loaded parmesan and cheddar cheese into my basket.

"Those would be good," I said, making a mental note to grab cans of imported tomatoes. "Jack would probably like it, too."

I directed the conversation back to my relationship with Jack. "I think part of it is the convenience. I'm right there in the tower; I'm easy. Maybe I'm too easy. My oma always said you should never give up the milk before making the man buy the cow, just give him a little dab of butter."

"That's a very specific cow metaphor," Nina said.

"She grew up on a dairy farm," I explained.

"I think Jack likes you more than just milk—am I using that metaphor correctly? I'm assuming he bought you that ridiculously expensive coat I saw on your Instagram."

"Yeah," I grimaced. "It was too expensive."

"You should gain something out of dating a billionaire," Nina said. "If he wants to shower you with expensive gifts, let him."

"That coat is beyond expensive. It costs more than the prize money for this bake-off."

Once we had all our ingredients, we lined up to check out. I tried to be sneaky about buying my ingredients for the muffins and the bake-off separately, but Hartleigh still wormed her way beside me.

"I know you're buying things for Jack." She looked at my hand. "Is that his credit card?" She tried to snatch the heavy black metallic card from me.

"That's not yours, Hartleigh," I warned.

"It should be," she hissed. "Our parents want us to be together."

"Don't argue with her," Nina told me. "Grow up, Hartleigh. No one believes you're going to marry Jack."

"I will," she protested, "as soon as Chloe is gone and he will stop being so distracted. She's trying to sabotage my relationship with him."

"Excuse me?" I screeched. "I'm trying to sabotage you? I know you did something to my egg whites. You're trying to sabotage me!"

"You can't prove anything!" she shrieked. "It's bad karma. You are stealing my boyfriend."

"He's not your boyfriend!" I yelled at her. I couldn't believe I was in a screaming fight with Hartleigh in the middle of the nicest food shop I had ever been in.

"He is, but you're leading him astray," she cried. "You and those sexy outfits. I bet they aren't from your fans. I bet you buy them yourself. Why else would anyone send that to you? You're not even that pretty!"

"Cut it out!" Dana yelled. "Honestly. You two are like little tween girls fighting over who has the biggest crush on a boy-band pop star."

There was a Santa Claus standing across the street. I saw him when I left the shop. He waved, and I sagged.

"Chloe!" Cody called. "Chloe!"

Needing him to stop drawing attention to me, I jaywalked across the street and was almost hit by a taxi.

"What are you doing here?" I demanded.

"Please," he begged. "I'm hungry and cold. I slept outside last night. Can't you spare something for your cousin?"

"You and your junkie friend just spend anything I give you on drugs," I spat.

"I promise I won't, Chloe, honest. We're family. We help each other out."

I shook my head. I needed to stop enabling him. "We're family, but you stole from me. You stole all of my life savings," I said.

"And I'm sorry," Cody said. He sounded annoyed and exasperated, as if I was the one at fault here.

Kevin, his junkie friend, walked up. He was also dressed in his dirty, shabby Santa costume. I hated to say it, but this whole business with the Santas was almost making me wish for a little less Christmas in my life. Maybe I should go to the Bahamas to escape the insanity. Oh, right, no I couldn't, because I had no money, so I was stuck here being stalked by Santas.

"You could help your cousin out," Kevin said. "We know all about you and your billionaire baby daddy."

That last bit of his comment caused my thoughts to come to a screeching halt.

"Excuse me," I hissed.

"I heard the rumors," Kevin said. "I can read. It's all over the internet."

Did I really look pregnant? I looked down at my stomach. Maybe I did need to lay off the sweets.

"Please," Cody begged. "I don't have any money, and you clearly do."

"I don't! You stole it!" How was he not hearing me? He was so fixated on my giving him the money he felt like he was owed that he wouldn't listen to reason.

"I have nothing for you. Do not contact me again," I told him.

"Oma is rolling over in her grave!" Cody called after me as I hurried back to the waiting SUV.

CHAPTER 40

Jack

Hunter and Greg were in the Platinum Provisions boardroom bright and early.

"Late again," Liam said when I walked into the meeting.

Greg pounced on that comment. "Is there a new pattern of lateness?"

"Chill, Greg," Liam said to his brother.

"You need to offload that tower," Hunter said. If Greg was a jerk, Hunter was a cold-hearted bastard. He was in high demand to be on companies' boards because he could ferret out inefficiencies and foresee problems long before they blew up.

"He's distracted," Greg said.

"It's not the tower, he has a girlfriend." Liam said.

"He does, does he?" Hunter remarked.

"Not helping, Liam," I said. "What I do on my personal time is my business."

"Not if it starts to affect my business," Hunter said in a low voice.

"Platinum Provisions is doing very well," I said. "There is no cause for concern."

Hunter leveled his gaze at me. I debated telling them about my lead with Mark Holbrook, but I didn't want to say more until I had more concrete information.

I wondered how Chloe was doing with the muffins. I would have texted her, but I realized I didn't have her number. We lived in the same building, so I never thought to call her, since I knew I would simply see her in person.

"I did want to talk to you about expanding your lab equipment division," Hunter said. "Svensson PharmaTech is trying to move into new spaces and drop drug prices. Mace's company needs better tools and a wider variety of more robust ones."

"Interesting you should say that," Liam said. Was he going to pitch his factory idea? We hadn't discussed it yet. I hoped he knew what he was doing.

"I was thinking that we needed to own the means of production. There's a lot of land out there in Harrogate near where PharmaTech is located. You guys own most of the town, correct? It would be a good fit, especially if we start supplying Svensson PharmaTech."

"Are you suggesting you want to move out into the country?" Greg asked.

"Harrogate is like two hours from Manhattan," Liam countered. "It barely counts as another town."

"I think it could be a good move," Hunter said. "I'll start looking into the logistics."

"Wait, wait a minute," Greg interjected. "You can't just unilaterally decide that Liam is going to move."

"Liam is an adult, Greg, and if he wants to live with me, then I think we should encourage that."

I sank down in my chair. I did not want to be in the crossfire of one of the legendary fights between the two elder Svensson half-brothers.

"I'm not moving permanently," Liam said, "and I'm not living with you and all the kids, Hunter, no offense."

"It's very much offensive that you care so little about your family after everything I have done for you," Hunter said, the expression on his face clearly broadcasting his disappointment.

Liam swore.

After Liam and I escaped the boardroom, Liam rubbed his hands together. "That went well, all things considered. Now we just have to find some tenants for your tower and select a ring so you can propose to Chloe."

"I'm not—" I sputtered. "I barely know her! We aren't going to marry each other."

Liam looked at me and placed his hands on my shoulders. "Jack, we have been friends since freshman year when you kept my drunk self from falling out a window. And you will never, ever find anyone else as good as Chloe. You need to lock that down. Girls love a Christmas proposal."

"She's not like that," I said. "She's not a gold-digger—she has ambitions. She doesn't want some guy to take care of her."

Liam snorted.

"You want to grab something to eat?" I asked, hoping to change the subject.

"Can't," Liam said. "I have to meet my brothers for lunch. Hunter brought a gaggle of the younger ones to New York City to go to a few museums. I think he assigned them reports."

"I don't know how you keep track of all your siblings. I only have five, and it feels like I never have enough time to spend any time with them," I told my friend.

When we arrived in the lobby, there were about two dozen teenage-and-younger boys. They had the same blond hair and grey eyes that Liam had. The younger ones were adorably cute, whereas the older ones were gangly, with big hands and feet. They hadn't filled out yet, though I knew that they would end up looking just like Liam and his other brothers. The Svensson male genes were strong.

"Did you have fun at the museum?" I asked, walking over with Liam.

The kids were visibly excited and chattered on about the dinosaurs they had seen. I could see why my parents might have wanted a big family. Liam's little brothers were noisy but fun, like puppies, just completely excited to see me. I also knew that Hunter sacrificed a lot to take care of his younger brothers and had a strict schedule and method of enlisting the adult Svenssons to watch out for and engage the younger half-siblings who were shipped to Harrogate every few months.

"It was so awesome! And we rode a train!" one of them said, bouncing up and down.

"A train," I said, crouching down to talk to him. Kids were cute; I liked them. I just knew I couldn't handle a dozen of them. Two kids would be perfect, though. Chloe could teach them how to cook, and I could teach them how to beg Chloe to cook, I supposed.

"I have another board meeting," Hunter said as he and Greg walked up. "I trust you have this under control, Liam." His tone implied that Liam had better have it under control.

The manager of the Japanese restaurant that was located at the base of the Platinum Provisions tower hurried over. "There is a gentleman here to see you about your tower," he said to me. "He's waiting in the restaurant and asked me to have you come over."

"Go make me proud!" Liam said.

As I followed the manager across the lobby into the low lighting of the Japanese restaurant, I wondered who it was. Was it Mark Holbrook? Maybe it was someone who had heard he was interested in Frost Tower. Wouldn't that be great? I could even rent everything out by the end of the year.

As I approached the booth, a tall, silver-haired man stood up and smiled at me.

"Dad. What are you doing here?"

"Sit," he said.

I ignored him. "I was told there was someone here to see me," I said flatly.

"Yes," my father replied. "It's me."

"I take it you aren't interested in the tower space," I said. I couldn't believe my father. "Aren't you supposed to be doing surgery right now?"

"I just finished with an operation," he said, sipping his water. "It took me thirty-six hours to do a spinal surgery on a premature infant. It was lifesaving stuff, and I used Platinum Provisions equipment, I might add. The surgery was very innovative. The New York Times is doing a full-page piece on me," he bragged.

"Well, congrats," I said. "I have a business to run, so since you don't have anything of value to add, I'll be leaving."

"I did such a good job with you and your brothers," my father said in that self-satisfied tone that made me want to punch something. "It's too bad Belle didn't understand the value of hard work."

I wanted to throw the glass of water at him. How dare he insult Belle after everything he had done to her?

"You and Mom were terrible parents," I told him. "The only reason I'm successful is because of Belle and the sacrifices she made. Not you."

"You are a productive member of society," he countered. "Tough love worked. You worked your way through college—"

"No, I didn't," I interjected. "Belle slaved and sacrificed to pay my tuition. I couldn't qualify for a student loan or any scholarships because you and Mom made too much money."

"Yes," he said. I could tell he hadn't really been listening to me. "It taught you the value of hard work."

"No, it didn't. Instead, it made me hate you."

"You say that, but you're here talking to me," he said smugly. "You know your children need their grandfather."

"There are no children," I said as I massaged my temple. I didn't know who was worse, my mother or my father.

"Your mother wants grandchildren," he continued.

I hated talking to my father; he was so frustrating. It was his way or the highway.

"Diane and I deserve grandkids. I know one of the women you're sleeping with is pregnant. People talk, Jack."

"Who is talking?" I demanded. Chloe would kill me if someone was spreading rumors that she was pregnant.

"Hartleigh would be the perfect mother," my father said, leaning back. "You know, your mother and I are friends with her parents. It would be great. We always planned for our kids to marry each other. It's a perfect ending to a perfect life."

"Your life was perfect at the expense of Belle," I said. "And as far as Hartleigh goes, burn that notion out of your head right now. She would be a horrible mother. She's crazy and violent."

"She is a wonderful young woman!" my father said. "I don't know why you're carrying on this way. I thought I raised you better than that."

"Hartleigh is a stalker," I told him.

"Men can't be stalked," he scoffed.

"We're done," I said, standing up. "You never protected me, you certainly didn't protect Belle, and you could never be bothered to do right by your own kids."

CHAPTER 41

Chloe

I was test-baking for the box of goodies for Mark Holbrook, and Jack was my taster.

"The potato–and–cheddar soup ones are definitely perfect," he said through a mouth full of muffin.

"What kind of cookies should I make?" I asked him. "I was thinking sugar, but maybe they like some other kind?"

He shrugged. "I wish my old assistant was still here. She knew the Holbrooks' assistant, Kate. Well I don't know if she's still the assistant, since she married her boss's son."

"Scandalous!" I said in a singsong voice then added, "Not that I can talk. I'm banging the judge of the competition I'm in."

Jack gave me an impish grin and kissed me.

"Try this," I ordered, shoving a pumpkin soup muffin into his mouth. "I don't think it's as special compared to the potato ones."

"Tastes fine to me," he said. "The grilled-cheese-and-tomato soup muffin is amazing."

"I'm not sure about these clam chowder ones," I said. "They're a little fishy."

"It's late," Jack said. "You can keep working on it tomorrow."

"You can't wait too long to send the box," I told him. "I wish I had more time."

Jack grabbed another muffin, and I sighed. "I guess I'll just send the tomato-soup muffins, the French-onion-soup muffins, and the potato-and-cheddar soup muffins."

There was a knock on the door. "At least we're all dressed," Jack said.

Eddie was there with another package.

"Another present from Chloe's fans," he said.

Jack gave him some cash, and I took the package into the bedroom and opened it. Inside was a ridiculously skimpy outfit. I stripped then put it on.

"I think it's a little small," I said when Jack walked in. Jack looked like he had just been run over by a reindeer.

It was a glittery little outfit. The skirt could barely count as a skirt. The red-and-white top had little zippers over the boob cups, not that the outfit needed them. My breasts threatened to spill out.

"I think it's supposed to fit like that," Jack mumbled.

"Try not to drool," I said and pulled a giant lollipop from the box and pretended to bop him on the head with it.

"What is this, some sort of Christmas candy slut outfit?" he said.

I reached down to try and adjust it. "I think there's a rip," I said. "Oh wait, nope, just crotchless." I looked at Jack's crotch—his cup also runneth over.

"I'm glad we're in the bedroom," he said, his voice low and gravelly. "I need to stop fucking you in the kitchen. It's dangerous. Someone could get burned."

I leaned back on the bed, and one boob popped out of the cup. He went after it, kissing the soft flesh. I shivered from the slight scrape of his teeth.

"The nice thing about this outfit," Jack said, his fingers slowly spreading the slickness between my legs, "is that I don't have to rip your clothes off to fuck you."

He moved down and hooked my legs around his neck. He kissed me, the slit giving him an all-access pass to my pleasure center. He licked me, his tongue teasing me. I strained against him. I felt a little slutty between the outfit, the gorgeous man, and the high-pitched moans and little screams that came out of my throat.

Jack pulled his mouth away, and I groped for his head.

"Don't stop!" I begged.

He flipped me over so I was on my front on the bed, my legs splayed for him. His fingers were back, dipping into me then teasing my clit, bringing me close to the edge then back.

"I can't believe how wet you are," he murmured in my ear. He put his hand in my hair then moved behind me.

"Are you ready for my cock?" he growled.

"Yes," I choked out.

"Tell me what you want."

I moaned. "I want you."

"Beg," he ordered, pinning my wrists above my head with one hand, his other stroking me forcefully.

"I want your big thick—"

I let out a cry of pleasure as he entered me, and sugarplums danced around my head. I felt totally dominated by him. Every thrust was accompanied by a high-pitched cry from me.

I came with a scream. Jack was still hard. I felt him fucking me, and I strained against his hands on my wrists. I felt raw with pleasure.

"Can you come again for me?" he asked. One hand was back teasing my clit. My hips rotated in little circles, and I wanted to feel that same wave of pleasure wash over me. He moved his hand to the scrap of a skirt. I heard it rip.

"Fuck," he said, his voice low and ragged, rubbing his hands over my torso and hips.

I needed his hand back on my clit.

"I want you," I whimpered.

"You want what?" he asked, his voice gravelly.

His two fingers teased around my clit, eliciting a moan from me. All the while he fucked me slowly, letting me rub against him, making me feel all of him. When I finally came, my whole body seized, and I could feel his cock spasming inside me.

"You're the sexiest little piece of Christmas candy I've ever had the pleasure of fucking," he said, nibbling on my ear.

"You ruined my outfit," I told him. I felt limp and sated.

"I'll buy you a new one," he said. "A sexier, skimpier one."

CHAPTER 42

Jack

Chloe lay sprawled on the bed, half asleep. She was still wearing the partially ripped slutty Christmas candy outfit.

I was a little concerned about the stuff people were sending her, but she did look amazing in that outfit. The slit in the panties was driving me crazy. I let my fingers play in the slit for a few minutes and smiled when I heard Chloe whimper. My cock surged to life.

I straddled her. She was still slick from our lovemaking that had ended only moments ago. I kissed her deeply, moving inside of her. Her whole body shivered with tremors, the aftershocks of an orgasm.

"Can you come again for me?" I asked her.

She moaned from the back of her throat, arching her hips up to mine as I pushed into her.

"You're so tight," I told her, kissing her breasts, which heaved, uncontained, in the little scrap of red–and–white fabric. She came with a cry.

"Fuck," I said as I came. I rolled us both over, letting her lie on top of me.

"This is the most sex I've had in I think forever," I murmured into her neck.

"I think I'm addicted to you." She kissed me on the nose.

We slept like that. She was a cute blonde bundle in my arms the next morning. I pulled her to me as she pushed out of bed.

"I have to go to the bake-off," she said, slapping my hand away.

"Screw the bake-off, just stay here with me," I told her. "You can be my live-in chef. I'll give you a credit card with an unlimited line of credit, and you can buy whatever baking tools and ingredients you want."

"I don't need a handout," she told me, her face serious. "I'm with you because I like you, not because I want your money."

She stalked to the bathroom, and I groaned. I needed to stop putting my foot in my mouth. I couldn't lose Chloe.

I swung out of the bed and looked around. There was glitter all over the bedroom, along with little fluffy bits of lace. I left a generous tip for the maid and a note apologizing for the mess. Between Chloe's baking and the sexy outfits and the subsequent sex, my poor housekeeper was doing a lot more work than she usually did.

After Chloe left to prep for the bake-off filming and I walked Milo, I went down to the production studio. They shot a video of me at the beginning of the challenge, as well as some shots of my walking around, then I left the tower for the day. I had to take Milo to the groomers', and then I had to go into the office. Between Frost Tower, the bake-off, and Chloe, I was neglecting my company.

Milo was happy to be outside. I needed to up his exercise routine. One more thing to add to the list.

The Scottie Dog Groomers and Pet Boutique was packed. It was fairly close to my tower and somewhat new. Ginny, the young woman who owned it, was washing a chunky-looking corgi when I walked in with Milo. The corgi barked at my husky.

"Gus, stop it," Ginny commanded. "I'll be right with you," she told me and wiped her hands.

"How's my handsome boy?" she said to Milo. He whined and licked her face.

"Congratulations," Ginny said to me.

"For what?" I was confused. Was she talking about the Platinum Provisions baking tools?

Ginny handed me an envelope.

"You won," she said.

"Excuse me?"

"The contest," Ginny explained.

I looked in the envelope. There were two tickets to the *Nutcracker* ballet.

"I didn't enter a contest."

"Your email is entered automatically," Ginny said. "It's something fun I'm doing for clients this year."

"I don't have anyone to take," I said automatically.

"No one special in your life?" Ginny asked. "No bakers?" She winked.

I was taken aback. How did she know about Chloe?

"I watch *The Great Christmas Bake-Off*," Ginny gushed. "I must have seen all the episodes like five times each. You and Chloe are adorable. You two have your own fan page, did you know that?"

"I don't even want to know," I muttered.

"Yeah, you probably don't," she said thoughtfully. "The implications people make about you two are, quite frankly, graphically sexual in nature."

I tried to keep my face cold and emotionless. She smirked. Clearly I had failed.

"I will pick Milo up this afternoon," I said.

"Sure thing. He's a well-behaved boy, not like Gus."

The corgi howled.

I left the groomers, tucking the tickets into my suit-coat pocket.

Should I take Chloe? I knew she liked Christmas, but she had been angry when I joked about buying her stuff and insisted she didn't want handouts. But she was happy about the gifts I had bought her. I was a little frustrated when I walked into the office.

"Look who decided to join us," Liam said loudly. The marketing team was assembled in one of the large meeting rooms. I didn't like to make people wait. That was a douche power move that was reserved for less successful people. I liked to be on time. I checked my watch and stifled a curse. I was two minutes late.

"Apologies for my lack of punctuality," I told them.

The marketing director waved away my apologies. "It's all pine needles under the Christmas tree. Sorry," he said sheepishly. "In my house, it's all Christmas all the time. My kids are obsessed. I had a nightmare about a talking snowflake last night."

Liam snickered. "Down to business," he said, clapping his hands and gesturing to the graph on the screen.

"These are preorders for the product," the marketing director said. "The factories have finished the first round of production, and it's all being boxed today and will be shipped off tonight." He pulled up another picture. "This is the line outside Williams-Sonoma of people waiting to buy the product."

"Wow," I said.

"The news is running stories about it," a young woman said, holding up her tablet. "Platinum Provisions special Christmas kits are the hot item this year."

"It's also translating into our medical sales," the VP of operations added. "We've had interest from hospitals as far away as Japan and Australia inquiring about our products."

My life was looking up. If I could convince Mark Holbrook to rent in my tower, this would be the best Christmas ever.

CHAPTER 43

Chloe

I forced myself to concentrate on the Meet the In-Laws challenge and not let my mind wander to Jack.

"Meeting your significant other's parents and family for the first time can be nerve wracking, especially if his mother asks you to bring a dessert. What do you bring?" Anastasia said to the camera. "We are challenging the contestants to make their perfect dessert to impress the in-laws during the Christmas season."

I had wanted to keep my ingredients safe in Jack's penthouse, but we had to have them down in the sound studio kitchen so we could pretend to go shopping. Hopefully Hartleigh had not messed with them.

I was going to make a mille crepe cake with an orange liqueur crème and cranberry jelly alternating between the paper-thin crepe layers. The whole cake would be covered with chocolate ganache, and I was going to make pear caramel pieces in the shape of tiny snowflakes to decorate the cake. Each person would have an individual tiny cake; therefore I would have to make a lot of crepes. One single large crepe would yield three small circles. We had to make at least four plates of desserts, one for each judge and one for the production crew to film. I checked the clock. I would spend most of my time today making crepes.

My ingredients seemed fine, and I made caramel. I was going to use it in the piping gun to make caramel pear snowflakes. The device from Platinum Provisions could pipe hot liquids as well as cold. I'd used it before for making candy. For frosting, one could easily use a plastic bag with a nozzle, but to pipe anything hot or sticky, Jack's machine was the best. As I funneled the piping-hot mixture into the chamber of the device, I smiled to myself, thinking about being with him.

The gun sat on my hand so that I could more easily control it, and after making sure I had a good grasp on it, I began to pipe the caramel. It sizzled as it hit the parchment paper. I heard a crack then felt burning-hot caramel run over my hand. I screamed in pain.

"It's burning!" I yelled. Nina rushed over and grabbed me, dragging me to the sink and turning on the cold water full blast.

"Oh no!" I cried. Anastasia hurried over.

"What happened?"

"The piping gun broke," Nina said.

"It's a very expensive piece of equipment. It doesn't just break, does it?" Anastasia asked.

One of the production assistants hurried over with a first aid kit. The other contestants had all stopped their baking and were watching me. I regarded Hartleigh through the tears in my eyes. She looked as if she was stifling a triumphant smile.

"I'm going to kill her," I seethed. "Hartleigh messed with my piping gun. Every station has a box of identical Platinum Provisions equipment, and she must have snuck in here and tampered with the one at my station somehow. I am seriously going to kill her!"

"Don't kill her," Nina hissed. "They'll kick you out. You can't prove anything."

"How bad is my hand?" I asked her, not daring to look.

"It's red, but it's not blistering or anything," Nina told me.

Another contestant, Maria, came over with a plastic bag holding some sort of thick green plant. She slit the spiky green plant down the length and rubbed it all over my hand. The gooey green gel smelled a little bitter, but my hand felt better.

"Leave it on," Maria said, coating my hand in the gel and sliding a glove on. "It will help the burn. You'll be good as new. Can't be a baker without being burned!"

I sniffled.

"Don't cry, mamí. There's no crying in the kitchen!" she said, wiping my eyes.

Zane was up close in my face, filming my reaction. I wanted to scream at him but knew that wouldn't do any good. I managed a shaky smile.

My hand felt stiff—I didn't know if it was the glove or the burn. I hoped it was just the glove. I forced myself to limp along. Because my hand was so stiff, I knew I needed to change my dessert to something simpler than the elaborate little crepe cakes. I settled on a flourless chocolate cake with ganache and candied pears. I hoped it would be enough to keep me from being kicked out.

The production assistant swept up the broken equipment.

"Save it," I told her. I wanted Jack to look at it.

Or did I? I wondered as I baked. Jack had a lot on his plate. He was dealing with finding tenants and running his company. Did I really want to burden him with my problems?

While my cakes baked, I took the glove off. My hand seemed okay, if a little red.

"Put the glove back on!" Maria called out while she whisked various sauces.

I put it back on after smearing more aloe vera on my hand.

Thankfully my cakes came out beautifully. I let them rest while I candied the little pieces of pears and made the ganache. Determined to at least bring something Christmassy to my dessert, I made a bright-red cranberry sauce and a bright minty-green sauce and painted little sprigs of holly on each of the plates. Then I placed the little round cakes on the plates and doused them with the glossy chocolate ganache, finishing them with a sprinkle of candied pears.

I looked at the plate sadly. It seemed a little basic. I knew it tasted good, but it wasn't what I had wanted to make.

CHAPTER 44

Jack

The tension was high in the studio when I walked in with the other judges. Chloe looked angry; she was wearing a glove on one hand and seemed to be favoring it.

I wanted to smooth the tight look on her face. But she and the other contestants were whisked off to the holding room, leaving Hartleigh remaining. It seemed she would go first. She smoothed down her apron, staring at me as her hands lingered on her body.

"For our esteemed judges," she said, "I made a cranberry and chocolate tart."

I didn't even want to eat her food. I broke it into pieces and moved them around on my plate, hoping the camera would have enough footage. Hartleigh looked annoyed when she saw I wasn't even tasting her dessert.

"If you're going to make a tart," Anu said after taking a bite, "remember that it's one of those things that's deceptively simple. Everything, the pastry, the filling, everything has to be perfect. Unfortunately, this falls flat."

"You should ask Chloe for some tips on pastry," Nick said. "Even though it wasn't even her dessert, that pie crust she made for that apple cranberry pie—you remember that, Anu—that was some of the best pastry I've ever had."

After that statement, Hartleigh looked steaming mad.

"Chloe," she muttered and stomped out before the judges could finish the critique.

"All, right then," Nick said after a moment. "Next contestant."

Nina was next with a cranberry chocolate cake with candied almond sorbet.

"You would impress anyone with this," Anu told her.

"Thank you," she said.

"Though it's tasty," Nick told her, "I think the presentation could be better."

They had similar comments for Chloe.

"I'm glad you didn't burn yourself too badly," Anu said. "Unfortunately, it's part of life as a chef. I have scars from some very bad burns."

"I was planning something else," Chloe explained.

"I think that's why your dessert isn't quite there," Nick said.

"You were able to finish, which shows a level of professionalism," Anu said. "And it's a fine dessert. However, it's not spectacular."

I was still reeling from learning she had been burned.

Maria presented last, and it was clear that she was the winner in Anu's and Nick's eyes. She had made a variety of churros with little dipping sauces.

"It's festive and fun and feels like something you would do with friends and family," Nick said.

"I agree," Anu told her. "It feels casual but still has a nice presentation. These churros are cooked perfectly."

I caught Chloe after we finished taping.

"You burned yourself?" I asked her. "Let me see your hand." I took it gently and eased the glove off. She winced.

"Does it hurt?" I asked her. I didn't want to touch it.

"Maria gave me aloe vera," Chloe said. "I think it's helping."

"I am going to take you to the emergency room," I told her. "You need to see a doctor."

She scoffed. "I am made of sturdy Midwestern stock. We don't go to doctors."

"Why are you being so stubborn? And what happened? How did you burn your whole hand?" I demanded.

"I was using your piping gun to make caramel snowflakes, and it broke," she retorted.

"My products don't break," I snapped. I couldn't believe it. "Let me see it! I'll take it to the engineers."

"It's fine," she said, not looking me in the eye.

"Give it to me," I ordered.

She sighed unhappily.

"Would you bring me the broken equipment?" I asked one of the production assistants.

She scurried off and returned with a box. The piping gun was in several pieces, and it looked like it had failed under pressure.

"This was not supposed to happen, Chloe. I'm so sorry. I'm going to figure out what went wrong," I promised.

"Just leave it alone, please," she hissed.

I looked at her incredulously. "You were hurt with something I made. No, I will not just leave it alone."

"Do you want to hang out tonight?" she asked me.

I held out a hand to caress her face. "I have a dinner meeting scheduled with Liam," I explained. We liked to touch base about the company without being in the office. It was a way to bounce ideas off each other.

"But I can cancel," I told her. "Liam will understand."

"No!" she said loudly, then lowered her voice. "You're not skipping out on a business meeting because of me. I'm not coming to your apartment."

"But—" I tried to protest.

"La la la, I can't hear you," she said, turning away to go complete the postproduction interviews.

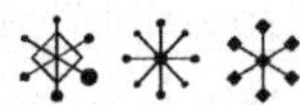

"Dude," Liam said after I scowled through the first round of drinks. "I know Christmas is a bad time for you, but you seem extra angry."

I handed him the box containing the broken piper. Liam whistled.

"Is this one of ours? It looks like it was run over by a truck."

"It happened at the bake-off. It burned Chloe's hand."

"Chloe?" he said in concern. "This is not good."

"Don't worry, she didn't post about it on Instagram, thankfully. We would be in deep trouble."

"Do you think she's going to sue?"

"No," I said emphatically, but then I wondered. Would she? I didn't know her that well. No, I knew her. It would be within her right to sue, but I knew she wouldn't. If she was angry at the device ruining her chances at winning the bake-off, she would just kick me to the curb.

I cursed under my breath. "My product could have cost Chloe her baking career. We were lucky her hand wasn't maimed."

"Did she go to a doctor?" Liam asked. "We should pay her medical bills."

"She didn't want to go," I told him. "Her hand just looked red. It wasn't blistered or anything. I'll keep an eye on it."

My friend smirked. "Look at you, keeping an eye on things. Does everyone know you're dating a contestant?"

"The internet boards seem to think so," I said, taking another sip of my drink.

Liam chuckled. "So that's what Carl said when he was joking that people were shipping you two so hard."

The waiter brought us another round, and I ordered us food to soak up some of the alcohol.

"So," Liam drawled. "Your first girlfriend ever, not counting Hartleigh. How does it feel? Did you kiss her yet?"

"Of course I did." I snorted. "And I bought her expensive presents."

Liam looked horrified. "Dude, you are so clueless."

"Excuse me?"

"Did you give them to her right after you slept with her?"

I looked at him in shock.

He shook his head. "You're just making her feel like a prostitute, like Julia Roberts in *Pretty Woman*."

I swore again. Was that why she was mad at me? Or was it just her hand?

"I'm assuming she knows all about Hartleigh?" Liam asked.

"More or less," I said.

"And she still wants to be with you even though you have a stalker?" he prodded.

"I guess. I don't know. She cooks for me. She bought me a present." The waiter brought our food. They never gave diners enough food at these high-end restaurants. I would probably have to pick up something more to eat on the way home.

"She bought you a Christmas present?" Liam said, laughing.

"And she wants to throw me a Christmas party," I continued.

Liam almost fell out of his chair laughing. "Chloe's going to drag Jack Frost kicking and screaming into the holidays! I love it!"

CHAPTER 45
Chloe

I was sort of glad that I wasn't going to Jack's tonight. I wasn't feeling particularly bubbly. In fact, I was feeling murderous. I wanted to push Hartleigh out the window.

"You need to calm down," Nina said. "You weren't sent home, thankfully. Now we're down to the last four. Don't do anything crazy. Also, don't say anything to Jack. He seems like the type of person to go completely ballistic. He'll go after Hartleigh, and she'll play the victim. You don't want him to end up in jail."

I saw motion in our bedroom doorway.

"You are a horrible witch!" I screamed at Hartleigh. Hartleigh smirked as Dana peered around behind her.

"Chloe, could I come speak to you for a moment?" Dana asked.

I followed her outside into the hallway.

"Look," the producer said. "You have to cool it with Jack."

"Nothing is happening," I lied. "We're friends."

Dana looked frustrated. "You know, I have quite a bit on my plate right now. I'm sure you've seen the tabloid articles about my brother and me."

I nodded. Talk about family drama.

"This show is almost over, and I would like us all to make it out in one piece."

I started to protest, but she held up a perfectly manicured hand to stop me.

"The other contestants are expressing anger at the perceived favoritism," Dana said.

"Other contestants?" I fumed. "There are only four of us left. It was Hartleigh, wasn't it?"

Dana glared at me. "Our show is relying on a number of advertisers, and we can't afford a scandal. We need this show to be profitable. People need to be paid. You don't want to be the reason people don't have a paycheck so close to Christmas, do you?"

I shook my head.

She patted my hand. "Just keep concentrating on your Instagram. It's almost Christmas! You're our little Christmas star. *The Great Christmas Bake-Off* fans love you, because you're wholesome. The more adventurous fans can pretend you and Jack are in love, but we can't actually have you two making out on screen. Light flirting is fine, but no more than that. No more bedroom eyes."

Hartleigh was smirking at me when I returned to the apartment. I couldn't stand being in the same room with her, and I didn't trust myself around Jack. I went down to the lobby.

There was a Santa standing outside. He was standing across the wide street, and I threw open the door to confront him. I was so tired of this.

"Leave me alone!" I screamed at him.

The Santa didn't seem fazed to see me. He was wearing sunglasses. Was he the same Santa from the mall? I couldn't tell in the dark. I could swear he smiled at me before he turned and sauntered away.

Eddie came into the lobby.

"Aren't you supposed to be here guarding this place?" I snapped at him.

Eddie was wearing a cleaner-looking Santa suit and smelled as if he'd showered. He pulled out a flask—so he wasn't completely redeemed.

"Sorry, Miss Chloe," he said. "There was a report of two vagrants outside trying to get in by the loading bay. Had to deal with it. They said they knew you."

"I'm sorry for snapping at you," I told him. "If you see those two, I'm not here, and they need to understand that they can't show up at Frost Tower begging for money."

"Understood. There's another package for you," he told me, plopping a box down on the counter.

I was starting to tire of the outfits, though Jack liked them. I took this box upstairs. I didn't want to go back to the apartment. I was still furious at Hartleigh and Dana for assuming I was sleeping with Jack—which I was, so what was I mad about?

I rode the elevator up to the top floor and stuck the package in the trash chute without opening it.

"Sorry, crazy fan," I said. "No Instagram pictures tonight."

I punched in the key code to Jack's penthouse. Jack had given it to me so I could stash the muffin ingredients in his fridge. I didn't want to misuse it, and I hoped he wouldn't mind that I was up here. I also hoped Dana didn't find out.

They wouldn't really kick me off the show, would they?

I crept into Jack's bedroom. It was late, and I assumed Jack was back from his business meeting. But Milo was asleep, alone, on the bed, so maybe not. The dog's nose twitched—he must have smelled me—then he woke up and wagged his tail.

"Where's Jack?" I whispered to the dog.

The penthouse took up almost the entire top floor, though I hadn't really explored it. I mainly stayed in the kitchen and occasionally in Jack's bedroom.

As I padded through the penthouse, Milo glued to my side, I heard clanging and someone cursing.

He must be up here, I thought and headed toward the light spilling from an open doorway.

"Jack?" I called, my voice sounding uncertain.

"Chloe," he said, standing up from a workbench. We stood there awkwardly, looking at each other.

"How's your hand?" he asked.

"It's fine," I said.

"I took a look at the piping gun," he began.

"I don't really want to talk about it," I said. "I'm trying to lift my bad mood."

He nodded. I picked at a fuzz ball on my sweater. Jack came over and hugged me. He smelled like metal and oil.

"Working late?"

"Just trying out some new robotics attachments for surgery."

"Aren't you tired? It's late."

I wanted things to go back to being easy between us. This thing with Jack was supposed to be fun. It was part of my authentic New York City experience before I inevitably failed to achieve my dreams and had to return to the Midwest, tail between my legs.

"Are you tired?" he asked.

"Not really."

"You want something to eat?"

"I guess I'll make some eggs."

He looked at me with concern. He had goggles pushed up on his head. They were messing up his hair, so I pulled them off and smoothed his hair back. He grinned and bent down as if he was about to kiss me, our faces centimeters apart.

"Can I kiss you?"

"Do you want to?"

"Yes, but I don't want you to bite my head off."

"I'm just grumpy," I said.

He bent down and pressed out lips together. I felt a little better.

"You're just hungry," he said.

I wrapped my arms around him, and he picked me up, carried me through the kitchen, and put me on the couch. Then he wrapped a blanket around me and turned on the TV.

"I'll pick a movie for you," he said. "How about *The Nightmare Before Christmas*?"

"That's a classic Christmas movie," I said. "Good choice."

"I'll bring you something to eat."

"Are there any soup muffins left?" I called after him. "That would be fine for me."

"I have something better," he replied.

I heard the microwave go, and Jack brought over a large bowl of steaming curry and a plate of naan.

"Indian food. Yum!"

"I hope this isn't too delicate for your Midwestern palate," he teased.

"Please," I snorted. "Indian curry is practically mainstream. We have a thriving immigrant population in my oma's town. There is a factory out there, and tech engineers, usually Indian, Bangladeshi, or Eastern European, would rotate through. Oma would always invite new arrivals to our house for Thanksgiving or the holidays. She said that it was a good way to learn about your neighbors. She believed that there was always room for one more. A lot of times, they would bring their traditional food with them there. My oma loved it. She never met food she didn't love. She was a big woman, but she had a big heart."

Jack handed me a box of tissue, because I was crying into the curry.

"You were really close to her."

"Yeah," I said. "She raised me. My parents were checked out. This is my first Christmas without her. It just feels empty and lonely. I don't even know what I'm going to do on Christmas. Now I'm the stray with nowhere to go."

"You can stay with me," Jack said, sounding slightly hesitant. "Not that I'm doing anything. My brothers will be back from Harvard. Last year I ordered Chinese food, and we played video games."

"That is, like, the saddest Christmas ever," I said, blowing my nose.

"You are such a Christmas snob," he said, feeding me little bites of curry.

"I'm not a snob," I said around the food.

"You are," he said, kissing me. "The sexiest Christmas snob."

CHAPTER 46

Jack

The next morning, after kissing Chloe goodbye, I headed to the Platinum Provisions tower. It had been a nice surprise to see her, even though she clearly wasn't impressed with my offer to spend Christmas with me and my brothers.

Before a meeting with the marketing team, I took the bag with the broken piper to the engineers.

"Can you guys help me figure out what happened?" I asked one man. "This exploded all over a baker, burning her with hot caramel."

The engineer hissed as I took out the device and laid it on his desk.

"To me, it looks like the pressure was too much, but I don't understand how that happened," he said. "We performed rigorous stress testing on this device."

"We have product out there on the shelves," I said. "If people believe that our baking tools maim people, then we will lose not only that business but our medical supply business."

"I'll look into it," the engineer said.

Later that day, after my meetings had concluded, Greg called me.

"I heard there was an accident," he said.

"We're investigating it," I assured him.

"This tower is too much of a distraction. You could lose everything with Platinum Provisions," he told me.

"I have it under control."

"I highly doubt that," Greg said.

Chloe was in my penthouse when I returned. I had given her the key pad code to go there and work on the muffins. I had to admit, it was comforting to have her there when I returned. The penthouse also smelled amazing, which was an added bonus.

"I'm making the soup muffins," she called out, "and fancy sugar cookies."

I snagged a muffin off the tray.

"You know, I shouldn't keep seeing you," she said. "Dana told me not to."

"Yet here you are."

"I couldn't leave you hanging. I promised to make muffins for bribing Mark Holbrook."

"Bribery is such a strong word," I said, kissing the back of her neck.

Then I tested the muffins.

"These are perfect," I said, eating a reddish-looking muffin with little cheese crouton pieces on it. "It tastes just like grilled cheese and tomato soup."

"Hence the name!" she said with a wink.

I ate more muffins until she slapped my hand away.

"I hope this is enough," she said, gesturing to the muffins.

"French-onion soup, potato-cheddar-and-bacon soup, and grilled-cheese-and-tomato soup," I said, listing the muffins. "I think it's plenty." I kissed her, then let her go and watched her put the sugar cookies carefully in little clear cellophane bags.

"Are these snowflakes?" I asked, holding up one of the cookies and inspecting it. "Hey, that's my tower! You must have spent a lot of time on this." The snowflake had a perfect drawing in delicate lines of icing depicting my tower and said FROST TOWER in loopy cursive.

"I hope this is enough to win you the contract," she said, taking the cookie from me.

Chloe fluffed up the tissue paper in a large box. There were little cutouts to hold each muffin. I watched as she carefully placed a variety of them inside the box, added another cardboard layer, and filled it with muffins too. She put a final layer of tissue paper on top and placed a card with little drawings and the names of the three different muffins in the same cursive script.

"This is an insane level of detail," I said, looking at the card.

"I wish I had made more," she fretted. "A variety of three is hardly a variety."

"It's perfect," I assured her.

She carefully closed the box and tabbed it with clear stickers that had little snowflakes on them. The box also said FROST TOWER. She put the little white box of the large snowflake cookies on top and tied the whole thing together with blue and silver ribbons.

"This is amazing," I told her.

"I'm taking a picture," she said, "because I think it looks fabulous, but don't worry. I'm not going to post it online."

I kissed her on her neck and nose and forehead and mouth.

"You are amazing. You're going to be the talk of the town when you open your restaurant."

"Bakery," she corrected. "I don't think I can handle a restaurant. That's a lot of work. I just want a cute little bakery."

The doorbell rang. Eddie was there with a courier.

"You have a car, right? I don't want these balanced on your bike handlebars," Chloe said as she handed the man the boxes. "Do not, under any circumstances, drop, tip over, or otherwise jostle those baked goods. Here's an extra muffin for your trouble."

The courier left with a big smile on his face as he munched on the muffin. Chloe dropped onto the couch.

"Thank you," I told her, sitting down next to her.

"Don't thank me until something is signed," she warned. "I want your tower to be successful."

"You are seriously the best thing that has ever happened to me," I told her.

She yawned. "You can thank me after I take a nap."

"You can't nap yet," I said. "I have something for you that you're going to love."

CHAPTER 47

Chloe

 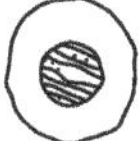 

"I wanted to do something nice for you," Jack said and came into the room carrying a stack of big white boxes.

I opened one, and inside was a slinky little black dress. The additional boxes held heels and a silvery-grey cape and hat in the same fur as the coat he had bought me.

"You have to stop buying me this stuff!" I exclaimed. "I'm a baker. The flour and dough will ruin these clothes! They're so nice. I really don't know where I'm going to wear them. I had pinned them as more aspirational than anything. I was feeling very *Breakfast at Tiffany's* that day."

Jack grinned. "Funny you should say that because…" He pulled out an envelope, "I have tickets to *The Nutcracker*."

"*The Nutcracker*! I love *The Nutcracker*!" I said, jumping up and down in delight. "We're actually going to see it! Jack, this is amazing! And you claim you don't like Christmas."

"I actually won them in a contest I didn't even know I had entered." He sounded a little sheepish.

"Hey, no harm in that. It means the universe likes you and wants to send good things your way."

I showered and changed then slipped on the fancy clothes.

Jack wrapped the cape around my shoulders. "You look very elegant."

I sighed as I looked at myself in the mirror.

"I feel very Audrey Hepburn," I stated.

The outfit was exactly as I had imagined it when I saw it on Pinterest. Jack was dapper in a tux minus the bow tie. He looked elegant but not fussy.

There were cameras outside taking pictures of people as we entered the luxurious theater. Jack scowled.

"I hope Dana doesn't see this," I told him.

"I don't care what Dana thinks," Jack said. "This evening is about you and me."

The Nutcracker was perfect. It was a far cry from the community-theater version that had been put on in my town. They had arranged it differently too. It was staged more like a historical drama—Clara was an Austrian princess about to take the throne, the prince, Alexei, was her lover, and the Rat King was her traitorous uncle who kidnapped Clara in order to take the throne for himself.

The nutcracker was simply a toy, which Clara broke apart and dropped like breadcrumbs for Prince Alexei to follow. The international dances actually had meaning. During every dance, we saw Clara drop a piece of the nutcracker out of the carriage as her uncle forced her through this or that country. In pursuit, Prince Alexei came by later and collected the dropped pieces. Watching the hero searching for his lost love, I started to tear up. I had never seen anything so clever or so poignant.

As the dancers bowed and curtsied, I dabbed tears from my eyes and blew my nose.

"I brought you here to have a good time, not to cry," Jack said jokingly.

"It was so perfect," I told him. "Everything was perfect."

He looked thoughtful and a little sad. "My sister loved *The Nutcracker*. My parents never took us, so this is the first time I've seen it live. My mother didn't want Belle to be obsessed with girl things. She wanted her to be a scientist like she was. So she purposefully never indulged Belle's more feminine inclinations, as she called it. "

I was about to tell him how horrible that was when the conductor came over.

"I had to introduce myself, Mr. Frost, and make the acquaintance of your lovely lady."

A shorter man had come over with the conductor, and he introduced himself as the president of the ballet center.

"Mr. Frost has recently become a very generous benefactor," he told me.

Jack looked embarrassed. "I only contributed a small donation in my sister's name."

"I'm so sorry for your loss," the conductor said.

"She's not dead," Jack said irritably. "Just gone. I think she's in Thailand."

"Ah." Awkward.

"The performance was beautiful," I said enthusiastically.

"So wonderful to see someone moved to tears," the conductor said, taking my hand. "That's all we ask for as an artist, isn't it? I believe you are a pastry chef, so you have an idea of what I speak."

“I don’t make things that are all that fancy,” I demurred.

“On the contrary, I am a big fan of your show,” he said. “The Middle Ages dessert—it was inspired!”

“My wife and I religiously watch *The Great Christmas Bake-Off*,” said the president of the center. “Come, let me take you on a tour of the theater if you’re so inclined.”

“I’d love to,” I said, looking at Jack, who nodded.

The conductor bid us farewell, and the president took us around the theater, showing us the backstage area, explaining the various priceless art pieces displayed around the building, and taking us up to the roof to look out over the skyline.

“This was a perfect evening,” I said to Jack, giving him a peck on the lips.

“It’s not over yet,” he said. He tilted my head up and kissed me like he meant it. When he drew back, it was like being in one of those old Dentine Ice commercials; I could see the steam in the air between us.

“What do you mean?” I said, a little breathless.

“I have a very fancy hotel booked.”

“But who will take care of Milo?” I exclaimed. “He’ll be all alone.”

He looked at me a moment. “It’s cute that you’re so concerned about Milo. I have Liam coming to stay with him. I’m going to have you all to myself the rest of the night. And,” he added thoughtfully, “tomorrow morning too.”

I smiled at him. A car drove up, and he pulled me in beside him. It was decadent, riding in the back of a limo down Fifth Avenue. Jack poured me a small glass of champagne, but I barely touched it since we could barely keep our hands off each other for the duration of the ride.

The limo stopped, and the driver coughed loudly, then knocked on the partition.

"We're decent!" I called, hastily straightening my dress. Jack turned his laugh into a cough.

When Jack helped me out of the car, I saw we had arrived in front of a historic-looking hotel.

"Mr. Frost," the manager said, greeting us. "And…"

"My girlfriend," Jack said forcefully. I didn't know how to feel about that. He squeezed my hand. It was a bit presumptuous. But then, he was attractive, and this was a nice hotel.

"Here is your room," the manager said after we followed him to one of the top floors.

I gasped. The whole suite had been decorated for Christmas. Real garlands were draped everywhere, and there was even a tree that glittered with little white lights that reflected off the sparkling glass ornaments.

"Wow!" I exclaimed. "This is how I want to decorate your penthouse." There was a tray laid out with light snacks, and Jack poured us glasses of Prosecco.

"You don't have to cook," Jack said. "There's room service."

I giggled, and Jack gave me a confused look.

"You look so proud of yourself! This is amazing. And they have cookies." I laughed.

"Not as good as yours," Jack said.

"You like my cookies, Mr. Frost?" I said playfully, grabbing him by the nape of his neck and dragging him down to crush his mouth to mine.

CHAPTER 48

Jack

I was so happy Chloe liked the room. It was a lot of Christmas for my taste, but it didn't come across as kitschy at least.

"I can't believe you did all this for me," she said. She hopped between kissing me, taking pictures, and exploring the excessively large suite.

"There's a whole living room with a piano!" she called out. "I can't believe this is a hotel suite. I haven't even found the bedroom."

I picked her up in my arms and kissed her. "Let me take you there." One of her shoes clunked to the floor as I walked her through the suite. "Nope, that's not the bedroom." It was another small office.

Chloe was giggling.

"That's not the bedroom either," I remarked as I went into another bathroom. Then I found stairs. "Maybe it's up here."

There were two bedrooms and an enormous bathroom on the second floor. I set Chloe on the bed, and she struck a sexy little pose. I kicked off my shoes and pulled off my jacket as I kissed her.

"Don't rip it!" she exclaimed as I pushed at her dress.

"You know," I said, kissing her breasts through the fabric, "you keep telling me not to rip your stuff, but I don't think I ever have."

"That time when I was"—she stopped speaking to moan—"when I was wearing that little candy cane outfit."

"Are you talking about the one with the crotch missing?" I said. "Yeah, I liked that outfit. I didn't rip it though. You were spilling out of it. In multiple places."

My hand was under the dress now. I just wanted to tear the fabric off of her. She made little whimpering noises, moving almost inadvertently against my hand, seeking the friction.

I hitched the dress up so she could splay her legs, giving me better access. I pulled her panties down. They were soaked from the slickness between her legs.

"You really want me," I marveled, pushing two fingers inside of her, a third on her clit. "I love how wet you get for me."

She gasped as I stroked her.

"If I didn't know any better, I would say you want me to fuck you," I said mildly.

"Please!" she moaned.

"That's what I'm doing," I said, bending down to kiss her, my tongue tracing around her mouth.

I could seriously do this all night, sit there fully clothed, teasing her, touching her. I unzipped her dress. It fell down, exposing her tits, and I reached out, letting my other hand pinch and roll the hard nipple between my fingers.

"I want..." she panted, her hands running over my chest and down to my crotch.

I unzipped my pants. "Is this what you want?"

"I need you," she said.

My cock was rock hard and fully erect when I stripped off my boxer briefs. I wanted her, but more than that, I wanted to give her the most intense pleasure of her life, to make her mine, and to make sure she never wanted to leave me.

I rolled on a condom and rubbed my cock between her legs, teasing her. Chloe moaned, her hips arching up, inviting me in. I couldn't resist the invitation, and I pushed into her. I was rewarded with a cry from deep in her throat.

"That feels so good!" she gasped.

I fucked her for a few minutes then withdrew.

"Why did you stop?" she panted, reaching for me.

"I want to feel all of you," I said as I took off her dress the rest of the way and the lacy black bra underneath. Kissing the curves of her body, I shrugged off my shirt, then I pressed her to me and pushed back inside of her. She clung to me as I fucked her, each thrust telling her she was mine, that I needed her and wanted her and couldn't live without her.

The next morning, the hotel staff discreetly left breakfast out.

"Yum, eggs Benedict," Chloe said. "I'm starving. You definitely gave me a workout last night."

I felt a satisfied smile creep up my face.

After making more use of the hotel's bed, we went back to Frost Tower later that morning. It was the weekend, so we didn't have to rush.

As we walked through the lobby of the hotel, Chloe said, "I wish we had a change of clothes. I feel like I'm doing the walk of shame."

"You look fine."

"People are judging me."

A woman ran over to Chloe.

"Chloe! Oh my God! I love you!" the woman grabbed Chloe in a hug. "I love your show and your Instagram." She turned to look at me and clapped a hand over her mouth. "Is that—"

"He's just a ghost," Chloe chirped. "Nothing to see here."

The woman gave her an exaggerated wink. "I totally feel ya. Selfie?"

"Do you want me to take it?" I offered.

"It's a selfie," Chloe said. "The people in it have to take it."

They made duck faces for the pictures.

"You look so chic!" the woman gushed. "Very New York." She seemed like she could carry on for hours, but I didn't want to be there all day.

"Chloe. Can we?"

"Sorry! It was great to meet you."

Chloe seemed tense as the car stopped in front of the tower. She looked around almost nervously.

"I don't think Hartleigh is out here," I told her. "Besides, I have Eddie to keep her away."

Eddie was passed out at the security desk when we walked in.

"So much for that," Chloe said.

When we walked into the penthouse and discovered Liam was lounging on the couch with Milo, Chloe asked, "Did you have a nice boys' night?"

"Look who's back! You guys are all over the internet," Liam said, jumping up to greet us.

"Dana's going to be mad," Chloe said, biting her lip.

Liam chuckled. "She's a Holbrook. They're always up in arms about something. They're even more uptight than Jack."

"I don't know if we've formally met," Chloe said, offering her hand for Liam to shake.

Liam swept her up into a hug. "You're basically family now! Also, I ate all your soup muffins and the leftover cookies. Jack can tell you the way to my heart is food. Especially sweets."

"You like sweets!" Chloe said excited. "Jack doesn't really."

"I love desserts," Liam said solemnly. "Crème brûlée, anything chocolate, cookies, cake. I will eat it all."

"You're lucky your teeth haven't fallen out," I remarked.

"I eat a lot of fish, and I've never had a cavity," Liam said. "And I floss."

Chloe and I spent a quiet night together after Liam left. Simply lounging next to her as she ate popcorn and watched Christmas movies made me the happiest I'd been in a long time.

Unfortunately, real life had to intrude. The next morning was another bake-off challenge. Chloe woke up early, and before she left, I grabbed her hand.

"If Dana gives you trouble, tell me."

CHAPTER 49

Chloe

The weekend with Jack had been magical, but now I was back in reality. At least my reality included cookies and sugar and chocolate, so it wasn't all that bad. I smiled to myself, thinking about Jack. He had called me his girlfriend. I giggled as I triple-checked all my equipment.

Dana wasn't the one I was worried about. The only reason she had said anything to me was because of Hartleigh. Nina swore she had slept in front of our bedroom door to keep Hartleigh from tampering with our stuff, but I was paranoid.

"This is the Twelve Days to Christmas challenge," Anastasia announced. "We have less than two weeks to go until the big night, and we want to mark the festivities with a countdown. This is going to be a grueling challenge, which is why we're starting early. Judges, do you have anything to add?"

"The key to this challenge," Anu said, "is that you have to make twelve distinct desserts. But they cannot be too disparate—they should build off of and complement each other. It will be quite difficult, I think."

"Yes, but these bakers can handle it," Nick said.

"Once again, you have all day to complete this challenge," Anastasia said. "Pace yourselves."

The four of us contestants left—Nina, Maria, Hartleigh, and me—hustled to start baking. I heard Maria tell Anastasia she was making some little fried pastries among other things.

Instead of making a set of large desserts, I wanted to serve the judges tastes of twelve desserts. I decided to make my twelve desserts constructed on a spoon, essentially one bite of flavor. They should range from more salty desserts to sweet, with maybe even a piece of candy for the last one. The first spoon would be cheese and fruit, which was what people in Europe sometimes served instead of a sweet dessert after dinner.

So that I wasn't just serving a piece of cheese, I decided to make a sherry reduction to drizzle over the cheese. Next in the lineup would be a mini cheese soufflé topped with cranberry compote. Another spoon I knew would be chocolate mousse. The next would be orange shortbread with a custard. I wasn't sure what the others would be. Maybe an ice cream? I should have been thinking about this instead of spending so much time with Jack. I looked over at the judges' table.

He was about to leave, but he was lingering, looking at me, a possessive light in his eyes. When he saw me watching, he grinned and licked his bottom lip. I shivered slightly.

Because the mousse needed to set, I started on it first. The custard also needed to set, so I made that next. For the rest of the day, I worked on making various cakes and little tarts that I cooked in one of the wide spoons. I tasted one, and it seemed all right.

Hartleigh was skipping around the studio, flitting from the fridge to the fryer to the pantry. I tried to ignore her and concentrate on my desserts. Unfortunately, I wasn't happy with the way they turned out, and Hartleigh's nonsense was adding to my irritation. The progression of my dessert bites was not convincing—they were all somewhat soft. The tart provided a little more crunch, but maybe it was all too one-dimensional.

When I looked at the clock, I saw we didn't have much time left. I hastily made a tempura batter and dipped some fruit in it, then made some little round pies.

"Are you frying those?" Nina asked me.

"Yes, I think my spoons don't have enough diversity of texture. I wish I had planned a bit better," I confessed to her.

"Too busy with Jack?" she teased.

I smiled to myself, remembering just how much of a distraction Jack was.

"Something like that," I said and took the platter of my additions over to the fryer and started adjusting the temperature.

Maria walked behind me a moment later. She had a large tray of pastries to fry.

"I need to deep fry some of my desserts," I said to Maria. "I'll be quick—I just want to try something out—but I don't want to mess up your frying schedule."

She chewed on her lip. "But I've been waiting for Hartleigh to finish. But you have less, so go ahead," she told me.

"No, no," I said. I set my plate down. "Here, I'll help you."

Maria smiled at me gratefully and dropped in the first few pastries.

The fryer immediately went up in flames.

Maria screamed and jumped back, banging into me, causing the large tray of pastries to scatter all over the floor. One of the production techs ran over with a fire extinguisher and sprayed white foam over the fryer and us.

Coughing, I wafted the smoke and chemical mist away from my face and looked at the carnage.

"It's ruined!" Maria cried, her eyes wide and wet with tears. She and I were both covered in little flecks of white foam, and I wrapped her in a hug.

"It's okay," I told her.

"My dessert is ruined!" she sobbed.

"You'll make more," I said, trying to be consoling. Would she, though? The fryer was obviously out of commission.

"What am I going to do? This was my whole dish!"

I petted her head. I at least could pivot a little more easily. Maria had had hours of work ruined.

Zane and the other camera guys roamed around taking footage of the dessert carnage on the floor, our dirty clothes, and Maria's tear-stained face.

The fire department showed up, the men dressed in heavy boots and protective gear. Jack was right behind them.

"Are you all right?" he asked me, holding me gingerly. I was covered in batter, fruit filling, and fire extinguisher foam.

"I'm fine," I said. "Everything's fine. You didn't have to come here. There's no fire."

"The alarm company calls me whenever there's an emergency," he said. "I'm still trying to secure tenants, and it wouldn't look good if I wasn't on the premises."

Gunnar hurried over with the fire marshal, and Jack left me to confer with them.

"You all need to evacuate the premises," the fire marshal said loudly.

"Is that really necessary?" Dana asked. "We are in the middle of filming."

"I have a smoke-evacuation system in place," Jack said. "This building was designed to handle small industrial incidents. See?" The smoke and mist that had gathered were being sucked out by the huge fans in the ceiling.

Jack handed the fire marshal a tablet. "This is the information on the system. I already explained when going through the permitting process that my tenants cannot be expected to evacuate whenever there is a minor incident. That's why I spent millions of dollars putting this system in place."

The fire marshal seemed skeptical as he read through the literature. I wondered if the contest would be called off.

"Fine," the marshal said at last, "but I'm leaving one of my men here. And you will of course be paying the department for his time."

"Of course," Jack said smoothly.

As Jack and Dana went to work out details with the fire marshal and his man, Gunnar scowled and turned to us.

"Maria, what happened?" he snapped. "You're supposed to be able to use a deep fryer without burning down the studio."

Maria only sobbed harder.

"It was my fault, so stop yelling at her," I said. "I set the fryer, and it should have been fine. I don't understand what happened."

"Go change," Gunnar said in disgust. "Three more episodes. We only had to last three more episodes."

Across the room, Hartleigh was watching the commotion with a self-satisfied smile.

As I changed, I fumed about Jack's stalker. "She did something to the fryer," I hissed to Nina when I returned to the studio.

"Of course she did," my friend snorted. "How are you going to prove anything, though?"

Jack was cold and professional as he dealt with the fallout of the fire.

"I love a man in a suit, don't you?" Hartleigh said as she walked past me. "He's so dashing and protective."

"Stay away from him," I told her.

She smiled at me. "Shame about that deep fryer. Those things are finicky, aren't they?"

CHAPTER 50

By the time I finished filling out paperwork with the fire department and dealing with the insurance company, it was time to judge the contest. The contestants looked frazzled—everyone except for Hartleigh, that is. She seemed rather pleased with herself.

Hartleigh was the first to present, and Anu and Nick seemed to think her dessert was passable. She made a set of little miniature cakes, which I said I hated on principle.

"It's bland," I told Hartleigh. "And boring. You had an entire day to make twelve desserts. These are all just cakes."

"Yes, Jack, but they're different," she said.

"Not that different," I replied, pushing away the plate. "It's not impressive."

She should have been sent home, but unfortunately Maria hadn't even finished her dish. She presented us with three little pastries each.

"I really like them," I told her. She looked like she was going to cry any minute.

"So there was a fire," Nick stated.

"Yes," Maria replied. "Most of my desserts were ruined."

"I sympathize, I really do," Anu said. "It can be chaotic in the kitchen, but you can't fall apart. You have to pivot and keep going. What you made is very good, but you didn't complete the challenge."

Chloe presented us with little spoons each holding a bite of dessert. I thought it was very clever.

"This is very good," Nick said after tasting each one. "I believe you also lost several hours of work in the fire."

"Yes," Chloe said, "unfortunately."

"I wish we could have tasted what you had planned," Anu said. "Your array of sampling is smart, but it needed some more salty, fried types of foods to offset these softer, sweeter foods."

"I completely agree," said Chloe.

"Nina's dish was most complete, I think," Nick said after we sampled Nina's shot-glass dessert samples.

"I like the way she used the shot glasses, but not everything was like a parfait," Anu remarked. "Some desserts were balanced on top of the glass, some on a skewer in the glass. It was a nice way to present it, and everything was well done. There was a balance of flavor and texture."

Nina was declared the winner, and Maria was sent home. Chloe hugged her as we told her the news.

"I'm sorry, Maria. You're a great pastry chef," Anu said, "but you can't lose your head. Bad things will happen, that's just life. You have to shrug it off and just keep baking."

Maria nodded, and we all shook her hand.

In the lobby outside of the studio afterward, I wrapped my arms around Chloe.

"Come upstairs when you're done," I told her.

"Okay," she murmured. I could still smell burnt sugar in her hair.

"I'm so tired," Chloe groaned when I let her into my apartment.

I picked her up, kissing her. "You had a hard day," I said and carried her into the bathroom.

"You're the best," she told me, punctuating the words with kisses. When she saw the tub filled up, she immediately stripped and stepped into the warm water.

I wanted her, but she seemed like she wanted to relax.

"I'm having my engineers look at the fryer," I told her. Her face had a sour look for a moment. I smoothed out her features, running my fingers lightly over her face. I would never get tired of having her in my penthouse.

Chloe half dozed as she soaked in the bath. I kissed her in between running my hands over her temples and shoulders. Every so often, I would let one hand go farther down, caressing her breast.

When the water started to cool, I wrapped Chloe up in a blanket, and she sat on my couch drying her hair. I had sushi and a yakitori noodle dish ordered in.

"Sorry Liam ate all the desserts you made," I said as I unpacked the bag of food Eddie had delivered, "but there's Japanese food."

"That's for the best," Chloe said. "I think even I could use a break from sugar. It was a lot today."

"Say it isn't so!" I exclaimed.

We shared the food, and after we finished, she yawned, her jaw cracking.

"I should Instagram," she said, closing her eyes and resting against me. "But I'm so tired."

She was half asleep when I carried her to bed and wrapped around her while she slept.

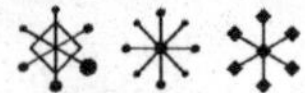

I woke to someone kissing me. Chloe was straddling me, and I let my hands come up and rest on her hips. She was a delicious weight on top of me.

"Good morning," she said. "I spent all night with you, and I didn't even see your cock."

That got my attention.

"I know you wanted another taste of my cookies last night," she purred.

"I did," I said, letting my hand drift under her shirt to cup one of the round, perfect breasts. She slowly ground her hips against mine. I could feel the wetness through her panties. The smell of her lust was driving me wild. My hand drifted between her legs.

"You want me, don't you," I said, pushing aside her panties and stroking her. The heat from her was invigorating my erection. I stroked her as she ground against me, her hips rising and falling.

I want this every morning for the rest of my life, I thought as she rolled a condom onto me.

CHAPTER 51

Chloe

A whimper escaped my lips as Jack slid his cock into me.

"Your pussy is so tight," he groaned. He sounded as if he was about to lose control, but he maintained a steady rhythm. My nails raked down his chest, catching on the ridges of muscle, as Jack rocked me down on him, our skin sliding together.

Jack flipped us over, his thrusts growing more erratic. I knotted my fingers in his hair, tilting his head down to kiss him. His dick was hot and thick, and my legs were splayed, my hips arched, begging him to claim me. I was lost in the sensation, moaning and dizzy and surrounded by Jack. I bit his shoulder when I came, and he thrust a few times more, milking the aftershocks from my too-sensitive skin.

After Jack had me good and fully awake, I made him breakfast then baked more of his favorite cookies.

"Don't you want me to make something different?" I asked him.

He looked horrified, his mouth full of cookies. "No!" he said after swallowing. "Why would you even suggest that?"

I snuggled next to him on the couch, talking with fans on social media while he took a conference call. I was pressed up against him; he had a blanket draped over us. The door to the balcony was open, and Milo lay half inside and half out. The air coming into the penthouse was chilly, but it was warm under the blanket. Jack kissed me then nuzzled my neck.

I shrieked. "Your nose is cold!"

"I want you," he said, leaning in to kiss me.

My phone started ringing.

"I've been summoned," I told him, waving my phone. "Dana wants to talk to us."

Dana was waiting impatiently in the tower lobby.

I bumped my hip to Nina's in greeting. She ignored me—she was glaring at Hartleigh.

"She stole Maria's spot," she said angrily.

"The show has blown up," Dana said. "It's viral. Everyone is talking about it. All the morning shows want you all to be guests."

"That's wonderful news!" Hartleigh said, clapping her hands together. "It's all thanks to you."

Nina made a gagging noise, and Hartleigh glared at her.

"Just dust leftover from the fire," Nina said with a fake smile.

"*They* are calling *us*!" Dana continued, giddy. "Do you have any idea how rare that is? This is totally organic and totally unprompted."

"So now we are expected to make TV appearances?" I muttered to Nina.

"You will be compensated, of course, for your time," Dana said, looking at me.

"If I'm paid, I'll do anything," I said loudly.

"I know you will," Hartleigh growled, "including other people's boyfriends."

"Jack is not your boyfriend!" I yelled.

"He's not yours either!" she screeched. "He is going to marry me. His parents don't even like you."

Even though I knew Jack had said he had a bad relationship with his parents, Hartleigh's words stung.

She smiled triumphantly when she saw my expression. "I hear these things. We're very close. They already think of me as their daughter-in-law," she said.

"She's lying," Nina said. "You're such a horrible person, Hartleigh. I know you sabotaged the deep fryer."

"Girls!" Dana yelled. "I swear, I should have been a middle school teacher. Stop fighting over men and stop blaming each other. We have a packed schedule for the next few days for your TV appearances. And you all have to try to act friendly in front of the cameras. Understood?"

We spent the rest of the day going from show to show. During most of our appearances, they wanted us to do a little baking demonstration. They also wanted to talk about Jack.

"How is it to have Jack Frost as a judge?" one host asked.

"I wouldn't mind having him judge my cookies!" her cohost joked, and the audience roared in laughter.

"Are the rumors true?" another talk show host asked me.

"Excuse me?" I choked out.

"About you and Jack having a relationship," she said.

A picture of us at *The Nutcracker* came up, then several more pictures of us together.

"I… we're just… I was just working on a side baking project for him," I said lamely.

"Oh, a *side* project," the host said, exaggeratingly winking at the camera.

"They aren't together," Hartleigh said snottily. "Besides, Jack has too much integrity to let any previous relationship affect his impartiality as a judge. He and I grew up together, we're very good friends. Our parents want us to get married. Hopefully we will start a family soon one day." She preened for the camera.

"So, you two have a history?" the host said, turning her attention to Hartleigh. "Can you tell us, what was Jack Frost like as a kid?"

"I cannot believe her," I fumed to Nina after filming the segment.

"Everyone will see that she's clearly insane," Nina said. "Besides, Jack's is the only opinion you should care about."

We filmed several more segments, including a couple that evening for the late-night talk shows.

I was tired, and my feet hurt when we returned to the tower.

"Don't forget," Dana said as we walked out of the cold into the lobby. "You all need to be down here at three thirty in the morning to go on the early-morning shows. Wear something cute. The crew people there will do your makeup, so have a fresh face."

Eddie came out from behind the security desk. Hartleigh scowled and skittered to the elevator. Eddie, with an unfocused look in his eyes, watched her, then swiveled towards me, almost losing his balance.

"Package," he said. He reeked of alcohol. If Mark Holbrook did rent space in the tower, Jack was going to have to find a new security guard—though Hartleigh seemed to find him disgusting, so that was one plus in Eddie's favor, I supposed.

He pushed a large box towards me. I thanked him and took it upstairs.

"Open it," Nina said. "I want to see what the outfit is. I bet Jack is going to be very happy."

I opened the box. Instead of a fun outfit, there were handcuffs, a rope, and a gag along with a typed note about tying me up like a Christmas present. It was all a bit sinister. I threw the package and its contents in the trash after taking a picture for evidence.

"You need to tell Jack," Nina said seriously. "And the police."

"This stuff is probably just from Hartleigh," I said, laughing it off. "She's trying to worm her way inside of my head and throw me off my game."

"Maybe, or maybe you have a stalker."

CHAPTER 52

Jack

Mark called me while I was in my office at Platinum Provisions.

"I talked it over with my board," he said, "and we would like to proceed with negotiations for leasing space in Frost Tower."

"That is great news," I said, trying not to sound as giddy as a kid on Christmas.

"Under one condition," Mark warned.

"Anything."

"The restaurant in the ground-floor retail space."

"I'm working on finding a tenant," I promised.

"We want Chloe. Her muffins were a big hit. My cousin Grant gave my brother Carter a black eye fighting over the last of the French onion soup muffins. Also, all the women in my family adored the cookies. They spent about an hour photographing them then carefully eating them. They looked great, but I didn't want to risk my health asking for a bite. Chloe is a huge draw, and we need her to be there baking and cooking."

"Of course, she does want to open a bakery, so she would be delighted, I'm sure," I told him. I stood up to pace around my office. I could barely contain my energy.

"No, you don't understand," Mark said. "A café is not sufficient. We need a full restaurant similar to the Japanese restaurant you have in the Platinum Provisions tower."

"Wouldn't you rather have a restaurant from a proven restauranteur? I know Nick Mazur, he has several successful restaurants, and I'm sure he would be glad to open one in Frost Tower."

"No," Mark said. "The same fifteen people run all the restaurants in this city. I'm sick of corporate restaurant food that all tastes the same. I've informed you of my needs if I am to relocate my company to your tower. If you can't manage to secure one girl to run a restaurant then you may cause people to wonder what else you are incapable of doing, Mr. Frost."

"I can of course accommodate you, Mr. Holbrook. Chloe would be glad to open a restaurant," I said. I knew Chloe had told me she hadn't wanted to run a full-service restaurant, that her dream was a franchise of cute little bakeries. But I needed her to open a restaurant so that Mark would lease space in my tower. I would have to broach this with her carefully. She might be mad if I just told her right off the bat that I had pinned all my hopes and dreams on her running a restaurant.

Mark asked, "I am looking forward to it. Her muffins were—"

"I need more of those muffins!" another voice said.

"Carter, go away! I'm on a call!" came Mark's muffled voice.

There was the sound of a scuffle, then I heard Carter shout into the phone, "I bet she can cook if she's living in your penthouse, Jack. We did research on Chloe, and she hasn't been in New York City that long. So either she's a witch and working a spell on you, or she's feeding you something amazing. Sex is magical, but not enough to have someone move in and play Christmas shows while having crazy loud—"

"Shut up, Carter!" I heard Mark yell at his brother. I wasn't sure if I should end the phone call.

"That's what you said, isn't it, Mark?" I heard Carter say in a voice that sounded farther away. "They were having sex while watching *Rudolph the Red-Nosed—*"

"What the hell is wrong with you, Carter?" I heard Mark say. Then his voice became clearer. I assumed he had regained control of the phone.

"My apologies," Mark said. "My brother is a bit of a loose cannon. But yes, if Chloe can open a restaurant, that is what we will need. I have to attract a certain type of talent to grow my company, and Chloe's restaurant would be a big draw for recruitment. I know it can take a while, what with the health department, but I trust you can make this happen."

"Yes, it's already in the works," I lied.

After I ended the phone call, I yelled, "Yes! My tower is saved!" And it was all thanks to Chloe and her amazing cookies. After this, I would never say a bad thing about sweets ever again.

Chloe was sitting cross-legged on my couch drawing that afternoon when I returned. I pulled her up into a hug.

"You are the best thing that has ever happened to me. Mark just called me," I said between kisses. "He wants to rent the tower in large part because of your muffins and cookies."

"Oh, I don't think it was all that. You have a nice tower," she said. "And I'm sure you offered him pretty competitive rent for the city, since you're trying to find tenants."

"All he did was rave about your cooking."

She blushed and mumbled, "I just bake stuff."

"It's transformative," I told her. She was acting bashful. I didn't want to bring up that I had promised Mark she would run a restaurant. It seemed like a lot to spring on someone. I needed to build up to it slowly.

"You were a hit on the morning shows," I told her.

"I plugged Platinum Provisions for you," she said.

"That's because you're always looking out for me," I said and kissed her.

"What are you sketching?" I asked, looking at the notebook that rested beside her on the couch.

"Just some ideas for the gingerbread house challenge."

"That's the next one?" I asked, kissing her again. She always tasted slightly sweet.

"You know," she said, not quite looking at me.

My heart dropped a minute. She couldn't be breaking up with me, could she?

"I was thinking. I wanted to have a Christmas party, just something small, I just… I love Christmas and I could decorate your penthouse. You wouldn't have to do anything," she said in a rush. "We could invite your siblings." She sighed and looked up at the ceiling. "Wait, never mind, ignore me, I'm tired."

"Yes," I said. "Have the party."

"No, you don't like Christmas."

"You should have a Christmas party," I insisted.

"Are you sure?"

I kissed her. "Yes," I said against her mouth.

She clapped her hands together in delight.

"Under one condition," I said in mock seriousness. "That you bake and cook." Then I mentally kicked myself. "Not because you're, you know, a woman."

"Keep digging that hole there, bud," she said.

"Just you're really good at it."

"I'm just teasing!" she said, laughing and wrapping her arms around my neck. "I know the way to a man's heart—food!"

I grinned at her.

"I'm serious about the party," she said sheepishly.

"And I'm serious about you having it," I told her. "Plan whatever you want."

"Great!" she said then gave me a slightly guilty look. "I just so happen to have some little email invitations ready to go." She opened her laptop. "I have it scheduled for Christmas Eve."

"Go ahead," I said, typing in my brothers' email addresses.

"What about your sister?" She asked. I frowned.

"Not Belle. I'll ask her myself."

Chloe sent the email, then looked at me with concern on her face.

"Are you sure you're okay with this?" she asked.

"I want you to be happy, and if this is what you want—" I told her, taking her hands in mine.

"If it's not what you want…" she mumbled.

"I'll be fine. I'm happy if you're happy," I said firmly. And I wanted her to be happy enough to agree to run the restaurant.

CHAPTER 53

Chloe

"There's nothing that says Christmas more than a gingerbread house," Anastasia said the next day. It was just Nina, Hartleigh, and me in the studio. One of us was going home. It had better be Hartleigh.

I knew Jack liked gingerbread, so I wasn't worried about him hating my dessert. Instead of a gingerbread house, though, I was making a whole village. I wasn't making a traditional Swiss Alps–type village though. I wanted to go all out for Christmas, so my gingerbread town was going to look like Whoville from *The Grinch*. To create that feel, I was going to make little curved roofs and whimsical shapes. Baking the gingerbread itself was easy. I whipped up a quadruple recipe in the giant mixer I had at my station. The air was pungent with cinnamon, cardamom, and nutmeg.

Jack came into the studio for a minute to watch me.

"You're distracting me," I told him. He gave me a look that could melt sugar.

"Jack, don't you want to see what I'm doing?" Hartleigh called.

"Have to run," he said to me. "Good luck."

While the gingerbread was still warm, I cut out the shapes for the buildings. I didn't make the buildings too large; I didn't have time to do an adequate decorating job. I kept them small so the level of detail would be appropriate.

Platinum Provisions made a little press that let you create curved shapes in warm cookie dough, and gingerbread worked very well for it. My gingerbread recipe was different from my gingerbread cookie recipe. The dough I was using for the village was similar to what I used for Pfeffernüsse. It was malleable when it came out of the oven, but once it cooled, it was rigid. It was like biscotti almost. My oma would make them so people could let them swim in their tea or coffee when they came to visit.

I had to work fast with the 3D press to make the roof curves right. Then I lost myself in decorating my gingerbread village. Each little building in my gingerbread village needed to be unique. I used a modified royal icing to glue the gingerbread building pieces together. Once I was satisfied, I began to decorate. The icing piper made it easy to quickly and neatly draw on the little icicles, colorful lights, and whimsical decorations.

I also made various colored fondants to create winding paths, stairs, and a giant Christmas tree (relatively speaking) in the center of town. As I carefully arranged my houses, Anastasia came over, and the cameras that followed my every move panned to her.

"This is a beautiful little village," she cooed.

"My gingerbread village has to be lovely, but it still needs to taste good," I said. "So something unique I'm doing is adding little dipping sauces. Dipping gingerbread in various sauces gives it a different flavor profile and is something fun to do. Some of the chimneys and wells I'm filling with little custards or chocolate sauce or cream cheese dip. There should be something bitter, fruity, or a little sour to cut the sweetness of the gingerbread and the frosting."

"That is unique," said Anastasia, watching as I lined the chimneys and little wells with folded parchment paper. I didn't want the dipping sauces to melt the gingerbread.

I made the sauces, and while they were cooling, I put on the snow. It would look strange to dump powdered sugar over everything, so I used the snow-maker attachment on the air injector pump that Jack had made to my specifications. It made me feel special to use it, and the texture was amazing. It was almost like cotton candy but not. Once I had finished, it really did seem like the whole village had been snowed on. It was magical.

As I surveyed my work, looking for any missed spots, I was so into it that I didn't realize until right as she was behind me that Hartleigh was carrying something dangerously close to my workstation.

"Whoops!" she shrieked. I instinctively flung myself over the village. A cascade of soupy frosting coated my back. I could feel it in my hair, dripping down my neck, and in my eyes. Some of it was dripping on my gingerbread village, but fortunately it seemed mostly okay. It wasn't anything I couldn't fix.

"You did that on purpose!" I hollered at Hartleigh and slapped her. I didn't hit her that hard, but my hand left a pink icing mark on her face.

"You bitch!" she screamed. "It was an accident! Your gingerbread isn't even ruined and you *hit me*!"

"You tried to ruin her village!" Nina yelled.

The camera guys hovered around like flies.

"She hit me!" Hartleigh yelled again. I hoped I wouldn't be thrown out for assault. I was starting to regret striking Hartleigh.

"This is uncalled for!" Dana said as she and Anastasia came over. Anastasia was trying not to laugh.

"This isn't funny," Dana snapped at her. "You three need to cool it. Stay at your own stations."

Hartleigh stomped away.

"Chloe, change, shower, then fix whatever's wrong with your village, and let's go. Are you all almost done? I want this judged, and then one of you is gone," Dana said. "If we weren't making so much money off of this show, I would just end it all right now."

When I returned from toweling off the worst of the frosting, I was able to cover up the little red splatter marks on my town. Nina and Hartleigh put the finishing touches on their gingerbread creations, and I poured my sauces into their holders.

Then it was time to see who the finalists would be.

CHAPTER 54

Jack

When I met with the engineer I had assigned to the faulty piper investigation, he pulled out another piper. Then he unscrewed part of the holder for the liquid, gouged parts of the seal, filled it with frosting, plugged it in, and pressurized it. I heard it vibrate slightly, then it exploded.

"This wasn't a product failure," he said. "Someone tampered with it. I was suspicious when I saw the seal. I thought maybe the broken glass had messed with it, but this seems to mimic what happened."

"Sure looks like it," I said, inspecting the machine.

"Who would tamper with the piper?" the engineer asked. "They're pretty pricy just to destroy it like that."

I knew exactly who. Hartleigh.

I had a few more hours until it was time to return to the tower and judge the competition, but I returned early to talk to Dana. Hartleigh had to be removed from the competition.

She probably had messed with the fryer too. The engineers were still working on it. It wasn't one of our products, so they had to do more research.

But in my gut, I knew the answer.

"Thank goodness you're here," Dana said. "We're moving the judging up early. I can't take these women anymore."

"I need to talk to you about something," I told her.

"Tell me after you judge," she said, prodding me into the studio.

Chloe presented first. She had a pleasant demeanor, but I could tell something was bothering her.

"It's almost too pretty to eat," Anu said, inspecting Chloe's gingerbread village.

"I'll eat it," Nick replied and broke off a piece of a roof. I did the same. The gingerbread was the same spicy, slightly sweet taste I remembered.

"I love what you did with the sauce," Anu said to Chloe.

"I see you used the new Platinum Provisions snowmaker attachment," I said, pointing to the snow.

"That's such a great product," Nick added, scooping up some of the fluffy icing with a piece of gingerbread. He held it up to the camera. "Do you see that consistency? It still is moist, but it's almost whipped. This is a really a great way to pull out interesting textures from icing, which tends to be fairly one-dimensional in texture. Great job!"

While Chloe had made a whole village, Nina had made a very intricate Victorian house.

"It's like an architectural model," Anu marveled. "This is very high-precision work. I'm very impressed." Nina's Victorian gingerbread house had a little garden, too, and delicate sugar fencing.

"How did you make this lacework of the hard caramel so intricate?" Anu asked.

"The icing piper from Platinum Provisions," Nina explained.

"Your company is on a roll," Nick said to me. "I love what you did with the candy, Nina."

"I made all of it myself," Nina said. "I candied the fruits and the citrus peels and hand-made the candy cane lights."

"You can taste the care you put into the gingerbread house. There is also the complexity of flavor," Anu added. "I can taste the flavors of the candy; it's not just stale sugar like what you taste from drugstore sweets."

"And last but not least," Nick said when Hartleigh walked up.

I recognized the house. She had made a gingerbread replica of my childhood home.

I clenched my jaw. I knew she wanted me to say something.

"I made a gingerbread *home*," Hartleigh said, looking intently at me. "A *home* where you can have a family, and a husband. See, there's a Christmas tree inside."

"It's interesting you decorated the inside," Anu said.

Nick pulled off a piece of the house. "The gingerbread is a little dry."

After she walked off, I turned to the other judges. "So Hartleigh is out, correct?"

"I think so," Anu said.

"She's never won a round," Nick said. "She's always been average, and that's just not good enough when you're talking about the finals."

Hartleigh did not take the news well.

"Jack!" she cried, sinking to the floor, "How could you let them do this to me? I trusted you."

Dana had to come into the studio and lead her away.

"Well," Anastasia said. "Clearly emotions are high. It is Christmas, after all. Now we have our final two contestants, Chloe and Nina. The finals are in two days, so rest up."

Chloe left to film more interviews, and I stood up with the rest of the judges, stretching my legs.

Nick turned to me. "See, that's why I don't sleep with employees or contestants."

"I didn't sleep with her," I snarled at him. I was a good head taller than Nick, and he gulped, looking up at me.

"Okay, man, okay, that's cool, man."

When we left the studio, I heard Hartleigh screeching in the interview room.

"I guess you won't be able to film any usable footage of her," I said to Gunnar.

"Are you kidding?" he said. "Crazy people make reality TV. Shoot, I might even give Hartleigh her own spin-off show. She's a pretty controversial character. Haven't you been watching the episodes?"

"No."

"Right, you don't need to," he smirked. "You have the real thing in your apartment."

I looked at him darkly.

"I'm not hating, man, just pointing out a fact," Gunnar said. "Where's your security team? I think Hartleigh is going to have to be escorted off the premises."

Eddie was somewhat sober when I went down to the lobby to tell him to remove Hartleigh.

"So the wicked witch is finally being tossed out!" he said, putting on his Santa hat.

"Can I ask you something, Eddie?" I said. "Why are you wearing that Santa suit?"

He looked at me as if I was crazy. "It's furry and warm. Have you seen how cold it is outside? We're in the middle of December." He shook his head, muttering to himself, as he walked off the elevator.

"Because clearly I'm the crazy one," I said to the empty elevator.

Chloe still seemed busy, so I went back up to my penthouse to collect Milo and take him for a walk. While I let him run around in the park, I called Greg to tell him about Mark Holbrook's offer.

"A Holbrook, huh," Greg said. "If he pays, he can stay."

"He had one condition," I told Greg.

"What's that?"

"He wants Chloe and her restaurant to occupy the retail space."

"I mean, I guess she can have a little bakery cart," Greg said. "It can't hurt anything."

"No, Mark said he wanted her to run a full-service restaurant."

"Absolutely not," Greg said.

"Mark said he wants one, like the Japanese restaurant in the Platinum Provisions tower."

"I don't care," Greg snapped. "I'm in talks with the New York Bread Company and Starbucks."

"Those are chains!" I protested. "I don't want a chain in my tower."

"Your tower?" Greg sneered through the phone. "My company invested in the tower, so really it's *my* tower, and I have the power to negotiate tenant deals in *my tower*."

"Chloe is a good cook," I said through gritted teeth, resisting the urge to throw the phone against a nearby tree.

"Chloe is not a viable solution," Greg said in a clipped tone. "She has no experience running a restaurant. You can go back to Mark Holbrook and tell him Chloe is not opening a restaurant."

The phone clicked. Greg had hung up.

I wasn't going to give up this easily. I was so close. All I had to do was convince Chloe she could run a restaurant, then we would come up with a business plan and present it to Greg. Greg would see the genius of the idea, Mark would sign the lease, my tower would be saved, and Chloe would be with me forever. Easy, right?

Right.

CHAPTER 55

Chloe

"We made it to the finals!" Nina crowed after we finished our interviews. I hadn't been able to clean all the frosting out of my hair. I sighed when I thought about trying to wash it out in our tiny bathroom.

"I'm going to meet a friend for drinks," Nina said as she changed.

I grabbed some clothes. "And I'm going to Jack's to use his shower."

Nina grinned at me. "The only thing that would make Hartleigh's exit more satisfying is if she knew that you had free access to Jack's penthouse."

"I'd rather not poke the bear," I replied.

Jack and Milo weren't there when I went into his penthouse. I decided to go ahead and take a shower. As I was pulling a wide-toothed comb through the tangle of curls to loosen the frosting, Jack surprised me in the shower.

"You're the sexiest baker I have ever met," he breathed.

I was already relaxed and half aroused from the warmth of the shower. His hand stroked me, and then he was inside me. I moaned, feeling lightheaded from the heat and the sensation of him.

"You like my cock, don't you," Jack murmured in my ear as he fucked me. I braced myself against the wall of the large glassed-in shower. He kept two fingers on my clit, stroking and teasing as he moved inside me. I came quickly. Jack continued to thrust in me, fucking me, still stroking me. I came again, and he swore as his body shuddered.

Feeling lightheaded and too warm after the shower sex, this time I was the one to throw open all the windows.

"I want to make a gingerbread home with you," Jack said as I crawled into bed next to him.

And I wanted to make a gingerbread home with him. More importantly, I wanted to give him one of the warm, loving family-oriented Christmases I remembered as a child with my *oma*. Jack deserved that, and if I could be the one to put the Frost family back together, I felt like I wouldn't be as depressed that my oma wasn't here with me this Christmas.

I looked up Jack's parents' address while he slept. I was going to surprise him tomorrow.

"You're off again?" he asked the next morning.

I was standing in the foyer, trying to leave, but he kept kissing me. "I have to do stuff with the show," I lied. "I'll be back this afternoon."

The drive to Connecticut, where Jack's childhood home was located, wasn't too long. Traffic was light, and the Uber made good time. I gave the driver five stars on my phone as I walked up the neat stone path to the front door. Jack's parents' house was a large Colonial-style home, the gleaming white wood siding punctuated by large windows with charcoal-grey shutters. A large front porch with columns welcomed me up to the front door.

The doorbell chimed. Maybe they weren't even there.

The large door eased open.

"You must be Chloe," said an older woman. She had Jack's intelligent blue eyes, but instead of his silvery-white hair, his mother's hair was a long, rich chestnut. She was tall, though. I could see where Jack had inherited his height.

"Come inside," his mother said. "It's very nice to finally meet you."

"You have a lovely home," I said, walking in.

The house was huge. The entryway was a double-height space with an impressive dark wood staircase up to the second floor. There was a sparkling chandelier punctuating the space. I tried not to drool. This was the house I'd always envisioned raising a family in—elegant, beautiful, and tastefully decorated. My oma's house had been small, well worn, and full of mismatched furniture. It had been well loved and welcoming, though, and was decorated based on the holiday. Oma had always gone all out for Christmas.

The Frost house, however beautiful, was bare of any personal welcoming touches. There were no Christmas decorations; there weren't even a lot of knickknacks. There was nothing personal except for one small family portrait of the two parents and six young children.

I heard heavy footsteps on the polished hardwood floors.

"And who do we have here?" a man said. I assumed it was Jack's father.

He was even taller than his wife, with the same platinum, almost silvery, blond hair like Jack, the same broad shoulders, and a strong jaw. If this was what Jack would look like when he was older, I had no complaints.

"This is Chloe," Jack's mother said.

"Hi!" I said. "Nice to meet you, Mr. Frost."

"Doctor," he corrected. "Both my wife and I are doctors. I am a doctor of medicine, and she has two doctorates, one in neuroscience and one in microbiology."

"I am one of the leading researchers of brain cancer in the world," Jack's mother said. "And my husband, Dr. Frost, is an internationally renowned neurosurgeon specializing in brain and spinal surgery."

"Wow," I said, "you are very accomplished."

"He has several patents," Jack's mother told me.

"Dr. Frost sells herself short," Jack's father said. "Diane also has several patents on cancer drugs."

"That's very impressive," I said, not sure what else to say when someone was bragging. "Your son is also impressive."

"Yes. He attended Harvard, and he went to Stanford for an MBA," Jack's father said.

"Where did you go to college?" Diane asked.

"I took a few culinary classes at the local technical institute," I told them, "but I never finished."

"I see," his mother said, looking down her nose at me. She was wearing heels, and she was so much taller than me that I had to crane my neck to look into her eyes.

"Do you have any ambitions?" Jack's father asked.

We were all still standing in the foyer. If they had been at my oma's house when she was still alive, she would have already brought them into the kitchen, sat them down in the least rickety chair, and served them an array of snacks and drinks. Yet Jack's parents were quizzing me about my mediocre life.

"I'm a baker," I explained. "I'd like to open a café one day."

"A baker," Diane said, a slight frown around her mouth. "Not what we hoped for our son."

Well. What can you say to something like that? As my oma would say, "Beauty is only skin deep, but ugliness goes to the bone." Did I really want to invite them to Jack's Christmas party?

"I didn't want to bother you," I said. "I only stopped by to pick up some of the cookie cutters, ornaments, and other special decorations Jack talked about."

"Is he having a party?" his mother asked, finally leading me out of the foyer and back into the house. The rest of it was just as beautiful and just as cold. There wasn't a pillow out of place, nor was there anything to inspire warmth.

"We keep the boxes of Christmas things in the storage room," she said, leading me to a door near the kitchen.

I expected the basement to be cluttered, but it was neatly organized, like an industrial warehouse. All the storage boxes were the same size and placed neatly on identical shelving units.

She pulled out five large plastic boxes labeled CHRISTMAS. I picked up one, she took two, and Jack's father took the two heaviest, and we carried them upstairs.

"So, a party," he said.

"You're welcome to come. It's on Christmas Eve," I said.

Jack was probably not going to like the fact that I had invited his parents. In fact, I *knew* he wouldn't like it. *I* didn't even like it. These were the last people I wanted to spend Christmas with.

I was a little winded from carrying the box to the foyer. Jack's mother didn't seem fazed at all.

"You should lift weights and work out," she told me. "And stop eating so many carbs. I'm not surprised you didn't go to college and you like sweets. Did you know that several studies suggest that a woman's risk for diabetes and heart disease goes up as her level of educational attainment goes down?"

"I did not know that," I replied.

"I want my grandchildren to be healthy," she said as I followed her to a sitting room.

"Which means the mother of our grandchildren needs to be healthy as well," Jack's father added.

"Oh, well, I..."

"That's why we want Hartleigh to be Jack's mate."

His mate? Was this a Steve Irwin show? I wanted to call an Uber and leave this cold, strange house, but I didn't want to be rude.

"Yes, she is the perfect person to be Jack's wife," Diane said. "She is well educated, we know her family, she grew up in this very fine neighborhood, and she is thin but not anorexic."

"I'm sure he'll take your opinion into consideration," I said. *Not*. No wonder Jack didn't much care for his parents. I was starting to regret coming here.

"May I be blunt?" his mother said. I thought she *was* being blunt but, okay. I braced myself.

"I don't care for you. You disgust me with your roundness and your baking and all that sugar. How much can we pay you to go away?"

"Go away?" I exclaimed in disbelief. "Where?"

"Away. Away from Jack," his father said.

"Would you take a hundred thousand dollars?" Diane asked me, pulling out a checkbook.

"Um..." They wanted to pay me to stay away from Jack. I was tempted to agree, take the money, and then shack up with Jack anyway.

But no, I shouldn't take their money. That would be fraud, which was what my cousin had done, and I would not stoop to his level.

"Jack is a grown man," I said. "I don't think you should try to manipulate his life like this—"

Slam!

We all jumped as the front door to the house was thrown open and banged against the opposite wall.

"What in the world!" Jack's father exclaimed.

Jack swept in, bringing all the anger of a winter storm with him.

"*What the hell are you doing here?*" he roared. He marched over to me and grabbed me by the arm, yanking me up. I yelped, more from the shock of seeing him than from any pain he caused me.

"You had no right," he snarled at me, "I told you—"

"I'm sorry," I cried. "I didn't mean—"

He dragged me towards the front door.

"What were you even doing here, going behind my back like that?" he growled.

"I wanted to surprise you..." I tried to explain, reaching for the boxes of Christmas decorations.

"You're so emotional, Jack," his mother said, shaking her head as she followed us out of the sitting room. "You should be with Hartleigh. She's level headed. She would be good for you, not this baker. All that sugar is bad for your endocrine system."

Jack's father started picking up the boxes, but Jack grabbed them out of his father's hands.

"Come on, Chloe," Jack ordered. "Don't even engage them. They're just trying to manipulate and control you."

"Honestly, Jack," his mother admonished. "You can't act like this around our future grandkids."

"I don't know why you care. You'll never see your granddaughter." He had a mean look on his face. I didn't like where he was going with this.

"That girl isn't pregnant, is she?" his mother exclaimed in horror as she followed us out of the house to the car.

"Yes, she is," Jack said, turning towards his parents, his teeth bared.

She is? I looked down. Why did people think I was pregnant? With all the walking I was doing, I thought I was actually losing weight.

"We're having a daughter, and you will never see her," he spat at his parents. He shoved his boxes into the back of the car and snatched the one I was carrying.

"We have grandparents' rights," his mother warned, grabbing my shoulder. Jack slapped her hand away and pulled me to the passenger's side of the SUV.

"You ruined my life, and I'm going to make sure you never have what you want!" he roared, slamming the car door and making me flinch. "You can sit here in this cold house and think about all the awful things you did to make your own son not want you to ever meet your grandchild."

The car peeled away.

"I am not pregnant. This"—I gestured to my general oven area—"is a barren wasteland."

Jack's hands were tightly gripped to the wheel. "You're worse than Hartleigh," he said in a low voice. "You just barged into a part of my life that I *told you* to stay away from."

"I didn't mean—"

"*Let me finish!*" Jack yelled.

I cringed and started crying.

"Do you know why I told you to stay the hell away from them? I thought I explained this to you, but clearly you weren't listening."

"I was trying to do something nice," I sobbed.

"I didn't ask for you to butt into my life!" he shouted. "It's *my* life, I've lived it, I know what kind of people they are, and I know there's no hope of reconciliation. There is no such thing as Christmas magic."

CHAPTER 56

Jack

I didn't know Chloe had been lying to me until I went downstairs and happened to run into Nina in the lobby. "Where's Chloe?" I asked. Nina looked confused. "I thought she was doing something with the show?"

"She left," Eddie said.

"Left where?"

"She said she was fetching some Christmas decorations of some sort to surprise you."

My stomach sank. I had a hunch that she had gone to my parents'. Unfortunately, I still didn't have her phone number, and I couldn't call her. Even as I drove to Connecticut, I thought to myself that there was no way she would be that stupid, especially after I had told her how terrible my parents were.

When I walked in and saw her there, in the sitting room, talking to them, I lost it.

And now here we were, sitting in my car, in traffic on the way back to Frost Tower. I was too angry at my parents, Hartleigh, Greg, and my life in general to make conversation, polite or otherwise. Chloe was sniffling next to me in the passenger seat, which only made me feel worse.

We pulled into the garage in Frost Tower, and I turned off the car.

"I'm sorry," she sobbed. "I was trying to give you a nice Christmas like how you had when you were a kid."

"That will never happen," I said, tilting my head back and looking up at the roof of the car. "Actually, it was never real. It was all a farce, a veneer my parents forced my sister to create."

She looked confused.

I sighed. "I think I explained this to you in bits and pieces, but let me lay it all out."

She blew her nose, and I turned to face her.

"Look, Chloe," I said. "I did like Christmas; I loved it, actually. Christmas was nice because of Belle. She would decorate—she had these antique glass ornaments she loved—she would cook a nice meal, and we would open presents. Did you know my sister lived with my parents until she was in her thirties? I always thought it was odd. My parents didn't pay for our college education. They believe you should work for it. Of course, they made too much money for us to qualify for any scholarships or loans, so Belle lived at home and worked her way through school. She wasn't able to go away for college because my parents wanted her to raise me and my brothers. So she stayed. She could have left, but she didn't want to leave us. She made home safe, warm, and fun."

"Your mom just let that happen?" Chloe asked.

"My mother and my father—he shares some of the blame—they both worked. They put a lot of time and effort into their careers and their own relationship. Belle picked up the slack with us kids."

"It's hard to have a career and a family," Chloe said diplomatically.

"If you aren't willing to make the sacrifice, you shouldn't have children, or at the very least hire a nanny and don't make your underage daughter do all the work," I snapped.

"Yeah, that's unjust," Chloe said, gingerly placing her hand on mine. "But it's not your fault."

"Belle is the reason I'm so successful," I said, trying to explain. "You remind me of her because you are both such hard workers. Belle did computer software coding remotely at night, and during the day she was investing in stocks. She also invested some in bitcoin, I think. She still found time to help me apply to Harvard. She even paid my tuition."

"That was very generous," Chloe said.

"My parents didn't even allow her to come help me move in, because they wanted her to stay and take care of my younger brothers. They were just so horrible to her. And I wasn't helpful either. I share a portion of the guilt and the blame."

"You were just a kid," she said sympathetically.

"Yeah, but later on I wasn't. I had a job, I could have done *something*. I'm paying for the youngest two's education now, of course. I hate myself for not realizing how bad it was for Belle. I was totally oblivious. I would come home for Thanksgiving and Christmas and allow Belle to make it nice and homey." I closed my eyes, the shame and anger washing over me. "I should have bought her a house or something, I don't know. I could have taken the kids at that point."

"Your parents would have fought you," Chloe said.

"I guess. But I could have figured out some way to make life easier for Belle." I yanked my hand away from Chloe. "I'm not stupid. I'm a billionaire, and I run a very profitable company. I mean, my tower is a dumpster fire, but I should have done better. Belle sacrificed everything for us, and I did nothing for her."

"So what happened? Why did she leave?"

I shifted in my seat. This was painful to talk about.

"When the youngest was in his freshman year, Belle sent out an email to us telling us how much she hated being forced to take care of us, how she never had a life because of us, how she was trapped in her childhood bedroom, and how she was tired of holding up the veneer for our parents' life and she was done. Then she left. This all happened right after Thanksgiving. That was two years ago, and I haven't seen or heard from her since."

"Someone should have gone to find her," Chloe said, her eyes wide with concern. "What if she's trapped or hurt somewhere?"

I grimaced. "She talks to the youngest two. I think she still considers them her babies, but she hasn't contacted me or my other brothers."

"Have you tried to reach out?" Chloe asked.

"No," I admitted. "I'm too ashamed."

"I understand you feel that it's your fault, that there was more you could have done," she said, stroking my arm.

Her phone buzzed. I still needed to put her contact info in my phone. But now did not seem like the time to ask. I didn't want to put her in the position of wanting to say no and feeling like she couldn't.

"Sorry, I have to go, I have a meeting," she said softly, patting my leg.

I let her leave. I was wrung out from seeing my parents. After sitting in my car in silence for a while after she left, I gathered myself enough to unload the boxes of Christmas decorations to my penthouse. Then I sat on the balcony in the snow with Milo.

CHAPTER 57

Chloe

I could have gone to see Jack after meeting with Dana, Gunnar, and Nina about the final bake-off challenge, but I didn't. I was mortified that I had gone over to his parents' house without asking him. What had I been thinking?

"I'm sure he'll forgive you," Nina whispered to me in the dark.

"He said I was just like Hartleigh," I groaned. "And I guess I am. I just barged into his life."

"You aren't like Hartleigh," my friend assured me. "Just give him a chance to calm down."

"He's clearly a private person, yet I practically moved into his penthouse. Maybe I pushed him too hard."

"He likes you!" Nina exclaimed. "It's close to Christmas. Emotions run high. Concentrate on the bake-off."

I tried, but I couldn't sleep. I wondered what I could do to make things right with Jack.

I still felt strongly that I needed to foster some sort of reconciliation with his family, but his parents weren't the issue. Belle was. I needed to contact her somehow.

Jack had said Belle was travelling. I messaged a few big travel bloggers I knew from Instagram and asked them if they had ever met a Belle Frost with platinum-silver hair and ice-blue eyes. Surely someone would have seen her. I sent them the invitation to the Christmas Eve party at Jack's penthouse and asked them to please pass on the message if they found her or knew someone who knew her.

My contacts promised they would, and I settled back to sleep. If Jack saw that I had brought Belle back, maybe he would forgive me for going behind his back to talk to his parents.

I was a little sleepy the next morning when Nina and I walked down to the studio.

"Good morning!" Anastasia greeted us. "This is the last round of *The Great Christmas Bake-Off*, then we have to say goodbye. Christmas is in just a few short days. Because this is the final round, we're calling it the Showstopper Christmas challenge. Throughout the bake-off, Chloe and Nina, you two have created some of the most beautiful desserts I have ever seen, and I've been reviewing high-end restaurants for years. Congratulations on making it this far! This is your last chance to see who will make the most show-stopping dessert. As usual, you have until this afternoon to finish your dessert."

Now that Hartleigh was out of the kitchen and I never had to see her again, I was able to relax and fully concentrate on my dessert. Usually the judges assembled in the morning before the competition started. Anu and Nick were there, but Jack wasn't. He was probably still angry at me.

I sighed and focused on my dessert.

"What are you baking?" Anastasia said. I couldn't believe that would be the last time she asked me that. It felt like *The Great Christmas Bake-Off* had only begun yesterday.

"A winter garden," I told her. "I want to capture the taste of winter, the coldness, the gloom, but then the hope of Christmas that is a bright spot in the darkness."

"Sounds ambitious. I can't wait!"

Anastasia went to talk to Nina while I assembled ingredients.

For the bright spot of Christmas, I was going to make little pagodas. After melting colored sugar, I made little puzzle pieces and melted the edges then stuck them together to form the structure. When those were done, I candied flower petals and carefully stuck them onto the pagodas. It was a little burst of color, and the sugar made the flower petals look as if they were covered in a layer of frost.

For the various sauces I was going to use to draw patterns on the plates, I made reductions of cranberries, pears, spiced oranges, plums, holly, pine, and spiced wine.

The dessert couldn't just be melted sugar, however. There had to be some dimensionality to it. I made a series of desserts, cookies, two kinds of cakes, two kinds of tarts, and also some candied nuts. These I would cut up or crumble up and place the pieces around the garden.

After I had everything baked and set, I was ready to plate my dessert. First on the plate, I spooned swirls of the sauces I had made. The cameras zoomed in on me as I carefully constructed the dessert. For the garden's "plants," I had made flavored mousse and custards that I spooned carefully in between the swirls. For visual interest, I placed pieces of the cakes, shortbreads, and candies I had made around the plate. Finally, I used a small machine from Platinum Provisions to create a layer of pine-scented fog on the plate around the treats.

The judges applauded when we were finished, and Nina and I hugged.

Jack had come in some time during the challenge. I hadn't been paying attention. He saw me looking, and he quickly averted his eyes. I felt sick. Winning the competition wouldn't mean anything if I lost Jack.

CHAPTER 58

Jack

I had missed Chloe last night. The penthouse felt empty without her. The boxes of Christmas decorations she had gone to collect from my parents sat on my dining room table, mocking me.

Though I knew Dana wanted me to be there in the morning for the last competition of *The Great Christmas Bake-Off*, I didn't know if I could face Chloe. I felt terrible for how I had acted. I cringed, remembering how she had cried in my car then run away after I tried to explain.

Ignoring Dana's phone calls and deleting her furious voicemail messages, I went to the Platinum Provisions office instead of the studio. The marketing team was grinning broadly when they walked into the conference room.

"Check out these numbers!" the marketing director said. "We practically sold out of the first round of product we shipped to the stores. The factories are working overtime to make more. There are millions of dollars' worth of preorders for the next deliveries."

"Thank you for your hard work," I told them. "You will of course be receiving massive Christmas bonuses." There were big smiles and applause.

"Great way to end the year," Liam said as we walked out of the building.

"For Platinum Provisions," I told him grumpily. "I still haven't figured out a way to save my tower."

"I thought Mark Holbrook was going to move in?" Liam asked.

I scowled. "Mark Holbrook specifically asked for a full-service restaurant that was run by Chloe. She sent him a box of special muffins that his whole family loved. But Greg doesn't want Chloe to open a restaurant in the retail space. He wants to put the New York Bread Company there instead."

"He wants a chain!" Liam exclaimed. "That's horrible."

"It's not like I even asked Chloe if she would be open to the idea of running a restaurant," I admitted. "She always said she wanted to have a little bakery or café, not a restaurant."

"Did you ask her if she wanted to run a restaurant in Frost Tower, specifically, though?" Liam asked.

"No," I confessed, "I didn't. And I think she's mad at me." I told Liam what had happened with my parents.

Liam whistled. "That's insane. Your parents are crazy, dude."

"I need to make it up to her somehow," I said.

"She'll win the competition, then she'll be super happy," Liam said confidently. "You can rub her feet, offer her a killer restaurant space, and she'll like you again."

"I hope so."

I walked into the studio right as Chloe and Nina were finishing plating their dishes.

Chloe had made a delicate dessert called Winter Garden with a little pagoda made out of melted sugar.

"It's beautiful," I told her. It was like a perfect miniature garden. It wasn't a replica, though. It was just abstract enough not to look kitschy but to still evoke the feeling of a winter garden. There were tendrils of sauces, studded with little bits of chocolate, cake, mousse, and other desserts. There was a little layer of fog that smelled like pine that clung to the plate, swirling in tendrils as you moved your fork around.

"I'm speechless," Nick said. "This is just amazing. The fact that you did all of that in like, what, five or six hours? Incredible."

"It's really like watching a master class on desserts," Anu said. "The attention to detail, the fact that all of the flavors work together. I mean, you made, what, seven different types of desserts to create this? You can feel the complexity. But everything works together like a symphony."

"Also," Nick said, "if you have any of this pear tart left back there that I was only given one small sliver of, I'm going to need the rest of it."

"Thank you," Chloe said then walked out, giving her friend a quick hug as Nina stepped up.

Nina's dessert was just as beautiful.

"It's called Sugar Plum," she said. On the plate sat a chocolate sphere studded with little bits of candied fruits and flowers. She cracked it open, and tendrils of fog crept out, revealing the jewel-like dessert within. The sphere held little pieces of fruitcake and colorful sauces.

"This is very impressive," Anu said. "Both your dessert and Chloe's look like they belong on the cover of a magazine. This is Michelin-star cooking."

"Thank you very much." Nina beamed as she walked back to the holding room.

Anu and Nick chatted about the desserts for the cameras. Then they turned to me.

"They both had wonderful desserts," Nick said. "Nina's, however, was a bit better, we think. It was well thought out and restrained. Chloe's was beautiful and tasty, but there was a lot going on."

"Okay," I said, not understanding why they felt the need to tell me. Normally they just decided who the winner was, since they were the experienced chefs.

"You're not going to be upset?" Anu asked in concern. "I heard you and Chloe are… ah… an item."

"It's fine," I said brusquely. "Chloe's an adult." Even as I said the words, I knew she would be heartbroken. She would probably blame me for not sticking up for her. But I didn't want to cause a scene.

When it was time to announce the winner, Chloe and Nina linked arms as they stood in front of us. I couldn't look at Chloe. She was going to be so unhappy.

"Both of you created excellent desserts," Nick said. "Not just today but the entire competition. Unfortunately, someone has to win, and that person is Nina. Your dish was modern but classical, and we think it just barely edged out Chloe's winter garden."

The crew and the judges applauded.

"Oh my!" Nina said, clasping her hands to her mouth.

Chloe hugged her friend. She was smiling, but I could still see the tears in her eyes.

"Chloe and Nina, thank you for all your hard work," Anastasia said. "*The Great Christmas Bake-Off* from Romance Creative is a unique show in that it is hosted only online. This gives fans of the show and of the bakers all unprecedented access. We wanted to acknowledge that, so we had a fan favorite poll going around on social media. Chloe, you are the winner of the fan favorite award. So congratulations on that."

Chloe smiled and mouthed "Thank you" to the camera and blew a kiss.

I breathed a sigh of relief. At least she didn't walk away with nothing.

"Both of you have done an excellent job," Anastasia said. "Thank you for your enthusiasm, thank you judges, and thanks to all the fans of the show for watching."

I didn't have a chance to see Chloe after the bake-off was officially over. She and Nina were whisked away for interviews, and then, I supposed, they would have to make more rounds on talk shows.

Gunnar came over to me. "We made it!" he whooped. "You made it, I should say. Still have all your teeth? The sugar didn't rot them away?"

"I've had my lifetime supply, I think. Though it wasn't all bad," I added, thinking of Chloe's Austrian wedding cookies.

"I hope you're not upset that Chloe didn't win. She won the fan favorite at least." Gunnar looked thoughtful for a moment, and I could practically see dollar signs spewing out of his eyes. "You know what would be great? Since we're doing the next production as somewhat Valentine's Day-themed, maybe we can convince Chloe to marry one of the men."

Rage. Icy cold rage.

"*No*," I said.

"But she's a fan favo—"

"No! *Absolutely not!* Don't even ask!" I thundered.

"Geez, you're scary when you're mad. You must have it bad for that girl," he said.

I couldn't take any more of the bake-off, so I went to my penthouse and started putting together a plan for Chloe's restaurant until I realized I didn't actually know that much about running a successful restaurant. The internet wasn't all that much help, and I desperately wished I hadn't ruined everything with Chloe.

CHAPTER 59

Chloe

While Nina had her interview, I talked to Dana.

"Don't be too upset," she said. "It's better that Nina won. Otherwise you would have been fan favorite and bake-off winner. Now you're both winners. Nina has a big following too, and no one wants to see their favorite lose, especially not this close to Christmas."

"So it was rigged," I stated.

"It's TV. It's all fake," Dana said. "But still, thank you for all the hard work. The check will be deposited in your account in the New Year. I bet you land an advertising deal at least! And hopefully a good job."

"Yeah," I said, rubbing my arms. "I don't know if anyone will want to hire the runner-up."

Dana patted me on the shoulder. "At least you have Jack. You could just set up in his penthouse and live a life of luxury. You seem to have him wrapped around your little finger."

I glared at her. "I'm not after him for his money."

Dana rolled her eyes. "It's TV. Everyone sleeps around for one favor or another," Dana said. "No one looks down on you."

Before I could protest, one of the production assistants signaled her.

"Must be off!" she called over her shoulder.

I went up to the shared apartment and slowly packed. Tears started rolling down my face. I couldn't believe I had lost! I hadn't won the competition, and I had made Jack angry.

"How is this my life?" I groaned, sinking down on the bed.

"There you are!" Anastasia said, coming into the room. "Don't be too sad!" She hugged me, but all that did was succeed in making me start sobbing.

"I'm happy for Nina," I insisted.

Anastasia stroked my hair. "I know you are! Don't cry. You will still be awarded money."

"It's going to be enough to pay off my credit card debt, but not much else," I sniffled.

"Don't fret. It's only a few hours after the competition. The finale hasn't even been uploaded yet. Watch, you'll be offered a job."

"I guess. I just want to stay in New York City."

"You will," she told me. "Let me know when you start at a restaurant. I'll come give you rave reviews."

After Anastasia left, my phone dinged with an email. It was from a manager at a restaurant in Brooklyn. He was interested in hiring me. Heart pounding, I looked up the restaurant online, and it seemed legit, so I called the number on the email.

"Maybe I could stay in New York City after all," I reassured myself, feeling slightly better.

A man answered after a few rings.

"Hi, this is Chloe. I'm calling about the job offer?" I said, my heart racing.

"Wonderful! We're big fans of yours," the manager said. "We're looking for a dessert chef. This is a relatively new restaurant in Brooklyn. I'd love for you to come out and take a look. Pay is competitive, but the hours are long, unfortunately. Again, we've already seen what you can do, and I'm a big fan, so the job is yours if you want it."

"Great!" I said. "It sounds like a wonderful opportunity. If you still want me after meeting in person with me, I accept the job. I'm a hard worker, and I can handle whatever you guys can throw at me."

"I know you can," the manager said with a chuckle. "I'm a huge fan of the show, your biggest fan maybe."

"When would I start?"

"After New Year's, but you may want to come in before that just to get a feel for the place. Stop by tomorrow and check it out."

"Thank you," I said.

After I hung up, I looked out the window at the snowy city below. I would miss this tower, and I would miss Jack. I sighed. I knew it couldn't have lasted. I wondered if I should have waited for other offers, but I had been receiving emails from the credit card company that I was almost at my limit. I couldn't afford to wait for the potential perfect job offer. I had to take what was offered now. If I didn't like it once I started, I could apply for a job at another restaurant later.

"Oh, Chloe!" Nina said as she walked in. "I'm so sorry!"

"No, you deserved to win," I insisted then started to cry. "It's okay, honestly. I was just offered a job at a Brooklyn restaurant."

"That's wonderful," Nina said. "Is that what you want?"

"I really just wanted to stay in New York City, so this helps me achieve that."

"I thought you wanted to own a bakery," she said.

I exhaled. "I don't know if that's ever going to happen. I'll take this job and work for a few years and see where it goes."

"What about Jack?" she asked.

"What *about* Jack?" I countered.

"Brooklyn is a bit far away," she said.

"It is?" I asked. I honestly didn't know.

"You need to be more familiar with the city if you're going to live here," Nina admonished. "It's a good hour by train, and that's if the subway is running on time. And an Uber or a taxi from Brooklyn is also really expensive unless it's at some weird time."

"I don't have any other options right now," I told her.

"You should slow down and think about this. You might have more offers after Christmas," Nina said.

I shook my head. "I need money now, and I need to start the New Year certain of where I'm going to be. This will be good," I assured my friend.

She hugged me. "One day soon, you'll have your bakery. Or even a restaurant."

"I don't know if I could handle that," I said.

"You can cook!" Nina insisted. "Besides, cooking regular food is so much easier than desserts. You'd be great at it."

"Only if you come work with me," I joked.

"Totally. You let me know when you start your restaurant. I am so there."

I hugged her. At least I had gotten one good thing out of the contest—a best friend.

CHAPTER 60

Jack

I waited around in my penthouse after the contest, hoping Chloe would show up, but she never did.

My phone rang. It was Mark Holbrook.

"We need an answer from you on the lease," he said. "I want to get this locked down before the break between Christmas and New Year."

"Yes, I understand," I said, cursing myself for yelling at Chloe. I needed to find some way to smooth things over between us.

"Is Chloe on board?"

"They just finished filming, but we're hammering out an agreement."

"I want a copy of it," Mark said in a clipped tone. "The space is unique, and the price is very attractive, but my company won't be a tenant if Chloe's restaurant isn't in the tower. I need assurances that you have amenities in place.

We are growing aggressively, and I can't attract talent if they can't even go somewhere for coffee or a bite to eat. I also need somewhere nice to take clients without having to take a car or the subway somewhere."

"I understand," I said. "I'll have something sent to you before Christmas Eve."

"See that you do."

I ran a hand through my hair. I needed to convince Greg to allow Chloe to run that restaurant. I could not lose the Holbrook deal.

I collected the work I had done on a business plan and went over to the Svensson Investment tower.

"Is Greg in?" I asked the secretary.

"Let me see if he's available. Please wait here."

I ignored her and followed her down the hall to Greg's office. I knew he would probably just tell her to send me away unless I saw him personally.

She knocked on his door and looked at me irritably.

"Mr. Frost is here to see you," she called into the room.

"Tell him I'm not here," I heard Greg say.

"Greg, I need to speak with you," I said, pushing past the secretary.

"What is it?" Greg barked, setting down the papers he was reading.

"I need Chloe to take the restaurant space. I'll lose the Holbrook deal if she doesn't."

"New York Bread Company is very interested in the space," Greg said.

"But Mark specifically asked for a restaurant run by Chloe."

"I heard she didn't even win the contest," Greg said.

"Only because Dana and Gunnar wanted her and Nina to both win," I tried to explain.

"Who is Nina? Oh, wait, I don't care," Greg said. "If Mark Holbrook isn't moving in, then we will proceed with finding a buyer for the tower."

"Why are you being such a dick?" I yelled at him.

"I don't like the Holbrooks," Greg said, a look of disgust on his face. "I'm certainly not bending over backwards for one and taking a chance on this girl."

"She's not a girl, she's an accomplished pastry chef," I countered.

"Pastry chefs," Greg said, "do not run full-service restaurants."

"She can do it," I insisted.

"Just because you're fucking her doesn't mean that she's qualified to run a restaurant," Greg sneered.

"So I'll find her a manager."

"Oh, so now that you've failed at real estate, you're going to fail at being a restaurateur, is it? Well, not on my dime. You don't even have a business plan."

I threw the plan on his desk, and he scowled at it. "You didn't even bring her in here to pitch. Does she even know you're making promises on her behalf?"

I glared at him.

"She doesn't, does she?" Greg scoffed.

I resisted the urge to punch him in the face.

"Your tower is not the only fire I'm dealing with right now. I'm about done with helping out Holbrooks, what with this business with Wes Holbrook and all of his father's random children that keep popping up. I'm not risking the financial solvency of Frost Tower because the Holbrooks have to have Chloe there."

I started to argue, but Greg cut me off.

"I'm sick of entitled billionaires, you included," Greg spat. "Get out of my office before I just decide to sell the whole tower to the Qataris."

CHAPTER 61

Chloe

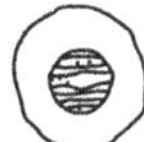 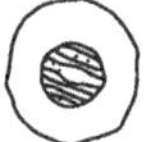 

I knew I needed to see Jack before I left; I didn't like the way we had left things. My bags were packed, and my cookware was wrapped up in newspaper and packed safely in a large heavy-duty plastic box.

I felt nervous as I stood in front of his door. Was he still angry at me?

He didn't smile when he opened his door and saw me. He just looked concerned.

"Chloe," Jack said. "I… didn't expect you."

"Is this a bad time?" I asked him. I felt jumpy, and my stomach was churning.

"No, come in. I wanted to talk to you, actually," he said once we were standing in his living room.

"I wanted to talk to you too," I said. "Just let me go first." His mouth snapped closed. "I'm sorry I went behind your back to your parents. I was just trying to help. I didn't want you to think I was just freeloading off of you."

He started to protest, but I held up a hand. "Let me finish. I'm not like Hartleigh. I don't want you for your money or your name. I just like *you*." I looked down at my boots. "I think we probably took it a little fast. I barely know you. I'd like to keep seeing you if you still want to."

He nodded, and I blew out a breath. "In the spirit of being independent, I will most likely be taking a job in a restaurant in Brooklyn as their pastry chef. It's like a cool pop-up restaurant; it will be fun." I tried to make the new job sound hip and upbeat, but really, I was nervous. What if it was a huge mistake? It felt like a huge mistake. Maybe I shouldn't have accepted the offer so quickly. Why did I always rush into things without thinking?

"I see," he said. Jack looked dejected. He crossed his arms over his chest and looked down at the floor.

"We can still see each other," I told him, putting my hand on his arm. "But it will be on a bit more equal footing. We'll set a date and a time then go to a movie or a wine bar. We'll be like classy, normal people. I won't show up at your door wearing some ridiculous Christmas outfit." I was trying to elicit a laugh, but Jack didn't even crack a smile.

"So that's all I have," I finished lamely.

"Right," Jack said. "Well." He worked his jaw. "Is this what you really want? To work for someone else back in the kitchen making desserts for the next decade, receiving no recognition?"

I was taken aback. Who did he think he was?

"Hey, this is my dream!" I said loudly. "Just because you're a fancy-pants billionaire with your nice cars and a tower doesn't mean you can pooh-pooh what other people do with their mediocre lives."

"You're not mediocre," he said softly.

I felt a little mediocre. I hadn't won the bake-off after all, and the restaurant in Brooklyn wasn't *that* great. But still. My dream was to live in New York City, and this was how I was going to accomplish that goal.

"This is what I want," I said firmly. But even to my own ears, it didn't sound like I meant it. I tried to shake off my apprehension. My emotions were all askew because I was sad that I was leaving the tower and disappointed that I hadn't won the bake-off.

He looked away from me then back with a strained smile. "If that's what you really want."

I shuffled my feet on the floor.

"I'll miss you," Jack said finally. "I don't know what I'll do without you sneaking up to my door at odd hours of the night."

"We can still visit each other," I said. "Brooklyn's not that far away."

"It could be closer," Jack said. "It's not the same as your being downstairs."

I nodded. I knew what he meant. But it was not like I could just move into his penthouse. I barely knew the guy.

"Can you stay for a bit?" he asked.

I shook my head. "I need to meet with the Airbnb host to pick up my key."

"You're staying in an Airbnb?" he asked.

"It's in Brooklyn near the restaurant. I'm going to stay there until Romance Creative sends me the prize money and I can find an apartment." I didn't have to meet the host right that second, but if I stayed at Jack's penthouse, it would only be delaying the inevitable. I needed to start on the next chapter of my life, and my relationship with Jack needed to either evolve to something more sensible or end.

"I understand," Jack said smoothly.

A part of me was a little upset that Jack didn't declare his undying love for me and demand that I tell the Brooklyn restaurant to go to hell and come live in his penthouse. But then I had just told him that I didn't want to stay and take advantage of him. Also, he was a gentleman; he wouldn't order me around. Jack was being respectful of what I claimed my wishes were.

"Um…What did you want to say?" I asked, remembering that he had wanted to tell me something.

"Nothing," he replied, "Just that I liked you and I wanted to keep seeing you, if you would be open to that."

"Oh." We looked at each other. "I like you, too," I said awkwardly. Then I reached up on my tiptoes and gave him a somewhat chaste kiss. I didn't feel all that happy, and Jack didn't look that happy either.

"I have to go."

"Let me know if you need anything," Jack said. He stepped forward and pulled me close and kissed me again. The kiss was deep, and he was making all the right motions, but it still felt cold somehow. I couldn't shake the feeling that I was making a big mistake.

CHAPTER 62

Jack

"Dammit!" I yelled when Chloe left. I picked up a nearby glass vase and threw it at the wall. Milo barked. I didn't know what I was angrier about, that I was going to lose my tower or that Chloe didn't want to stay with me.

"Of course she doesn't want to stay here. You scared her. You yelled at her and made her cry." I went to the closet, grabbed a broom, and started cleaning up the glass shards.

I looked around the penthouse. It seemed cold without Chloe. In fact, the whole tower felt cold without her. Maybe I should just let Greg sell it. I didn't want to be here if Chloe wasn't here. The whole place would only remind me of her. I know she didn't say she was breaking up with me, but Brooklyn was far away. It wouldn't be the same as having her here.

Feeling grey and depressed, I put on my suit jacket and headed off to Platinum Provisions for the last board meeting of the year.

Hunter seemed annoyed when I entered the boardroom. I didn't know if it was directed at me or his brothers.

"Christmas seems very profitable," Greg said after I gave an update on the latest earnings. Hunter scowled at him.

"We're also making progress on preliminary research for moving a factory to Harrogate," I added.

"I can see after looking at these production numbers how it may be prudent to own at least a percentage of production capacity," Hunter remarked.

Liam smiled. At least someone's dreams were coming true.

"New Year's goals," Hunter said. "Liam is going to be spending more time in western New York, and Jack is going to have his hands full with his tower, I presume?"

"I don't know," I said. "Maybe we should just sell it. The Holbrooks won't move in."

"Look," Greg interrupted me, "the New York Bread Company isn't working. And, well, it makes financial sense to accommodate Mark Holbrook in the restaurant."

Liam was grinning ear to ear.

"Why the change of heart?" I asked after I recovered from the slight shock of hearing Greg Svensson change his mind.

"It's Christmas," Greg said. Hunter was smirking.

Liam slung an arm around my shoulders. "I complained to Hunter about what was happening. He threatened to send all our younger half-brothers to live with Greg instead of with him and my other brothers in Harrogate." Liam doubled over laughing. "Can you imagine Greg taking care of a bunch of eleven- and twelve-year-olds?"

I smiled slightly. "I appreciate it, but I think it's a bit too late. Chloe is taking a job in Brooklyn at a restaurant."

"That is unacceptable," Greg said. "I want this tenant deal locked down by Christmas. I have a preliminary agreement drawn up for her restaurant. It should be enough to satisfy Mark Holbrook while you call her and tell her that she needs to run this restaurant."

"I'll try," I said. Chloe had seemed adamant about wanting to take the Brooklyn job. But maybe if I begged and pleaded, she would agree to run the restaurant.

"I want an update by tomorrow," Greg ordered.

On my way back to Frost Tower, I started to panic. I still didn't have Chloe's number, and she hadn't offered to give it to me before she left.

I had to make this deal work. I forced myself to calm down and make a plan. I sent Dana a message begging for Chloe's number, then I sent her a message through Instagram. While I waited to hear back from Dana, I wondered if Chloe was only trying to let me down gently. Maybe she didn't actually want to continue our relationship. Maybe she would disappear like Belle.

Seeing Hartleigh outside the tower when I returned jolted my thoughts out of their downward spiral.

"Jack!" she cried, wrapping her arms around me. "Tell me it isn't true!"

"What isn't true?" I asked, irritated, as I struggled to peel her off of me.

"About Chloe! She's not carrying your baby, is she? My parents said..." Hartleigh started sobbing. "They said she was pregnant."

Ah, yes. The lie I had told to my parents to make them angry had now come back to bite me.

I was still feeling sour, so instead of telling Hartleigh the truth I replied, "Of course Chloe is pregnant. You were never the one for me. I would never in a million years allow you to be the mother of my child."

Hartleigh started screaming and crying. She yelled and swiped at my face with her nails. I pushed her off and ran inside the lobby, locking the door against her.

"Eddie!" I yelled, but the Santa was passed out at the security desk.

CHAPTER 63

Chloe

The Airbnb I stayed in that night was small, cramped, and smelled funny. It was nowhere near as nice as Jack's penthouse. After a fitful sleep and a lackluster breakfast, I went over to the Brooklyn restaurant. It was in an old industrial complex. The space was nice, with high ceilings and old brick walls covered in artwork.

"This is going to be nice," I told myself. "It's a little hipster, but it's cute. You can work with this."

My good feelings evaporated when I walked into a small office. There, waiting for me, was a man in a Santa suit, minus the beard and the hat.

"I'm here about the job?" I said to him, feeling apprehensive.

"Chloe!" he boomed, crushing me to him in a hug. Then he kissed me on the cheek. I laughed nervously.

"I'm Herbert, the manager here," he said, a wide grin on his face.

"I see you have the Christmas spirit," I said, wondering if I should cut my losses and run. But I needed this job. I had to pay for the Airbnb.

"I work at the mall as a Santa," he told me as he crossed the small room in two steps, cutting off my access to the door.

"You work at the mall?" I asked, feeling slightly faint. Alarm bells were going off in my head.

"I enjoy it! I love to help make Christmas memories for people. That's why I think we're perfect for each other. You like Christmas as much as I do."

He had stepped towards me, and I huddled back against the desk. He wasn't the Santa at the Christmas market—I knew that much. He wasn't tall enough. But I knew he had stalked me in the mall and the grocery store.

"Where's the chef?" I asked, trying to diffuse the situation.

"He's not going to be here until later," Herbert said. "I wanted us to have the chance to chat. Alone."

The alarm bells were deafening.

Herbert shuffled closer to me. I could smell the everything bagel he'd had for breakfast. "Did you like my presents?"

"What presents?" I asked faintly.

"The outfits. You didn't post pictures of the last two." He licked his lips.

"You were sending me the packages?" I kicked myself for posting those online. I never should have done that. Now here I was, trapped in an office with my stalker Santa.

"I really wanted to see you in the last outfit," Herbert said. I could practically see him salivating. "That skimpy little number, your hands tied up, pretty mouth gagged."

"I, um... I think I need to go," I said, trying to keep my voice from shaking. "I forgot I had another meeting."

"I'm in love with you, Chloe," Herbert said, looking at me intently. He reached out to stroke my hair, and I flinched.

"Uh huh, sure, well, again, I really need to be going—"

"Are you pregnant?"

"*Excuse me?*" I said. The anger inspired by that question bolstered me, and I stood up straighter.

"The rumors say you're pregnant with Jack's baby."

"No," I snapped. "Those are just rumors. That thing with Jack wasn't real. There is nothing between him and me. It was all for the show."

Herbert smiled at me, the relief plain on his face. "I'm glad to know you weren't with Jack," Herbert said, visibly relaxing. "That would have been bad." He pulled out a handkerchief and patted the beads of sweat on his forehead. "Now you can be with me." He grabbed my hand and stroked it with a sweaty palm.

I was starting to wish I had gone to the police when the packages started showing up.

"I follow you sometimes," he said.

I needed to escape that office somehow. I started inching my way to the door.

"I'm glad you did," I lied. He didn't stop me from moving around him. "It makes me feel safer knowing you're around." Herbert grabbed me, hugging me. I pushed him off and grabbed the doorknob.

"It was great to meet you, Herbert. Like I said, I have to go, but you and I are going to have a great time. I know it!" I practically ran out of the restaurant.

"It's a step up," I told myself as I walked around Brooklyn, burying my face in my scarf against the cold. "The pay is okay. The hours seem long. There's no time for work–life balance, not that Jack seemed like he wanted to work–life balance with me. Oh, also the manager is a creep and has been stalking me and sending me creepy sexual presents." I felt like I was going to cry. I really wanted a drink, but it was early. Also, my credit card was maxed out. I had been shocked when the Airbnb reservation was approved. I was sure the bank had me on its naughty list.

"Hey!" a man in a pizza shop said. "You're Chloe from the bake-off! Come try our pizza!" He gave me three slices, and I took pictures and posted them on Instagram. I was willing to trade publicity for free pizza.

After I ate, I walked around the neighborhood, feeling at a loss. Here I was, at yet another low point. What was worse was I missed Jack. I wished he would swoop down and… do what, exactly? Save me?

After he had yelled at me and said I was just like Hartleigh, New York could freeze over before I asked Jack Frost for money. I'd even left the presents he'd given me at his penthouse. The clothes, especially that coat and those shoes, were expensive. It wouldn't have felt right to take them.

I sat down on a bench in a small park and kicked at the leaves by my feet.

I wondered if I had moved too fast. Maybe I should have held off, played harder to get. Give a mouse a cookie, and he'll sleep with you then not care to continue the relationship. Or maybe Jack had wanted to have a relationship with me, but then I had ruined it all by talking to his parents behind his back, and now he thought he couldn't trust me.

As I walked through the neighborhood back to my Airbnb, I was approached by a Santa. I steeled myself, but this Santa wasn't as short and fat as Herbert.

"Why are you following me?" I yelled at him. He was wearing dark sunglasses, and I couldn't see his face.

"So it's been confirmed that you are indeed pregnant." He smiled through the fake beard. "I am watching you."

I peered at the Santa. He looked very familiar. He saw me studying him, and he turned and walked quickly away.

"Why is everyone so concerned with the state of my womb?" I yelled irritably. A woman walking her cat gave me a dirty look.

Maybe I should just move back to the Midwest, I told myself. *I clearly can't handle myself alone in New York*.

I scrolled through the thousands of messages people had sent me, needing the boost to my self-confidence. There were declarations of love—and declarations of other things. I closed the app.

"Stop taking the easy way out," I said to myself. "There are other restaurants. You'll find something."

But would I? I felt sick. I was locked into this Airbnb for the next few days, I didn't have any more money, and I had no job lined up.

The sad reality was that I just wanted Jack. I knew I was safe with him. But Jack had his own problems. He didn't need mine.

As I was tucking my phone back into my purse, a Santa jumped out at me. I screamed.

"Chloe," he said. It was my cousin. He seemed as if he needed drugs immediately. I remembered the look from my mother. His friend Kevin wasn't with him at least.

"I need help," Cody pleaded. "Chloe, you have to help me. I need money. Just a little bit. I'll do anything."

"I don't have any money," I yelled. "I am flat broke. You need to leave me alone."

"You may not have money, but I know who does," Cody said as someone put a bag over my head. I screamed as I felt myself being dragged into a car. A door slammed, and we drove away.

CHAPTER 64

Jack

I couldn't believe Hartleigh was still hanging around. Why did she have to be here and yet Chloe wasn't?

My phone rang, and my heart jumped, thinking it was Chloe.

"She doesn't have your number," I told myself as I answered the phone.

"Who are you talking to?" said the voice on the other end of the call. It was Owen.

"Uh, no one."

"I see. Are you actually having a Christmas party?" my brother asked.

I slapped a palm to my forehead. I had completely forgotten. That was why Chloe wanted the decorations. Why had I been so awful to her? She was only trying to help.

"Are you still there? Are you even listening?" Owen snapped.

"Yes, yes," I said. "There's a Christmas Eve party, I think."

"Are Matt and Oliver coming back from Harvard today?"

"I guess."

"You don't seem to know what's going on," Owen remarked.

"I'm very busy. I am a billionaire. I'm running a company. And I am trying to keep a multimillion-dollar real estate deal from imploding!" I yelled into the phone.

Owen snorted and hung up. The phone rang again.

"What is it?" I snapped.

"I hope that's not how you answer the phone for potential tenants," Greg Svensson said in a clipped tone. "No wonder Frost Tower isn't making any money."

I sighed. "Can I help you, Greg?"

"Has Chloe confirmed that she will be running the restaurant? We need her in that space as soon as possible. Carl has had interest from several tenants who seem intrigued about your baker running her own restaurant. Apparently my brother's bake-off show has been farther reaching than previously anticipated."

"You know, if you had let me do it when I asked originally, we wouldn't have this problem."

"You didn't sell it well enough," Greg said. "Call me as soon as she confirms."

There was a knock on the door, and I flung it open, expecting to see Chloe.

"Jack!" exclaimed my brothers. I hugged Matt and Oliver. My third-youngest brother, Jonathan, walked in behind them.

"Was the drive okay?" I asked as I hugged him.

He shrugged. "Traffic was fairly light. I think most people are out of the city for the holidays already."

"I thought there was going to be a party," Oliver said, dramatically flopping on the couch and turning on the TV. "There aren't even any decorations up."

"We're running behind," I explained.

"Where's your girlfriend?" Matt asked.

"What? That's not—"

"One of the Svenssons lives in the dorm down the hall from me. He said that Liam said you had a girlfriend, and she made the best food ever," Matt countered.

"I'm hungry!" Oliver complained.

I rummaged around in my nearly empty fridge.

"There's two soup muffins left," I told them. I microwaved the muffins to warm them slightly, and my younger brothers ate them in two huge bites.

Jonathan snickered.

"When is Chloe going to be here to make some more?" Matt asked.

"Maybe this evening," I hedged.

But was she?

Maybe moving to Brooklyn was her final "screw you." Maybe she was angrier than I had thought. I hadn't realized Belle was that angry, hurt, and resentful until she'd left. Maybe the same thing was happening with Chloe, and I was too dense to see it.

Milo bucked at my hip.

"I'm going to walk him. I'll tell Owen to pick up some food for you guys since he's on his way over, so make sure you're downstairs waiting to help him carry whatever he buys you," I told them as I clipped the husky into his harness.

My three brothers were glued to the football game on TV and grunted in acknowledgment.

I took Milo on a long walk to the park and back. I thought the dog could sense my anxiety, because he didn't want to stay and play in the snow drifts.

There was a Santa Claus in sunglasses standing in front of my tower when I returned.

"You have ten seconds to scram or I'm calling the police," I growled at him.

"Where is Chloe?" he asked.

"Not any of your concern." I studied him. "Hey, don't I know you?"

But his gaze wasn't on me. The Santa was looking down the street, where a junky-looking car was slowly creeping towards Frost Tower. Then a door opened, and a familiar blonde baker tumbled out and ran towards me.

"Jack!" Chloe yelled, running into my arms. I held her close then swore as the Santas descended on the scene.

CHAPTER 65

Chloe

 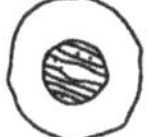 

"This is insane!" I yelled when Cody took the hood off my head. We were in an abandoned warehouse, and I was lying tied up on the floor. The sad thing was that I was thankful I had been kidnapped by my junkie cousin and his friend and not Herbert the perverted Santa.

"It's not insane. We're going to ransom you for money. It's the perfect plan," he replied.

"I don't have any money," I repeated slowly. "You kidnapped a broke woman."

"I need you to make Jack give me money," Cody said. "Call him and tell him to give us a hundred thousand dollars."

"He's not going to give you that much money!" I screeched. "He won't even believe this is real unless we talk to him in person. He's a billionaire; he's not going to just make a deal like that over the phone."

"But he needs time to go to the bank and take out the cash," Kevin said dubiously.

I laughed. "Are you kidding? He has a safe full of cash." I could see Cody's eyes light up with greed.

"Take me to Frost Tower," I ordered. "You can wait with me in the lobby. Jack will go upstairs and fill a shopping bag full of cash for you, and then you can be on your merry way. Easy peasy."

Kevin looked at Cody. Thankfully, their drug-fried brain cells decided that this was, in fact, a great idea. I shook my head. This was the jankiest kidnapping ever.

"Okay," he said. "We'll go to the tower. But no funny business."

I had to bunny hop to the car because my feet were taped together.

The ride to Manhattan was painful. The car was moving slowly down the street, and people kept swerving around us. My cousin was high as a kite and driving slowly. I was sure that in his mind, he was trying not to draw attention.

As we approached Frost Tower, I looked out the window and saw Jack. I had to escape the car.

Cody's friend, Kevin, wasn't paying attention to me, and they didn't even have me tied up all that well. I pulled my feet out of my boots. My hands were still tied, but I was able to open the car door and jump out.

"Jack!" I yelled.

"Chloe!" he said in surprise while Milo barked.

"Where are your shoes?" he asked as he hugged me against him. "Why are your hands tied?"

Jack broke the duct tape on my hands as Cody and his friend jumped out of the car.

"You need to pay us if you want her back," they said, Santa hats bobbing in the wind as they jogged across the street.

"The hell I am!" Jack yelled, pushing me behind him.

Kevin lunged at me, but before he could touch me, he was tackled by a man in a Santa suit. Jack let Milo off his leash, and the dog guarded me while Jack went after Cody, punching him in the jaw.

The other Santa stood up, grinning. His beard had been ripped off, and his sunglasses were bent.

"Dad?" Jack said in disbelief. "*What are you doing here?*"

"Just watching out for my future grandchild," he said cheerfully. He walked over to me and rubbed my belly. I slapped his hand away.

"Don't touch her!" another Santa said, running up to Jack's father and tackling him. "She's mine! I love her. Chloe, we're going to be together forever." It was Herbert, the mall Santa. Both men went down, and another Santa came sprinting out of Frost Tower.

Jack shook his head in disgust as Eddie jumped into the fray. The stalker Santa and Jack's father were fighting. Eddie was taking on Cody and his junkie friend.

"I'm surprised Eddie is sober enough to see where to hit," I commented as Eddie socked my cousin in the stomach. I didn't feel sorry for him one bit.

Dr. Frost punched Kevin with a powerful uppercut. I could hear his jaw crack.

"Ooof. Maybe you should do something?" I said to Jack.

"I just..." Jack said. "I don't even want to involve myself."

"You would think a surgeon would be more careful with his hands," I said as Jack's father punched another one of the Santas in the face. It might have been Eddie, but at this point, I didn't even know which was which.

Dr. Frost disentangled himself from the fight. Eddie was wavering slightly, but he was still standing. I watched him take a swig from the flask in his pocket, and he flashed me a thumbs-up sign. Dr. Frost straightened his Santa suit and strode over to me. Jack stepped in front of me.

"Don't touch her," Eddie hollered.

One of the Santas grabbed him around the ankles, and he crashed to the sidewalk.

Dr. Frost looked down his nose at them then turned back to Jack.

"Step aside, son," he said. "That girl is carrying my grandchild, and she is walking around with no shoes on. She needs to come home with me so that she's safe."

"No, she doesn't," Jack yelled.

"She shouldn't come with you, I should!" screamed Hartleigh as she ran towards the fighting. Because of course that was exactly what the situation required.

"I am the mother of Jack's child," Hartleigh said, latching onto Jack's arm.

"She's not!" Jack said, turning to me, his eyes begging me to believe him.

"I know," I said, disgusted. I pulled at Hartleigh, trying to drag her off of him.

"You don't love her, Jack," Hartleigh pleaded. "She drugged you or put a spell on you. She was seducing you. She is only after you for your money."

"Chloe, don't you see Jack Frost isn't worthy of you?" Herbert the stalker Santa told me. "You belong with me. I sent you all those nice presents."

My cousin was out cold on the ground next to his junkie friend and my stalker. Jack's father was standing over them. He was watching Hartleigh and me fight over Jack in mild amusement.

"Jack," he said, "I'm going to take Chloe home with me. You and Hartleigh can work things out on your own. How does that sound?"

"That is not going to work," Jack growled. His father stepped up and latched onto my upper arm.

"Let go of her," Jack said, straining to escape Hartleigh's grasp. His stalker had her fingers twisted on his shirt collar and in his hair. I had heard stories about people being so strung out on drugs that they had superhuman strength, but I didn't know it could happen if you were just plain crazy.

"Jack, you're mine!" she shrieked. I could see little pricks of blood on his neck from where her nails had sunk into him.

Jack's brothers came running out of the tower towards us. But before they could reach Hartleigh, a black town car pulled up. We all turned to see who it was.

A woman stepped out. She was tall, with toned arms. They were bare in the cold. She had piercing blue eyes and platinum white hair in a thick braid down her back. She looked like something out of *Game of Thrones*—she just needed the dragons and a direwolf.

Traffic had stopped due to drivers rubbernecking to watch the Santa Claus brawl. Belle—that was who I assumed the woman was—slowly made her way across the street, ignoring the honking.

The police chose that moment to show up. Sirens blaring, they hustled over to us.

Belle reached us first.

"I thought you were gone," Hartleigh said, eyes wide. Belle didn't say a word.

Hartleigh started babbling. "I'm sorry, I just wanted a family, I just wanted—"

Belle reached out and grabbed two of Hartleigh's fingers, twisting her arm. Hartleigh screamed, and Belle made some sort of Jedi motion and Hartleigh was on the ground, clutching her side in pain.

"Let go of her," Belle said to Dr. Frost, her voice icy.

"I thought you were… I thought you were gone for good," Jack's father said.

"Hardly," Belle said coldly.

Dr. Frost released me and slowly stepped away.

"No!" Hartleigh sobbed, "This isn't happening. You ruined my life, Chloe. Jack is supposed to be with *me*! That's supposed to be *my* family. That's supposed to be *my* baby."

"*I'm not pregnant!*" I yelled. "I stress eat!"

Hartleigh ignored me and pulled out a gun from under her jacket. Her hand was shaking as she aimed it at me. I raised my hands and watched as Hartleigh was promptly tackled by a Santa.

"That was my boss," I said mournfully.

"Not anymore," Jack replied.

CHAPTER 66

Jack

The police officer on the scene couldn't stop snickering as he and his partner started arresting Santas.

"Can we not arrest some of them?" I asked.

"Which one would you like to take home?" the officer said, gesturing dramatically to the line of handcuffed Santas.

"For starters, I need my father," I said.

Dr. Frost smirked at me. "I knew you respected me."

"I don't care about you, but I don't want the Frost name smeared across the tabloids. I can still press charges," I warned. "So stay away from me."

"Do as he says," Belle hissed. "I know things about your finances and your tax evasions. Don't try me. I lived in your house for decades. I have enough blackmail material to gut you and sink you in the Hudson River."

My dad looked mildly concerned. He put his Santa hat and his sunglasses back on.

"You're free to go," the police officer said, "right after you give the detective your statement."

While Jack's father talked to the detective, an ambulance showed up, and the paramedics strapped Hartleigh into a neck brace and gingerly loaded her onto the stretcher.

Chloe's Santa stalker boss, who had tackled Hartleigh, was loaded into the back of a police car.

"Chloe!" he called. The news media was hovering around, and one photographer snuck up to the stalker Santa. He turned to the camera. "I want the world to know that I am Chloe Barnard's number-one fan! I love you! I'll always love you!"

Thankfully, the police shooed the cameras away and slammed the car door on the stalker Santa.

"I need that Santa too," I told them as the police officer dragged Eddie to another car. "He's my employee."

"Mr. Frost," the arresting officer said, "this man is clearly inebriated."

"He's not dangerous," I replied.

"Public drunkenness is not acceptable."

"I know," I said, pinching the bridge of my nose. "But it's Christmas. I won't let him sleep on the streets; he supposed to be my security guard."

The police officer shook his head incredulously.

"If you're willing to assume responsibility for him," he said and released Eddie from his handcuffs. Eddie grinned and stumbled over to me.

"I didn't even lose a tooth!" he bragged and took a swig from the flask.

"Eddie, put it away," I hissed. "If they see you drinking, they're going to arrest you."

Fortunately, Chloe's cousin started making a commotion, and the officer's attention was diverted.

"Chloe!" her cousin yelled to her. "Please don't let them take me."

I looked to her.

"Sorry, Cody," Chloe said, "but I'm pressing charges."

"Oma would be so angry at you," he screamed. "We're family! Family takes care of each other!"

"You didn't take care of me, you kidnapped me!" she yelled. Her face was red, and I knew she was upset. "I'm not enabling you anymore." She looked sad as she watched the officers load her cousin into the back of the police car.

I noticed my four brothers hovering around the periphery, watching the action.

"Belle!" Jonathan said. The two youngest boys ran over to her, and she hugged them.

"You're back!" Matt exclaimed. My two other brothers slowly walked over to her. They seemed nervous, but Belle hugged them too, then she hugged me.

"You came back," I said. "How?"

"Chloe summoned me," she said wryly.

Chloe looked at me sheepishly. "Sorry to meddle. I wanted you to have a nice Christmas. I know you're close to your siblings, and I wanted you all to be together."

"I can't believe you actually came back," I repeated. I was still stunned to see my sister standing in front of me.

"Are you staying for the party?" Oliver asked.

"We'll see," Belle said. "I have a few things to take care of first." Then she returned to the waiting town car.

I sagged. Oliver and Matt were visibly distraught that Belle had just left again. Owen and Jonathan hid their disappointment a little bit better, but I could tell they were still disappointed.

"I guess she's still angry," Owen said.

"Can you blame her?" Jonathan replied. "She probably hates our guts."

The police finally let us leave, and we walked back inside dejectedly. Eddie was half propped up on me. I couldn't tell if he was drunk or injured. He seemed physically okay, though, so probably just drunk.

"She'll come back," Chloe said, rubbing my back as we walked into the lobby. The Christmas decorations she had set up mocked me. How could I have believed that pretty décor and cookies would be enough to make Belle forgive us?

"How can you be so sure?" I asked Chloe as I sat Eddie at the security desk.

"It's Christmas," she said. "You have to have faith."

"That's a bit in short supply around these parts," I replied.

"How did you convince her?" Jonathan asked Chloe.

"I had some Instagram friends forward her an invitation."

"You didn't even talk to her?" Owen said, as he picked up a paper sack that smelled like cheesesteaks from the security desk.

"No," Chloe replied. "She came of her own volition. That's why I think you'll see her at the party. I bet she missed you guys. I don't have siblings, but I have my cousin. He stole money from me and broke promise after promise, but I still forgave him. I'm sure Belle doesn't hold a grudge against you."

We watched through the window as the ambulance carrying Hartleigh sped away.

"This is probably the most violent Christmas ever," Jonathan said, breaking the silence, "since Grandma got run over by a reindeer."

"Not helpful, Jonathan," Owen growled. "Not helpful."

CHAPTER 67

Chloe

"Is it weird that I feel bad about Hartleigh?" I asked Jack as we sat in his penthouse. I was curled up on his couch, rubbing my wrists. They still felt a little tingly. Also, my stockings were ruined from running on the street.

"Head injuries are bad," Jonathan said. "They make you crazy."

"Hartleigh was already crazy," Jack added. "Now she's hopefully going to jail when she's released from the hospital."

"I feel bad for her parents," I said. "That must be awful, to have your daughter arrested so close to Christmas."

"They knew she had mental problems," Jack said. "And they did nothing."

The TV was on, and a football game showed on the screen. Owen and Jonathan were watching the game, but Oliver and Matt were arguing in a corner.

Jack's two youngest brothers were in sweatshirts and jeans. They were still baby-faced teenagers, but I could see the angles of their faces slowly coming into relief. In another couple of years, they would be as handsome and broad shouldered as Jack and the other two older Frost brothers.

Matt and Oliver stood up, pushing and shoving each other as they got near me.

"Stop it," Owen snapped.

"You ask her!" Oliver said to Matt.

"Are you making Christmas?" he asked.

"What kind of idiotic question is that?" Owen said.

"Leave her alone," Jack yelled at them. "She's been through a lot today."

I fiddled with my hair. It felt frizzy.

"Of course we're having Christmas," I told them. "Jack is just being a Grinch."

"I'm not," he said, glowering. His brothers snickered.

"Before I can do that, I need to go back to the Airbnb. All my cooking stuff is there, along with my fancy pens."

"Why do you need fancy pens?" Jonathan asked.

"To write out what's in each dish," I told him. "Honestly, I don't know how you all function."

"I'll drive you to Brooklyn and help you gather your things," Jack said, standing up and grabbing his keys and wallet.

The boots he had bought me, along with my other presents, were still in his closet. It was nice to see the fur coat and dress hanging up next to his suits.

I tugged on my boots and followed Jack to his car. He kept his arm wrapped around me in the elevator.

"So no more Brooklyn restaurant job since your boss was your stalker, I take it?" he said once we were on the road.

"I don't think it's going to work out," I said sadly.

"Huh," he said. "Well, I—" He seemed about to ask me something, but then his phone rang.

He seemed irritated as he answered. "Yes, I know, I know, you're hungry. I don't know if she's cooking tonight. How can you be finished with the food Owen brought already?"

I smiled. "My brothers are starving," Jack explained.

"They're teenagers," I said. "Of course they're hungry."

"They want you to cook. I told them to order more takeout."

"They can't eat takeout," I protested. "They need a home-cooked meal."

We made good time to the Airbnb. I hadn't unpacked, so it was a simple matter of carrying my things to the car. I dropped the keys in the mailbox.

"Listen," Jack said. "I want you to know you don't have to cook or hang decorations or anything. My brothers will live."

I gave him a scathing look. "Tomorrow is Christmas Eve. I will have a Christmas celebration for the ages. Now take me to the grocery store."

He grinned.

But Jack's grin faded as I dragged him through the store. I wanted to buy things for the dinner that night, and I also wanted to shop for the Christmas Eve party.

"This is too much food," he complained as he dragged the two grocery carts while I dumped in bags of cranberries, flour, dozens of eggs, and other ingredients.

"You and your brothers are giants," I reminded him. "Plus all the Svenssons are going to be there. You guys are going to eat a lot. The stores are closing for Christmas, and we need to have enough food."

Jack loaded up the bags in the car then called his brothers and told them to be waiting downstairs to help unload.

"Wow!" said Matt. "That's the biggest turkey I've ever seen."

"And there are two of them!" Oliver added.

Jack's fridge could barely hold all the food. I prepped the meats then washed my hands and told the Frost brothers, "We need to decorate. I want Jack's penthouse to look like a Christmas card."

I unpacked the boxes and started rifling through them.

"You have nice Christmas decorations," I remarked.

"Belle picked all of that out," Jack said. The brothers all looked sad. I didn't know where Belle had run off to, but I hoped she would return soon. She had come all this way. Surely she would show up for the Christmas party.

"She'll be here," I told them firmly. "But first we need to make this place sparkle for her."

I put Owen and Jonathan in charge of hanging garlands.

"They have to be hung evenly," I said, taking out a tape measure. "See? You just have these tacked up all wonky."

The younger two were in charge of hanging up lights, and once I was sure they had the hang of it, I told Jack to help me hang the crystal snowflakes in the windows.

"These are so beautiful," I said. "Tack them up firmly to make sure they don't fall down."

I watched him easily hang the snowflakes from the window frames. "It's nice to have a tall person around to help decorate. You don't even need a ladder."

"You do!" he snickered. "You need a step stool and stilts." He leaned down to kiss me.

"I'm not that short," I said, swatting him playfully. "You're just freakishly tall."

"It's that Nordic blood," he said, striking a pose.

When the boxes were empty, we all stood back to admire our handiwork. Jack wrapped an arm around me.

"It looks fantastic," I said. Owen dimmed the lights. Garlands punctuated by white and gold bows ran around the perimeter of the open kitchen and living area. The lights twinkled, making the crystal snowflakes sparkle.

Jack kissed me on the mouth, and I wrapped my arms around him and kissed him back. Jonathan let out a wolf whistle.

"Get a room!" Owen said with a smile.

"Food! Food!" the younger brothers chanted.

"Okay," I said, laughing. "But I'm going to need a helper."

CHAPTER 68

Jack

My brothers went back to watching TV, claiming they were too tired and famished from decorating to help cook.

I didn't mind. I wanted to spend the time with Chloe. She had started assembling all the ingredients for the fried pork chops she was going to make, but I stopped her before she could start chopping.

"I have a proposition for you," I told her. "Just please keep an open mind."

She looked at me in confusion. I ran to my workroom and returned with a 3D model of the empty two-story retail space in the ground floor of the tower.

"What is this?" she asked, wiping her hands.

"First of all," I said, "just know this isn't a handout. I'm not offering you this restaurant because I feel sorry for you. I need you to run it."

"A restaurant?" She sounded shocked and not all that enthusiastic, so I launched into my pitch.

"I know you can do it," I said. "You can hire whoever you need. I already promised Mark Holbrook you would run a restaurant. Also, the Svenssons said that several tenants wanted to rent in Frost Tower because of your appearance on the show, and they are really excited about having your restaurant as an amenity. It's a huge space. There's room to do commercial cooking as well as catering to supply desserts to other restaurants, hotels, and events. And—"

"I accept," she said.

"Oh. But I'm not done with my spiel."

She kissed me lightly.

"I'm sure it was a nice spiel. If my running a restaurant will help you, then absolutely."

"I know you didn't want to do a restaurant," I said.

"What's wrong with a restaurant?" she asked.

"Well, you told me you didn't want to run a restaurant, that it was too much work."

"That was hypothetical," she snorted. "But now someone is offering me the space, and I'll have a captive audience in the tower, so to speak."

"You don't want to think about it?" I asked. I didn't want her to wake up a month from now and feel like I had pushed her into doing something she didn't want.

She looked thoughtful. "I'll obviously have a bakery component in the restaurant. Also, my oma always said, 'If a man gives you a cow, don't sit there and complain he didn't bring a butter churner, too!'"

I chuckled.

"You know," Chloe said, "I wonder if Nina and Maria would be interested. It will be fun. If a stalker mall Santa can run a restaurant, certainly I can."

"I know you can," I said, feeling relieved. "I'll give you anything you need."

"I'll have to commute in from Queens, I guess," she said. "I can't afford rent near your tower."

"You could live with me," I offered then regretted it. Chloe was probably tired of men assuming she wanted to be with them forever and ever. Having a stalker could ruin one's whole outlook on life.

"Seems soon," she mused. At least she didn't seem horrified at the idea.

"In New York, you move in practically after the first date because rent is so high," I told her. "By Manhattan standards, we've been dating for years."

Chloe looked around. "It *is* a nice penthouse."

"We can remodel the kitchen, and you can have a craft room," I offered.

She seemed intrigued.

"I did always want a craft room. You really are selling this, Mr. Frost," she said.

I cupped her face, kissing her deeply. My hands drifted down her back to her waist.

Our kiss was broken up by my phone ringing.

"It's Mark Holbrook calling," I said, looking at my phone. "Sorry, I have to take this."

"The Svenssons tell me that Chloe is confirmed for a restaurant," Mark said when I answered.

"Yes, she is."

"The paperwork that Greg sent over seems incomplete," he said.

"We still have to hammer out the details," I replied.

"Let me speak to Chloe," Mark ordered. "I need to confirm for myself."

I put the phone on speaker.

"Chloe," I said. "Mark Holbrook wants to talk to you."

"Merry Christmas!" she said.

"Can you confirm you're going to be in charge of the restaurant?" Mark asked.

"Yes," she said. "It will be full service like you requested. I'm envisioning more upscale bistro–style food with larger portions. It won't be too fussy, but the food will be tasty and nicely presented. I'm picturing a place you could take clients but also meet with coworkers for a quick lunch."

"Perfect," he said. "And the cookies?"

Chloe laughed. I would never tire of hearing her laugh.

"There will be a counter with coffee and baked goods, maybe soups and salads to go."

"Oh, good," Mark said. "I think my entire family is addicted to your baking."

"I'm glad you like it."

"You are amazing," I said after I ended the call. She laughed, and I picked her up and spun her around. "This is going to be the best Christmas ever."

CHAPTER 69

Chloe

I seasoned the pork chops, cut up the green beans, and made the macaroni and cheese and put it in the oven. Then I made sugar cookies and Austrian wedding cookies for dessert.

Jack put on the last episode of *The Great Christmas Bake-Off*, and I watched from the kitchen. His brothers laughed whenever Jack appeared on the screen.

"Your comments are terrible," Oliver joked.

"It's almost as if he knows absolutely nothing about baking," Owen said.

Jack snagged a cooling cookie. "I know enough to eat it."

I slapped at his hand playfully. "No dessert before dinner!"

"Chloe's stuff looks legit, though," Matt said.

I preened when I saw my finished winter garden dessert on the screen. It did look amazing.

"Your dish is so cool," Oliver said.

"Yeah, you should have won," Matt agreed.

"My friend Nina won. Besides, I can't complain. I have a restaurant now, apparently." Jack smiled at me. "So I have everything I want—family, friends, good food, and the ability to keep doing what I love."

Dinner was coming along, and the cookies had cooled.

"Dinner will be ready soon," I told them. "Why don't you all help me decorate these cookies? The pork chops need to slow cook a bit in the oven first. Then it won't take long to fry them up and make some gravy."

The Frost brothers all washed their hands then settled down at the table. I laid out the icing piper and several other tools for decorating.

"Do you even know how to use that?" Oliver asked Matt as he picked up the icing piper.

"Of course I do!" He squeezed the handle, and icing shot out all over his brother's face.

"You two can use the knife," Jack said, mopping icing off the walls and their faces.

"I'm an adult. I can clean my own face," Oliver said, trying to push off Jack's hands.

"Can you? Because you looked a little rough when I picked you up from the train station," Jonathan said. "Almost as if you hadn't, oh, I don't know, showered or bathed or even washed your face in days. It's no wonder neither of you has a girlfriend."

"You don't have a girlfriend either," Matt shot back.

I couldn't help but laugh at their antics. I'd always wanted a big family, and now I sort of had one.

While they joked around, I spooned the buttercream frosting and the royal icing into piping bags for them and showed them how to carefully outline the cookie with frosting then fill it in for a clean, even look.

"I'm putting the *Fortnite* logo on my cookie," Oliver said.

"You're supposed to put Christmas themes on the cookies," Owen chastised them. He was carefully drawing an intricate geometric pattern on his snowflake cookie.

"Wow, Owen," I said, "you need to come work for me at my restaurant. This is a beautiful cookie."

Owen looked smug. "See, Jack. I'm the smartest, most gifted Frost brother. Look at that cookie. That's a work of art."

"I think you got some art on your suit," Jack said.

Owen cursed and looked down at the icing on his expensive clothes.

"I'll grab a rag," I said.

"Your cookies look like garbage," Jonathan said to Jack as I dabbed at Owen's suit.

"I think I cleaned off all of the frosting, but," I said, pulling out a frilly apron. His brothers all roared in laughter. "I think you need to wear this. We don't want to ruin that suit."

"Don't laugh, Jack," I said. "I have one for you too. This is why I wear a crappy old T-shirt when I'm baking for real and not taking an Instagram picture. It can be messy."

Jack tied the apron around himself. It was red with ruffles and said KISS THE BAKER. I kissed him on the mouth.

"Yum, you taste like cookies."

We finished the cookies. Rather, I finished them, and the Frost brothers tried their best.

"I don't know if we should serve these," Owen said. His cookies looked the best of all of them. He had only been able to finish two, though. None of the cookies Jonathan had decorated made it onto the platter. He had eaten them all. The cookies Oliver and Matt had made were just a straight-up mess. They were dripping with frosting and looked like a knockoff Jackson Pollack painting. Jack's were okay. His frosting job was a little wobbly, but he more or less stayed in the lines. The rest of the cookies I had decorated.

"Don't worry," I said. "These are just for dessert tonight. I'm not serving these for the party."

"Wow, vote of no confidence," Jonathan said.

Milo belched.

"Sounds like Milo had his share of cookies too," Owen said, patting the dog on his furry head.

"Ready for dinner?" I asked them, pulling the meat out of the oven and starting to dip it in the egg wash and peppery breadcrumb mixture I had prepared. The oil in the fryer was hot.

As the brothers cleaned off the table, the doorbell rang.

"I bet it's Eddie," Jack said, wiping off his hands to answer the door.

"Your drunk Santa security guard?" Oliver asked.

"He saved Chloe's life, so he's not that bad," I heard Jack say from the hallway as he opened the door.

I heard his voice fade away, then I heard him say, "Belle?"

CHAPTER 70

Jack

I stood in the doorway, staring at my sister. She looked just like I remembered her. Her hair was a little longer, but it was still in the French braid she always wore.

"Merry Christmas," she said. "Can I come in?"

I stepped back from the door, allowing Belle to enter. She had a well-worn backpack, a duffle bag in one hand, and two large red paper sacks in the other.

My brothers all stopped and looked at her when I led her to the open living area.

"You're back," Owen said.

"Of course," she replied. "It's Christmas." She set the bags in a corner and turned to face us, spreading her arms wide. "Come here, you guys."

My brother and I ran to her, and all the Frost siblings met in a big group hug. I felt my eyes starting to tear up.

"I thought we weren't going to see you again," I told her.

"You're my little brothers. Of course I was going to come see you," she said, looking slightly offended.

"I'm so sorry for everything," I told her.

"None of that was your fault," she replied, ruffling my hair.

"You gave up your life for us," I insisted.

"Just my childhood," she quipped.

"And your twenties and early thirties," Owen added.

Belle stepped back and made a face. "Don't remind me how old I am," Belle joked. Then she looked serious. "You guys are my brothers, so what could I do?"

"You didn't have to slave to make sure we had a nice childhood and pay for our college," I told her.

"I'm wasn't going to let you not attend college," she scoffed. "The last things we need are more idiotic, uneducated men running around. No, our parents are totally oblivious to the way the world works if they thought they could just dump you out on the street and expect you to make something of yourselves. I remember how hard it was working and going to community college. I knew you guys wouldn't be able to handle it. So I did what had to be done."

"But you never fulfilled your dreams," I said.

Belle shrugged. "I put five kids into Harvard, made enough money to help you and Owen launch billion-dollar companies, and just spent the last two years traveling to exotic places in the world. I did okay."

"Are you going to leave again?" Matt asked. He was the youngest, and I knew it had hit him hard when Belle left.

Belle looked out the window.

"She can't, can you, Belle?" Owen said darkly.

"Explain," I demanded.

"You're not really happy to be back, and you know you have to stay to keep Mom and Dad away from Chloe and Jack," Owen said.

"I can protect Chloe," I protested.

Belle rolled her eyes and looked over at Chloe, who was watching the exchange from the kitchen island as she methodically fried pork chops.

"Owen's right, I have to stay. Narcissists like Mom and Dad can go nutty when they think people aren't paying attention to them or they feel like they aren't being given what's rightfully theirs. New York City's not a bad place to live."

"But you don't want to be here," Owen said. "Admit it. You're still angry that you had to raise us, that you were forced to give up your life for us."

"Stop being so dramatic," Belle said. "Our parents hold all the blame for what happened. I don't resent you guys at all. I am angry, I'm not going to lie, but I'm angrier at our parents. They didn't just steal my childhood and young adulthood, they stole my chance to be your sister and not your mom. I really want to be your big sister."

"Well," I said. "You can have an apartment."

"And a job with me or Jack," Owen said.

"I'll pass," Belle said. "I'm going to do some work with Romance Creative. They need some software engineers. I'll travel around but mostly stay based out of New York City."

"Is that really what you want?" I asked her.

"It's fine," she insisted. "I missed you guys."

"We'll do anything for you, Belle," Owen told her.

"Yeah, Jack and Owen are billionaires," Jonathan said. "They can buy you a ticket to the moon if you wanted."

She laughed. "I'll think about it."

We stood around looking at her.

"Look lively, boys," she said. "This could be worse. The poor Holbrooks had three of their younger family members die in a horrible house fire a few Christmases ago. We still have each other." She hugged us again.

"And we have Chloe," she added. "Speaking of which, is it time to eat? That smells amazing."

"It's ready," Chloe said, beaming. She had all the food set out on the long kitchen island with a stack of plates, buffet style.

The food was amazing as usual.

"Are you going to make these for your restaurant?" Jonathan asked as he went back for his seventh pork chop.

"Don't eat so much," Belle admonished. "Leave some for other people."

"It's all right," Chloe said. "I have two more pans. Eat away! It's better when it's fresh."

"We decorated," Oliver said proudly.

"I see that," Belle said, looking around with a critical eye. Belle always did like decorating.

"Now, I think this place looks great," she said, "but it looks like we are missing a Christmas tree."

After dinner, we waited for Chloe to bundle up in a coat. The rest of us stayed as we were.

"None of you are wearing a jacket?" she asked in disbelief.

Belle shrugged. "It's not that cold outside."

There was a Christmas tree lot a few blocks away inside an abandoned warehouse complex.

"Are you thinking about buying this property?" one of my younger brothers teased.

"Absolutely not," I replied. "Frost Tower is the last real estate deal I will ever do. In fact, when I die, don't even bury me in the ground, that's how much I hate real estate. I am sticking with what I know—high-precision metal fabrication."

Belle smirked.

There was one nice-looking tree left, and we bought it. Jonathan and Owen carted it back to Frost Tower.

"What are we going to use to decorate it?" I asked as we watched Owen and Jonathan wrap strands of lights around the large, full blue spruce. Chloe was tucking more garland around the room that she had bought at the Christmas tree lot.

I hadn't seen the antique glass ornaments among the boxes Chloe brought from my parents, but Belle went into the duffle bag and pulled out several small boxes.

"I saved the ornaments," she explained. "I didn't want Mom and Dad to have them. I left them with a friend of mine."

We carefully unwrapped each glass ornament and hung it on the tree. Then Belle laid the presents she had bought for each of us under the tree. Chloe added the one she had bought for me.

"Beautiful," Belle said. I watched her, and she seemed a little sad as she contemplated the tree. I tentatively reached out and hugged her, and she patted my arm.

CHAPTER 71

Chloe

"I don't think Belle is that happy to be here," Jack said, looking out over the guests in his living room.

Greg, Carl, Liam, and several of their other brothers had stopped by for the party, and they waved to me.

"It's a lot for her, I bet," I told him.

"I know she resents us," Jack said.

I smoothed the frown lines on his forehead. "Maybe, but she's here, and that counts for something," I said. "She'll have to work out her own demons. She probably wants to just have a nice Christmas and make some good memories. At the very least you can give her that."

"You're right," he said, squaring his shoulders.

I hadn't invited a lot of people to the party, but between the Svenssons and the Frosts, we had a good-sized gathering.

"I had to taste the famous Chloe's desserts and food since now she is the lynchpin of the Frost Tower development," Liam exclaimed.

I handed him some Christmas punch and made him a plate.

"This is amazing!" Liam said, his mouth stuffed with food.

"Mark says he's going to sign. Word is already out that he wants to move his company here. I've had several more inquiries," Carl said. "Not that that newspaper article about your Santa stalkers did you any favors." He pulled up the article on his phone. There was a picture of the Santa brawl.

"They just made it sound funny, not dangerous, at least," I said. "But Anastasia posted on her blog about the new restaurant, so there's some positive news floating around."

"Of course I did," Anastasia said, walking over and hugging me. "I told you I'd promote you!" She had a half-eaten cookie in her hand.

"Cheers," I said, tapping our cookies together and raining crumbs all over Greg's shoes.

Liam laughed as Greg cursed. "I'm going to be over here all the time eating at your restaurant," Liam said to me.

"We had several people ask about condos because of it," Carl added. "That show made Frost Tower really attractive."

"It just needed a little boost," Greg said. "I think it will prove to be a profitable investment. Depending on how much we can lease out, we might even think about doing another tower with a similar type of high-bay creative manufacturing space."

"I hope you aren't suggesting more real estate deals," Jack said with a grimace.

"You have to roll with the punches on real estate," Greg told him.

"I'll stick with engineering from now on," Jack said.

"And restaurateuring," I reminded him, wrapping a hand around his waist.

Belle handed Greg a cocktail. He stared at her.

"Don't look at my sister," Jack snapped.

"He can look if he wants to." Belle winked.

Greg inhaled some of his food and started coughing. Liam wacked him on the back, while Carl snickered into his drink.

"Did we miss the party?" Dana called out as she and Gunnar walked into the living room.

"Mistletoe!" Gunnar said and kissed her playfully. She shoved him off with a half-smile.

"You look like you need a drink," I told Dana.

"Don't mind if I do."

Gunnar went over to his brothers.

"Are you doing Christmas in Harrogate?" Jack asked.

"Yep, driving over there after this. The car is packed full with presents for the kids. My brother, Remy, apparently has a huge Christmas tree in the house."

"How many brothers do you have?" Belle asked.

"There's close to a hundred of us. My father is on wife number nine or ten," Liam said.

"Good gracious," Belle said. She turned to Jack. "And we thought we had a big family."

"You'll be seeing more of us if rumors are true and you're joining my no-count half-brother on his quest to create the trashiest reality TV known to man," Greg said.

Belle smiled. "I'm looking forward to it. I enjoy a little creative romance."

Liam and I stifled a laugh as we saw a slight flush creep up Greg's neck.

Belle grinned toothily at him. "Who knows? Next year, you could be the Grinch that learns to love Christmas."

"I like Christmas," Greg protested.

"Are you kidding me? Greg, you complained nonstop about coming to this party. You hate Christmas," Liam said. "I had to listen to a rant from you not even five hours ago about the sheeple who overdo Christmas and wait to break up with their significant other until after Christmas and how much you hate having to go to three holiday parties a week and—"

"Thank you, Liam, that's enough," Greg said.

"Greg," Jack said, putting an arm around the investor's shoulder. "Take it from a reformed Christmas hater—you need to relax and let the spirit of Christmas fill your heart."

"Or you could just have some more Christmas cheer punch," I told him, topping off his glass. "That will make you feel warm and fuzzy inside."

"You make me warm and fuzzy inside," Jack said, wrapping his arm around my waist.

"The mistletoe is that way," Liam said, pushing us towards a doorway.

"I don't need mistletoe to kiss you," Jack said, tipping me back and kissing me deeply. "I love you, Chloe."

"I love you too, Jack." I felt tears prickle in my eyes.

"Don't cry," he said and kissed me. "Stick with me, Chloe. I promise it will be Christmas every day of the year."

The End

EATING
HER
Baked
Goods

CHAPTER 1

Jack

"This has to be the fastest that a restaurant space has been permitted and approved," I said as Chloe and I walked through the newly remodeled space. The formerly cold and barren two-story retail space in the base of Frost Tower was now bright and cheerful. The second floor held a more elegant private dining space, while the ground-floor level contained some casual seating. On one side was a bar where during the day you could buy coffee and baked goods and at night you could drink cocktails.

We walked back through the kitchen, where there were stacks of baked goods on trays each sporting a sign saying DO NOT EAT written in her perfect cursive. I snuck one—okay, more like three—of my favorite cookies.

"You're going to get crumbs all over your suit," she said. I kissed her, leaving powdered sugar on her mouth.

"I'd like you eat you up… or out," I said in a low voice. Chloe blushed.

"Later," she squeaked. "I have to finish setting up. There's already a ton of people saying they're going to come tomorrow for the opening. Everything has to be perfect."

I followed her back into the restaurant space. The contractor was fixing a few final things on the punch list. When Frost Tower had been built, the two-story glass-enclosed retail space had been harsh and corporate. Chloe had worked her magic, however, and now the space felt warm and inviting. Wood and dark navy-blue walls with bronze accents gave it a casual, high-end feel.

We stopped to look at the white lettering spelling out Grey Dove Bistro on one of the large walls.

"It looks nice," I told her, hugging her.

"I'm ready for tomorrow but almost dreading it. What if the restaurant is a failure?" Chloe fretted. "Some of my fans are flying in from other states to come to the opening. What if they're disappointed?"

She waved to a group of people standing outside the restaurant.

"This restaurant is going to be great," I told her. "You can cook, and you can definitely bake. Your restaurant is the most successful thing in this tower."

She wrinkled her nose.

"The bar looks nice," I said. It had a glass front to display the various baked goods during the day.

"What are you going to do at night?" I asked her. "People sitting at the bar are going to scuff up the glass," I told her.

"I know, but we have panels that pop into these bronze brackets," she pointed. "It helps change the feel of the space. It was hard making the space work for a casual lunch or snacks and for more formal cocktail hours or dinners, but I think it works."

"Can I have a muffin?" I asked, looking at the tantalizing bakery items in the glass case.

"I thought you had to go meet Mark Holbrook?" she asked, rummaging around behind the counter. "Aren't they moving in today?"

"Yes, I suppose I should go see that he has everything he needs."

"Take him this," Chloe said and handed me a little navy-blue box with a gold bow on it. "I made him some snacks. After what happened with him and his girlfriend..."

"It sounded like she was never his girlfriend," I said, taking the gift. "She was just trying to ingratiate herself with the Holbrooks to destroy them."

"That's so awful," Chloe said.

"Their family has the worst luck," I said, hugging her close to me. The newspapers had treated the Santa brawl as a funny Christmas story, but as the Holbrooks could attest, stalkers and family drama could be dangerous, deadly even. I was glad Chloe was unharmed.

"Chloe, you need to look at this," Nina called.

"You're in high demand," I said. "I'll let you go."

"I'll see you tonight," Chloe said. "Wait, sorry, no, I won't. I promised Anastasia I would meet with her for an interview."

I laughed. "I understand. Don't worry about me."

"I meant to cook you dinner," Chloe said guiltily.

"This is the night before your big opening. You're needed here. I can fend for myself," I promised. "I'll order pizza."

"That's what I'm afraid of," she said with a grimace.

I kissed her again and smoothed down her features.

After Chloe ran back to the kitchen, I walked out the side door into the lobby of Frost Tower. The Christmas trees and other décor were gone. In their place were sculptures and various plants Chloe had selected.

"Boss," Eddie greeted me. He was sober, alert, and out of the ubiquitous Santa suit. I resisted the urge to shudder as I thought about the holidays. I hoped I never saw another Santa again.

I had hired a new security firm at Mark's request, but Eddie was still the official greeter and doorman for Frost Tower.

"Mark Holbrook is already here," he said. "I told him you would be right up. He had some questions to ask you. Also, Greg Svensson's assistant called to say more tenants were coming by at some point to look at space in the tower."

Mark's people were already moving in when I walked into the space his company was renting from me. Mark and his business partner, Finn, were standing in the middle of the action, fielding questions and directing movers. Finn cast worried glances at Mark. The CEO seemed tense around the eyes and more on guard than he had been the last time I'd seen him.

"Are you finding everything you need?" I asked Mark, shaking his hand.

"Yes, I think we are. I'll want to go over the security protocols. You can't be too careful," Mark replied.

I winced. I knew he was thinking about what had happened not even a week ago with his girlfriend.

"I'm sorry for your loss," I said. "That must have been a shock."

"My feelings are irrelevant," Mark snapped. "My whole family could have been killed, and now my cousin has run off."

"I'm sure Wes will be back," I said. "I'm looking to collaborate on some of his robots for search and rescue. We're making new types of drills for uneven debris piles such as in the case of earthquakes."

Mark didn't look that reassured, so I held out the little box of baked goods.

"Chloe made these especially for you," I said.

"Tell her thank you," Mark said. He didn't smile, but he accepted the present.

"I'll let you all return to setting up," I said finally. "Let me know if there's anything else I can do to make this a smooth transition."

I wanted to go back down to the restaurant, but I resisted the urge. I knew I would only be in the way, but I just loved watching Chloe work. Also, I was hoping I could steal her away for a moment. I'd barely been able to spend time with her in the last month. She was always at meetings. And even when she was home, she was busy trying out recipes or on the phone.

When I walked into the penthouse, I saw stacks of plastic containers filled with baked goods, random buckets of frosting or glaze, and piles of various ingredients like fruits, nuts, and chocolate bars.

I was happy for Chloe and proud of what she had accomplished, but I missed spending time with her. I had food delivered and split some with Milo. It felt like being a bachelor again.

CHAPTER 2

Chloe

The restaurant was opening tomorrow. All day, people had been stopping outside in front of the glass to take pictures. It was a little nerve-wracking, if I was being honest. I tried not to freak out in front of everyone. Running a restaurant was very different from a bakery. With a bakery, all you had to worry about were cakes, pies, cookies, maybe some coffee. Now it was liquor licenses and menus and flatware and wait staff.

"The menus finally arrived," Nina announced, handing me a sheet of the thick cardstock.

"Better late than never," I said. "They look nice."

"I'm so glad we went with a simple rotating menu," Nina said, looking over my shoulder.

I nodded. "There's no way we could have done several pages of appetizers, salads, pasta, and multiple courses. This way it's better, too, because it keeps the menu fresh. We can adapt the dishes to what's in season and make it more likely that the tenants in the tower will keep coming if they know they aren't eating the same thing every day. But we'll still keep some of the most popular dishes on the menu, of course. "

Maria came over with a glass. "Andrew is testing cocktails," she said. "Drink."

I took a sip. It was sweet but not too sweet. I ate the preserved cherry that garnished the drink. Maria had made several jars of them, and they were delicious.

"Perfect," I said.

"Do you want a cookie to go with it?" she teased.

"You know I love sweets, but I think I've been eating cookies and desserts for weeks," I told her as Anastasia walked into the restaurant.

"Ready to go?" she asked.

"Oh, uh, yes," I said, looking around. The restaurant still seemed a little in disarray. "Is this going to work? Tell me it's going to work," I pleaded.

"Have another sip of this cocktail," Maria said. "You need to calm down."

"It's okay, we can reschedule," Anastasia told me.

"You should go, Chloe," Nina said. "You're so frazzled, you're not even being much help. Maria and I will finish up. It's just last-minute stuff. We're almost there!"

"I am so glad you two are here helping," I told Maria and Nina. "I could not have done this without you."

"Hey, as long as everything is ready to go before tomorrow morning at seven when the Grey Dove Bistro opens, then we're golden," Nina told me.

I took off my apron, checked my hair, and followed Anastasia out into the cold evening.

"Soon I can just come downstairs for a nice meal and not have to walk for twenty minutes to find something nicer than a pizza place," she said.

"I think that pizza place is doing a lot of business from Jack lately," I told her. "I haven't had time to cook for him."

"He'll survive," Anastasia said with a laugh as we climbed into a waiting car.

"I just feel bad," I admitted. "He's been very supportive."

Anastasia snorted. "Supportive? Jack isn't patronizing you and giving you a pretend restaurant to play with. He knows you're running a serious business. It sounds like he and Greg are making millions selling the restaurant as an amenity to tenants. Don't sell yourself short. Jack loves you, and he respects what you do. You're very fortunate."

"I know," I said. "That's why I feel bad that I've been working so much."

"After the restaurant has the big opening, you'll find your rhythm."

The car had stopped in front of a cute little restaurant. We walked in then followed the hostess to a table, and Anastasia ordered. I twisted my napkin. Everything here seemed to run so smoothly. Who was I kidding that I would be able to pull off a restaurant?

"Don't be too jealous," Anastasia said. "The food here is nothing special."

"That's what my food is," I said, panicking. "Edible but nothing special."

"It *is* special," Anastasia countered. "It's high-end casual bistro food. You aren't chasing Michelin stars, you're trying to make money. Still, your food is actually quite good, and your presentation is nice too."

The waiter put down a dish of scallops for us. I waited impatiently while Anastasia photographed everything. Then she snapped a picture of us.

"For the blog," she said.

"How is that going?" I asked her.

"It's going. Blogging isn't as profitable as it used to be. If things keep heading this way, I might have to start working in your kitchen."

"You just need to find a billionaire to marry," I quipped. "There's Jack's brother Owen or his friend Liam."

She laughed—she knew I was joking.

"I'm not looking for a handout. I just need to work a little harder. Maybe Romance Creative will have me host another show," Anastasia said. "Maybe now that Jack's tower is a popular spot, I can sell my condo and move somewhere a little smaller."

"No!" I protested, "We have to be neighbors! I'll find something for you, I promise."

"You're so sweet, Chloe. Don't worry about me. Maybe my father will die and I'll inherit all that narcissist's money," she said lightly, though I knew her relationship with her father was a sore point for her. Anastasia and I had traded horror stories about our parents over many a wine-fueled girls' night.

"I'll make a post on my blog about the opening," she promised. "I've already contacted some people I know to mention it as well. But don't worry, no one is going to do a review yet. Usually when reviewing a new restaurant, people wait a few months after you've opened so you have your sea legs."

It was still chilly outside when we walked back to Frost Tower.

"I really need it to go well," I said, trotting to keep up with Anastasia.

There was a line of people outside of Frost Tower when we arrived.

"What on earth?" I exclaimed as we approached the large group.

"What are you here waiting for?" Anastasia asked them.

"We're waiting for the Grey Dove Bistro to open," one woman said.

"Chloe!" someone yelled.

"I'm your biggest fan!"

Though I wanted to go up to see Jack, I stopped to hug my fans. These people were standing out in the cold to see me. It would be rude to just walk past with a wave.

"Wait just a minute," I told them and went inside.

Maria was sweeping, and Nina was straightening the bottles on the shelf behind the bar.

"This place looks great!" I gushed.

"That last little bit of tidying was just what it needed," Maria said.

"Maybe we should have had more of a soft opening," Nina remarked. She sounded slightly worried.

"Anastasia recommended just hitting the ground running," I told them. "We have a bit of an advantage given that we're the only decent-ish restaurant in the area. When the new tenants are fully moved in, I expect we'll be packed for lunch and probably dinner most days."

"Looks like there's already a line," Maria said.

"I know, isn't it crazy?" I told her. I already had a big pot of hot chocolate made, and I heated it up then put a tray together, carted it outside, and started handing out the steaming cups. Everyone sipped the hot chocolate gratefully.

"I can't believe you all are waiting outside in the cold!" I exclaimed. "Thank you for your support. This means a lot to me."

We took more pictures, then I carried the tray and empty cups back inside and started washing them.

"Leave it," Maria said. "Garcia will wash them in the morning."

I smiled at her. "I'm so happy your cousins agreed to help work here."

"It's nice to have family around," she said. "Plus it's easier to commute together. My other cousin is working at the security company that won the contract for Frost Tower. We can all travel together."

After telling everyone I would see them in a few hours, I grabbed one more cup of hot chocolate and walked through the lobby to head upstairs. It was very late—after midnight—I wondered if Jack would still be awake. He usually woke up early, so maybe not.

Eddie was still at his post, and I handed him the drink.

"Package for you," Eddie said, giving me a box. "I hope it's not another creepy gift."

"I ordered this one, so it should be fine," I assured him.

Eddie sipped the hot chocolate I had given him. He was sober and seemed a lot healthier.

The penthouse was dark when I walked in. I saw a pizza box in the kitchen, and several of the cookies on the trays I had made for tastings were gone. I smiled. For someone who claimed he didn't like sweets, Jack sure was eating a lot of them.

After clearing off space on the table, I opened the box. It contained dried sakura blossoms and a bottle of sakura blossom essence I had ordered from Japan. Spring was coming, and I wanted to make cherry blossom cookies. I'd had the idea bouncing around in my head. I itched to start baking.

There was also a surprise for Jack in the box, but I would have to give it to him later.

I tiptoed to our bedroom. I was still tickled that it was ours. I lived here with Jack, and he loved me. All the more reason I felt bad for neglecting him lately.

Jack was sprawled out on the bed, Milo, his husky, next to him.

"Chloe," he said sleepily.

"I didn't want to wake you," I told him, going over to kiss him.

"Come to bed," he said, tugging me down towards him.

"I will," I assured him. "Go back to sleep."

I closed the door. I was too wired to sleep, and I didn't want to disturb Jack by tossing and turning. So I did what I loved to do—I baked. I tied on my apron and started mixing up a batch of sugar cookies. I made a batch of royal icing with the sakura essence and added some vanilla to bring out the flavor and added a few drops of food coloring to turn it blush-pink. After the sugar cookies cooled, I frosted them and decorated them with a few of the dried petals.

The cookies looked great. After snapping a few pictures, I bit into one and was enveloped by the faint scent of cherry blossoms.

Unfortunately, it still didn't taste exactly how I wanted. The flavor of the cherry blossom wasn't strong enough. I decided not to bake the rest of the batch and put the dough in the fridge to see if I could experiment some more with the flavor. The fridge was jam-packed, and I couldn't fit the pink icing in, so I covered it and stuck it on a shelf along with the precarious stacks of boxes and other random containers from the shop.

I felt bad for the cleaners. After the restaurant calmed down, I would need to sort through all of this baking stuff.

I checked the clock. It was almost four a.m. I was still too wired to sleep, and I needed to be down in the restaurant in an hour, so I made some strong coffee and took a freezing-cold shower. Jack swore by them for waking you up in the morning, and though I hadn't liked icy showers at first, I'd had to admit that he was right.

Trying not to wake him up, I put on my white and black uniform in the dark and headed downstairs. The line had grown. People bundled up in coats stood waiting outside my restaurant. I stuck my head out.

"Two hours, everyone!" I said cheerfully.

They all cheered.

CHAPTER 3

Jack

Chloe didn't come to bed that night. I was worried about her. Her Instagram showed me she had spent the night talking with fans, making hot chocolate, and baking more cookies. She baked when she was stressed, and our apartment was filled with boxes and containers of sweets. When I walked into the kitchen, there was another batch of cookies, along with a big tub of pink royal icing perched on a shelf.

Someone knocked furiously on the door, then I heard it unlock as someone punched the code into the keypad.

"Hi, Liam," I called out.

"How did you know it was me?" he asked.

"You're the only one besides Chloe who has the code. And Chloe is, I presume, downstairs overseeing the opening day of her restaurant."

"Wowza," said Liam as he walked into the kitchen. "Are you sure the restaurant isn't up here?"

"Have a cookie," I said wryly, gesturing around the kitchen. "Chloe stress bakes."

"And you're stress eating," Liam said, poking me in the stomach.

I wouldn't admit it to Liam, but I missed having Chloe around, and if I couldn't have her, then her baking would be a substitute. I looked down at my stomach.

"I upped my daily workouts to counteract the cookies. I can still count my abs through my shirt," I told him.

Liam made himself a plate of a variety of cookies. There were a lot to choose from.

"How's Harrogate?" I said. "Are you acclimating to living with all your half-brothers?"

Liam made a face then bit into one of the cookies. "My brothers are kind of exhausting, to be honest. At least I won't be living with them for long. I'm looking to buy a property and renovate it. The factory is in the works. I'll tell you more about it at the board meeting today."

"I should come out and visit you," I told him, "after Chloe has a chance to find her groove with the restaurant."

"Unfortunately, there aren't baked goods like these," Liam said and took a bite out of one of the sakura cookies. "Though there is a baker."

"Is she cute?"

"Yeah, I guess."

"But I know you have your eye on someone else," I prompted. Liam never talked about dating. Like me, he was always too busy and too wary of running into a woman like his mother. But I knew he had met someone special in Harrogate. He just wouldn't admit it.

"Just because you're all set in the girlfriend department doesn't suddenly make you an expert, dude," Liam said.

"Chloe basically fell into your lap. You had no game to speak of."

"I have game," I protested.

"You don't. You're like a little turtle stuck on its back. Chloe had to come rescue you," he teased and helped me snap Milo into his harness.

Plate of cookies in hand, Liam walked downstairs with me. Milo needed the exercise, and I wanted to see how Chloe's restaurant was coming along.

It was absolute chaos. Between the news crews, her fans, and all the Instagram personalities taking pictures with the food, it was insane. I waved to her from across the restaurant, and she gave me a harried smile.

"Guess you're low priority," Liam said, cookie crumbs spraying out of his mouth.

"I think there's enough going on in here without you and me added to the mix," I told Liam. "Plus Milo wouldn't be allowed inside."

We walked to the park instead, and Liam gave me a rundown of what was happening in Harrogate.

There was still snow on the ground, but spring would be arriving soon.

"It's going to be boiling this summer," I said with a shudder. "Maybe I should pack up and go to Argentina or someplace on the other side of the world to hide out from the summer."

"Or you could go to Alaska," Liam said.

I turned away from watching Milo and looked at Liam and the empty plate in his hand. "Did you eat all those cookies?" I said in shock.

"Dude, my life is a straight-up disaster right now," he said. "Also, Hunter and Greg aren't really speaking, so I think this board meeting is going to be awkward."

The board meeting was definitely awkward. Greg and Hunter sniped at each other, and when Liam admitted that the factory had run into some snags, Greg yelled at Hunter and told him he needed a better grasp of what was going on in Harrogate.

Though I wanted the factory to be successful, I missed having Liam around. I wondered if he would come back to Manhattan after the factory was up and running. Maybe not if he had a girlfriend there.

I wondered about my own girlfriend. I texted her but didn't expect to hear back.

Greg followed me out of the room after the meeting.

"I have two groups of tenants coming by Frost Tower this afternoon," he said. "Make sure you're ready to show them around. I have an older couple looking to purchase a condo. They ate at Chloe's restaurant today, loved it, and decided they want to move there. Give them the VIP treatment and make them feel special."

"Why is Jack dealing with tenants?" Hunter said, coming out of the room with his arms crossed. "There should be a leasing agent."

"Yes," Greg snapped at his brother, "but we want tenants to feel special. They need to sign. This tower has gone unprofitable for too long. If having Jack spending an hour showing them around convinces them to pay in cash, then that's what he's going to do. But I wouldn't expect you to understand anything about real estate."

"I understand plenty," Hunter said in a clipped tone. "I also understand that the restaurant has only filled one of the retail spaces at the base of the tower and that neither of you have made any moves to fill the rest."

"I'm working on it," I interrupted them before they could spiral into another fight. "I've had interest, but I need to poll the tenants to see what types of retail would work best for them. We need a good mix. Also, just send me the files of the prospective tenants and what their needs are. I'll make sure the space is ready."

Chloe's business was still packed when I returned to the tower. All the tables were full, and the wait staff was hurrying back and forth. A few times I saw her personally seat people.

"That was really great," said a group of people coming out of the restaurant. They walked over to me. "You must be the famous Jack Frost," one woman said. "We're here to look at some of your office space."

"You must be from Harrington CyberTech," I greeted them smoothly. I was glad I had read over their file in the car on the way back from the Svensson Investment tower. "Right this way, please."

"We are currently located in Brooklyn," the woman said, "but it's far away from the finance center."

"That it is," I said as we stepped into the elevator. "You will find that we have the space here that can accommodate you." I took them to a few floors below where Mark Holbrook's company was setting up.

"That restaurant is great," the woman gushed. "Honestly, this tower is so cool. I had no idea it was here!"

"And they have condos," one of her colleague said.

"Yes, our CEO, Steve Harrington, mentioned we might purchase a few of those."

"They're going fast," I told them. "I have people coming in later today to look at some."

"Oh, we'd better jump on it. I'll talk to Mr. Harrington today," the woman said.

They took pictures of the space as we walked through it.

"We'll be in touch," the Harrington CyberTech representative said as we shook hands.

The older couple showed up next. The older woman had a cookie from Chloe's bakery. It was one of the special ones she'd made that said Frost Tower.

"I couldn't resist," the older woman told me with a big smile. Then she wrapped me in a hug. "I feel like I know you from Chloe's Instagram!" she said, squeezing me.

I wasn't sure if I wanted them as my neighbors, but a sale was a sale, and they seemed nice enough. The elderly couple also seemed very much in love, and I hoped that would be me and Chloe when we were that old.

"Look, Bernard!" the woman said to her husband as she gushed over the condo. "Isn't this view fabulous?"

"What is the policy on renovations?" her husband asked.

"Right now, there aren't that many people moved in yet," I explained.

Chloe and I could handle any noise, and Anastasia would probably take a discount on her HOA dues if I gave it to her in exchange for tolerating construction noise. Chloe had said Anastasia was having some financial difficulties. I thought about offering her a loan or at least introducing her to my brother Owen, who was a cryptocurrency billionaire and who I thought Anastasia would like. But I knew the woman had too much pride for that.

"Frost Tower can accommodate any construction you need completed," I assured the couple.

"I love this space! It's perfect."

"I think we'll take it," Bernard said and offered his hand for me to shake.

"Wonderful," I told him.

"I can't wait to be neighbors!" his wife gushed.

"I think it's commendable that you live here," Bernard told me as we headed downstairs. "To me, that says something about your integrity that you stand by your project so much that you live in it. A lot of these real estate types are fly-by-night investors from China or the Middle East. Trudy and I have been looking at condos in a variety of buildings, and you never know who you're dealing with. I like to look a man in the eye and shake his hand and have him guarantee what he's selling me. That's how it was in my day. It's reassuring to see there's still honest men left in this city."

"Yes, sir," I said and waved at them as they left the tower. I looked over into the restaurant space. It didn't appear as if the restaurant was experiencing a lull at all. I checked my watch. Soon it would be dinner time.

"Pizza again, I guess," I said to myself.

CHAPTER 4

Chloe

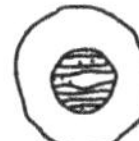 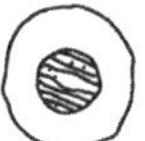 

When we opened at the Grey Dove Bistro promptly at seven, the place was immediately packed. "Please don't let us run out of food!" I begged the kitchen gods. That was my worst nightmare, what kept me from sleeping, and probably why I frantically baked. I did not, under any circumstances, want to run out of food. That was the ultimate faux pas and the ultimate insult in the small Midwestern town in which I had grown up. To run out of food was to be a bad hostess. To not have enough food for everyone meant you were inconsiderate and probably a little dense.

My oma had liked to brag that the whole town could show up at her house unannounced and she would have enough food to feed everyone and give them seconds. The whole city of New York might not have shown up at my restaurant, but it sure felt like it. Nina, Maria, and I had spent the last week baking thousands of cookies, cakes, and tarts in the large commercial kitchen.

The baked goods were going quickly. There was a constant stream of people at the counter and waiting to be seated in the dining area. The wait staff were professional and were quickly taking orders and bringing food. Maria and Nina had also enlisted family members to come help out.

"You guys are a lifesaver," I told them while doling out muffins, cookies, and cups of coffee. I saw Jack across the room. He smiled at me, and I gave him a frantic wave then turned back to my customers.

In front of me was a representative from a large hotel chain. She waved one of the special Frost Tower cookies in front of my face.

"I need to put in standing orders for thousands of special cookies each day. We want to give them to our hotel guests," she said. "We want ones just like the Frost Tower snowflakes except with our branding, obviously."

"We can accommodate that," I lied. Those special cookies were time consuming to make even with the Platinum Provisions tools. I would need to talk to Jack about renting more space in his tower. The commercial kitchen we had in the restaurant was not going to be able to handle all those cookies and desserts.

"Schedule a time when you can come back and talk with us about what you're thinking, okay?" I plastered a smile on my face, and the woman seemed satisfied and left.

She was quickly replaced by another man who I recognized as a restaurateur.

"I'm going to email you about supplying my restaurant with desserts," he told me while I was trying to ring up customers and tell my back-of-house staff where I had stored more of the soup muffins.

"Yes, absolutely, we can do that," I told him.

"I want a special dessert only my restaurant will have," he demanded.

"Talk to that woman over there and schedule a time," I said with a tight smile. One more thing to add to the list.

I recognized other restaurant owners from around the city. They had also come in to sample desserts. I knew when I opened up my email account that night, I would have more requests.

"It will calm down after lunch, right?" I said to Nina when she brought me some water.

It did not calm down. Four p.m. came and went. The coffee crowd died off, but the dinner crowd picked up. Maria's cousin and brother quickly switched the bakery counter over to a wine bar.

"I can already see that this is not a viable solution," I told Maria.

"Maybe we can expand into a nearby retail space and keep that open as a coffee shop and bakery?" Nina suggested. "Jack's tower has other empty retail spaces. They're a little smaller than this one, though."

"We're going to need to do something," I said as more people came in looking for baked goods and coffee. I sold them some because I felt bad, but the bartender had arrived and needed the space to start making drinks. Then some people asked for cookies *and* wine.

"I should make a cookie cocktail or something," the bartender joked.

"Can you?" one customer asked. "That's all I ever wanted."

I made more mental notes for what I would do in the future, then I jumped in to help the hostess seat people. There was a line for dinner, and I did not want people to have to wait for a table.

I recognized an older couple who had come in for breakfast then come in again for a cookie, and now they were back for dinner.

"We want to support you!" the woman said, waving when she saw me.

"Thank you," I told her, grabbing two menus and leading them to a table.

"We're going to be neighbors!" she told me. "We just talked to your husband."

"Jack's not my husband," I said, smiling.

"He will be, though," the woman said and winked at me. "What's that song? Put a ring on it?"

"You're going to live near them? Good luck," Nina snickered after I came back from seating the couple at a table near the window. "Expect to have her ask you when you're having kids every single day."

"I'm glad Jack sold a condo, but honestly," I sighed, looking at them.

"I'm sure they'll travel a lot," Maria said diplomatically.

"We can only hope," I replied.

"We're almost sold out of all the baked goods," Nina said. "We'll have to bake more for tomorrow before we leave."

"I don't know how we will be able to bake everything," I fretted.

"I called my family," Maria said. "They're in the back starting to mix the batter and dough."

With the bakery traffic dying down and the chefs on their game making savory food, I wasn't needed as much. The wait staff were experienced, and after the initial rush, things hummed along smoothly. With the lights dimmed and the bartenders slinging drinks, the Grey Dove Bistro felt like a relaxing, upscale establishment.

"I feel like I can breathe," I said as I tied on an apron and started baking. With Maria's mom, grandmother, and sister helping us, we managed to bake and decorate enough items for the next day.

"You need a bigger kitchen!" Maria's grandmother said. I started to choke up a little. That was what my oma would have said.

"I'm working on it," I assured her.

I offered Maria's sister a job on the spot and begged to have her mother and grandmother come by to help bake as well. It was after midnight when we finished.

"Do it all again tomorrow?" I said to Nina.

"You know it!" she replied cheerfully.

One of the chefs gave me a box of leftovers, and I hobbled out into the lobby to go upstairs to see Jack.

CHAPTER 5

Jack

After the older couple left, I took Milo for another walk, and then I met Owen for a drink. I was tempted to go to Chloe's restaurant, but I didn't want her to feel obligated to entertain me. I knew it had to be stressful. I remembered when Liam and I had first started Platinum Provisions—we'd barely slept for weeks. There was a constant churn of product design meetings, emails, and conference calls.

Owen was at the bar with Jonathan when I arrived at a restaurant near the Svensson Investment tower.

"You have the worst taste in bars," Jonathan was saying as I walked up.

"I didn't know you were coming," I said, hugging my younger brother.

"Belle says I need to be more proactive about being a member of the family," he replied.

I wished Belle were here, but she was off with Dana and Gunnar, filming the next Romance Creative production.

"She said she's coming back into town next week," Owen told us. "She wants to try Chloe's restaurant."

"It's a big hit," I said. "The place is packed. I think she'll need to expand."

"That hotelier I know, remember Mike with Greyson Hotel Group?" Jonathan said. "He was asking me about Chloe doing cookies for his hotels."

"How much is he talking about?" I asked him as the bartender handed me a whisky.

"The entire group in the Greater New York area has like ten thousand keys or something insane. He owns all these boutique hotels. They're all over the city. He said his group is moving away from the bigger hotels to better compete with Airbnb. He wants special cookies for each hotel to give them that personal touch."

"The restaurant kitchen won't be able to handle that much," I said. "I mean, every single day? That's a lot of cookies."

"Give her some more tenant space," Owen said. "You can put in a big factory-style kitchen."

"Chloe is not going to accept industrialized cookie production," I said. "Her cookies are all hand made."

"I'm sure she could find people to come decorate cookies," Jonathan said.

"I guess."

We drank and talked. It was nice to hang out with my brothers. Since Belle had returned, it was as if the tension that had existed between us had dissipated.

It was late in the evening when I returned to the penthouse, but Chloe still hadn't come home. A few people had still been eating in the restaurant when I walked by, and I knew she wouldn't leave until the last person was gone.

I ordered in some food for her, and though it was close to midnight when it was delivered, she still hadn't come home. I watched TV with Milo while I waited. I was starting to drift off when I heard the door open.

"Chloe," I said. "You should have told me you were coming. I could have had a bath ready for you."

"You're so sweet," she said as I wrapped her in my arms and kissed her.

"I feel like I haven't seen you in years," I said into her hair. It felt good to hug her.

"I'm so sorry," she said, her expression serious.

"Do not ever apologize for success," I told her, tilting her chin up and kissing her mouth.

"I still want to spend time with you," she said, wrinkling her nose.

"Are you hungry?" I asked her. "I ordered you some food."

She smiled and held up a box. "I brought you some too."

I made a plate for her while I heard the shower run. I expected her to come out in a bathrobe and thick, fluffy socks. Except when she walked into the kitchen, she was not in a bathrobe. Instead, she was wearing a very sexy outfit.

"What are you supposed to be?" I asked, feeling my mouth grow dry. My pants were uncomfortably tight.

"It's a sexy French pastry chef outfit!" she exclaimed. I could tell she was loopy from lack of sleep, but she struck a pose, and it was all I could do to keep from ripping the tight-fitting costume off of her.

CHAPTER 6

Chloe

I walked over to him. I had seen the sexy French maid outfit when I was shopping on the Japanese store for the sakura flavoring, and I couldn't resist. I was larger than the typical Japanese woman, but the costume had a little bit of give, plus I knew I wouldn't be in it long.

"That's… quite an outfit," Jack said. He was looking at me as if he was hungry for more than cookies.

Then Jack seemed suddenly angry. "Did your stalker send you that?"

"No," I snorted. "I bought this just for you."

He smiled and relaxed. "In that case, then…" He pulled me close to him, running his hands over my body, the forcefulness of his kiss telling me I was his. He pushed me up against the kitchen counter. I felt his hand creep between my legs, and I spread them, offering myself to him.

"I think your costume is ripped," he said when I felt his fingers in the wet warmth.

"I bought it that way," I whispered in his ear then bit it gently. He ripped the bodice of the costume, his mouth hungry at my breasts. He rolled a nipple around with his tongue, the feel of his mouth sending a shock straight down through my body.

His hand was still between my legs, stroking me. It had been a spell since we'd made love, and my body was on fire for him.

"I want—" I moaned.

"I know you want me to fuck you," he murmured, "but I want to take my time."

He hoisted me onto the counter. Boxes toppled to the floor.

"My cookies!" I gasped.

"I'm going to eat your cookie right now," he said, his voice deep with lust.

He spread my legs even wider, and I moaned and arched back as his mouth kissed and licked between my legs. It didn't take much for me to come. My chest heaved against the costume. My fingers slipped out of the tangle in his hair as he stood up.

"I'm not done with you yet," Jack said.

I was still seeing stars as his belt slid out of the loops and he stepped out of his pants and boxer briefs. I reached out to stroke his cock, hard and thick in my hand. I wanted it.

Placing a hand on my lower back, he brought me closer and teased me with his cock.

"Please," I begged.

He put two fingers in the crotch of the little outfit then pulled, ripping the slit longer. He ran his cock around the hot flesh revealed by the slit in the costume. I moaned, and he kissed me, stifling the sound. Then he entered me.

The sensation drove me wild.

"Jack!" I cried, repeating his name as he thrust into me. He wasn't even trying to go that slow. His movements were pure lust. Jack wanted me, and I loved him for it. I was letting out high-pitched gasps and whimpers with every thrust from him. The stuff on the counter was jostled. More boxes crashed to the floor, and I smelled sugar in the air.

He kissed me sloppily, and I panted against his mouth. His cock rubbed against my clit with every thrust, and I angled my hips towards him, needing to feel him. I felt my whole body tighten once more, then I came from the sensation of him. My legs, wrapped around him, needed him to milk all the pleasure from me.

Jack buried his face in my neck when he came. He kissed up my jaw then up to my mouth to kiss me long and slow.

"That was fantastic. I missed you, and I love you," he said against my mouth.

"I love you too," I said. My legs were still wrapped around him. I didn't want to let go.

He nibbled my ear as we slowly untangled. "You want to come to bed and do this all again?" he asked, nuzzling my neck as he spun me around to direct us to the bedroom.

Unfortunately, the tub of royal icing I had made last night finally gave up its precarious grasp on its perch and toppled off the shelf, covering Jack with pink frosting. He stood there in shock, blinking at me.

I snickered then laughed as he started guffawing. Giving me a devilish look, Jack wrapped me in his arms, covering us both in the sticky pink icing.

"I think I might bake too much," I said.

"Never," he replied and kissed me, covering my face in streaks of pink.

"You're the best-tasting thing in this kitchen," Jack said with a chuckle.

I smiled and swiped a finger through the icing on his forehead. "And you're my Jack Frosting!"

Austrian Wedding Cookies

My father claims these cookies are the reason he married my mother! Enjoy!

Ingredients:
1 cup unsalted European butter
6 tablespoon confectioners' sugar
1 1/2 cups finely chopped pecans from Georgia
2 cups sifted flour
1/2 teaspoon good vanilla extract
Pinch of salt
1/3 cup confectioners' sugar for rolling

Directions:

1. Preheat oven to 350° F
2. Cream butter in a bowl, gradually add confectioners' sugar and salt. Beat until light and fluffy. Gradually add flour, salt, and pecans
3. Shape into balls (a little smaller than a golf ball). Place on an insulated cookie sheet and bake for 15-20 minute until a slight golden brown. Do not over bake. Cool slightly, then roll in the extra confectioners' sugar. (They should still be slightly warm when doing this but not too warm or they will crumble.)

Acknowledgements

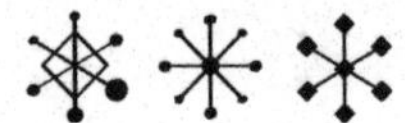

A big thank you to Red Adept Editing for editing and proofreading.

And finally a big thank you to all the readers! I had a great time writing this book, and I hope it put you in the Christmas spirit!

About the Author

If you like steamy romance novels with a creative streak, then I'm your girl!

Architect by day, writer by night, I love matcha green tea, chocolate, and books! So many books...

Sign up for my mailing list to get special bonus content, free books, giveaways, and more!

http://alinajacobs.com/mailinglist.html

Made in the USA
Monee, IL
12 November 2019

16707756R00262